P9-DUR-080

No Good-byes

Also by Elaine Kagan

Somebody's Baby

Blue Heaven

The Girls

No Good-byes

A Novel

Elaine Kagan

William Morrow
An Imprint of HarperCollins*Publishers*

HarperCollins books may be purchased for educational, business, or sales promotional use. For information please write: Special Markets Department, HarperCollins Publishers Inc., 10 East 53rd Street, New York, NY 10022.

FIRST EDITION

Designed by Fearn Cutler de Vicq

Printed on acid-free paper

Library of Congress Cataloging-in-Publication Data

Kagan, Elaine.
No good-byes : a novel / Elaine Kagan. — 1st ed.
p. cm.
ISBN 0-688-15746-7 (acid-free paper)
I. Title.
PS3561.A3629N6 2000
813'.54—dc21 99-44731

00 01 02 03 04 BP 10 9 8 7 6 5 4 3 2 1

FOR EVE

ACKNOWLEDGMENTS

A special thank you to Razel Ronne for her kitchen, her ear, and her knowledge—in and out of books,

to David Francis for listening, listening, listening,

to Carole Smith for being my personal reference desk,

to Jeffrey Fiskin for shoving me down the right path (and thinking I can sing),

to Eddie Barnett for putting his uniform back on, and opening his heart,

to Jeff Ramsey, the master of stunts,

to my dear doctors: Lynne Turner, Dorothy Doyle, Mal Hoffs, and Paul Silka who helped me with my characters inside and out,

to Gena Rowlands for reading and seeing,

to Ginger Barber for believing,

to David Freeman for never hanging up.

John Cassavetes,
always and forever, Bob Gottlieb,
and my dearest Eve.

CHAPTER 1

"It happened in Italy," the young woman said.

A bus changed gears on Glendon. Eleanor could hear it surface through the normal hum of the street, through the click of the air conditioner and the unopening stretch of windows across the west wall of her office; the *whoosh* of cool air hit her at her knees. She studied her cuticles, shifted her ass in the black-leather swivel chair, and wrote "cotton balls" on the pad where she had written "cottage cheese." Then she drew a box inside a box and then a lid, an open lid flipped back to reveal the contents, which was nothing because if you drew something inside the box then you wouldn't see the lines that made it a box. How did they do that? Eleanor caught her lip between her teeth and drew a moon. Not in the box, but up in the corner. Floating, as it were.

"Have you ever been to Rome?" the young woman asked Eleanor.

Eleanor didn't answer.

"Well, it was in Rome." And then in a rush, "It's not like I think about this, you know, dwell on it. I mean, it happened a long time ago." She hesitated. "I was only twelve . . . I don't even know if I can remember the details."

Twelve, she was twelve.

Quiet. The young woman's eyes were somewhere on the wall behind Eleanor, either on her framed degrees or on the black-and-white autographed photograph Jimmy had given her of Colette.

"Go on," Eleanor said.

"She was holding my arm. Not exactly holding it, but we had kind of crossed arms for a second"—a slight lift of the eyebrows—"not like a mother and daughter, but more like two girls, two girls . . . in a film," the young woman said, turning her head to one side, away from Eleanor, "like in a musical," she said.

A musical. The light fell across her hair, straight beige hair with golden streaks. Golden streaks that Eleanor knew cost an arm and a leg to have put in like that, as if they'd been painted in by God. You could do that when price was no object.

"*My Sister Eileen,*" the young woman said to the wall of unyielding windows, and then an intake of breath. "I don't know why I thought of that, I don't remember anything about *My Sister Eileen.* Did they sing in it? It was a musical, I think."

If it was a clown in the box it would be one of those things where you turn the handle and then the lid pops open and the clown doll flies up. All around the mulberry bush, the monkey chased the weasel, that hollow plinkety sound and then that doll popping up. It was awful. Who would have bought her such a thing? Eleanor tried to envision turning the crank on the box. It was red, she remembered, with a particular smell. Tin? Does tin smell? In her mind's eye, she tried to see who was sitting next to her. Her mother would never have bought her something so scary. Eleanor drew four dots and connected them with a single line. She could never draw a clown in the box. Too difficult. You had to be an artist to draw a clown. Or Red Skelton.

"Technicolor," the young woman went on, "very technicolor. And an apartment where you could see the windows up at the tops of the walls, a kind of basement New York apartment, I guess it was supposed to be, very stylish, you could see people's ankles as they walked up and down the street. It was a set, of course. High-heeled shoes and taxis honking. It must have been a musical, I think I remember singing . . ." Her voice drifted off and then came back again. ". . . she must have shown it to me, Mommy, she must have run it." The slender legs in running shorts lifted now and crossed at the skinny ankles; her enormous marshmallow sneakers didn't reach the end of Eleanor's couch. "They used to run movies at the house when I was little. Sundays for company, whatever was new, and whenever Daddy was working on something he wanted to show her, but she loved to run the old ones. 'Watch what she does now, Chassi, watch what she does.' " Eleanor looked up. The girl's imitation of her mother's voice was unmistakable, the honeyed cadence of Texas and the memorable face of Sally Brash filled the room.

"Not in a fancy screening room like people have now," Chassi continued in her own flat accent, "just in the second living room. This screen would float down from the ceiling with a hum and old Max, the projectionist, would be behind that funnel of light in the little square hole in the wall. Go ahead, Max." Chassi threw out the last three words as if there was someone behind her. "He'd come from the studio, you couldn't see him, just his silhouette, and then the sound of the projector in the dark." She sighed, with her mouth open, a smaller *whoosh* than the air conditioner. "Nothing was on tape then, all film. So different"—she exhaled—"glamorous." The girl ran her hand through her expensively streaked hair and continued the stretch, the hand reaching above her head; a delicate arm, thin, short fingers, tiny elbow just a little pinker than the rest; no folding skin, no wrinkles, just a pale, young, ivory arm. "I wish I could have been in one of those, not that anybody would make a musical these days." A shrug of a laugh. "Who would make a musical these days? No one in their right mind. Well, Woody Allen, but he's in his own category. He can do anything he wants."

Eleanor drew another moon. This one with a star next to it. Two stars. What the hell kind of a name was Chassi, anyway?

"My mother never did a musical. Just dramas. Black and white, even if they were in color, if you know what I mean, very—" She stopped and turned her head, her lovely green eyes wrapping around Eleanor, her pale cheek against the black leather of Eleanor's couch. "Did you ever see *No Trumpets, No Drums?*" A slow, deep breath. "Incredible. So desperate, so breaking, but absolutely still. She managed to pull it off as if it was"—a soft frown tilting her eyebrows—"as if it was her." The little shrug laugh again. "My mother was certainly not known for being still." Her eyes searched Eleanor's. "You must have seen it, she won the Academy Award. You do go to the movies, don't you?"

"Your mother had her hand on your arm," Eleanor said.

Chassi blinked. Blonde lashes up and down; her eyes weren't really green when you saw them full on, they were amber, the luminous shade of antique amber. Bigger than her mother's. No, not bigger, a different shape—almonds. Amber almonds, as if her father had been Chinese and Eleanor knew that Saul Jennings was certainly not Chinese, she'd seen his picture in the paper a number of times. A large, showy man; heavy, dark-rimmed glasses and big, thick, wavy hair, an elegant topcoat man with a trace of gangster in his smile, and certainly not Chinese.

"She had her hand on your arm," Eleanor said.

Chassi's spider legs of blonde lashes opened and closed again and then she nodded and turned her face away, rested the back of her beautiful head on Eleanor's black leather couch. A couch that had also cost an arm and a leg, for that matter; something from the thirties, fifties, Eleanor couldn't remember, but something done by some la-de-da who was postmodern, the decorator said, and it would "make the room." The couch probably cost the same as the sunbeams in sweet Chassi's hair.

For godsakes, how could the incredible Sally Brash give the name Chassi to her only child? Eleanor scratched her leg at the top of her boot under her long knit skirt, silenced her bracelets, and drew a triangle next to the moon. A triangle could be the hat on the clown's head. That was all it was, a clown hat, just a triangle, after all. You didn't have to be an artist to draw a triangle.

"My mother liked to get close to me," Chassi said, the edge of her mouth lifting. "She liked to smell me is what it was." A smile, wide and lovely. "You know, it was this big joke between us, she'd cuddle up to me and I'd say, 'I know what you're doing, Mom.' " Chassi ran the back of her hand across her nose and sniffed but she didn't say anything. Eleanor watched her and then looked back at the drawing.

That's it, the triangle could be the hat on the head of the clown. Put a pom-pom on top and then a circle under the pointed hat for the face, and then eyes in the circle. Will you look at that? Who said she wasn't artistic? Her mother, that's who.

"It didn't look like a cab, it just looked like another Italian car."

Eleanor stopped drawing.

"It wasn't yellow or white or with writing on it," Chassi said, "I mean, except for the little thing on top it just looked like another fast little Italian car. Of course, I didn't see it until after. It was wrapped around a tree."

Eleanor watched the young woman on the couch hold her breath. "She had her hand on your arm."

"Yes."

The air conditioner clicked off and now you could hear the clock on Eleanor's desk. Jesus. How could such a little clock be so loud? It was a mistake. She had to replace it, she had to get another clock at lunch. There were a million places to get a clock in Westwood. Did she have a lunch today?

"And then?" she said to Chassi.

"I let go of her, uncrossed our arms, I mean."

The clock was louder than the goddamn air conditioner. "Go on," Eleanor said.

Chassi sat up, she didn't look at Eleanor, didn't turn, just sat up. The young back straight and perfect, the slender curve, the poke of shoulder blades under the straps of the pink tank top, tanned and smelling of lotion, hovering in the air. Chassi's mother liked to smell her. Well, of course she did. Sure she liked to smell her, she probably smelled like Eleanor's daughter, Caroline. Not the lotion, although it was probably the same lotion that Caroline used, all the kids used whatever was *in*. Movie stars' daughters, psychiatrists' daughters, plumbers' daughters, turning the pages of the same slick magazines. They were the same age, Chassi and Caroline, Eleanor knew that, she had known it from the very beginning when the studio called. "We've got a real problem here, Eleanor, think you can help me?" Matt Fishburn, who used to play softball with Jimmy, she'd shared a lot of pizza and beer with him and his wife, Moon, after a lot of games. "She'd be my patient, Matt," Eleanor said, "if she'll see me. It would be about me being her doctor, not about getting her back to work."

"I got it, Eleanor, I understand."

"As long as you understand. I won't care about your picture, I'll only care about her being okay."

"Well, she's not okay, she's acting crazy, not like her, not a bit—yelling, throwing things, normally she could melt butter and suddenly we got shades of Judy Garland here. The kid's actually got the door wedged with something, won't come out of her trailer, won't let us in."

Who was this kid anyway? "Who's your problem, Matt?" Eleanor said.

And now Matt's problem, the most talked about young box-office phenomenon in Hollywood, lay quietly in running shorts and a tank top on Eleanor's couch.

Twenty-five. Chassi and Caroline were both twenty-five. If circumstances had been different they could have gone to the same school, they could have had sleep-overs and play dates, they could have been best friends.

"Go on, Chassi."

Caroline had actually needlepointed Eleanor a pillow many Christmases ago with "GO ON" written across the front of it in yellow and purple script. Eleanor had bopped her in the rib cage with it. "I can't take this to the office, you silly," she'd said, laughing, but Caroline hadn't been laughing with her, feelings hurt like always, you had to always watch what you said, and Jimmy had piped up from behind the green and tinsel, "Well, I don't see why not. You can flash it at them, El, save your voice." Eleanor put the cap on her pen. Christmas. Well, Caroline wouldn't be home with her this Christmas. If she wasn't speaking to Eleanor, how could she come home?

"I crossed the street," Chassi said.

Eleanor caught her lip in her teeth. *Tick, tick, tick,* and Eleanor's own breath in her chest and Chassi's thin back hovering, the light caressing the same bones as on Chassi's mother's famous face, the similarities eerie except the child wasn't as tall as the movie star or maybe the movie star had only been tall on screen. Didn't Alan Ladd stand on a box? "Go on, Chassi," Eleanor said.

". . . she was behind me . . ."

Eleanor waited, her eyes on the girl.

Chassi lifted her knees suddenly, clasping her arms tight around her naked kneecaps, the soles of her big tennis shoes dropping bits of dirt on Eleanor's ridiculously expensive couch. "How could a person have so much blood?" she said.

Quiet.

"Via Emelia, that was the name of it, the street."

Eleanor watched her.

"We had gone to eat in the same place as the night before, they made this artichoke that I liked with crumbs . . . I'm a vegetarian."

An intake of Chassi's breath and the annoying ticking.

"Not my mother, just me. God, certainly not my mother. My mother was"—she laughed—"I don't know, the queen of Spenser steaks, the duchess of prime rib. I mean, she even did one of those meat commercials, you know, voice-overs like Robert Mitchum did, for, I don't know, the American beef thing."

Eleanor couldn't reach the clock even if she wanted to, she could see it but she couldn't reach it, she would have had to fall out of the chair and crawl to the edge of her desk on her knees. So unbecoming for a doctor.

"I never liked meat," Chassi said softly. "She always had to cover it with sauce if she wanted me to eat it, I mean, even when I was little, before I became a vegetarian, she covered everything in tomato sauce, well, told *them* to, but I didn't like it anyway . . . meat." She inhaled and blew the exhale out of the side of her mouth, the air stirring the blonde silk against her cheek. "I never knew blood smelled."

Jesus. Eleanor felt her own body stiffen, closed her eyes and could see the blood.

"It spread out from under her. Just like in the movies."

They both waited.

"She'd said she wouldn't take a movie no matter what it was, we would go away together, just her and me. My graduation present from sixth grade. So grown-up, I thought. I was always the youngest in my class, but Mommy said the most grown-up."

She was remembering, you could see her remembering, you could practically see the blue and the gold of Italy on the girl's face.

"She said we could go anywhere I wanted. I picked Italy, I did a report on Italy in school; you know, you had to pick a country and I got Italy. It wasn't what I wanted, I wanted Ireland but I got Italy instead."

The girl didn't move, just sat there, her eyes somewhere on a street called Via Emelia, off the Via Veneto near the famous Excelsior in Rome. "Go on."

"Anita Blackman got Ireland."

Eleanor's lip caught between her teeth. What a gyp. Did good old Anita Blackman ever get to go to Ireland? And where was her mother today? Chassi's face in perfect profile, the light catching one amber eye.

Silence.

"You know, we rode home with her. Daddy came, I guess they called him . . . I don't know, he was just suddenly there . . ." She stopped and then started, ". . . Daddy and me in first class and Mommy underneath somewhere with the luggage, and I kept thinking the whole time that maybe there was a puppy down there with her, you know, one that somebody was taking back to L.A., because I wouldn't think they'd have special compartments." She turned and faced Eleanor. "I mean, they don't know when they're going to get a body, right? They'd have to put all that stuff together. Puppies, people, Louis Vuitton bags . . . I envisioned it . . ." And then she gave a half smile. "Of course, in my envisioning, Mommy was alive. You know, not in a casket, not broken and . . ." She didn't finish. . . . "but up, you know, and laughing and playing with the dog. Drinking her water in a stemmed glass with all her rings on and throwing the dog a tennis ball." Eleanor kept her face empty, and swallowed. Chassi's knees bent into a cross-legged Indian position. "My mother would have liked it if there would have been a puppy down there with her." She lowered her head. "My mother always loved dogs. Isn't it time for me to go?"

"No."

She opened her small hands, palms up, and laid one on each bent kneecap, the marshmallow shoes perched up and locked over her inner calves. It was the lotus position in yoga, Eleanor knew. Caroline's legs bent into the same arrangement in the middle of Eleanor's kitchen floor as Eleanor crossed behind her silently with the coffeepot, Caroline standing on her head in the living room, or frozen in what she called the warrior position at the foot of Eleanor's staircase, motionless and breathtaking, only missing a spear.

"Do you do yoga?" Chassi asked.

Eleanor didn't answer.

"It's supposed to relax you. Or keep you centered." She shrugged. "I'm just starting, I don't know."

"What happened then?"

Chassi arched her back straighter, pushed her body into the position, kept her open hands on her knees. "What do you mean, in Rome?"

Eleanor watched her; Chassi lowered her chin.

"The car hit her."

Neither of them moved and then the girl leveled her eyes at Eleanor. "She flew into the air like she was a stuntman, they had the number of feet in the newspapers, I don't know."

If she was waiting for a reaction, she didn't get one. Eleanor held the girl's stare. "Go on."

"Go on what? Do you mean the funeral? Was that a yes or a no?"

The first sign of anger, a flash of defiance, a slight flush across the cheeks and nose.

"Okay, look," Chassi said and broke position, "I've been shrunk before, it's not like this is the first time." She pursed her lips, squinted her eyes into the look of a cartoon psychiatrist, " 'Ve vill discuss ze guilt fhrom your muzzer's death, you zink you killed her. No?' " Her gaze was intense on Eleanor. "No. My mother died a long time ago. I didn't kill her, okay? I know."

She uncrossed her legs and stretched them out behind her on the couch and faced Eleanor, lying on her side on one hip. Her elbow poked into the leather with that arm raised, her hand holding her head up at the cheekbone. "I don't know what you think this has to do with anything," she said, "with my *episode*. That's what the suits are calling it. 'My God, she had an episode, Marty, we couldn't get her out of the trailer, we had to shut down.' " She used another voice this time, the cartoon voice of power and money, of a stubby man with a pinkie ring and wide lapels. "They only have two scenes left with me and the movie is insured; it's not like it's going to cost them. And I'm fine now." Her eyes were on Eleanor's, appealing, the same way they appealed on screen. "Look at me, aren't I fine?"

"Tell me about the funeral."

The blonde hair fell across her face and she lifted it and tucked it behind her ear. "Huge," she said, "I don't know, cameras clicking behind the barricades, I could hear them, they tried to keep me back, away, but I could hear them, you know . . ." She waited, as if she thought that would be enough for Eleanor and then she sighed. Her eyes shifted off Eleanor, glazed somewhere in between the two of them on the pale dhurrie rug. "It was hot"—she replaced a hunk of hair that had fallen—"and the pallbearers nearly dropped the casket going up that stupid hill"—an intake of air—"my heels, she'd let me buy them, he said I was too little, but she'd said . . . they were just these tiny heels, they sank into the sod. Daddy was wobbly, I don't know, his hand was wet"—the pink tank top raised and lowered as Chassi breathed—"gardenias and they were turning brown, you know how they do and the florist people must have known that they would, but Daddy insisted on gardenias and what could they do, walk alongside the casket and sprinkle water on the gardenias?" She breathed out. "My mother, always walking around with gardenias as if she was still in the land of Louis B. Mayer." The girl ran her other hand fast across her cheek, kept her eyes down. "The heels are still in the box in the closet, little pieces of mud and grass stuck to them like moss in a science experiment. So stupid . . ." And then she was quiet and she lowered her arm and her head, buried her cheek on the inside of her elbow, settled into Eleanor's hard couch as if it were a down comforter, and said in her mother's twang, " 'Sally Brash, east Texas's own darlin', three-time Academy Award winner, wife of the mogul Saul Jennings, mother of the nothin' Chassi, was buried today in the City of the Angels.' " She took another long breath and exhaled. "Fade-in, fade-out."

• • •

IONIE WAS LATE and she knew it and she knew Rudy knew it too, uniform or no uniform, and no matter how she stood there acting as if she'd been waiting on customers since ten-thirty, no matter how everyone had covered for her, Rudy knew. She adjusted her Cuppa Joe shirt under her apron. It wasn't bad enough that the shirt was purple, which went awful with her red hair, then they had to go and make it even dumber with the Cuppa Joe lettering and the cup with the steam coming out of it stitched in red. Red and purple, who came up with such colors? Ionie could see her mother, one hand on her hip, the other lifting a cigarette. "Honey, that just don't go." "I know, Mama." "Well, baby, you just tell them you can't wear that, not with your hair." Ionie smiled to herself. "I'd rather be pecked to death by ducks than wear this," she could tell Rudy in her mother's drawl.

She pushed lids on the three lattes, one with *"very little foam,"* the lady with the teeth had enunciated, as if too much foam would kill her. Ionie bagged them, and handed the ticket to Rudy, who gave her a look. Go ahead, say something, she yelled back at him with her eyes. He punched the register and smiled his crap smile at the lady with the teeth.

She'd only been twenty minutes late, for cripesakes, and it wouldn't have been such a big deal except she'd left early last week to make an audition at Fox and he'd caught her. The parking was a bitch at Fox and Rudy had caught her walking out the door. "Leavin' a little bit early, aren'tcha, Ionie?" he'd said in his singsong with a lot of emphasis on all three syllables of her name. As if being the assistant manager of a Cuppa Joe could possibly be someone's goal.

Ionie mopped spilled coffee off the long white counter and scanned the room. Chassi Jennings was at one of the high round tables in the corner; she'd moved the stool so that her back was to the room. Just like last time. She was not wearing sunglasses. The two of them had exchanged glances twice, she'd been sitting there since noon. It was amazing to Ionie that she hadn't been stormed by idiots wanting her autograph, but then again, from the back it was hard to tell that she was a somebody; who would know that that tiny back and nothing blonde hair belonged to the same person you'd seen being interviewed by Barbara Walters the night before? Ionie straightened her shoulders, refolded her rag. She'd known about Chassi Jennings her whole life. Chassi Jennings, the daughter of Sally Brash, who was not only the biggest movie star to have ever come out of Texas, but was from Ionie's very own home town. Ionie's mama could give you the history of Sally Brash and her daughter, Chassi, as if she had made a biography on them for A&E. A lot of actors hung out in Cuppa Joe, but not anybody who had made it, or at least not anybody who was as famous as Chassi Jennings. Only dopes who lugged in *Variety* or sat poised behind a script pretending to be learning their lines; only Ionie knew that they weren't learning anything, only looking around the room. As if a real working actor would learn lines in a coffee joint anyway and not at home. You had to say lines out loud. "Sing them, scream them, say them until they're a part of you, until you turn blue," Joan preached to them in scene study. Ionie could recite lines to the beat of "Humpty Dumpty," sing them to the tune of "How About You?"

She tossed torn sugar packages and mixing sticks into the wastebaskets, working her way across the room. People were such pigs. The guy this morning at the audition was a pig, that was for damn sure. A producer pig in Armani. How could you not look at someone auditioning right in front of you? Kept his eyes glued to her 8 by 10 glossy when he could have reached out and touched her without wrinkling his suit. A pig, crumbs or no crumbs, a definite pig.

Chassi Jennings didn't move on the stool. She wasn't reading anything, she wasn't writing, she was just staring at a wall two feet in front of her. The funny thing was that she was probably the only one there who could really have been learning lines. Or maybe not—the skinny in class was that on *Hard Copy* they'd said Chassi Jennings had thrown some kind of fit on a picture and they'd had to shut it down. The other funny thing was that if you walked out of the door of Cuppa Joe and turned left, all you could see was the marquee of the Bruin looming in your face: "Chassi Jennings and Franco Ciovinni in *No Secrets*," fat black letters hovering above your head and here she was two doors down sitting behind a cardboard container of cold espresso staring at a wall. Ionie crumpled up some used napkins and swiped another table with her rag. Okay, she was good-looking, you had to give her that, petite and kind of honey-colored, with stunning bones. Her mother's bones. And her mother's career. Nothing like stepping onto a silver platter. Ionie pushed some loose red curls back up under her Cuppa Joe visor and lifted her head to her full five feet, nine inches.

Okay, that wasn't fair. Chassi Jennings was a good actress, no matter how much Ionie didn't want her to be. She was. Ionie'd seen *No Secrets*. Twice. No kidding. And only part of it was that she'd had two hours to kill in Westwood before she was supposed to sub for Sherry on her shift; the other part of it was that she'd wanted to watch her again, the truth, especially the scene in the closet. There was something about her that caught you, Ionie didn't know what it was. She brushed some scone crumbs onto the floor, turned, and caught Chassi Jennings looking at her. Ionie returned the look and Ms. Movie Star lowered her eyes. Well, don't worry, Ionie thought, walking across Cuppa Joe, her rag swinging, I'm not going to bother you, far be it from me.

• • •

AS IT TURNED OUT, Eleanor did not have a lunch, she had twenty minutes in between patients, twenty minutes and then The Shoelace. She studied the selection of yogurts in her mini-refrigerator. She shouldn't think of him as The Shoelace, it was awful, but she'd never been able to break the detailed image of his description that first session, his meticulously detailed description: rows of shoes lined up in his closet, he'd painstakingly managed to get out, all at the same *precise* angle, all the laces *tied*. "Wing tips to Nikes," he'd seethed through clenched teeth, poised, stiff hands out in front of him, his mortified eyes on Eleanor, eyebrows high, "and I have to untie them and then retie them, *perfectly*, before I can leave." He said again, in desperation, "Do you understand what I'm saying, Dr. Costello? *Before I can leave*."

Blueberry, not peach, and certainly not cappuccino. What had possessed her to buy cappuccino yogurt? Eleanor stayed where she was in the cold air, knees bent, crouched. A momentary blank— she'd bought it for Jimmy. She reached for the blueberry and gently shut the refrigerator door. Her right knee made a *clunk* sound as she stood up.

"No wonder the poor bastard is always late getting everywhere. Honey, tell him he doesn't need you, he just needs to get rid of some of his shoes."

"I'm not telling you about my patients again, ever." Eleanor, laughing, wiggling out of Jimmy's hug, "no matter how you try to wangle it out of me, never again." That was the beginning, that was when he'd started giving them names.

"What? What are you guys talking about?" Caroline, coming into the kitchen, always looking to see where they were.

"Nothing, Caroline."

"We were talking about a shoelace," Jimmy said, making a face at Eleanor over Caroline's head.

"Jimmy," Eleanor said.

"No, wait, just tell him to stick to loafers. No laces, no problem. Hey, El, you want a beer?"

Jimmy in front of the open refrigerator, Jimmy with his beer.

"Honey, what are you looking for?" She'd find him standing there.

"I don't know . . . a cheeseburger?"

Eleanor lifted the lid on the blueberry carton, grabbed a plastic spoon, and sat in her chair. She stirred the lavender cream, skidding the spoon against the cardboard. Dead people do not eat cappuccino yogurt, Eleanor, just let it be. That's what her mother-in-law had told her last week on the telephone.

"It's my new theory, dear, no matter what upsets me, I say to myself, 'Sis, just let it be.' "

Is your mother-in-law still called your mother-in-law if your husband is dead?

It was Jimmy's blood Eleanor could see when the child described her mother lying in the street. A flash of Jimmy in the bed at the hospital and a flash of the intensity of quiet as all the machines made an abrupt stop, the rise and fall of the sickening *squoosh* sound strangled into a horrifying flat green hum. She raised the spoon to her mouth. *Hey, Eleanor,* she could hear Jimmy's Brooklyn, *hey, honeybabe, just let it be.*

It had never sat well with Caroline that Eleanor had been the one to pull the plug, the vernacular of the hospital and the situation, "pull the plug." A simple three-pronged plug pushed into a socket or pulled out of a socket, as the case may be. As if you were disconnecting a lamp in the living room and not a husband of twenty-eight years. It had never sat well with Caroline that she wasn't the one the doctors had finally turned to with empty hands and eyes. After all, it was her daddy. Didn't it say "#1 Daddy" on a gold chain around his neck, a too-big, too-gold chain with too-big letters that Caroline had given him when she was thirteen and which he'd refused to remove. "It's a little flashy, don't you think, Jimmy?" His eyes bright as he turned to Eleanor, "Naw, it's great, babe, I like it fine."

"He'll never breathe on his own, he'll never do anything," the doctors had said to the beat of the *squoosh* sound, their scrubbed hands clasped behind their backs. Jimmy never do anything? The renowned infielder for the United-Jewish-Italians? The man who could rumba better than Tito Puente, make a perfect coffee milk shake, bench-press 250 without batting an eye? Her Jimmy Brooklyn Costello? Eleanor looked through the doctors into the pale green wall and held tight to Jimmy's lifeless hand. Caroline resented Eleanor for being the one to make the final decision, but more than that, she resented Eleanor for being the one who was still alive. The undermining of their relationship, it went everywhere with them, stitched as tightly as the thin silk inside a gabardine suit.

"Daddy wanted a Viking funeral."

"That was a joke, Caroline."

"Not completely."

Eleanor felt her lips tighten over her teeth, she wanted to swat her. "Your father wasn't a Viking."

"That isn't the point, you could do it for him. Somehow he'd know."

"No."

The set of her child's face across the table. "You're not open to anything that comes from me, are you? You think you know everything about him. You think you're the only one."

The set of her child's face across the table, the set of her child's back as they lowered the casket, the set of her child's jaw three months after the funeral. "I need to be separate from you, Mom, I can't do this. I don't want to see you. Don't call me. Okay?" And Eleanor, with no breath for words, sat there frozen as Caroline walked out of the house. "Don't call me," she said again, the door closing, the "#1 Daddy" chain swinging from her clenched fist.

Eleanor put the lid on the empty carton of yogurt, stood, and walked to the windows. The muffled din of Westwood stretched beneath her; she rested her cheek against the glass. Rain again.

Umbrellas opening and a curious bustle that was so unlike L.A. The light changed at the corner and the people surged across. She knew the tiny street, Via Emelia, she'd been to Rome. Once with Jimmy and once alone but alone before him. Pre-Jimmy, he would have said. "Before I lit you up, huh, babe?" Eleanor closed her eyes at the window. She hadn't known the girl had been with her mother when the mother had been killed. Had that been in the papers? She opened her eyes, kept her gaze steady on the stream of traffic, the back and forth of the windshield wipers. She had never taken Caroline on a trip, just the two of them, had she? No. What had they ever done together without Jimmy?

Eleanor leaned her forehead against the window. Bury him. That was it.

She turned. The light from the waiting room blinked yellow, The Shoelace had arrived. She promised herself she would not look to see if he was wearing loafers, she promised herself she would never again buy cappuccino yogurt, she promised herself she would not think about Jimmy; she walked across the room.

Chassi Jennings suffers the loss of her mother, Caroline Costello wishes her mother was dead. Eleanor sailed the empty yogurt carton around her back and up into a high arc. She hadn't seen or heard from her daughter in eleven months, she hadn't talked to her. Well, she'd talked, but with no answers, just Eleanor having pathetic one-sided conversations with Caroline's answering machine, the soft jingle of distant wind chimes and "Hi, it's Caroline, please leave the message," and then Eleanor fumbling to speak before the beep. "Hi, it's me, it's Mom, uh, it's your mother. Uh, I hope you're fine. Good-bye." Pathetic, stammering like a two-year-old, Caroline's words, "Don't call me, Mom," looming like neon in Eleanor's head. The yogurt carton landed squarely in the waste can.

"Two points, Brooklyn, babe," Eleanor said to the empty room and opened the door.

CHAPTER 2

"They're worried about you," Saul Jennings said to his daughter.

"They're worried about their picture, Daddy," Chassi said.

He raised the heavy crystal glass of scotch off the bar, lifted it to her in a wordless toast, a slight nod of the head. "They're worried about that too, they'd be fools not to." He took a sip of the drink. "It's called show *business*, sweetheart, remember?"

"I know."

He walked across the thick Persian carpet and sat in his chair, the larger of two beautiful old caramel-leather wing chairs angled toward the fireplace. The smaller chair had been Chassi's mother's; Chassi sat on the sofa across from the chairs. Saul ran his hand across the nail heads studding the chair arm, took another swallow of scotch and looked at his girl.

"What do you think of the doctor?"

"La Shrink? I don't know."

"Why don't you know?"

"She doesn't talk."

"Oh?"

"Okay, she talks; she asks, but she doesn't answer."

Saul made a "hmmp" sound.

Chassi imagined a red velvet rope tied from arm to arm across her mother's wing chair, preventing anyone else from sitting down. It was like that all through the house, a veritable Sally Brash museum, all they needed was a sign. An imaginary velvet rope across the wing chair and scalloped in and out: over the bottles and jars left scattered on her dressing table, looped through the big brass Chinese knobs on the doors of her closets, tied in a bow around the golden faucets of her deep claw-footed bathtub, pulled inside the sleeves of her pink monogrammed terry robe hanging on the back of the pool cabana door. As if her mother would breeze in and race upstairs, a clatter of high heels across the parquet, a cloud of gardenia and laughter where she had just stood.

"What?" Chassi said to her father. They could have a kiosk at the gates at the end of their driveway where people could buy their tickets, but where would they park their cars?

"I figure the doctor doesn't talk because she wants you to talk."

"I know that, Dad, but it's still disconcerting."

"Yeah, I guess so."

Chassi tried to imagine her father on the couch across from Dr. Costello; she swallowed her laugh.

"What does she look like?"

"I don't know, you mean if you had to cast her?"

Saul Jennings's faint smile behind the crystal and amber. "Yeah, sure."

"Anne Bancroft with all the angles and fire but with a little more meat on her, maybe five, ten years ago and with graying hair."

Saul nodded. "I always liked Anne Bancroft, hell of a gal." He lowered the glass. "Have you told her yet about the crying?"

"Not yet."

"I thought that's what you were there for."

"I thought I had to do it her way." She held his eyes.

"Right you are," Saul said, draining his glass and rattling the ice cubes. "I'm sure you're fine. A little sleep, a little fun; how about you come with me to dinner? I'm meeting the Fiskins and the Bernheims at Dan Tana's."

"Not tonight, Dad, I don't think so." She stood up, moved across the room. "Say hello for me."

Saul held out his hand. "So, what does she ask about, Chassi?"

She stopped where she was and looked at him. "Rome."

He thought it was crying, that's what she had told him, that's what she had let them all think. A crying jag, nothing. After all, didn't she have a right to be exhausted, hadn't she been shooting two whole months of nights? Chassi turned up the hot in the shower. She ought to move out, she ought to get her own place, it was more than time. There was no reason to live in a museum for her mother, walking around in a remake of *Sunset Boulevard* with her father doing a bad imitation of Gloria Swanson swathed in cinematic memories. Not that anyone saw it, she never asked anyone over; who would she ask? She just hadn't figured out a way to tell him, didn't want to watch him pretend that it was all right if she left. She had been here with him since they had returned from Rome, since the day after her mother's funeral, since the banner headlines had spread across the front of both trade papers: "Tidal Wave Stuns Pacific." *In an emotional speech that shocked the industry, Saul Jennings announced today that he would step down as chairman and CEO of Pacific International Pictures after a reign of twenty-two years.* He stepped down and his lawyers made him an independent-producer deal; he moved into a swank set of offices in a high-rise Century City building and never set foot on the lot again. In the fourteen years since her mother had died, Chassi always knew where her father was—in his office, out with friends for dinner, or sitting in the wing chair.

Chassi ran the soap across her breasts. No one lives at home with their father when they're twenty-five. She turned her back to the stinging water. Of course, she'd never had a normal life. And what do your mommy and daddy do? Oh, my mommy's a movie star and my daddy runs the big studio where she works. Chassi picked up the shampoo. Studio. "Daddy's late for the studio, punkin'," her feet dangling from where Saul held her in the air and kissed her; he lowered her to the driveway and got into his car. She'd been in and out of the gates of the studio since she'd been born, had her first birthday party at the studio, a garish affair on the back lot with clowns and real ponies that she didn't remember at all, her first job at the studio when she was only four, doing a walk-on in Howard Hall's last musical on stage sixteen, and her first man at the studio, a giddy, breathless, stand-up fuck with Marjorie Grissom's driver, Garris, against the door of Marjorie Grissom's dressing room, in the dark. The head of the sign shop in the art department had taught her how to hand-letter the backdrops for her science project with a brush and a stick, the head of wardrobe had made sure the designer instructed the seamstresses on each and every costume she ever wore for Halloween, and the head of transportation not only taught her how to drive a stick shift without letting the car jerk but coached her through the exquisite art of sucking a cock. Chassi Jennings grew up at the studio, she loved the studio and the studio loved her. The dizzy began; she put her head under the water to rinse out the shampoo; she had better get out before she fell down.

• • •

"THEY'RE AN HOUR BEHIND," the brunette said from the chair closest to Ionie.

Ionie put her gym bag, her purse, and her water bottle on the floor. "An hour? I practically killed myself getting here."

"They're not even here yet," said a blonde sitting on the floor. She rolled her eyes. "They're still at lunch."

There were seven of them lining the hallway outside the production office, seven women; three were around Ionie's age, late twenties, and four older, maybe forty, forty-five. Ionie sank to the floor. One line for seven women. That's all the part was, one line: "Dr. Mills, what are you doing?" The character's name was Woman No. 2. Ionie's fingers had made sweat marks on the flimsy piece of paper, she'd read the line so many times. It was fax paper from Al's machine on the job. She didn't have a fax, she didn't have a cellular, she didn't have a beeper. She didn't network, she didn't drink martinis, she couldn't get into the Bar Marmont. What was she doing in Hollywood anyway? She said the line to herself again, slumped against the wall behind her, and took a big swig of water.

"One line?" Al had said. "Is that all of it?"

Ionie studied the smudged piece of paper. "I guess."

"You're going to read for one line?"

"Yes."

"Jesus. You'd think they'd just give it to you."

"They don't do that, Al."

"Well, you'd think they would. I mean, what's the difference?"

He read over her shoulder, " 'Dr. Mills, what are you doing?' Who's Dr. Mills?"

Ionie looked at him. "I don't know."

"Is he, like, a main character?"

She was going to hit him, she was going to punch him right between his baby blues.

"I don't know, Al."

"So what's he doing, good old Dr. Mills?"

"I don't know."

"What do you mean, you don't know?"

She exhaled. "I mean I don't know."

"You don't have the rest of the thing?"

"No, Al."

"Well, how the hell do you know how to say 'What are you doing, Dr. Mills?' if you don't know what Dr. Mills is doing?"

She was going to cry, she knew it. She could feel it rising up out of her chest like a geyser; she would slug him and then she would cry.

"Have you seen the whole script?" she said to the blond. She was one of the ones who was Ionie's age, a blond with lipstick that was way too pink.

"Not me. She has." The blond nodded her head toward one of the forty-year-olds, one sitting on a chair all swathed in white. She was too chubby to be wearing all that white, she looked like the Pillsbury dough-boy. Was she wearing white because Woman No. 2 was a nurse? A lab technician? A nun? Ionie smiled at her. "Do you have the whole script?"

"Uh-huh."

Just uh-huh. Not "Uh-huh, sure, do you want to look at it?" Not "Yeah, here it is." Not "What do you want to know?" The woman turned away from Ionie and silently said the line. Ionie could see her lips moving to the tune of "What are you doing, Dr. Mills?"

"Do you, uh, happen to know what Dr. Mills is doing?" Ionie whispered to the blond.

A vacant stare, the pink lips moving. "Excuse me?"

"It's okay, never mind."

It was hopeless. Why did she care anyway? All these years of improv and Shakespeare, Meissner and tap, diction and Linkletter, Strasberg and singing, mime and jazz and ballet and voice. For what? To be Woman No. 2, a vision in white. To say "What are you doing, Dr. Mills?" Who the hell cares what Dr. Mills is doing? Who the hell really cares? What was she going to do if she couldn't be an actress? Her whole life she was going to be an actress, there'd never been anything else. The tears came now, not in front of Al where it wouldn't have mattered, not in the car when she'd practically killed herself getting there, but now in front of six other women who probably all cared deeply about Dr. Mills. Loved Dr. Mills. Respected Dr. Mills. They'd probably all done Dr. Mills, maybe all of them at once—

"Ionie St. John?" someone said. Ionie looked up. It was a young woman holding a clipboard, the clipboard Ionie had signed when she'd arrived.

"Your agent said you had another reading across town and could you go first. You ready?"

God bless Nicki for saying she had another reading. Yeah, right, she had a reading at Cuppa Joe with a cappuccino machine.

"Sure," Ionie said and stood up, wiped her cheeks with her fingers, and followed the clipboard down the hall.

She said "What are you doing, Dr. Mills?" to three people on a couch, two men and one woman, all three overweight and beige. They said nothing. She was on and off the lot before you could say Woman No. 2. She called Nicki later in the afternoon when there was a lull between the lattes and she was sure Rudy was in the john. Ionie would never know what Dr. Mills was doing because she didn't get the part and she knew she would never, ever watch the show.

• • •

THE DIZZY HAD COME OUT OF NOWHERE and it was getting worse. Chassi's first thought was that she had been hungry. Low blood sugar, have some orange juice, get a real Coke. But then she was dizzy after she'd had a sandwich and then she was dizzy after she'd devoured a big bowl of Tia's spinach and ricotta ravioli and apple pie. She covered it, she left the dining room humming, trailing her hand across the chair backs to steady herself; she could feel Tia's eyes on her. "Chassi, you have headache?" "No, I'm fine." And then she was dizzy on the set, kissing Lyle Marvin, so close up, the brown of his eyes melting into the pink of his face, like standing too close to a Seurat. She held on to him long after Ziggy had yelled "Cut." Clinging to his arm, reeling. They all thought it was the kiss; even Lyle, the fool. Talk about the male ego. But she was an actress, she could cover it, no one would know. And then she got dizzy in the shower, so dizzy that she slid down the glass holding on to the washcloth and wound up half inside and half out, water beating against the tile floor, soaking the rug. She pulled herself up, wet and trembling, holding tight to the towel rack. It was nothing, she told herself, she could stop it, it was in her head. And in between the dizzy were the nightmares. And the nightmares made her tired because she couldn't go back to sleep. And then she couldn't concentrate; the lines she'd memorized the night before would slip away from her, she couldn't grasp them, it was as if they were right on the edge of the frame. She'd always been able to remember lines before, it had never been a problem before. Before what? There was nothing, nothing had happened, there was no reason for this. But she was an actress, she could cover it, no one would know.

• • •

"How are you?" Eleanor said.

Chassi moved her feet on the couch. "Oh, a little tired, that's all."

"I see."

She sees what? Be careful, girl.

Silence.

"Do you sleep?"

"Oh, sure."

"Then why are you tired?"

Chassi ran her hand over her face, turned her head slightly away from Eleanor. "Sometimes I wake up."

"Do you dream?"

"I don't know."

"Do the dreams wake you?"

Be careful, you know how to do this, watch your step.

"You don't remember?"

"No." It was true, she didn't remember, the dark dreams were lost shadows when she opened her eyes. Terrifying shadows.

"Do the dreams frighten you?"

"No." Oh, God, don't answer so fast. She shouldn't have said that, she should have said "What dreams?" Now the doctor knew she had dreams and she'd just said she didn't have dreams. Now she knew. You had to be smart. If the doctor thought there was something wrong with her, she wouldn't let her go back to work and she needed to go back to work, she needed to be okay and go back to work. Be smart, be smarter than the doctor, Chassi. Look at her diplomas, she went to Cornell, in Ithaca. There's nobody smart in Ithaca. Where did she go to med school? Chassi tilted her chin up slightly, looking backward over the top of Eleanor's head.

"Tell me what happened in the trailer."

"What? Sorry, I . . ."

"What?"

"I don't know, nothing."

"Is there anything you'd like to tell me?"

"Not really."

"Ask me?"

She tried a soft laugh. "Not that I can think of. Uh, what is the meaning of life?" She gave her most angelic smile to Eleanor; she knew what it looked like, she'd perfected it in the mirror, she'd seen it on screen. "That was a joke," she said sweetly.

"We can talk about life."

"No, really, it was a joke."

Johns Hopkins in Baltimore. Damn, that was not what she had in mind.

"I asked if you would tell me what happened in your trailer that day, the day you locked the door."

Oh, Jesus. "I was just, you know, overworked. Tired. We'd been on two months of nights." She looked at Eleanor. "Do you know what that is?" That's it, take her in, nonpros always love to hear about the day to day of moviemaking, it makes them feel *in*.

"Yes, I know."

Oh, great. "Well, we had just turned around." That's it, let's see what she does with that.

"Started shooting days again," Eleanor said. "I see; so you must have been very tired. It's hard to turn one's clock around, isn't it?"

"Mm-hm." Short answers, stick with short answers, don't get tangled up in her line.

"And what else?"

"Excuse me?"

Dizzy, just the slightest bit, just the smallest whoop. Sit up. Not too fast. There you go. Sit up, turn around, face her. Maybe it was from looking back over her head like that.

She let her legs dangle off the couch.

Relax. You can do this. Relax.

"What else were you feeling besides tired?"

"Nothing."

The doctor held her gaze. She was actually pretty, this Dr. Costello. Not a knockout like Mommy, but pretty. Late forties, maybe fifty, it was hard to tell. She needed a good haircut, she'd look much younger if it was chopped right at her chin. Great eyes. But why does she wear all those drippy clothes? Long skirts and boots, so seventies—

"Angry?"

"What? No."

"You weren't angry?"

"No."

"I understood you threw a hairbrush at someone."

Jesus. "Not *at* someone."

Eyes steady, the doctor said nothing, just waited for Chassi to go on. "Go on" was what she said most of the time.

"I just threw it. Kind of, I don't know, a little actor fit." She gave the smile again. "Can I get down?"

"What?"

"I mean, off this couch. Can I walk around?" Can I walk out of here and go home?

"I'd prefer it if you would stay there."

"And lay down?"

A faint smile pulled at the corner of La Shrink's mouth. "*Lie* down."

"Why?"

"So you won't be distracted."

"I wouldn't be distracted."

"It doesn't matter now."

"It doesn't?"

"No. Our time is up. I'll see you Thursday, Chassi."

"Okay." Oh, God.

Chickens lay, not people, Eleanor used to say to Caroline.

"Lie, lay, what's the difference?"

"One's correct, the other isn't."

"I don't care."

"Well, that's a good attitude." The shrug, the tilt of the head, Eleanor wanted to smack the smirk off her daughter's face.

"It's not going to change the world if I say lay or lie, Mom."

"Okay, Caroline, let's forget it."

"Fine with me."

Eleanor swiveled around twice in her chair. The walking wounded. Chassi Jennings ought to have sutures holding her heart together. A splint, a cast, a cervical collar. A sterile pad and sticky tape for each wound life inflicts. Eleanor smiled. Psychology, not philosophy, babe, who do you think you are?

She stretched, got out of her chair, hit the star key and 63 on her phone to kick it into voice mail, picked up her datebook and her purse. Lot of stuff going on with that Chassi. Eleanor yawned. Should she have dinner first or a bath? Maybe she could have dinner in the bath. What a concept. She flicked the light switch and her office dimmed, indigo haze from the windows. "What a concept" was not her phrase, it was Caroline's. Eleanor took a deep breath and walked to the door. How much gauze does it take to stop the bleeding if you see your mother die?

• • •

CHASSI SAT on one of the high stools in the back of Cuppa Joe, kept her eyes on the cardboard container of espresso.

A little coffee would fix her up. Maybe she would even have a muffin. Had she put in the sugar? Who would have thought that this would be her most important role? For best performance by an actress in a drama, the Academy Award goes to Chassi Jennings for *Hoodwink the Shrink*. She tasted the coffee and lowered the cup with a grimace; it was cold.

CHAPTER 3

"You're a wonderful actress," Al said to Ionie.

"Yeah? Well, then why won't they let me act?"

"It takes time, baby."

"Don't call me baby. I don't have time, I'm already too old to play the ingenue, soon I'll be too old to play the mom; I'll be playing the grandmother, the great aunt, the curmudgeon."

"Why can't I call you baby?"

"Because my father calls me baby."

"Okay, I'll call you curmudgeon."

She rolled over and faced him, put her naked leg over his. They'd been on the top of the bed for an hour, fooling around. "No, call me something sexy."

"Penthouse?" He squinted at her. "That's a magazine."

She grinned. "I know that, Al." She burrowed her face in the crook of his neck, put her hand on his chest.

"Uh, Playboy?"

"Al."

Zest and sweat and tanned skin. She ran her fingers down the length of his cock. She loved the smell of him, she loved her mouth on him, she loved his gray hair. He lifted her slightly, bent his head, ran his tongue around her nipple, took her breast in his mouth and softly sucked.

Her breath caught. "Al?"

She was wet. She'd been ready for most of the hour, wanting him but wanting to wait and waiting, but wanting him again.

"Mmm?" he said.

He moved her up on top of him. She bent her knees and slipped one leg over him, straddled him, took him inside. A little, just a little and then a little more. They watched each other, she moved against him, smiled.

"Well, ride me, Texas," Al said.

"The women's magazines say we're not supposed to be up here."

"Why not?"

"Because when a man looks up at you, you don't look so good. Bad angle." She spread her fingers wide under her chin.

"You look good to me." He gave her a broad smile. "You look like a curmudgeon."

They were quiet, his eyes on her. He took her hands in his, she held them out to the sides and he took them in his, she arched her back and moved. Hair fanning across her face, she could feel her breath.

"Wait," she said.

"What?"

"I want to know what you're going to call me. Something erotic, huh?"

Al pushed himself hard up into her.

"Wait, I'll come, Al, wait."

"That was the plan."

"But I want to wait for you. Tell me what you're going to call me."

"You can wait for me after the third time."

"Ha!"

"Oh, you don't think so, huh?"

"Al, wait."

He drove himself up into her. She locked into him, held tight to his hands and she didn't say wait again, she couldn't. His eyes on hers, the rush and the swell from inside, the flush as it spread and overtook her, the tremble, the heat, the honey; she rocked back and a sound came from deep in Ionie, a low sound, her chin tilted up and her head flung back and then forward, her eyes on his; she never looked away as she came.

She fell softly forward across his chest, a tumble of pink woman, the top of her head under his chin. He pushed the curls back from her face and kissed her damp forehead. "That's one," he whispered, pulling her close into him. "Hey, Ionie, hey, my love, I'll call you coconut cream."

He didn't know anything about acting; he was a finish carpenter, he said, he only knew about wood. And nails and sandpaper and—

"Finish?" Her eyes flashed. "You're from Finland?"

He laughed, it was an old joke but he laughed anyway and it caught her unaware. His eyes were blue, his hair was gray, and he was the exact same height as Ionie, no matter what he might tell her later, he was five-nine. She could see the muscles under his shirt and she could smell him. Lemons, she thought, the tang of sweet lemons. "Jersey," he said, searching her face with his baby blues, "Teaneck, New Jersey. Where are you from?"

"Tyler."

"Who?"

"Tyler, Texas."

The music was loud and it was smoky, he tilted his head toward hers. "You're kidding."

"Texans don't kid."

"They don't?"

"Nope."

"I never really knew anybody from Texas."

"What's it like in Teaneck?" she said.

"It's a model suburban town."

He was serious. He had this little frown thing going on in between his blue eyes. He was serious and he was adorable.

"How long has your hair been gray?"

"Forever. I'm really a hundred and three."

Ionie leaned forward. "What's your name, Jersey?"

"Al."

"Big Al, huh?"

A sheepish smile. "I guess so."

Her heart did this little zwoop thing up against her rib cage. "My name's Ionie," she said, and he looked right at her and in the most awful, phony Texas accent she had ever heard, he said, "Howdy, ma'am."

That was six and a half months ago. For their six-month anniversary he had given her a map of the state of New Jersey that he'd gotten from AAA and she had given him a Texas sheriff's badge that she'd bought at a dimestore.

• • •

"WHERE DO YOU LIVE?" Eleanor asked, her eyes on Chassi.

"Holmby Hills."

The sky darkened; the storm was moving in from the beach. They both had their eyes on the wall of windows as the ink rolled in.

"I live with my father."

"I see."

"Do you disapprove?"

Eleanor didn't answer.

"I know I'm too old to live at home." Chassi blinked, then sighed. "It's a big house . . . I don't know . . ." She shrugged.

A big house. Eleanor had a big house too. A big, fat, empty house halfway up a mountain. Coyotes and deer did a parade at sunset, spiders and squirrels brought rats to tea. "This sure ain't Brooklyn, babe," said Jimmy the day they moved in, downing a beer from the bricked garden. "I got to build us a stoop." The squeal of delight from Caroline—"Daddy, baby de-ahs on the mountain, Daddy, look!" Their California-born baby with Jimmy's accent coming out of her mouth.

"I live in my room," Chassi said. A short laugh and she turned her head to look at Eleanor. "I mean, I'm still in my room, the room I had when I was a baby. That's weird, I guess, huh?" She watched Eleanor. "Not that it looks the same."

Caroline's room had looked the same when she'd left for college and returned, dropping out somewhere during the second semester of her junior year without telling them, showing up one random Tuesday evening right before the pork chops to surprise them with the news. It looked the same when she left again, leaving only a scribbled note and some dirty laundry, to follow some boy they had never met to San Francisco. It looked the same when she returned shell-shocked but refusing to divulge details. It looked the same when she left to seek her New-Age-airy-fairy life, as Eleanor thought of it, and the same when Eleanor had asked her to return, after Jimmy died. It was then that she wanted to change everything in the house but Eleanor had said no. To have Jimmy gone was all the change she could take. Nothing more.

"I'm not there a lot, I'm usually shooting, you know, kind of just there to sleep." Chassi frowned. "I'd like to go back to work, you know."

"All right."

All eyes, she sat up. "I can?"

"Yes, you can."

A roll of thunder. They watched each other, they didn't look at the sky.

"Wow," Chassi said.

"Tell me about your room."

"My room? It's"—the almond eyes on Eleanor—"you know, I'm really happy to go back to work . . ." She smiled and then covered her smile with the fingers of her right hand. ". . . uh, my room is, it's two rooms. The bedroom part and the sitting room part, that's the way all the bedrooms are in the house, except theirs, which has two sitting rooms, you know, one for her and one for him." Her shoulders softened, she leaned back down on Eleanor's couch. "It's mostly blue, my room."

Caroline's room was "eclectic"—her word, not Eleanor's. Eleanor's word would have been "godawful." A lava lamp, of all things, swap-meet-painted furniture, a hook rug that was in the process of unhooking, from Sis's old house in Brooklyn, a whorish curtain of red glass beads that clattered in the doorway as you went from the bed to the bath, dried flowers hanging by ribbons from the ceiling, a ratty recliner chair. "You're not putting that in your room." "But I love it." "Where did you get it?" "Brentwood." "Caroline, you did not get that awful chair in Brentwood." "I did too, someone left it in their trash." Her daughter, the garbage collector. "I don't want that filthy thing in my house." "It's not filthy and it's my room." "It's her room," Jimmy had said. "El, don't make such a big thing." Caroline did not take the precious chair when she left, she took none of her treasures. Her new place was probably just an empty white space where crystals hung alongside burning sage and candles, with a telephone wire stretched across the floor. And an answering machine where a mother could leave messages that were never returned.

"I'm mostly in my rooms or in the kitchen; not the kitchen, the smaller dining room, there's this window seat . . ."

Quiet.

"I'm hardly ever in the kitchen; I don't cook."

The rain began, a wash of it across the windows, fast and hard.

"Go on," Eleanor said.

"Go on what? I don't know, I don't cook . . . I never learned. Tia cooked, cooks, she still does . . ."

Quiet. Nothing. Just the rain.

"Did your mother cook?"

Chassi laughed. "My mother? My mother barbecued. 'If it doesn't barbecue, I sure ain't interested,' " she whined in her mother's twang.

"Do you barbecue, Chassi?"

A catch of breath and the child's eyes filled; Eleanor could see it from her chair.

"Chassi?"

Nothing.

"Are you thinking about your mother?"

"No."

"What are you thinking about?"

"Nothing." She struggled. "Going back to work, that's what I'm thinking about, just going back to work."

A barbecue, a million barbecues. Her mother the movie star, whose face was on the cover of three magazines at any given moment, stood in short shorts, a halter top, big sunglasses, and a ripped straw hat at the stone barbecue pit she had had built at the far corner of their lawn. Beyond the pool and before the tennis courts, in the middle of a huge expanse of garden, Sally Brash stood barefoot in the grass basting pork ribs over charcoal with a brush and a pan of sauce. Chassi stood in front of her in a one-piece, too-small bathing suit. Her stomach stuck out. She had no breasts, she would probably never have breasts, and her legs were skinny and her knees were bony and clunked together and her hair was straight. She would never be as beautiful as her mother, she was nine and she already knew. "Beer is the ticket," her mother said in a breathy whisper, "it's the magic ingredient but you mustn't tell." Sally's eyes flashed. "Not anybody, not ever. Okay?"

A delicious wave of pleasure washed over Chassi. To be included, to be in on the secret, to be a confidante of her mother was the best there was. "Okay, Mommy."

"Sally, get out of that hot sun," Saul yelled from the cabana.

Her mother didn't answer, just gave Chassi a wink. She took a swig from the bottle of Budweiser and poured some into the pan.

"And you have to stand here and baste them if you want them juicy, I don't care what anybody says." Sweet smoke and cut grass and Coppertone as Sally leaned in close. "Here, baby, taste"—extending the pan to Chassi—"go ahead, stick your finger in." Chassi dipped her finger into the warm sauce and then into her mouth. "Good?" Her mother's smile, her hair, and the barbecue sauce were the same red-orange. "You'll see, I'll teach you, baby," Sally crooned. "I'm goin' to teach you everythin', you'll always have me."

Barbecue sauce and Coppertone and gardenias. But it was a lie.

Chassi heard the soles of her own shoes squeak across the marble lobby of Eleanor's building. She took a left and walked out fast through the swinging glass doors into the February rain.

• • •

LAMB CHOP, one lamb chop, didn't somebody do a routine about one lamb chop? Eleanor poured herself another glass of Nozzole and cut into her second lamb chop. She had made herself three. She hadn't broiled them in the stove, she'd done them on the grill in the backyard even though it was pouring, stood there in the dark under an umbrella with the grease and the rain spattering into the hot coals and grilled them the way she liked, rubbed with salt and then marinated in Dijon. Charred on the outside and bloody on the inside. Chassi's mother would have been proud. Eleanor sat in the dining room alone, at one end of the long table. Crystal, china, silver, linen, a whole bottle of Nozzole, Ella on the CD, orange gerber daisies in a cobalt blue jug; she'd even stopped at Sweet Lady Jane's on the way home and bought herself one piece of bootleg cake. If Jimmy had been alive they would have been married—okay, don't add it, talk about negative addition. She shouldn't even be thinking about it, no more red circles on the calendar, that's what her mother-in-law had said.

"It's two years since he's gone. You should be out, you're a young woman."

Eleanor had given a short laugh.

"Well, you are," Sis had said, "and you know it."

"I don't have anybody to go out with."

"You're just not being open. If you're open, he'll come."

Just like the ball field in that movie. Eleanor put another pat of butter into the baked potato and eyed the sour cream. What the hell. Three men had asked her out in the last six months. She'd gone out with all three of them. Yuk. Yuk. Yuk. He'll come. Who he? He who? It would be easier to build a goddamn ball field than to be open for someone to come. Eleanor laughed out loud, rolled the wine around the inside of the glass. She was slightly tipsy. Did they still say tipsy, the kids?

The kid hadn't called. Their one and only, their loving Caroline. You'd think she would have remembered, remembered all those cards she'd made with her Crayolas: "Happy Anniversary, Mommy and Daddy, I love you very much, Love, Caroline." Construction paper cut into hearts, something always spelled wrong, sparkle dust shaking off into Eleanor's hands, all over the rug. Caroline loved to cut and paste, pieces of ribbon or lace stuck to the hearts with Elmer's glue. Eleanor finished the second lamb chop, took another swig of wine.

She could have gone out, she'd actually been asked out to dinner at Matt and Moon's tonight but she'd declined. She told herself it was because she didn't want Matt to ask about Chassi; he'd sent the girl to her, he would be itching to ask. Eleanor didn't want to refuse to answer in the middle of Moonie's pot roast but that wasn't the real reason; she also didn't want to be the *one*. The United-Jewish-Italians' famous infield and their wives: Matt and Moonie and Bob and Maria and David and Judy and Jimmy and, oops, Jimmy's dead, remember? No Jimmy, just Eleanor. Seven chairs instead of eight. No thank you.

"Are you sure?" Moonie had asked.

"I'm positive."

"Eleanor."

"What?"

"We miss you. Why won't you come?"

"It's my anniversary."

Moonie had been quiet on the other end of the telephone.

"Not much you can say to that, is there?" Eleanor said. "Really, I'd rather be alone."

"Greta Garbo."

"God bless her, she had it down."

"You'll be all right?"

"Absolutely."

An audible sigh from Moonie.

"Moon, just think of it this way: I'm planning on getting shitfaced and this way I won't have to drive home."

She finished all three lamb chops, gnawed on the bones; she finished the potato, including the skin; she finished the wine, tilting the dregs up and into her mouth. She washed the dishes, blew out the candles, climbed the stairs. She didn't wash her face, didn't brush her teeth, she didn't say any prayers. She came with her own hand in the darkness, in the middle of their big bed when she woke at four. She came twice; she thought that's what he would have wanted. "At least twice, babe," Eleanor could hear Jimmy say in her head as she watched the dawn.

CHAPTER 4

It was all she needed to add to her week. A latte in a big china cup, "not *to go*," was the order, and a water bagel, toasted lightly, with cream cheese. Ionie bit down on her lip and walked across Cuppa Joe with the tray. Chassi Jennings sat on her regular stool in her regular position, her back to the room. "She's here again," was the skinny when Ionie had come on shift. No sunglasses. Jeans, a black T-shirt, the blonde streaks pulled up into a stickout ponytail with a few pieces loose, black boots. No script, no newspaper, but this time a magazine. Ionie set the latte to the right of the slick, colored pages. Chassi Jennings tilted her head, lifted her hands in front of her; Ionie put the bagel plate next to the latte.

"There you go." No makeup.

"Thank you."

"Sure," Ionie said.

It was French, a French *Vogue*. Wouldn't you know? A French *Vogue* cost anywhere from $11.50 at the newsstand on Fairfax to $17.00 at the Beverly Hills Hotel. Ionie knew because she couldn't afford to buy one, just glanced at the pages and replaced it in the stand.

"Miss?"

She was halfway back to her post. "Uh-huh?"

"May I have some sugar?"

The sugar packets were with the Equal and the Sweet'n Low and the low-fat and the half-and-half and the cinammon and the chocolate and the stir sticks and every other thing you could put in your coffee on three separate counters around the room. All Miss Movie Star had to do was get off her stool and walk maybe four steps.

"Sure," Ionie said.

Two sugars, the plain kind, not the cane, and a stir stick. Ionie put them down next to the cup.

"Thank you."

"Uh-huh. Calendra." It had thrown her, so out of context, her mother's scent on someone else. Chassi looked up; Ionie felt her face flush. "Oh. I didn't mean to say that out loud."

"It is Calendra."

One completely beautiful smile. No kidding. "Sorry," Ionie said and turned. She wasn't going to stand there.

"Do you wear it too?"

Ionie did a little pivot. "Uh, no . . . my mother does. I . . ." She stopped herself; what was she doing? Oh, sure, have a perfume conversation with a movie star. Like Chassi Jennings really wanted to know what perfume Ionie wore.

"Is she a blond?"

"Who? My mother?"

"Uh-huh."

"Sort of. Strawberry, I guess you'd say."

"Calendra works on blonds."

Ionie stood there, her mind blank. The smile, but softer, and then Chassi looked at her as if she was somewhere else. "My mother had red hair."

Of course her mother had red hair, everyone knew that, everyone alive knew that Sally Brash had had fire-red hair. Quiet, motionless, Ionie could see a wisp of her own red hair at the corner of her eyebrow.

A couple of seconds and it was over. Ionie moved one foot and Chassi picked up a sugar packet and said, "Thank you," and Ionie said, "Sure."

It was all Ionie needed to remind her, the appearance of Miss Movie Star in Cuppa Joe. The audition she'd had on Tuesday had been for a guest-star lead. Ionie had nailed it. She knew she'd nailed it, it had been a cinch right from the start. After work, no worries about getting off, no sneaking around Rudy. The show was *Queen of Angels*, about a hospital, its patients and staff, and Ionie not only knew the show, she watched it, every Wednesday night, cross-legged on the couch in front of the box by ten. The part couldn't have been juicier—a young, single mother with leukemia. Oh, boy. An office full of stone faces and Ionie had had them crying. Producers, who never show anything at an audition, had shown everything, they'd practically walked her to the door, practically thrown flowers, and they'd called Nicki and asked for Ionie's availability, Ionie St. John's availability, as if she had something else to do. Besides make milk foam. And they'd put a hold on her. A hold on her, a hold. There was just one little hitch. "Oh, really?" Ionie said to Nicki, bile rising in her chest, "what's that?" "Oh, they want Daisy Monk." Daisy Monk, who was doing a show Off-Broadway, Daisy Monk, who had two series under her belt and was doing a show Off-Broadway where they were standing in line to get in. Daisy Monk, a *name*. "Uh-huh," Ionie had said, her fingers rigid on the back of the chair. Oh, but they were sure it wouldn't work out, assured Nicki. Monk did have a clause to get out of the play but there were technicalities, Nicki said. "Hey, kid, don't worry," and on Wednesday they'd put Ionie on hold. "A hold," she'd said to Al as he held her. "You bet," he'd said. And on Thursday they'd asked if they could send her to wardrobe. It wasn't legal, Nicki explained, on their part, to send her to wardrobe without booking her for the job, but they were so sure Daisy Monk wouldn't work out. "Send me," Ionie had said. Oh, God, send me. On Thursday before Cuppa Joe she went to wardrobe, the little Chinese lady on the floor in front of her with a mouthful of pins. On Friday they'd sent her the script, pink pages with blue additions, they were so sure Daisy Monk wouldn't work out. She'd learned the lines over the weekend; by Sunday Al could say them too. On Sunday night a driver had knocked on the door of her apartment with a new script in pink, blue, green, and yellow, a scene breakdown, and a day-out-of-days—everything that was sent to an actor when a part was for real. Nicki had called to reiterate, oh, they were sure Daisy Monk wouldn't work out. Al fell asleep covered in pastel pages, Ionie learned the rewrite while he snored. On Monday they'd delivered buff pages and on Tuesday Daisy Monk had worked out.

"What do you mean?" Ionie had said, her face wet, clutching the crumpled Kleenex and the telephone.

"They owed the understudy."

"What?"

"They had a deal with Daisy Monk's understudy to go on; they put it into the play so that Daisy could come out."

Ionie couldn't breathe.

"Ionie?" Nicki had said. "We'll get another one."

Another one? So fast? A sound came out of Ionie. A sob?

"Okay, kid?" Nicki had said. "You were close. Remember that."

Ionie shook her head up and down.

"On to the next, babe. Gotta go."

Dial tone, a dead receiver filled with dial tone, alone in a room.

All she needed to remind her now was Miss Movie Star in Cuppa Joe reading a $17.00 magazine.

"Don't forget your daddy knew her mama," Kitty Ray said.

"You're kidding."

"Ionie."

"Mama, I know the story my whole life."

"Well, you could bring it up, give you somethin' to talk about."

"I don't think so."

Kitty Ray took a breath. "I certainly don't know why."

"It would be embarrassing."

"What do you mean—embarrassing? Your daddy didn't do anythin' embarrassing. It's a way to talk to her."

Ionie circled the couch with the phone. "That's not what I mean."

"Then explain what you mean; I guess I'm not smart enough to understand."

"Mama, don't do that, I hate it when you do that. It would be embarrassing for me to walk up to her and say, 'Oh, guess what, my daddy knew your mama in high school.' "

"Why?"

"Well, what do I say after that? It's not like we know the same people, live the same lifestyles. What do I say then?"

"You'll think of somethin'."

"Mama."

"Ionie."

Ionie flopped on the couch, held the phone between her ear and her shoulder, and pulled on her socks.

"I thought you wanted this more than anythin' in the world. Your dream," Kitty Ray said. Ionie didn't respond. Her mother took a drag from her cigarette, Ionie could hear. "He knew her uncle Joe too, died in Vietnam. Poor thing," she said and exhaled.

"Mama, you're smoking."

"I am not."

"You're lying."

Silence on the line. It was a waste of breath to go into it, her mother would be smoking from the grave. Ionie reached under the couch for her shoe. "I'm not going to bring up her poor, dead uncle. Where's Daddy?"

"In the garage. It's just a way to strike up a conversation, you never know where it could lead."

"Oh, Mama."

"Oh, *Ionie*. If she likes you she can give you a part in one of her movies."

"Maybe I should do a monologue for her in the parking lot."

"I don't see why not," Kitty Ray said with another exhale.

Ionie took a breath, held her temper. "That just isn't how it's done here."

"Well, pardon me."

"You don't have to get mad."

Quiet. Ionie bit her lip and then Kitty Ray said, "So who's this Al?"

• • •

"DO YOU HAVE A BOYFRIEND?" Eleanor asked.

Oh, Jesus, here we go.

"Chassi?"

She couldn't just sit there. "I've never had a boyfriend."

Eleanor didn't say anything.

"I mean, I've gotten laid. I've just never had what anybody would call a boyfriend, whatever that is."

They were both quiet. Chassi watched the specks of dust move in the light hitting her legs. She wasn't dizzy. Maybe it was really going away, maybe it was gone. Cured by the amazing Dr. Costello, who had no idea who she really was. No, maybe it was because the doctor had let her go back to work; she had finished the last two scenes of the picture and they'd wrapped. That was probably what it was. Having to work with Lyle Marvin was probably what had made her dizzy in the first place, it was surprising it hadn't made her puke. The next one didn't start until August, she was free and clear. Maybe after she'd finished with wardrobe she'd go away to work on the script. Someplace hot, someplace desolate, desert. Not Palm Springs. Not Hawaii. Barren, where was it barren?

"Does that upset you?"

Does what upset me? "I'm fine."

"I think we should explore what's stressing you."

"I'm fine."

Mexico? Mexico was barren.

"Chassi?" The clink of Eleanor's bracelets behind her. Chassi smiled to herself; she liked the sound.

"What? I'm fine."

"A person doesn't behave in a manner so contrary to their usual manner unless something is wrong."

Jesus. What was it now? She thought she'd already convinced her about the episode in the trailer. No, she wasn't angry. No, she wasn't upset. No, she wasn't anything. Now what? Now she was going to blame it on the fact that she didn't have a boyfriend? She should have told her she had a boyfriend, she should have made him up.

"What do you think about what I just said?"

Chassi's eyes scanned the bookshelves in the corner of the room. What kind of boyfriend could she have? Not somebody in the business, too boring. A doctor? A lawyer? God, no. An Indian chief. She could have used a character from something she'd done . . . Lyle's nitwit character from the movie she'd just finished, or even Lyle himself. Lyle in a full headdress of feathers with a hatchet and a pony—

"Chassi?"

The doctor had little black clay sculptures across the top of the bookcase. Crude ones, simple, as if a child had made them; they weren't very good. There was a picture of someone in a frame on the second shelf but she couldn't make it out. That girl probably had a boyfriend, that waitress in the coffee place. She probably had a boyfriend and an apartment and a normal life. Friends and dinners and going to the movies on Saturday, whatever one did with a boyfriend. If she'd known, she could have asked her. Excuse me, Miss, do you have a boyfriend? What's he like? I have to tell my shrink.

"Chassi?"

Damn. Why did she keep coming here? She didn't have to, the picture was over, she was off the hook with the insurance people. Why?

"You know I don't have to keep coming here," she said out loud. She wouldn't look at her, she'd keep her eyes faced front.

"No, you don't," Eleanor said.

She felt a rush of something, she didn't know what it was. "Well, then maybe I won't." But that wasn't what she wanted. There was something good about coming here.

"Is that what happened the last time you had therapy?"

"What?"

"You left before you were through?"

Is that what had happened? Was it true? She was trying to concentrate, because even if she didn't tell her, she could still think about whether what she'd said was true. Her mind was blank, she couldn't remember anything, she was stuck on that sound. "You know, you have a very loud clock," Chassi said and from behind her Eleanor let out a laugh.

Chassi turned; she'd never heard La Shrink laugh before.

"I'm sorry," Eleanor said, still laughing.

Chassi sat up. "What?" she asked, and then she began to laugh with her, she couldn't help herself.

"I have to replace it," Eleanor managed to say.

"You sure do, it sounds like fucking Big Ben."

And that set her off again, and then they were both laughing, that contagious laughter that spreads back and forth between two people, catches them and they can't stop or speak, that fabulous buzz in the chest and finally Chassi managed to say, "I was going to see how long we were laughing but then I'd have to look at your clock," and Dr. Costello said, smiling, "It's okay, our time's up."

She had laughed with her mother. She had also laughed at her mother. Sometimes it was hard to tell which was which. You couldn't help it, her mother was that kind of person, her mother was a hoot. That was one of the words people used: a "hoot," a "pistol," a "firecracker," "snappy," "hot," a "corker," a "humdinger," a "knockout," "feisty," "racy," a "real doll." Chassi put another pillow behind her back, sat up straighter in the window seat and looked out across the lawn. Her mother had charisma and sex appeal, her mother had zing and pizzazz. The sprinklers sent the water in soft arches up and over the grounds. The sprinklers were on and it was raining. What a waste. "Lollapolluza," she'd left out lollapolluza, her mother was a "lollapulluza," they said. The script for *No Trumpets, No Drums* slipped off her knees and she righted it. She would do all the wardrobe fittings and then she would go away to someplace hot and dusty to learn the lines; it was clear she couldn't concentrate here.

CHAPTER 5

"I can't make it by five," Ionie whispered into the pay phone next to the rest room, "Pacific's all the way across town, can't they see me at six?"

"At six they're going to producers."

"Can't they just let me go to producers?"

"Ionie, May Weber isn't going to let you go to producers until you read for her."

"Okay, okay." She looked to make sure Rudy wasn't slithering down the hall, moved the phone to her other ear.

"Well?"

Nicki was irritated, you could hear it. Just what she needed, an irritated agent and no chance to make it because of this crummy job.

"I can't make it by five unless they take me on a stretcher after I've had an eight-car smashup on the 101."

"Then you lose it."

"Oh, Nick . . ."

"I can't help it if you can't make it, Ionie, I can only do the best I can do."

"I know."

"It's important for you to read for May Weber."

Ionie bit her lip.

"It's an MOW, Ionie, a real-life movie of the week, and they want a *redhead* and they want an *unknown*. They're not looking to get another Daisy Monk, they specifically said an *unknown*."

"What do you want me to do? Quit my job and get thrown out of my apartment and have to move in with you?"

Silence.

"Are you thinking about it?"

A half-hearted laugh. "You're not my type, honey."

"My luck," Ionie exhaled into the telephone.

"Can you make five-thirty? I'll call and beg for a five-thirty."

"Oh, Nick, five forty-five, I promise."

"Jesus, Ionie."

"Five forty-five, Nicki, I promise. I'll do you proud."

"Call me in five minutes," Ionie's agent said and the line went dead.

She made it by five forty-five but only because she flirted outrageously with Tony, who was working the main gate, who she was lucky enough to have actually met because he'd gone with a girl in her scene study, and he let her drive on, park in a red zone, and run to bungalow 10. She read for May Weber, who showed absolutely nothing and didn't say a word and then practically floored Ionie by mumbling could she stay to read for producers as Ionie was walking out the door. Ionie's theory was that if you were even vaguely pretty, all female casting directors hated you on sight, especially the Jewish ones. They all looked to Ionie like would-be actresses who had had the unfortunate fate of being put on God's earth ugly, fat, and mean. But she would rethink that now in the light of May Weber's brilliant observation of her extraordinary reading and her genius decision to ask Ionie to stay. Of course she could stay to read for producers. "Thank you, May. Thank you, thank you." May I kiss the hem of your skirt?

She went over the lines in front of the bungalow, her back up against a palm tree. A younger redhead did them sitting on the steps of the bungalow and an older redhead did them silently with her lips moving, in a chair across from May Weber's assistant's desk. She had done this before, read against others who looked just like her but, oh, to have a string of days where every writer in town sat in his room and wrote "redhead" across the blank page instead of "blond" or "brunette." Once she was one of three redheads and they'd all read against this big black guy and the casting woman's assistant had explained that it was because the producers weren't sure, they might *go another way*. "Another way, I guess so," Ionie said to one of the other two girls.

That time she had read second, this time she went in third. Both of the other redheads threw her a "good luck" as they left. If everybody wanted the part, wasn't it ludicrous to wish each other good luck? Ionie hadn't figured it out yet, maybe the good luck was an actor's way of telling another actor good-bye. This was her first time reading for a television movie but the sixth time Nicki had sent her out in the last eight months. She hadn't gotten anything and then the Daisy Monk thing. This was a substantial role and there was probably no way she could possibly get it, her resumé was practically blank, but if she didn't get it, Nicki would probably lose interest and stop sending her, and if she didn't get it, she would probably go off the way craz-ohs did in the post office and open fire in Cuppa Joe. There were five people in a semicircle around the table. She didn't get any of their names, she didn't know who the producer was or who the director was and she only did the scene once, reading with May Weber who not only continued her low mumble but never lifted her eyes from the page. So much for ingratiating herself with ugly, fat, casting directors.

Silence. Ionie stood there.

May Weber shuffled the pages from the scene. One of the five looked at another one of the five and then gave Ionie a blank gaze. "Thank you," that one said. The other four kept their mouths shut. No notes, no nothing. No Could you do it again and break down in the middle? Could you do it again and be defiant? Could you do it again standing on your head?

Ionie drove off the lot decidedly sinking; why had she come to L.A.? There were a million actresses as good as she was and that wasn't even counting the blonds and brunettes. Or the black guys.

The night air from the open windows blew her hair around and she could smell shampoo, gas fumes from her '78 Datsun, and her own sweat. She was twenty-eight years old, twenty-nine come September. "You better do it if you're gonna do it, honey"—Kitty Ray's eyes sizing her up through the goddamn cigarette smoke—"you look good but let's face it—" "I know, Mama, you've told me a million times, I'm no spring chicken anymore." Was she right? Had it passed her by already? How old is too old? How old is old enough to give up your dream?

She stripped off all her clothes and left them in a damp pile at the foot of her bed. She walked around the apartment naked. The kitchen faucet leaked and the oven was never as hot as it said it was. There was a rip in two squares of the linoleum that she tripped over at least once a day. The shower door stuck because the strip at the bottom was loose, and you couldn't get the rust off the tile no matter what you used. The closets were minuscule; she had to wedge herself in between things with a hip and a shoulder to pull a skirt out. The paint was so thick on the trim around the windows that you could make a mark in it with your fingernail; she'd already tattooed "I.St.J." in three places on the sill by her bed. The toilet flushed of its own free will. You could hear the morons upstairs. You could hear the morons on either side. There was only one electrical outlet in the living room. There was no cable. There was no dining room. There was no yard. *Go west, young woman, and be an actress. Find fortune and fame.* Were you still a young woman at twenty-nine? Ionie stood naked at the kitchen window, pale arms crossed over her breasts and wrapped around her rib cage. What would she do if she couldn't be an actress? Since her first tap shoes, her first taste of people applauding, which happened to be one night in her aunt Dorothy's backyard where she had sung and danced the entire score of *A Chorus Line* for the neighborhood; crickets and cicadas and people clapping, and she had stood there loving it, flushed and bowing and loving it, on a piece of cardboard her uncle Gene had set up on the grass under Aunt Dorothy's clothesline. She was an actress, then and now and always, that's all she was. Ionie stared out at the night sky. No stars. There were no stars. There were probably stars from Chassi Jennings's windows, she was probably way up high. Oh, to be a movie-star daughter of a movie star. Oh, to be able to buy a $17.00 magazine.

She would have to go back to Tyler, she would have to sell cosmetics at the Wal-Mart or give permanents at Lucille's Beauty Salon. She would have to give it up, this dream that was maybe out of her reach . . . she'd end up a mean old woman with no scrapbook . . . The phone rang.

"Don't quit your day job," Nicki said.

Ionie folded to the sofa. "Oh, God. I didn't get it, huh? I thought I was good, Nicki, really."

"You were good, kid, you got it, but you're only the third lead and no matter how much I danced and screamed I could only get you thirty-five. How many cups-a-joe do you have to sell to make $35,000?"

"Oh, Nicki, I got it?" Ionie said and burst into tears.

The part was perfect: a trailer park redhead from somewhere south of Podunk whose husband repeatedly beat her senseless, whose three babies were hysterical, and whose mother finally lost it one fine summer morning and blew the bastard's head away with a big gun. The mother would be played by Eileen Patton, a consummate actress who only worked in TV when it was something that was considered important. The swine of a husband would be played by Marc Raymond, who was in a hot cop series and was everybody's latest throb. The money seemed to have no significance to Ionie, the only thing that mattered was that she'd gotten the job.

"It's me, Mama," Ionie told her mother on the telephone, "the part is me."

"It's you, except you are not married, nobody ever beat you, and I gave all your daddy's guns away to his cousin Bill," Kitty Ray said back at her daughter.

"Metaphorically, I mean. The basic debased Southern mentality and I can just speak with my accent, not have to watch that it's slipping."

"You have never been anywhere near a trailer park, and what do you mean, debased Southern mentality? I certainly never raised you up to be a libertine."

"I mean I understand it."

"Don't make fun of where you come from, Ionie."

"I'm not, I'm not. Hey, aren't you excited?"

"Of course I'm excited, I just want you to make sure you don't turn into another Yankee makin' fun of us nitwit down-home dummies or whatever they think we are down here. Here, tell your daddy. LYMAN, I SAID SHE WANTED TO TELL YOU SOMETHIN', GET OVER HERE!"

"Hey, Daddy, I hear Mama gave all your guns away," Ionie said, smiling into the telephone.

"That's what she thinks," Lyman St. John said. "Go ahead, baby, tell me all about your job."

• • •

ELEANOR TOOK HERSELF to see *No Secrets;* she never told the girl. She had it, whatever that *it* was, it was there. Different from the mother, the mother was bigger. Snappy, Sis would have said. A bit of the nasty in the gold-green eyes. The daughter was not snappy, the daughter was what? Honey, taffy, peanut brittle . . . no, not brittle, but closed and covered. And what else?

Eleanor watched Chassi. The girl crossed her ankles, folded her hands over her stomach, shut her eyes. Comfortable, Eleanor thought to herself, and smiled.

"Why didn't you go away to school?"

The little shrug laugh. "Boy, I never know where you're going to start." She sighed, moved her hands up and across her face. "You mean college? God, I had already made three movies by then. I don't know, it suddenly didn't seem . . . feasible. A lost idea from another time. From before"—she twisted a piece of hair around her first finger—"before and after, that's what it was . . . there was no reason to go away to school."

Eleanor studied the child's profile against the backlight. Sun flooded the office, it was nearly too much sun, the first sun after weeks of rain.

"I couldn't see myself at some school."

Quiet.

"And he didn't care. I mean, if I went."

"Who?"

"My dad. You know, he needed me"—Chassi recrossed her feet at the ankles—"so I stayed."

Quiet.

"Did he want you to be in the movies?"

"My father? Oh, sure. I mean, why not? It's kind of the family business."

Eleanor's eyes refocused on her own hands, the light catching the gold of her wedding band, Jimmy's thick ID bracelet against the skin of her wrist. Jimmy teaching Caroline how to ring the register at the nursery, her little red tennis shoes in tippy-toe position on the stepstool.

"You get along."

"Sure."

Fathers and daughters getting along. Daddy's little girl. Jimmy and Caroline walking out the door without her. Jimmy siding with Caroline when she walked in that night out of nowhere and announced she had quit school.

"You spend a lot of time with him?"

"I guess. More when I was younger."

Eleanor's eyes on the girl. Where was she? What was she remembering?

"What did you do?"

"Oh, you know, he just took me along with him. Chasen's, Palm Springs, Broadway"—a breath—"wherever he went, he took me. After, you know."

Eleanor sat up straighter, flexed her leg at the knee. A soft look touched the corners of the child's mouth. "Go on," Eleanor said but Chassi said nothing. "What's he like?"

"Now? Oh, I don't know . . . like a father, I guess."

"And before?"

A tilt of the head in Eleanor's direction. "He was . . . complete, I guess is the way to put it." The sun moved, caught Chassi full on in a wash of light. "They were this, I don't know, couple, they . . . complemented each other"—a small frown at the edge of her eyebrow—"she was kind of zany, you know, and he was sound. She was wild, and he was, I don't know what you'd call it but she turned to him, my mother . . . they were, you know, the pieces of this puzzle." She hesitated and then went on. "Now he's just . . . half."

It caught Eleanor mid-breath. Her hands went to her face, her bracelets jangled, and Chassi turned. Still, frozen in the white light, neither of them said a word.

So what was the difference in being in the house alone and being in the house with someone else if the someone else was in another room? Eleanor sat in front of the silent television set, the clicker in her hand. She listened. A creak of the house, a car taking the corner. It wasn't the noise that made you feel complete, was it? It was the knowledge that the someone else was there.

Her life had been woven into Jimmy's and now it wasn't and it was ridiculous, all this yearning. For what? He certainly wasn't going to come back, appear in the doorway in a blue work shirt with one sleeve rolled, his hand wrapped around a beer. Eleanor shifted her body on the sofa, slammed her feet onto the coffee table, cleared her throat. Jimmy and Eleanor, Eleanor and Jimmy. And then Caroline. A threesome, he'd said, "El, let's be a threesome," and Eleanor had never wanted to be a threesome but that's what Jimmy wanted, so . . . so, where was the threesome now when she needed it? *Don't call me, Mom.* Eleanor clicked on the television set, spun the channels until they were just a blur.

She had walked in that night right before dinner, the pork chops in the pan. Jimmy sautéing pork chops with yams and apples, Eleanor's favorite, Eleanor sitting at the kitchen table, her boots off and one foot tucked under her, doing the *New York Times* crossword with a pen, not a pencil, and drinking a glass of red wine. Cozy and safe, sweet jazz on the radio, the sweet smell of baking apples, Jimmy telling her a story, and then a key in the door. He slid the pan off the fire, his long stride out of the kitchen, Eleanor at his back, to the sound of her "Hi" in the hall.

"Hi," their daughter had sung out gaily, as if life was fine, just fine. She had quit school the second semester of her junior year. Walked out without a wave in the middle of the second semester, meaning that after that semester she would have had only a year to go.

"I won't go back." Eyes defiant, posture resolute and angry, Caroline glared at her mother and held fast to her side. And as if Jimmy was the referee saying, "Go to your corners," they took their places like always, like two bantamweights waiting for the next round. "I can't be what you want," was where they were after the first hour. After the dancing and the punching and his staying between them, keeping them both in view. And he was spent by then, no more asking, no more pointing out the obvious, presenting his case, his argument with sound reason; he had run out of steam. Fading fast when it came to a fight, Jimmy didn't like to fight and especially not with his only child. He watched now from behind the ropes, slumped against the side of the stove.

"I can't be what you want, Mom," Caroline said again.

"I didn't want you to be a lit major," Eleanor said.

"I didn't want to be an *anything* major. Don't you hear what I'm saying? I went for you, not for me."

"What were you going to do? Sit upstairs for the rest of your life and watch TV?"

"It's all about you. What you want. It's never about me."

"And what do I want? Something bad for you?"

"You want me to be . . . a something."

"A something? I want you to be a something? You're damned right." So ungrateful, so selfish, so childish.

"I can't be what you want," her daughter had said again, her chin high.

Eleanor's heart was flapping up against her ribs, she wanted to smack her, she wanted to shake her until she got it through her thick head. "Caroline, be smart, you're a year away, get the degree and then decide. Get the degree."

"It doesn't mean anything."

"It means plenty."

"I already told you. Not to me."

"You're just going to take two and a half years at Berkeley and throw them down the drain?"

"What I learned won't go down the drain. Don't you see? You only care about the degree."

Take your time, take your time. Eleanor took a swallow of the wine. "Caroline, you're twenty-one years old."

"Everybody doesn't have to be like you, Daddy did amazing things in his life without a degree."

"Oh, Jesus," Eleanor said, "Daddy's life has nothing to do with you."

"We already talked about that, Caroline," Jimmy said. "I went to 'Nam, came home, and got a job. Things were different then, different for me."

The big brown eyes on her father. "I can't do it anymore. Don't you see? I'm dying there."

"Oh, don't be so dramatic," Eleanor said.

The flash of the eyes, the brown curls whipping around to her mother. "You can only give to your patients, only to the sickies. Do you know that? What do I have to do? Make an appointment for you to hear me?"

Eleanor's fingers to her mouth, the punch knocking more than the wind out of her, the punch slamming in way below the belt.

Eleanor's fingers to her mouth now, she punched the Power button on the remote with her other hand. The set went off. Remembering the night and the fight and how Jimmy had begged her in the weeks that followed to make peace with the child upstairs. "You be the big one," he'd said. "I know she hurt you, El, but you be the one." She sat now and remembered. Alone in the dark of the room and the hateful quiet, she remembered how she wouldn't be the one.

CHAPTER 6

Chassi made her first picture the summer before her fourteenth birthday. It was a thriller and the thriller was between two men, the bad guy and the good guy; Chassi played the daughter of the good guy. The part didn't amount to much screen time but there was one frightening scene when the bad guy was looking for the good guy and only found the good guy's kid. The camera didn't just catch her, it nailed her, people left the theater with Chassi's face stuck in their heads. There was no question as to whether she would grow up and become an actress, she already was. The only difference between Chassi and the other young actresses about town who were talented was that she was the daughter of Saul Jennings and Sally Brash; the doors swung open for her, she didn't have to knock any down.

She smudged the olive eye liner above her lashes with one finger, studied her face in the glass. She had stayed with him, her father. Of course she had stayed with him, there had never been any question that she would leave. She had become his confidante, he had become her aide. They relied on each other. He needed her and she would do whatever he asked.

"Chassi, you ready?" His deep voice from the hallway.

"Coming, Dad."

She got up from the dressing table, scooped up her diamond studs and evening bag, and met him at the top of the stairs.

• • •

Sally Brash made *No Trumpets, No Drums* in 1981. She was thirty-six; Chassi had just turned nine. A war movie to end all war movies, but no black-and-white tearjerker about how war is swell and in the end the lovers kiss close-up, superimposed over the waving red-white-and-blue. This time the gung ho soldier marches off to war singing "God Bless America," comes home maimed and broken, and turns into an antiwar radical after his affair with the flag-burning nurse. No studio would touch it. The filmmaker was John Nicholas Thalosinos, an unknown, a nobody who would later become one of the first of the independents, a smoldering, sexy, young Greek. He didn't have a deal, he didn't have a nickel; all he had was a script and plenty of passion and then he got Sally Brash. It rocked Hollywood. She was going to do it for no money up front, she was going to do it against the advice of everyone except her husband, she was going to do it because in 1968 her kid brother, Joey, a PFC in the 6th Battalion of the 45th Infantry of the 197th Infantry Brigade, twenty-two years old with freckles, a lazy left eye, a wide grin, and his sister's fire-red hair, had stepped on a mine near the muddy banks of the stinking Song Tra Bong and had been blown to smithereens.

Sally Brash won the Academy Award. It was her first in a long and solid career and the winning was memorable, not because of her gown or her jewels or her hair, but because of the way she accepted, the way she stood in perfect stillness, the statue locked in her arms, and said only her brother's name. John Thalosinos won for writing *and* for directing and so did the editor, the cinematographer, the composer, and the man who did the production sound. This shoestring budget of a picture that every studio had passed on became the talk of the town. Nominated for eleven Academy Awards, it won seven. "Eleven come seven. That's good. Right, darlin'?" Sally Brash had said to Saul. The money to make the sleeper had come from Saul Jennings, and not as head of Pacific International; against everyone's no's he had personally financed the picture out of his pocket. *No Trumpets, No Drums* had been a gift to his wife.

Saul Jennings had decided to remake the picture and remake it exactly the way it had been. He didn't want to morph the North Vietnamese and the South Vietnamese into L.A. street gangs, he didn't want to move it from straw villages and rice paddies to Fifth and Main. He didn't want to update, he wanted to do it the same. "Didn't they do *A Star Is Born* three bloody times?" he carried on. "Hang it. I'll do it the same."

There was no way any of the young turks who ran the town would make a picture with an old warhorse like Saul Jennings. He was a joke. Well, if not a joke at least he should be put out to pasture, they said to each other Monday night at Morton's at the bar. Oh, they would meet with him, they *had* to meet with him, how could you say no, each resenting the waste of his or her own inestimable time, but be assured they met him only because they had to, certainly not out of respect. A piece of shit whose picture grosses in excess of one million dollars commands more respect in Hollywood nowadays than a man who made class winners in days gone by. It is no longer about esteem or regard or honor, it is only a "how much have you made lately" game, and it is debatable, but probably accurate, that the only reason the ones who could get into Morton's on a Monday night even met with Saul was so they could rise to their feet and applaud themselves if the Academy of Motion Picture Arts and Sciences honored him with the Gene Hersholt Award. Unfortunately, in their fog of greed and power, they forgot one thing. If all else failed, Saul Jennings had a way to green-light his picture; the biggest box-office star of young Hollywood was sleeping in his house in Holmby Hills, right down the hall.

• • •

"GOOD MORNIN', MISS CHASSI," the guard at the main gate said. "You'll be goin' to wardrobe today?"

"Scotty, how've you been? I thought you'd be retired by now."

"Not yet, Miss, got to teach these young ones," he beamed. "Retirin' next spring. Sure is nice to see you all grown."

Chassi could feel the flush spread from her throat. "Thank you, Scotty." She'd known him since she was three. The younger guard in the gatehouse tried to angle himself around Scotty's shoulder but the older man held his ground.

"Your mother would be proud, Miss." He pulled at the brim of his hat, cleared his throat. "There's a spot reserved for you in front of wardrobe." The gate arm raised and Chassi drove on the lot.

Ionie had lunch in her trailer. Well, not a whole trailer, half of a trailer, "half a star" is what it was called. They had it waiting for her when they broke just like she'd ordered: a Cobb salad with no dressing and a diet Coke with no lemon, set up on the table in front of the sofa across from the television set. The little built-in refrigerator was filled with bottles of Evian water. There was a basket of fruit from the production company and a basket of fruit from Nicki and the agency, a crystal vase filled with lilies from the director, and one red rose from Al. It had taken her about twenty minutes to get used to all this luxury. The first morning when the PA had asked if she would like lunch in her trailer, that he was taking orders for the cast, she about fell on the floor. A tiny taste of the fantasy they call Hollywood; she didn't want to get too excited but it was hard not to—for the first time Ionie was actually chewing on a taste of her dream.

"Are you going to quit your job?" Al had asked.

"Leave Cuppa Joe? The land of lattes? Surely you jest."

"No, I'm not jesting."

"I can't leave, Al, not yet. I may not get another job in the business for months"—she took a breath and laughed—"for years, I may not get another one *ever*. I have to be realistic, I have to have an income, even if it's only in coffee beans, unless, of course, you want to take care of me in a manner to which I am definitely not accustomed—a penthouse in Westwood, a ranch in Malibu—" A solemn look in his eyes stopped her. "Hey, I was kidding."

"Okay by me," he said, and smiled.

The thirty-five thousand, less a major chunk in taxes and less a 10 percent commission to Nicki and the agency, wouldn't spread very far, especially with what Ionie owed on her Visa card.

She leaned against the phone booth and waited for Al to call her back, she had beeped him the number of the pay phone. Was Al the one? She hadn't gotten into it, didn't want to get into it, not yet. She had a career. Okay, that was pushing it. Not a career. You couldn't call three one-liners and two under-fives and now this MOW a career. But it was too soon, wasn't it? She'd known him less than a year. How could she know if he was the one? Ionie pulled the kimono from wardrobe snug around her middle, retied the sash. Did she want to spend the rest of her life looking into only those blue eyes? She was getting used to those eyes, falling for those eyes, but were they the ones? If only people could enter your life with labels, little white cards floating out from their necks on bits of string like price tags attached to sleeves: *Lover, Possible Husband, Enemy, Friend.* Then as soon as you saw them, you'd know how to behave.

Chassi Jennings drove right past Ionie, eyes front, one elbow bent out the open car window. She was wearing sunglasses and her hair was down. The car was black, a BMW 535i, new, with a subtle, thin dark-red racing stripe along the top of the door and mag wheels. Ionie laughed to herself. That would surely make her daddy proud; how many other girls would know those were mag wheels? She turned and grabbed for the ringing phone.

The uniform was white and stiff with starch. Tissue stuffed in the sleeves and under the bodice, tissue shaped into breast mounds as if her mother was still there. No arms, no head, no smile, but Sally Brash's form suspended from a hanger, the pale-blue plastic covering now in heaps across the floor.

Chassi took a long drink from the bottle of water they had handed her.

"She wanted me to keep it, even though there was no reason," said Ruth Marley, the designer. She cocked her head at the hanger. "It's just a nurse's uniform, after all. Not something I lost my heart on, or where I outdid myself"—she frowned—"but she wanted me to keep it." She pushed her glasses higher on her nose, exhaled. "Your mother could be very persuasive. I'm sure you know."

A lift of her shoulders as if she was done with it. "We'll duplicate it, of course"—eyeing Chassi—"you're certainly not your mother's size." She extended her hand. "My tape measure, Bud." Two steps up, onto the tiers of raised gray carpet, nimble fingers encircling Chassi with yellow tape, pushing her this way and that. Ruth Marley quarterbacking numbers to the kneeling, gay Bud as he scribbled them on a notepad. "Thirty-three bust, twenty-six waist, hut one, hut two, fourteen red." Chassi's eyes on the mirror in front of her; she and Ruth Marley and Bud going round and round together in the glass. She had seen her mother in that uniform. Playing with baby dolly outside the steps of Sally's trailer, tossing her up in the air and catching her and then tossing her up in the air and not catching her, letting her smash straight down, her rubber head bouncing on the pavement. "Oh, no, my baby, poor baby," she'd drawled just like Sally and cradled the doll, sitting cross-legged on the hot asphalt. "Whatcha doin', baby?" All she could see was the white of that uniform as she looked up to her mother's voice. White against a blue sky, with a cherry on top. Chassi tried to keep her eyes glued to one place on the mirror like she had been taught to do when you practiced turns in dance class. "Nineteen inches, hut, below the knee," Ruth Marley sang out to the smell of toothpaste, white toothpaste, the white of the uniform, the white smell of her mother's gardenias, the red of her hair, the white of the dress as they walked arm in arm up the Via Emelia. "Do you think I'm too old for this dress, baby?" Her mother's luscious figure doing a pirouette in the hotel glass. "You look beautiful, Mommy." The white silk of the skirt swirling. "C'mon, baby, let's buy you a artichoke," Sally said.

Chassi reached out her hand, saw her hand lift in the curve of mirrors to catch her mother's fingers as they left her arm. The yellow of the Roman sun, the yellow of the tape measure, the yellow of the pencil sticking out of the bun on Ruth Marley's head. "Wait, Mommy."

"Are you all right, Ms. Jennings?"

Focus, Chassi, you can do this. Don't look at the uniform, don't look at the dress as it flies through the air. Red blood across the white, red blood billowing across the parachute, bringing it down, soaking it red, her mother's tanned legs in peculiar angles jutting out from under the spreading red, red dots like at the end of a movie, descending like a theater curtain into a blanket of black. Chassi slipped softly to the right and slid unconscious down the shoulder and backside of a shocked Bud, who gave a small squeal as he broke his pencil and her fall.

• • •

ELEANOR WAS DREAMING about Jimmy but it didn't look like him; it was a little guy in a topcoat with Jimmy's face. She opened her eyes, then shut them again quickly but it was too late. The dream slipped up and over her lashes like a balloon taking off, smoke back into the genie's bottle in a teardrop shape, pouf, gone. No dream, just dawn. Furniture edges taking shape against the gray light. She nestled back into the pillows, brushed at the duvet until it was smooth. She flexed her toes up against the top sheet and then down, yawned, stretched, pushed at her hair. More rain. Rivers of rain gushing down her mountain gathering mud. Shades of a monsoon. She could hear it. It never rained in L.A. until it rained for weeks at a time. February, March, unrelenting rain. She had to call the boys at the nursery. Get out of bed, put on the poncho, the boots, get the flashlight, the shovel. Check that the mud was moving according to Jimmy's plan, stop-gapping over the parade of sandbags, splitting at the back of the house and going around it like a set of draperies around a window;

not collecting in the back, not oozing up the garden steps, sliding under the den French doors and seeping across the downstairs. Eleanor turned over onto her stomach, flattened herself against the sheets. She pictured mud covering the golden hardwood, waves of mud dyeing the turquoise Chinese rug in the dining room shit brown. She pushed her face into the pillows and let out a small muffled scream. "That's it, babe," Jimmy yelling across to her through the thunder as they sandbagged together, knee deep in the rain and the muck. How do you sandbag alone? Maybe she could ask her patients to come over and help her, be her troubled bucket brigade. The Shoelace and Mrs. Picket Fence and Sad Lady and Marty the Dog and Chassi—hey, she didn't have a name for Chassi.

Eleanor breathed into the darkness of the pillow, felt her own breath come back at her. Chassi, what would Jimmy have named Chassi? Miss Movie Star, Miss . . . what? She smiled into the pillow, felt her teeth against the case. Miss Mud Pie. Is that what Jimmy would have said or did she have mud on the brain?

Chassi on the couch, her voice smiling. "I don't know, we were in Texas at my nana's, I guess I was two." She swiveled her head at Eleanor. "How old are you when you can remember?"

"It depends."

"Well, I don't know, two, three. It had rained and it broke, you know, the sun came out, I think I remember, but it was real muddy."

Eleanor waiting, watching the child's face.

"She took me out to teach me how to make mud pies." She laughed. "Really. Had me sitting with her right in it. Sitting in the mud. Digging. Shaping them with our hands. Patting them. Mud everywhere. I guess I had on, what? Underwear? A diaper? We were filthy and my nana was in the doorway yelling, but Mommy didn't care. She's dead now, my nana." A flicker. "Well, both of them."

Eleanor lifted her head now from the pillow and sat up. She would have never done such a thing, played in the mud with Caroline. Made mud pies. She'd never made a mud pie in her life. *Get out of that dirt,*

Eleanor. Get out of that dirt, Caroline. Generation after generation, anal compulsives in a row. If Caroline hadn't said "Don't call me, Mom," Eleanor could ask her to come over and make mud pies with her on the mountain. Come over, daughter dear, forgive me for being the one you didn't love as much, come over and, I promise, we'll do all the things we've never done.

Eleanor punched her elbows into the pillow behind her and slumped back. Talk about ironic. The woman who'd never played in the mud had married the gardener extraordinaire. His words, Jimmy's, and his name across the long block from Dixie Canyon to Woodman in the valley, "Costello's Nursery," it read from end to end. A crack of thunder. Shit, damn. Eleanor threw back the covers and got out of bed.

• • •

SHE SHOULD TELL THE DOCTOR. Chassi studied the wall in front of her, moved her eyes around the Cuppa Joe logo without turning her head. Maybe it was a brain tumor. But if it was a brain tumor, wouldn't it be there all the time? Her shoulders slumped, she exhaled, lifted the cardboard container of espresso to her mouth. She hadn't been dizzy in weeks and now she was passing out. You had to face that, that wasn't a small thing, she had actually passed out. She should have done television; if she had played someone with a brain tumor on one of those doctor shows, then she would have known. Wouldn't the dizzy be there from the time she woke up until she went to bed? That made sense, didn't it? That wasn't rationalizing. Sugar, the coffee needed sugar.

Chassi turned on the stool and faced the room, her eyes scanning the customers, the guy behind the counter, the two girls next to him, clean and neat in their purple and red T-shirts, happy, having a wonderful life. Where was the girl she'd talked to? The one with her mother's hair? Chassi took a swig of the coffee. Cold. And it needed sugar. And it was ten o'clock and she was supposed to be upstairs. And it would probably never stop raining. And what was the point in going to a psychiatrist if she wasn't going to tell? All that carrying on with Ruth Marley and her assistant, all that saying she hadn't had lunch. Or breakfast. Such bullshit. People believed what you wanted them to believe, that was the truth. She got off the stool, scooped up her purse and car keys, slid the sunglasses down from the top of her head. It would probably be easier just having a brain tumor. Then she wouldn't have to worry about making the picture, all she would have to do is get sick and die.

CHAPTER 7

The cinematographer was definitely going to make a pass, it was just a matter of time and place now, Ionie knew. He'd stood next to her on the lunch line twice since they'd been on location, asked her to join him and his crew at their table, which she'd done, and she could feel his eyes on her whenever she walked on the set. That was from the beginning of the shoot, his eyes on her whenever she walked on the set. They were brown, his eyes, and not especially remarkable but he had a craggy face that somehow was remarkable and he was quiet and he had her father's hands. That's what had stunned her. He'd helped her down the steps of the makeup trailer that very morning because he happened to be standing there when she came out—which seemed unusual, was he waiting there for her?—dawn pink painting the darkness, a cold, dusty wind, desert quiet except for the low rumble of production trucks; she was holding on to her hairdo before it was whipped to nothing and her heels were rickety and high, she shouldn't have worn them to makeup but she was wearing them as much as possible, trying to make them her own. The cinematographer said nothing, just held out his hand to take her elbow and that was when she saw a replica of her father's hand, Lyman St. John's fingers coming at her, squared and marked and tan. She hadn't noticed the cinematographer's hands before. His name was David, David Jones, but she hadn't heard anyone call him David, only Jones or Jonesy; only "Jones" was stenciled across the back of his chair. She came down the steps and he released her, went toward the set without a word. She wobbled on the way back to her trailer, actually wobbled, she could feel the strength of his fingers still on her arm. He smelled of coffee and Sea Breeze. He was tall with a slight stoop and painfully thin, all bones; wicked shoulder bones and actor cheekbones and you could see the jut of his knee bones poking at the legs of his jeans. He was probably forty, forty-five. He was probably married. He was probably a daddy with three kids. Ionie made a face at herself in the elevator mirrors of the Ramada. The Ramada of her *first* location. Tah-dah. Not terrifically sophisticated, not terrifically far from Los Angeles, but a location was a location just the same. Some actors got April in Paris, Ionie was terrifically happy to get Palmdale in May. She was terrifically happy about all of it, this upside-down routine of a movie life that had slid over her and caught her like an invisible veil; bed by ten to face the dawn mornings or sleeping in the daytime and working all night, standing in line to order a breakfast burrito and the morning the fry cook in the truck knows, without saying, that you're the one who doesn't want the bacon and does want the cheese, learning who sits where and who talks to who, the politics of the makeup trailer and whether the key does your face, wearing something that opens in front so when you remove it to put on your wardrobe you won't muss your hair, hitting your mark for camera, not eating all the doughnuts on the craft-service table, learning lines, learning to wait for your scene, the sheer pleasure washing over you when the director says, beaming, "That was great, Ionie, just great; that's a print, let's do the reverse."

Ionie had become a part of this company, this team. Day by day a camaraderie had formed that was kind of unexplainable. A hundred strangers connected as if they were members of something intense and heady but something that wouldn't last, twenty-two days of seeing only each other with their regular lives on hold. No clocks, like in a Vegas casino, no reason to look out to see if it's day or night. No family, no ritual, nothing regular; no evening news, no going out with friends for dinner, no in bed with the wife. There is nothing and nobody that touches you except this picture and this cast and crew. A haphazard collection of people who never would have picked each other for friends, bonding as if they were what? A club? A family? Ionie didn't know, but against all odds they were there to make the picture, that was their only goal. Intense, Ionie said again, and Al had said oh, yeah, it was probably just like a platoon cut off from the rest of the company, trying to take a hill. Without the gunfire, of course, he'd smirked, without the possible loss of life and limb; no shells, no mortar, he'd laughed, and Ionie had felt herself turn off and get cold. Maybe there was no way to explain this movie business to somebody who didn't know, who hadn't been a part of it. Maybe she didn't want to. Maybe she would never try again. There were only two shooting days left now or really two shooting nights and she was already aware of the coming loss, that sinking feeling like when she knew summer was ending and she would curl up in her room and think her life was over and Kitty Ray would say, "Baby, you just got the Rotten Sunday Night Blues." They would wrap the picture in Palmdale, the spell would be broken. Ionie would shed her character's worn dress and rickety red high heels, wash away the makeup bruises, don her purple-and-red uniform and take her place behind the counter at Cuppa Joe. She had two days left as Cinderella before she turned back into a scone. The elevator doors slid open to a *bing* sound and Ionie crossed the lobby with her usual stride.

There was no earthly reason to order room service and spend the evening alone in her room, it was only six-thirty. There'd be lots of people from the company meandering around the hotel, she'd just look in the bar and find some, surround herself with other actors and stay away from the camera crew. Besides, she could certainly handle a pass from Mr. Jones if he made one and he probably wouldn't be in the restaurant anyway, he hadn't been at the pool. Maybe his wife had driven up. Maybe she'd brought the kiddies. Maybe they'd all gone to McDonald's to have a happy meal with fries. There was no reason to stay in her room and order room service, she had a late call, she didn't have to be in makeup tomorrow until three.

They would shoot the end-of-the-night stuff, that's all they had left, the fight scene where the husband goes after her in the kitchen, drunk, with the gun. She was ready. She knew the words of the scenes and who she was in the scenes; she and Marc Raymond and the director, with the stunt coordinator, had already choreographed most of it like a ballet. She wanted to take a break from the pages, not be too prepared. The sun and the swim had been delicious and then the hot shower and now the new sandals. Her hair was down and wet, russet curls skimmed her shoulders, she could feel her bare thighs up against the cotton of the sundress, her underpants brush at the back of the skirt. He was sitting at the bar alone, Jones. He turned just as she entered as if he had been waiting there for her. He smiled and extended one of those hands and there was no way not to go to him, to at least say hello.

The pass did not come during her beer or his martini. It did not come during her tostada or his *grande* combination plate or her second beer or his second martini or the decaf they had back in the bar. It did not come when he walked her to the elevator. He said good night and he'd see her *mañana*, he said he hoped she'd sleep well. She said, "Good night, Jones," and he leaned forward but didn't touch her, kind of nodded his head. Ionie pressed nine, he stepped back, the elevator doors slid shut with the *bing* sound and Ionie laughed out loud. She'd been nuts to think he would make a pass. There was no sexual energy coming from him, she must have made it up. He was dear and kind and he liked her, that's all it was. He was forty-two, he was married. Her name was Linda and she had just been made a partner at some chic Beverly Hills law firm. He showed Ionie her picture. Blonde and elegant and possibly as thin as he was, pearl earrings, the works. He had two boys, Ben and Adam, twelve and nine. He showed Ionie their pictures. Typical kid stuff, freckles, with their mother's hair and their father's eyes, softball uniforms, braces, and big, dopey smiles. His father had been a cinematographer before him, his mother had been a housewife. No pictures of them in the wallet. Ionie laughed to herself and relaxed. He talked about his work and his family, he talked about film and light, he talked about Ionie's face and body on camera but it wasn't personal when he spoke of her, it was more like going to a lecture at USC. No, that wasn't right, it wasn't like he was lecturing, more like teaching, sharing what he knew. He asked about her work and her family. He listened, he was interested, his eyes told you everything about him, he was what her gramma called a "finished gentleman," what her mother called "a class act."

Ionie went to her room happy, talked to Al in L.A., turned out the light after the eleven o'clock news. She slept soundly in the middle of the king-size Ramada bed and had pleasant, safe dreams. The pass came the next night when it was nearly morning, the last hour before dawn, but by then you couldn't call it a pass anymore and it wasn't Jones who made it, it was her.

She was shaking, she couldn't stop shaking. They'd taken Marc Raymond to the nearest emergency room even though the medic had assured everyone that it was physically not a big deal; some powder burns, bleeding, and what would amount to a mean bruise. "He never should of had *that* gun in the first place," Dansky growled at the director, "not till we got outside, I made that damn clear to *everybody*." Dansky was the stunt coordinator. The director said something that Ionie couldn't decipher and Dansky snarled something about props being *goddamn sloppy* and the prop man said something about too many hours and Dansky threw up his hands. Jones didn't say anything. Somebody moved Ionie into a chair. "He never should of had the gun anywhere near her face anyway, that wasn't the plan. Goddamn actors losin' their goddamn perspective." Ionie could feel Jones watching her. "Got hit twice myself in the face on *Enemy* with quarter loads, damn actor just couldn't keep the gun pointed at my chest where I told him, goddamn actors," Dansky said again and Ionie began to shake. "You okay, honey?" the wardrobe lady said.

That must have been who had moved her into the chair. "No two ways about it, a blank at close range is gonna break flesh," the medic said. "He never should of had *that* gun in the first place," Dansky said again. "How did he get it, anyway?" Dansky said right into the prop man's face. And the director said, "Okay, let's just wait a minute here," and somebody said, "Wait a minute, my ass," it must have been Dansky, and somebody said, "Fuck you," and then Jones moved, he was in front of Ionie, crouched at his knees, bent to her. "How about we take you to your trailer?" he said. She looked at him but she couldn't seem to say anything. He nodded at the wardrobe lady and together they lifted Ionie by the arms. Someone had put a blanket over her shoulders, she didn't even realize it until she felt it slipping and Jones righted it, his hand clasping her shoulder, his fingers holding her tight.

Marc Raymond was supposed to push her around the kitchen. Drunk, his character sits at the table with a bottle of Maker's Mark and a glass and a gun. The gun's a .38-caliber revolver. Middle of the night, her character happens into the kitchen and his character goes off like someone pulled his pin; gets her up against the stove, tussle, scuffle; up against the sink, chairs topple, dishes crash; up against the back door, and boom, out into the yard. That's the plan. The rest they're supposed to shoot the next night: a dance around the yard, a near rape against the truck fender, she fights back, and the gun goes off. He doesn't hit her, the bullet grazes his truck. Cut. Print. Wrap the picture, everybody goes home. They've already shot the scene where her mother kills him, they've already shot the end of the picture, they've already had guns on the set. Strict procedure with guns on movie sets, strict handling, everybody is forewarned. The stunt coordinator and the director work with the actors, the prop department is in charge of the guns. The gun in this scene is not supposed to go off until they're outside and then it will be the gun with the blanks, the gun with the flash load so Jones will get a nice white barrel flash on screen. When they're *outside*. The gun they use inside the kitchen will be the empty gun.

Somewhere around four-thirty, five in the morning, the director says he wants to do it again, just *one more time*, he says, which is what directors most like to say. They're about to lose their light anyway, or in actuality their darkness because the sun is about to come up. Jones is walking around with a light meter and he gives the director a look and Marc and Ionie are both bruised from knocking into stuff and more than exhausted and the director says, "Can you two just do it *one more time*?" and, "Sure," they say, "Yeah, sure, you bet." "Thanks, guys," he says, "just one more time." The producer looks at the director in such a way that the director knows it really is just one more time and the director looks at the first assistant director in such a way that he knows it too and the first says to the second, a smile spreading to his eyes, "It's the fucking martini," "martini" being movie talk for the last shot of the day, and word spreads across the set, building into a rumble because everybody wants to wrap and go back to the hotel already and get some sleep already because they have to get up and do this again tomorrow and the second yells, "Hold the work," and the rumble fades into a low hum. The hair guy fiddles with Ionie's hair to match it back to the beginning of the segment, comes out of nowhere, his hands on her, but by now she's used to it, some stranger rearranging her hair; the makeup guy is blotting the sweat off her face with a rolled powder puff but Ionie doesn't see him, she's concentrating on what she's about to do, as if she doesn't feel the powder puff or see the man standing there. The actors take their places. The director nods at the first and the first says, "We're on a bell, roll sound," and the hum fades to nothing, there is silence, and the sound man says, "Speed," and the camera operator says, "We're rolling," and the second camera assistant says, "Scene 44 Denver, take eleven, mark," and hits the clapper and the director says "And . . . action" practically under his breath. Marc grabs Ionie and does the dance from the stove across to the sink, shoving and shouting and pulling, yanks her hard by the hair up against the sink counter and then because he's either too tired or too edgy or thinks he ought to show the director something new or something different or his wife told him on the phone earlier she wants a divorce or he saw his father do it to his mother or all of the above or none of the above, because the list of baggage brought to a set is endless, he goes past the mark and over the edge of acting, he straddles her hard, pins her hard up against the sink countertop and puts the cold gun barrel into the soft flesh under the cheekbone in Ionie's face. Ionie St. John, who is Lyman St. John's daughter, a fourth-generation Texan, who has known how to handle guns since she was ten years old, who was a champion marksman winning seven blue ribbons by the time she was thirteen, this stupid actor from Long Island who has never even touched a gun before this picture, puts the gun in Ionie's face. And she reacts. It's not conscious. There's just a gun in her face that isn't supposed to be there and her instinct is to bat it away; she struggles, wrenches her right arm free, nearly breaking it, from behind her back where Marc's got her locked up against the sink, her arm swings out from behind her and she bats the gun away from her face. The gun that's supposed to be the empty gun, she bats it away. And it goes off in Marc Raymond's left bicep. A sound and a smell and smoke and blood and screaming, the gun goes off in Marc Raymond's arm.

"I can't stop shaking," Ionie whispers to Jones in her trailer and he folds her into his arms and holds her and she's lost the rickety red heels somewhere, he's so much taller, engulfing her like a big thin bird. She's crying and shaking, her teeth are banging, she can hear them as if they're a cartoon. "I shot him," and Jones is crooning, "It's all right, Ionie," and she looks up, sobbing, "I shot him," raising to her tiptoes, maybe to tell him closer because he's so tall, maybe she wants to get closer, and maybe he helps her because it seems she isn't touching the ground anymore, she only knows she's shot Marc Raymond, she could have killed him, she shouldn't have reacted that way, why did he put the gun in her face, and she's trying to tell Jones and then she's kissing him, clutching him as if she's about to fall or is she pushing him to fall with her? And where is the wardrobe lady? Is she in the trailer? What happened to her? Kissing Jones, sobbing, snot mixing with the tears running into her mouth and blood from somewhere, did she bite her lip? She crumples, doubles, bends and falls, sobbing and kissing Jones.

A forward pass made by Ionie. Definitely made by Ionie. Not just a pass, six points. Because it becomes a touchdown and it's not as if he instigates it but there is definitely not a lot of defense from Jones. "Hey, Ionie, wait a minute, honey," was all he said, she thought, somewhere lost in her ears with her breath and his kiss and the thrust of the first down on the floor of the trailer, and it's Ionie who makes the pass, Ionie who can't stop it, who fucks him, because that's what it is when she makes herself remember, when she can't sleep because all she can do is remember that she was out of control. The thin fabric of her character's dress ripping as she pushed his cock into her, hard, fast, no words, just breathing, smelling the dirty carpet, the fruit rotting in the basket and the black powder burns. It was Ionie fucking Jones on the floor of her trailer, her first trailer, not a whole trailer as she'd explained to her mother and father and Al and everybody, not a whole trailer but what they called a "half a star."

Sex on a set, sex during the making of a movie, affairs of the cast and crew. There should be a brochure given out to all first-timers, a pamphlet explaining the possibilities, no, the *likelihood*, the etiquette, pros and cons. The end of the rules, as if by mutual agreement. No rules, no past, no future, whatever you do here will not be held against you, come and get it, jump in. Sex permeates the atmosphere like sweet perfume. Sex among those above the line—actors, writer, director, producers—and sex among those below the line, which includes the whole rest of the crew, but mostly sex crossing the line, obliterating all lines with the speed and beef of a runaway truck. The actress, sitting on the steps of her trailer, deep in conversation with the transportation captain as he leans against the trailer, her leg decidedly grazing his leg on the step but neither of them noticing, as if their legs didn't exist; the director counting shots with the script supervisor, one strand of her hair falling lightly against his forehead, his fingers next to hers on the page; the dolly grip laughing with the female producer at the craft-service table where he eats nachos and she eats raw carrots and then they've somehow disappeared together behind the camera truck. The sound man with the wardrobe mistress, the gaffer with the production assistant, Ionie with Jones.

What had she done? How would she look at herself? How would she look at Jones? She would have to walk on the set, she would have to look at him, at his craggy face and the length of him, the sweetness of him, his smile. Don't think about it. Ionie rolled over. *What about Al? What about Al?* Like the lyrics of a bad song in her head. She punched the pillow, refixed her legs on the sheet, opened her eyes. She was sweating. Twelve o'clock, straight up, she didn't have to be at work until three. High noon in the darkness, the blackout drapes shut tight against the yellow glare of Palmdale, one thin edge of vertical bright light slipping through and cutting across the black of the bed. Why was she sweating? She could hear the air conditioner, feel the blast of it across her shoulder, she could hear the bedside clock flip to the next number: 12:01, it flipped happily in John Deere green. She had to sleep, she had to sleep so she could get up, be in that makeup chair at three. Shoot the last scene, finish the picture, walk on the set, look at Jones. Good-bye and thank you so much and I had a wonderful time. So long, everybody. That's what Gramma said instead of good-bye—*So long*. 12:02. The noon whistle, lunch time in America, "This is Paul Harvey. Good day." Her mother listening to the radio while she ironed her father's shirts. Ionie home from school for lunch, one shoe on top of the other, dirty fingers pushing pale gray prints into the soft white bread that you could mold into shapes, a peanut butter and purple jelly starfish, a cream cheese moon. "Finish your milk, honey," Kitty Ray's cigarette smoke mixing with the sweet smell of playground sweat and ripening peaches on the window ledge. Noon stock reports, soybeans up and hogs down, the smack and hiss of her mother's iron.

Ionie shut her eyes, pushed her hair off her face and onto the pillow. Next week she would be back to her regular life, cappuccinos and no more movie talk and regular hours and what about Al? *What about Al? What about Al?*

Ionie shoved her hand under the pillow, loosened the fingers of her fist, ran them along the pillow case, along the particular grit of sheets that have been laundered only in a hotel. She'd say *So long* to Jones, that's what she'd do. She'd never see him again. She'd never had more than one man at a time, she didn't do that, she wasn't that kind of girl. A bad girl. She was a bad girl only that one time when she'd told her mother the lie. "I didn't go there." The slant of Kitty Ray's eyes. "You didn't?" "No, ma'am." The yank out of the chair, the swift smack of Kitty Ray's hand against her backside, the shock, the revolting bile of turned chocolate milk as it backed up into her throat. "Don't you *ever* lie again, you bad girl." Ionie mortified, huddled against the bannister of the side porch right in front of her friends. The only time Kitty Ray had ever raised a hand to her was for a lie.

Ionie rolled to the other pillow, billowed the top sheet around her body and exhaled as it fluttered down around her like a parachute. No more a girl now, she was a woman. No more braids and no more peanut butter and jelly and no more the sting of her mother's hand. Ionie's hand skimmed the hot skin of her backside and found a place to rest in the dip between her hip and her breasts. The tattoo of her mother's fingers red on her ass when she pulled her panties down, stood on her Barbie stool, and looked backward in the mirror. Oh, for crissakes, Ionie, go to sleep. A breath, two deep breaths, slow, slow, don't think breaths but it was hopeless, her eyes opened again as if by remote control. 12:04, 12:06, 12:07 flipped the soft green glow.

He'd ridden in the van with her from the set to the hotel. They'd put her in the front seat next to the driver but Jones was right behind her, the press of his fingers steady against the back of her neck. If it hadn't been for those fingers, she might have flown out the open window of the van into the sunrise. Jones's fingers pressing at the back of her neck, the fingers that looked like her father's fingers. Lyman St. John's tanned, square fingers on the wheel of his John Deere green tractor, Jones's tanned, square fingers in the trailer as they clutched at her ass. Noisy voices, people crushed together being driven to the hotel, stale coffee breath and peppermint cover-up and everyone exhausted but jazzed from what had happened but Ionie didn't really hear them, not their words, only the rush in her head. *What about Al?* went the lyric and the gunshot and the roar of her come. *What about Al?* Jones had walked her to the door of her room. "Are you all right, Ionie?" "I'm fine, thank you"—because what could she say to him and what would she say to him? Either him, the other him, Al him, that was the one. "Tell me about the accident, honey." "Oh, sure . . . well, the gun went off and then . . ." Let me tell you everything except this one particular part. Because Ionie knew she would have to be a bad girl again like when she was seven, she would have to tell another lie. But not a real lie this time, a lie of—what did they call it? Omission. That's right, a lie to not hurt Al, because what was the point? She would never see Jones again, she would never behave like this again, there was no reason for Al to know. Ionie rolled onto her back. "Honey, try to sleep on your back," the makeup man had told her, "stop mushing your face, I promise you, you'll thank me later on."

She fell asleep, face up, somewhere after 12:20 and dreamed of her mother, only Kitty Ray was riding a tricycle and had Al's blue eyes.

CHAPTER 8

"What are you going to do next?" Eleanor asked Chassi.

"Learn lines."

Eleanor didn't say anything; her eyes moved from Caroline's photograph in the bookcase to the girl on the couch.

Chassi continued, "I have a picture to do in August."

She looked pale, Eleanor thought, spending too much time on that window seat and not enough outdoors. She smiled; funny when she caught herself imagining the things in her patients' lives that she had never seen: Sad Lady's evil husband, the lies slithering out from between his thin lips; The Picket Fence's bedridden mother's hopeless smile; The Shoelace's closet, in Eleanor's mind stocked with more shoes than the July Fourth shoe sale at Saks; and Chassi's Holmby Hills mansion that she shared with Saul. The sprawl of the lawns, the pool and cabana, Chassi's blue bedroom *avec* sitting room, the second dining room where the child sat curled in that window seat. Chintz, Eleanor imagined, costly chintz from England that went for $87.00 a yard, exquisite chintz with an ivory background, cabbage roses, antique bamboo, soft, thick carpets that toppled you when you crossed them in high heels, leaded windows, everything shining, meticulous, smelling of wax and money and cocktails, everything old Hollywood, a technicolor cinemascope 1957 dream.

"In the Philippines," Chassi said.

Eleanor was quiet.

"Rehearse here two weeks the end of July, fly to Manila for an eighty-day shoot. God, I won't see you until Thanksgiving." A small piece of smile above the shoulder. "So, will you miss me?"

"Do you like the picture?" Eleanor asked.

"It's *No Trumpets, No Drums.*"

"What?" *No Trumpets, No Drums*, and Eleanor could see Jimmy throwing the chair. She blinked. "They're remaking it?"

"Uh-huh."

Chassi was remaking her mother's picture. Flag on the play.

"My dad's remaking it."

Eleanor was quiet.

"He needs it," she said. "Not for the money, he's not doing it for the money"—hesitating and then going on—"most pictures are done for the money . . . I mean, there's always the money, but . . ."

Eleanor waited.

". . . but he needs a picture, he hasn't made a picture in a long time, you know. . . ."

Eleanor's eyes on the girl's profile. Nothing. "How come you're doing it, Chassi?"

"Why not?"

Quiet.

"Why would I say no to my father?"

Eleanor waited.

"It's just another picture."

Just another picture. "I see," Eleanor said out loud.

And Chassi angled her head around. Pale, translucent, the few freckles across her cheeks and nose prominent across the white. "You know, you should have a T-shirt with 'I see' printed across the front. 'I see' on the front and 'Go on' on the back." A flush of color now, a frown. "You could sell it at shrink conventions, it could be all the rage."

Rage is right, that's the ticket. "Are you angry?"

"No. Why should I be angry?"

Chassi's eyes on her face; Eleanor sat still in the chair, her palm pressed hard against her bracelets. "How do you feel about making it?"

"Fine," Chassi said.

Eleanor motionless.

"It's not like it belongs to my mother," Chassi said, "it's his picture as well as hers."

Okeedokey.

"It'll be fine, I can't wait to make it," Chassi said, turning away from Eleanor. "I feel fine."

• • •

JIMMY WAS WILD WITH ANGER. There had been no reaction in the theater in Westwood, in the row, up the aisle, into the street. He'd seen pictures about Vietnam before. Nothing. And they went to have a beer at the Bratskellar and she said something about how she understood, not meaning that she, Eleanor, understood, but that she understood how the character of the nurse felt about the war, and he went off. Jimmy's arm as he shrugged away from her, yanked his arm away from her, catching her off balance, she stumbled backward, hard, into the bar, after she'd slid off the stool. The sound of the money jangling across the wet wood in between the bottles, the look on the bartender's face. The angry clank of the keys hitting the ignition, his fury as he went from brake to gas, the jerk of the gearshift, the scream in his eyes.

"Jimmy?"

She shouldn't have tried to discuss it, he had discussed it only once before they were married and never again, that's what he said, "Don't ask me." Not even years later when she thought it was so long ago that how could it matter and Caroline had asked, "Daddy, were you in Vietnam?" and "Yes," just yes, was the clipped answer, and then he gave his beloved child a closed face, like the cigar store in the old neighborhood when they rolled that bumpy metal curtain down.

They were married in 1969. Eleanor was twenty-four and Jimmy was twenty-six, he'd already been back from Vietnam for three years. Drafted in August of 1964 when he was twenty-one. *Happy Birthday, Young Man, Love, America,* was how Jimmy put it, shipped out to Ton Son Nhut airport on the perimeter of Saigon after basic in Fort Jackson and a short stay in Texas at what he called the misnomer Fort Bliss. Two years of what he wouldn't discuss and then mustered out, back in the land of Brooklyn by September of '66. "Two years, babe, and I was back with the cannolis." No telling what he'd seen there because there was no telling. He wanted to segue back into his old life, he said, slide and slip in, as if where he had been and what he had seen didn't exist, and if he didn't acknowledge it, it didn't. That was that, end of discussion, about-face. Except that one time, the only time he would talk to her about it, a postcard April afternoon in the living room of Sis's house, on the blue sofa, two months before they walked down the aisle. Somebody was playing stoop ball, the windows were open, a breeze pushing at Sis's lace curtains, Eleanor could hear the *bonk* of the ball.

"But why did you go?"

A smirk. "Aw, El, you know, John Wayne bullshit."

"What?"

"You know, too many movies, good guys and bad guys, I wanted to be a good guy."

She touched his face, he grabbed her hand, pulled it across his mouth, kissed her palm.

"You could have gone to Canada."

"What was I gonna do in Canada, for crissakes, be a lumberjack?" She was laughing, Jimmy could always make her laugh. "You're supposed to commit to something, stand tall in the saddle, isn't that what they say? Not that I was tall," he said, grinning. He was very tall, six-four.

"Oh, Jimmy."

"Guys trying to learn how to wear panties, makin' like they were fags, tryin' to get their heart rates up so they'd keel over during the physical or give the doctor a goddamn coronary when he read the numbers on their chart. Hell, deferments up the ass, 'I gotta go to school, man,' 'I got a heart murmur,' 'I'm goin' to Montreal, man,' " his imitation of the bad guys accompanied by a sneer. "Canada, hell." He pushed the square diamond engagement ring he'd given her around her finger with his big hand. "I went. This country didn't get made by running." He shrugged. "I went."

He went, he wasn't wounded, he came home. End of story. There wasn't much else he would say. A little about the coming home part, how they flew them home on a commercial airline out of Saigon, how it was the first time he had seen regular women in such a long time but that wasn't what got to him. "It was the little pillow, El, you know the little pillow they give you for your head on the plane? It was so clean, I put it to my face and breathed through it"—the look on his face—"I just couldn't get over it, that it was so clean." How when they landed in Japan to refuel he got out in the dark and stood on the runway, just so he could say he'd been in Japan. How the airport in Fairbanks, Alaska, was so *air-conditioned.* He said "air-conditioned" with such emphasis you could feel the stink and the stick of the heat in Vietnam. And how they had landed in San Francisco to a fucking national airline strike. "Can you believe it?" he said, laughing. Here they were in America in an airport that had practically turned into a third world country like the one they'd just left, people stranded, people lying around everywhere on top of each other from end to end. They were home but they were in California instead of New York; the wrong coast, he said, the beach was on the wrong side, he said, his eyes bright, how the hell were they gonna get home? And how his buddy Eddie Lerman had said, "Hey, man, we were in *fucking Vietnam*, the military has *got* to fly us home." Jimmy laughed. "That was Eddie, you know, he said if he said something like 'a fucking Jew lawyer,' his words, excuse me, like if he said it with enough authority, it would be so. And damned if he doesn't turn around and call Travis Air Force Base and say, 'Hey, you guys gotta fly us home' "—his face breaking into a wide grin—"and they did it, you fucking believe it? We get out to Travis and they put us on a transport to McGuire in Jersey. Then it was only a bus to the city and the Long Island Railroad and bingo, I'm home." He was quiet a minute, didn't look at her. "I didn't want anybody to pick me up, you know, Sis or nobody, let them know exactly when I was coming, I just wanted to slip back in, you know, and let it go." He lifted his eyes to hers, kissed her fingers. "Hey, I love you, El."

Here and there through the years she'd gotten bits and pieces: how when he'd come home he'd only weighed 141 pounds, "Skin and bones, El, I was gorgeous," how Sis had wanted to make him a party, had the banner all ready to string up, "Welcome Home, Jimmy" in red, white, and blue, if you can believe it, across the front of the house and how she'd gotten in a real tizzy because he'd given her a flat no. How he jumped and was spooked by loud noises as if he were a newborn deer, how some mornings she would peel off a wet nightgown, soaked in his sweat when he'd bolted up in bed and she'd held him until the black became dawn. How some friend of his, "a real motherfucker," his words, had sent him a letter when he was in country saying, "Do you know what you're doing over there?" as if that would keep him alive, he said with a look on his face, if he got into that kind of crap that was going on in America, as if that would keep him alive, how when his big black sergeant had said to him, "Hey, Costello, did you have your 're-up' talk yet?," how Jimmy had just looked at him and said, "Excuse me, Sarge?" and that was the end of it. "Re-up, my ass," he'd told their friend Driskill when Driskill had brought it up. Little things, bits and pieces when somehow, somewhere, somebody brought up Vietnam. And then it was 1982, sixteen years since he'd come home and he had thrown the chair across their kitchen because she had tried to discuss it, because she had pushed him to go with her to see a movie called *No Trumpets, No Drums.*

Eleanor stood at the window of her office and looked down, watched the daughter of the movie star who had won the Academy

Award for *No Trumpets, No Drums* take a left at the corner and go out of sight.

"What do you mean, you understood her side?"

One of the four kitchen chairs she'd bought in somebody's driveway when they were first married, the muscles in his arms pushing against his T-shirt when he carried them home for her, one by one, over his head; one of the four kitchen chairs that he'd painted for her so lovingly, white paint drops across the newspaper, splattered like a Jackson Pollock across the front of his jeans; one of the four kitchen chairs that she had lugged from Brooklyn into the city and then all the way across the country to Los Angeles. "You want to take these old chairs, El? You gotta be kidding." "I love them," she'd said, and he'd pulled her into his lap in the chair, one arm settling around her, finding her breast, the other hand pushing at her skirt; one of the four kitchen chairs where he sat every morning muttering at his newspaper and drinking coffee with three sugars, one of those chairs lay smashed between them, splintered in a heap at her feet.

"I'm sorry," she said.

"What did you mean?"

Out front a car honked; Jack, the giant Bouvier from next door, started a mean bark, a door slammed.

His eyes on her, his big hands balled into fists, tensed at his sides.

Caroline would be home any minute, coming up the walk; Eleanor had driven the four giggling girls to the birthday party, the other mother would drive them home.

"Jimmy, it's just a movie, please."

"Hollywood assholes. Were any of them in the war? Huh, El?" His eyes on the chair and then up at her. "You want to know who went? I'll tell ya—my friends, not your friends, the ones who couldn't afford college, the ones who didn't have a rich father to buy their way out. It was a class war, don't tell me. A fucking class war; if your daddy had enough strings to pull, you didn't go."

"Jimmy—"

"Miss La-de-da in the city, what did you know, huh, El? You probably marched."

"I didn't march." She could feel her face pale, actually feel the blood go.

"You didn't march, you just understood. Is that it? Is that what you're tellin' me now?"

"Honey, Caroline will be home."

"God bless America, fuck you, welcome home." His face was so red. "You think I don't remember?"

"Jimmy, honey."

"Don't honey me, El, just don't honey me," he said, "and don't touch that goddamn chair." He left the kitchen, left her standing there shaking, the porcelain plates over the sink tilting as he slammed the front door.

What was the point in Eleanor telling, it was the past, pre-Jimmy, before he'd "jimmied" her, she'd whispered into his neck from the pillows that first time. What was the point? She couldn't help being born in Manhattan instead of Brooklyn, she couldn't help being born into "we have no right to be there" instead of "America gives us everything, we go, we defend." She couldn't help being the daughter of old-time liberals Eddie and Lisa instead of the son of old-time conservatives Sis and Sal. She had marched before him, oh yes, marched and coughed up tear gas and waved banners and screamed slogans until she was weak. She had marched and she had never told him; a lie, but just a little one, a little white one, the only lie between them in all the years.

No Trumpets, No Drums was only a movie, just another movie, Chassi had said, but a movie that happened to be about the only closed subject in Eleanor's marriage, Jimmy's personal taboo and their only booby trap: Vietnam.

• • •

IONIE SLID OUT OF THE BED. Al was asleep on his back, making that little *pouf* sound with his lips as he sank deeper, his arm flung up over his face. She pulled carefully at the crumpled sheets under his legs and feet, pulled them out from under him and covered him, he groaned and rolled to one side. She bent and touched her lips to his cheek softly, he smiled with his eyes closed. "Where ya going, Texas?"

"Bathroom," she whispered.

"Uh-huh." A sigh, and the rhythm of even breathing, asleep again.

She padded across the floorboards barefoot, closed the bathroom door, sat on the pot. She didn't flush, didn't want to wake him, lathered up a washcloth and ran it between her legs. She splashed water on her face, studied her shoulders and breasts in the mirror, squinted at her eyebrows, leaned forward and measured the whiteness of her teeth. Al didn't know. He didn't suspect and even if he questioned her, she would never tell. She would never see Jones again. It didn't matter, it had been nothing, less than nothing. Some kind of momentary madness, she decided, as if she had been taken over by aliens. She was back to her regular life now, slinging lattes and balancing acting class and yoga class and auditions and Al. He would never know. Never. After all, wasn't she an actress? Ionie studied her face in the glass at a three-quarter angle, lifted the hair off her neck, and smiled.

CHAPTER 9

The right side of the page was still blank; there was no reason to not do the picture, Chassi didn't know why she'd even started the list. Not that she would walk away now, she couldn't do that to her father, and what for? The "con" side of the page was blank; the scribbles on the "pro" side read: work, terrific script, hot director, great part. Chassi put the pen down. The pros and cons of doing the picture, the pros and cons of everything, her mother had said; make a list. Besides, what else did she have to do in August? What else did she have to do but work? She got up from the desk, crossed the room, looked out the windows at the pool. Work. She could hear them. Baudelio and his son, Andrew, were working in the gardens. Clipping, watering, raking, but as if they had been hushed, gardening sounds through a filter, as if they were in a library, as if someone had died. Baudelio and his son, Andrew.

"Andrew isn't a Spanish name."

"Yeah, I know, Chass, and let's talk about your name, the 'chassis,' as I recall, being the metal frame of a car."

"You shut up, Andrew."

"You shut up," and she would take off after him across the lawns. But he had the hose. But she was the daughter of the *jefe* so they were never allowed to play fair. *"Eso es todo, Andres, callese,"* Baudelio's voice cutting across the roses, bringing Andrew to a halt. *Don't get too close to the boss's daughter, watch it, boy.*

Baudelio's knee was too bad now to tackle roses, he coached Andrew from a lawn chair. "*Ya sí*, Poppi, I know, Poppi." Baudelio's eyes on the roses, waiting for the boy to make a mistake. The boy was twenty-four now, a year younger than Chassi, he had a degree from Santa Monica College in business but as he pointed out to Chassi, the only business he would ever be doing was taking over for his pop. Sweet Andrew of the long legs and the broad smile and the jet black hair, sweet Andrew smelling of fertilizer and plants.

"Hey, Andres," Chassi shouted from the window.

The smile covered his face. "Hey, Chass."

"*Cómo está*, Baudelio?"

The old man lifted his hat to shade his eyes. "*Bien, niña*," Baudelio said to her, "*bien*."

He wasn't *bien*, his leg was so bad they'd nearly had to take it off last year but that's what he always said, *bien*.

She waved. Baudelio said something to Andrew and the quiet clipping began again. Chassi left the window, returned to the desk, lifted the pen. They'd had their moments. *Ay, Dios*, she thought to herself and smiled. When they were five and six they'd buried baby dolly in the garden, sailed her across the pool, sunk G.I. Joe repeatedly with a rake tied to his foot. When they were seven and eight they'd pushed each other in the wheelbarrow, hid in Sally's barbecue pit coughing charcoal, and had to face Baudelio's wrath when they'd crushed the gerber daisies and the Johnny-jump-ups during a fistfight. When they were nine and ten they decided to be spies and spent the summer months driving everyone crazy by refusing to speak except in code. When they were ten and eleven they stole Baudelio's pickup out of the driveway and got three blocks before Andrew pulled over and turned around. When they were eleven and twelve her mother died, Andrew sat next to her in the potting shed, his fingers tentatively touching her arm as she sobbed. When they were thirteen and fourteen they kissed in the cabana; when they were fourteen and fifteen they sneaked past Tia in the kitchen and inspected each other inch by inch across the top of Chassi's bed. When she was sixteen she was sure she loved him and when she was seventeen he was sure he loved her and they did it for the first time and whenever they could all that summer, mostly in her car in the garage. When she was eighteen he found a Mexican girlfriend named Blanca because, as they both knew, there was no way.

"Chassi Jennings and her Mexican gardener," Andrew said as they stood together leaning against his father's pickup. "*Ay, Dios,* get the red-hot story, pick it up at the checkout counter with your razor blades and gum." He said it in the thick Spanish accent he used sometimes to make her laugh, because he didn't have an accent, he'd been born and raised in Los Angeles, he was a California kid just like her.

"Too on the nose," Chassi said, looking into his black eyes.

"Too Hollywood," Andrew said, his hands cupping her face.

But they weren't laughing.

When he was twenty-three he married Blanca. Chassi leaned forward to kiss Andrew's cheek in the receiving line and could feel his heart thumping through his tux front. They danced one dance. She proceeded to make her way to the bar and three margaritas. Now they were twenty-four and twenty-five and Blanca was pregnant. Chassi and Andrew kept their distance, the unspoken rule seemed to be at least four rosebushes between them at all times. Chassi sat motionless at the desk for maybe a minute, she pictured herself discussing it with Andrew, the pros and cons of making the picture between the blossoms and thorns, Baudelio watching, always watching; Chassi sighed. Okay, come on, do this.

Her eyes scanned the list again: work, terrific script, hot director, great part. Great part . . . she had just had her ninth birthday when her mother made *No Trumpets, No Drums.* She didn't remember much, it didn't have much to do with her, it was just her mother's work.

"Come do lines with me, baby."

"Do you know them?"

"Slave driver," Sally had said and laughed. "Come on, help your feeble mama." She patted the flowered loveseat next to her. She'd been doing this with Chassi since Chassi had learned to read.

"You have to know them or I'm not gonna."

"I know them, I know them."

Chassi narrowed her eyes at her mother. "Mommy . . . don't lie."

Sally narrowed her eyes back at her daughter. "How can I know them if you won't do them with me? You're not bein' fair."

"I am too, you're supposed to learn them first yourself."

"Am not," Sally said.

Chassi studied her mother from the doorway. "Ten minutes, that's all I'm giving you."

She crossed Sally's sitting room, sat next to her. Sally snuggled Chassi into her. Gardenias and lipstick, breasts and hips. "What are you doin' in ten minutes, you have a big date?"

"I have to meet Andrew in the garden."

"Ahhh, I see. Big doin's among the flora, huh?" Sally ran her fingers through Chassi's ponytail, gave it a yank.

"Mommy, cut it out."

"Touchy, touchy. You like that Andrew, don't you?"

Orange oval fingernails gently surrounding Chassi's scabby knee, curling around the kneecap like a spider, her mother's fingernails like spider legs back and forth. "Don't tickle me, stop it"—giggling, trying to get away—"don't do the spider," the delicious torment of her mother's hands. "Nana says you're not supposed to tickle." "Oh, yeah? What does she know?" Chassi's shriek, "If you don't stop, I'm not helping you." Chassi squealing, Sally laughing as they tussled on the couch. "Okay, I'm not helping you," Chassi slipping out of Sally's hands, flushed and happy, rolling off the pillows to the floor.

"Will you help me after supper, Uta Hagen?"

"Who's Uta Hagen?" Chassi tucking her shirt into her shorts.

Sally grinned. "You will give my very best to Señor Andrew, won't you?"

"Good-bye, Mommy."

"Don't do anything I wouldn't do."

Chassi turned on the heel of her sneaker with as much drama as she could muster. She could hear the ring of her mother's laughter as she skipped down the hall.

Good-bye, Mommy.

Sally's face lit with love for Chassi. Red and pink and green and gold. And now she had to learn the very same lines.

Good-bye, Mommy.

Chassi sat back in the chair, the list falling from her fingers, gliding silently to the floor.

• • •

THEY WERE CASTING FOR *No Trumpets, No Drums*; Ionie was desperate.

"It's a big picture, they want a name, honey."

A name, a name. "Okay, tell them I'm Carole Lombard, risen from the dead."

"Very funny."

"I am actually Drew Barrymore's twin sister, you know, we were separated at birth." Silence on the line. "A cousin of Winona Ryder?" Breathing. "Come on, Nicki, tell them I'm Daisy Monk."

"Very funny. They won't see you, kid."

"But it's not the lead. What if you show them tape from the MOW?"

"They won't give me tape from the MOW." A slight edge in the voice.

"Why not?"

"Because they're killing themselves to get it on for May sweeps."

"But couldn't they just give you a scene or something?"

"I tried, Ionie." A definite edge.

"But what if you tell them it's a job for me?"

Nicki laughed. "Oh sure, that'll get 'em."

Ionie ripped the piece of cuticle off with her teeth. "Nick—"

"The network doesn't give two hoots in hell about your getting a job. What are you to them? Nothing, nobody."

"But I thought they said I was great in it, I thought they told you the footage was great."

"They did tell me it was great, that's why they're breaking their backs—" And then Ionie could hear the loudspeaker echoing in Nicki's office, the assistant telling Nicki that so-and-so was on the line. "Tell him to hold on," Nicki said, her lips tilted away from the receiver. "Look, honey, I'm working on other things for you, okay? A guest star on *Boots and T.G.*, a pilot one of my writers is doing, really great, just sit tight, okay? I gotta take this call, I'll get back to you. Love you, okay?" A click and the line went dead before Ionie could return the okay.

They already had Chassi Jennings for the lead, this wasn't the lead, it was the sidekick, the third lead after her and the guy, why did they need another name? Ionie shut the flip phone, jammed it back in her purse and started the car. She backed out of the mini-mart parking lot, looking through the plastic hanging bags of Al's clean shirts. There were definitely gas fumes, the Datsun smelled like a moving Mobil, she didn't care what he said. She needed a new car. She needed a new apartment and a new car and she was going to be late for yoga, which would make her late getting back to the apartment to shower, which would make her late to the dreaded Cuppa Joe.

She had to get in for that part, no matter what Nicki said, she had to get in for that part. Ionie exhaled, took a left off Beverly at La Cienega and swung around a bus. She should have flagged down Chassi Jennings the day she'd seen her on the lot. But, of course, even if she'd done that, what good would it have done? Hi there, it's me from Cuppa Joe, you know? Where you sit and let your cappuccino get cold and study the wall? The one who brings you sugar. That's right. Listen, I hope you don't mind my bothering you but could I be your sidekick in your new film? Oh, I'm really an actress, didn't you know?

She tapped her fingers on the steering wheel, jabbed at the radio buttons. She'd paid off the Visa card, bought the cell phone, a few clothes, taken herself and Al to dinner at Toscana, which she'd thought would please him, talk about a mistake.

"Twenty-six bucks for veal, no way."

"We're celebrating."

"No way."

The maître d' passed their table, nodded his head.

"Al—" She smoothed the new dress, smiled at him, adjusted herself on the chair. Flowers, the din of people talking, the linen tablecloth touching her knees. Oh, to have the maître d' know you, to have your special table, to eat there at the drop of a—

"I could take you to places in Jersey, two veal chops, two side dishes, *and* a bottle of vino, you'd be outta there under twenty-six bucks." Two little frown lines in between the baby blues.

"Honey, we're not in Jersey."

"Well, then maybe we should be." He held her eyes, she lowered her look to the menu. "Okay, order something else if it upsets you."

"You could feed a whole family."

Was she supposed to spend the rest of her life in diners with him eating chicken fried steak?

"We are ready?" The waiter between them, checking his notes as if they were lines. He was probably an actor; Ionie looked up at him—was the Roman accent real? "Tonight for the specials we have a calamari fritti with a diablo sauce, delicious."

"Give us a minute here, okay?" Al's eyes steady on Ionie.

"Certainly, sir."

Absolutely an actor, and not very good. "Al—"

"I don't come from this, Ionie."

"Neither do I."

"Then let's go." He pushed back his chair.

"Al, please—"

"Please, what? Let's get out of here. I'm not paying twenty-six bucks for a veal chop."

Her heart beating hard up against her ribs. "But you're not paying." Her breath in her chest. "I am."

Oh, God.

What was the moron in front of her waiting for? An engraved invitation to make the left?

Al had spaghetti, just spaghetti, he said to the waiter, and he wanted it plain. A man who put Tabasco or Pickapeppa sauce on everything said he wanted it plain. A man who was wearing a new sport jacket and a new shirt that she'd bought him just for the occasion said he wanted it plain. Spaghetti with just olive oil wasn't even on the menu. She had risotto with shiitake mushrooms and radicchio, most of it left on the plate. She had lost her ability to swallow. No, not swallow, enjoy. It would have been better if they'd left, the celebration had turned into a showdown, the white linen tablecloth the dusty street. And when she wouldn't fight with him, he pushed the spaghetti around the Italian porcelain, he mumbled, he sulked; he didn't want wine or a beer, he didn't want water with bubbles. "Plain water, as in from the tap," he said to the waiter. Like a quick-change artist he had transformed into a seven-year-old brat. His lip was practically on the table. It was funny, oh, it should have been funny, if he could have heard himself he probably would have laughed. Or maybe not. He didn't understand Hollywood procedure, he didn't want to, he laughed at the idea that she should want to go to a particular place to be seen.

What was the moron doing? Homesteading? Ionie tapped the horn, the guy turned and gave her the finger. How quaint, how lovely, how very L.A. He made the left, she stepped on the accelerator and the Datsun died in the middle of the street. Died, as if someone had shot it. She hit the ignition. Nothing, not even a grind. Silence. Don't let this be happening, please. Sweat on the upper lip, she tossed her head as if it was all a mistake, don't be ridiculous, my car works fine. She turned the key. Dead, definitely dead. She could probably plant geraniums in it. There would be a small, tasteful funeral, possibly at Forest Lawn, they would lower the Datsun gently into the ground, she would wear black with a veil. The woman behind Ionie honked. Ionie turned, gave her the finger, and got out of the car.

My distributor, my ignition, my ignition, my distributor. "My sister, my daughter," Evelyn Mulwray said to Mr. Gittes as he slapped her face in *Chinatown*. Ionie smirked, smacked at the pillows on the back of the couch. It had been all too absurd. The distributor had come apart and torn up the ignition, or the other way around, the guy said, after the tow truck, $38.00 for a goddamn tow truck because she didn't have an AAA card, had meant to get one, was going to get one, Al had harped at her to get one but somehow she'd forgotten to call. Hopeless, totally hopeless, the Datsun was falling apart piece by piece, soon it would have Velcro holding up its wheels, a silk scarf tied around its hood, and she was going to get axed from Cuppa Joe, just one more time that she was late or couldn't make it, that would be it. "Your car again, Eye-oh-neeee?" He'd been on her case since she'd returned: "Could we trouble you to get some stir sticks from the back, Miss Bankhead? Could we have your autograph, Miss Davis? Could you foam up this milk, Miss Pickford? Mop that corner, Miss Bergman, please?" She could imagine the glee that would ooze across his slimy face when he gave her the ax. She paced the apartment. She would have to get another job. Why couldn't she get a job as an actress? She was an actress, she wanted a job as an actress. She didn't even like coffee. She had to get in for that part.

She punched open the bag of potato chips and stuffed a handful into her mouth. It wasn't a big deal. She circled the couch. Stop making it into a big deal. She paused at the coffee table and looked down. "David Jones," it read on the first page of the cast and crew sheet lying next to the telephone, "David Jones, Director of Photography, Home: 818-777-6823, Beeper: 818-587-6762." Ionie sat down, lifted the receiver, wiped the salt from her lips with the back of her hand.

She punched in the first three digits of his beeper number. It wasn't a big deal, she was only going to ask him if he could help her and that certainly wasn't a big deal. After all, she had to look out for herself, 5-8-7, she had to do whatever she could to get work as an actress, to get in for that part, 6-7-6-2, and the pound sign, and she lowered the receiver to the hook.

She stood up, exhaled, crossed her arms over her breasts. After all, Ionie thought, waiting for the phone to ring, after all, work was work.

• • •

SUNDAYS WERE HARD. You could read the *New York Times*, the *Los Angeles Times*, have coffee and a bagel, tidy up the mail from the week and the magazines and the catalogues, make another pot, hose down the front steps, punch the pillows in the living room, make the bed, wash the pot, take a shower, and it would still only be five after ten. Eleanor went to Fashion Square in the valley, all the windows down, hot air blowing her hair. She walked the aisles, picking up and putting down packages of panty hose, let her hand trail across the cashmere sweaters, tried on shoes. She people-watched in the food court in between bites of a teriyaki chicken bowl with rice. Everyone seemed cranky—babies whimpering and mommies punishing and husbands grumbling, as if they all needed a bath and a cold drink. She went to See's and stood in line for a scotchmallow and a mocha and maybe just one chocolate butter cream. Or a caramel. No, a butter cream, she said to the lady in the uniform with the puffed sleeves. She wandered Bloomingdale's clutching the little white bag of candy. Sweets were not Eleanor's usual downfall, she was much more of a pretzel and chip man, a salt man, but she was a sucker for See's. Solid chocolate bunnies for Caroline's Easter basket, chocolate almonds in colored silver wrap, chocolate Santas and reindeer with sprinkles on their horns, garnet velvet heart boxes from Jimmy for Valentine's, green chocolate shamrocks for St. Patrick's, the See's white metal toy truck filled with coffee lollies for her desk, and an occasional piece to carry home from the mall. Eleanor sprayed herself with Dolce & Gabbana and then contemplated going to the ladies' room and trying to wash it off before it gave her a headache worse than the one she already had. What had possessed her? She pushed at the hair that had fallen across her forehead, rubbed her temple, and there was Caroline across the store. Eleanor dropped the bag of candy but didn't bend to retrieve it, her limbs frozen in position like the plastic mannequins at the escalator stairs.

She was on the other side of cosmetics, her Caroline, at the Lancôme counter alone and, God, she'd cut her hair, all the loose curls gone, no wisps of sweet spirals escaping from the thick rope of braid, but clipped and short and looking very fashion model, standing up with some sort of gel like on MTV. Jeans, a pale blue T-shirt with a little vee at the neck. Eleanor couldn't see her feet but she knew it had to be sandals, and it was too far away to tell if she was wearing makeup. She just looked like Caroline: a compact package, thick brown hair in this new cut, Jimmy's huge round eyes, the little nose, bigger breasts than Eleanor, smaller hips, stunning posture, and the quick, open face that looked like Christmas was about to begin. *A present wrapped in brown ribbon, look how beautiful she is, El,* Jimmy had said from the moment she'd been born.

Eleanor stood nearly motionless for at least five minutes and watched. Like a spy without a fedora, Columbo without his trenchcoat, concealed behind a parade of Lancôme lipsticks; just like always, Eleanor watched.

"Can I help you with that?"

"No, Daddy will."

"I'll take you, Caroline."

"No, I want to go with Daddy."

"When's Daddy coming home?"

Jimmy's brawn stuffed into the pint-size pink chair at the pint-size pink table drinking invisible tea from miniature china cups with Caroline and two dolls, Jimmy's big paw pushing a wee plastic creature through the dollhouse, Jimmy's Brooklyn raised at least three octaves as he folded himself to the floor and pretended to be a dolly Southern belle. Eleanor watching with her back up against the door jamb, the plaster cold between her shoulder blades. Jimmy teaching Caroline how to plant a sapling, his big hand and her little hand on the shovel together as they dug the hole for the tiny birch. Jimmy pushing her at the swing, sprinkling her with the hose, drawing the hopscotch diagram in the driveway and jumping with her, pink chalk on his nose. Eleanor watching from the steps above them, the rough concrete under her bare toes. Jimmy running next to Caroline on the new blue bike, shouting when she maintained balance as if the old Dodgers had sprung to life. Eleanor down the street, left alone in front of the garage, her arms full of training wheels. Jimmy sitting with Caroline on the kitchen floor in front of two mixing bowls, painstakingly demonstrating how to separate the eggs from the shells. Jimmy reading the story again and again, holding Caroline's head over the toilet bowl, singing her to sleep. Eleanor watching from the dining room, from the backyard, from the hall. When had it started, this always watching, this peeking in as if she didn't belong?

Caroline bought what looked to be a mascara, had a quick exchange with the saleslady, signed the slip, replaced the charge card, and took her purchase away. Her usual gait of no dilly-dally, the determined Costello step.

"Come shopping with me."

"You take too long, Mom."

"What do you want, Mom?"

"Leave me alone, Mom."

"I have to separate from you, Mom, don't call me anymore."

Don't call me anymore and she blurred into the mall exit behind two women with identical blonde hair. There was no Daddy now. There was no husband. It was just the two of them, Jimmy's women, separated like the eggs and the shells.

Eleanor bent and scooped up the candies, finishing all three of them before she got to the car. When it came to Caroline, Jimmy was the meat and potatoes, Eleanor just a side dish; like the candy, she was Caroline's butter cream. Something that was good but if you already had the meat and potatoes, something you didn't really need.

CHAPTER 10

Ionie scooped up the phone on the second ring. "Hello?"

"Well, I see you don't need to talk to your mama now that you're a big movie star," Kitty Ray said.

"Mama—"

"I believe I have been sittin' here three days now since you hung up on me because you were gettin' a more important call. 'I'll call you right back, Mama,' I believe, were your exact words."

"I—"

"Your father said he was going to hang his hat on me if I didn't leave from this spot."

Ionie laughed. "Mama—"

"*Ionie?*"

"I'm sorry, I should have called you, I—"

"Okay."

Ionie smiled, flopped on the couch. It didn't take much to please her mother.

"So, what was the big phone call? Al?"

"No, it was"—Ionie stopped herself—"about a job."

"An audition?"

"Uh-huh."

"For what?" Kitty Ray said.

"What?"

Hesitation. "Honey, are you doin' somethin' else?"

"No."

"Then tell me, when's the audition?"

Ionie circled the room with the phone.

"I didn't get it yet."

"Why not?"

"What?"

"Ionie, what's goin' on with you? This conversation is like pullin' out your baby teeth."

She hadn't lost any of her teeth, no wiggling them out like the other kids, no pulling out with a small bit of thread; it was one of the St. John family stories, how Ionie's baby teeth just wouldn't fall out, how old Dr. Mark had had to pull each and every one of them, their roots so strong, her mama said, that he needed leverage, had his foot practically up on the chair.

"I'm sorry, I was kind of walking out the door . . ."

Silence.

"I have to go to class."

"Oh. But what did your agent say? Is it a big part?"

"I'll call you later, I promise."

"Is somethin' wrong, Ionie?"

"No, Mama, I just gotta go."

"Okay, I love you, you do whatever it takes to get in for that part. Don't forget, honey, time's a-wastin'."

"I love you too," Ionie said, and hung up the phone.

"I don't want to fall in love with you," Jones had said.

She'd just looked at him.

"I would never leave my family."

What was he thinking? "Well, of course not, I don't want you to leave your family, that isn't what I want."

He looked good, very tan. He'd been doing some awful shoot in the jungle. Mexico, he'd said, north of Manzanillo, nights, it was awful, lots of bugs.

"Like hundreds?"

"No," he said, "like tens of thousands. On everything, covering everything, crawling across the cameras, jumping."

"I'm glad I finished my sandwich."

He shook his head, grinning. "I never saw anything like it in all my days."

She smiled back. "You haven't had that many days, Jones."

Embarrassed, a little nod of the head—he had such sweetness, Ionie thought.

"They were everywhere," he said.

"Not on the people?"

"Oh, especially on the people, they had to give us hazard pay."

Ionie laughed. "You're kidding."

"Sixty bucks a day, or rather, a night."

She ate a tiny speck of potato chip left on her plate. "Why didn't you leave?"

"Oh, I wouldn't do that."

"Why not?"

"Well, it was the job."

Those hands of his on the table, tanned fingers circling the spoon. Small talk, meandering around what was really going on with them, what was between them that they were avoiding, like a bad smell in the room.

"More coffee?" the waitress said.

"No thank you," Jones said. "More Coke, Ionie?"

"No thank you."

"Dessert?"

"Never."

He laughed.

"Adria"—it said on her name tag—picked up a ripped sugar packet, put down the check, and left. She didn't notice them. Adria of the name tag in the Art's pink uniform with the lace handkerchief tucked in the breast pocket just so, she didn't notice them or care, she was just waiting for her shift to end, the same way Ionie felt at Cuppa Joe. Cuppa Joe and Rudy and the distributor and the ignition and Al and the apartment and she looked at Jones.

"So," he said, his eyes already waiting.

"So," she said, refolding her napkin; she took a breath and smiled.

"I never would have called you," he said.

"No?"

"I couldn't stop thinking about you, but I never would have called."

She put down the napkin. Oh, God. Wait a minute.

"I don't want to fall in love with you," he said again, his fingers leaving the table top, his thumb stroking the back of her hand. "I would never leave my family."

"I don't want you to leave your family, that isn't what I want."

What she wanted was for him to help her get in for the part, get a piece of the film to show somebody, or maybe he knew the producer, or the director, or anybody where he could put in a word. What she wanted was for him to talk to her, teach her, show her the ropes, he was forty-two, after all, he'd been doing this since he was her age. He probably knew everybody in town, he probably knew everything there was to know.

"We can just be friends. . . . Oh, God," she said, rolling her eyes, "I sound like a B movie. 'We can just be friends,' says the ingenue," she said again in a tone.

A soft smile tilted the corners of his lips. "You know, there's a lens called an *angenieux*."

"There is? You mean for a movie camera?"

"Uh-huh."

"What kind of lens?"

"Oh, it'll go from a twenty-five to a fifty-five, mostly a zoom. It's French."

She laughed. "I thought maybe you could use it only to shoot young women."

Jones's face melted. "I'm crazy about you, Ionie, you're just . . . extraordinary, I think."

His eyes so tender she wanted to run her finger over every line in his face. It was too much, she'd lost track of where she was and what she was doing. He circled her hand in his, intertwined their fingers. She let him, she didn't even begin to think why, she just looked at him, his sweet face, his bony shoulders, the length of him folded into the booth, he was dear and kind and caring, he was . . . what? Focused, and mature. That's what it was. A grown-up. Oh, God, was that what it was? A house, a car, a career, pictures of people in his wallet, and he made her feel . . . better. Just being with him two hours and she felt better, like everything would work out, and look at how he looked at her, and listen to what he said, and what difference anyway? Really, it was all so silly anyway, and so somehow Ionie meant it when she squeezed his fingers in return and said, "I'm crazy about you too, Jones."

• • •

THE LUNCH WITH ROBBY PERONI and her father was at Morton's; Chassi was ten minutes late and oblivious to the eyes that followed her as she crossed the room.

"Hello, sweetheart," Saul said, kissing her cheek, extending his hand toward the frowning man curled in the corner of the olive-green leather booth. "Chassi, this is your director." And encircling his daughter's waist protectively with his other hand he said, "Robby, this is my girl."

Small, pale eyes behind John Lennon glasses, a boot-camp flattop of beige spikes, and a button-down white shirt that looked to be from the fifties, the scrappy, California-born-and-raised Italian lowered his espresso cup, nodded, didn't shake her hand, and barely audible under the din of the restaurant, said only, "Whatsup?"

Robby Peroni, *Variety*'s hot "helmer," was Saul's pick to direct *No Trumpets, No Drums*. Blessed by both critics and box office, married three times with three kids while still in his late twenties, the notorious Peroni was often the town's item on the eleven o'clock news. After the lead, but definitely before the sports and weather—Peroni seen drunk and disorderly at, you name it: the Gate, the Key Club, the Viper Room, cloaked with an entourage of mostly females, none of them his three wives, and most often rumored to have punched somebody out. The wunderkind director with more heat and buzz on him than a lump of dog shit left in the garden—could this nothing-looking guy be him?

"You wouldn't believe it," Chassi said to Eleanor from the couch, "he looks like a telephone repairman or something, really, like a guy who fixes your cable or changes your oil, you can't believe it's him, and then he opens his mouth and he's like an encyclopedia about the business, well, not the business, but the filmmakers, it's like he eats and breathes film."

Eleanor had never seen the girl so excited, she'd never mentioned any of the other directors she'd worked with; actually, she never brought up anyone.

"He's seen *everything*. I'm not kidding, he must live in a dark room."

He must live in a cave, Eleanor thought, like all Neanderthals.

"I mean, I've read all the stuff about him punching people and sleeping with everything that walks, a real bad boy, but you can't believe that he could do those things when you listen to him"—she had whirled around and was facing Eleanor—"which is *verrry* difficult because he talks in this nearly whisper, but it's what he *says*"—her eyes were lit—"he knows everything. Did you know that once when John Ford was over schedule, and they came to reprimand him on the set, he just picked up the script in front of them, *ripped* out ten pages, and said, 'Now we're two days under,' and never shot them? The ten pages, I mean. Can you believe it?"

Eleanor didn't answer, but it was clear Chassi wasn't waiting for a reply.

"All these stories that, of course, my father knows, and I guess some of Hollywood, but not me, we sat forever after Dad left and he just went on and on." She smiled the luminous smile at Eleanor, the one that Eleanor had seen on screen. "Michael Curtiz, the man who made *Casablanca*, I love *Casablanca*, Robby said Curtiz's real name was Curtezsh, he was a Hungarian Jew, and he never really spoke good English, he had all these malapropisms, like when he was doing *The Charge of the Light Brigade*, he said, 'Bring on the empty horses,' you know, for riderless. Don't you love it?"

Chassi grinning now, doing her version of what she thought would be Curtiz's thick accent, which was somewhat reminiscent, Eleanor thought, of Myron Cohen's. "And then on, I don't know which picture, Curtiz said, 'If I wanted an idiot to do this I would have done it myself,' " Chassi said, tucking her legs up and under her now, cross-legged on the couch, laughing, as if she and Eleanor were girlfriends drinking Cokes in her bedroom discussing some boy. "He's studied them all: Fellini, Renoir, Truffaut, and Huston and Ford, and Orson Welles and Cassavetes, but then some Japanese directors I've never heard of: Yasujiro Ozu and Mizogushi, and Satyajit Ray from India—I've never seen his stuff—and do you know who Sergei Eisenstein was?"

Eleanor nodded, Chassi hardly took a breath.

"The *most* genius, Robby says, of all; one of his films, the one no one ever got to see because he never got to finish it, I mean, in the last thirty years two guys have tried to cut it the way they thought he would have, but how could they, not being the genius that he was; it's the one he called *Qué Viva Mexico!* Well, the guy who financed it, Upton Sinclair, the most famous big-deal American writer, major liberal—did you know he ran for governor of California once? He didn't win. Anyway, he financed it and he sent this idiot nephew of his down to Mexico to keep the reins on Eisenstein while he was shooting and it so infuriated Eisenstein, because the guy was totally inept, that he had made these porno drawings—Eisenstein, he drew all the time—these magnificent drawings, and one of these drawings, which was Jesus on the cross being"—she stopped, her eyes on Eleanor's—"you know, getting a blow job, from Mary, it was probably just something on his mind—he had such a mind, who could know what he was thinking? But because he was so pissed off at Sinclair's nephew, he left the drawing in with the footage that was being shipped back to the states and when Sinclair saw it, he wouldn't send the footage to Eisenstein to cut;

he was back in the Soviet Union by then, and Sinclair wouldn't send him his own film. I realize Eisenstein was being somewhat of a brat at the time but can you believe the hypocrisy of Sinclair, this politically active muckraker, to not send Sergei Eisenstein his own film?"

Chassi shook her head, took a breath. "He knows all these stories, Robby, it's so amazing, he's—"

"Who directed the film the first time?" Eleanor interrupted, she couldn't remember his name but hadn't the man also won an Academy Award? Besides Chassi's mother, hadn't he won?

Chassi blinked, midstream. "What do you mean?"

"The first time they made it."

"*Qué Viva Mexico!?*"

"No," Eleanor said, "*No Trumpets, No Drums.*"

Shoulders still raised, mid-breath. "*No Trumpets, No Drums*? Who directed it?"

"The first time," Eleanor said.

"Mr. Thalosinos."

"Was he like Mr. Peroni?"

"I don't know."

"Did he have lots of stories?"

Chassi just looked at her.

"You don't remember?"

"No."

"I would have thought you'd seen a lot of him. Didn't you visit your mother on the set?"

"I was little," Chassi said.

"Ten? Eleven?"

The blue jeans and marshmallow sneakers slowly uncrossing, Chassi didn't say anything.

"You don't remember him?" Eleanor asked again.

"Not much," the girl said.

CHAPTER 11

Chassi had been "shrunk" before, if you could call it that; mostly what she remembered was listening to a short, blonde, dumpy woman with a helmet hairdo go on about her mother and her mother's films. It was not clear to Chassi if Marion—*oh, you don't have to call me Dr. Ashley, dear, you can call me Marion*—had studied her mother's movies before she got the job of shrinking Chassi or after so that she could impress Saul. She even went so far as to recite dialogue, or at least what she thought was dialogue, from some of Sally's most noted scenes; luckily she did not attempt Sally's accent when emoting but did get up from her chair. It was Chassi's twelve-year-old opinion that Marion was a hideous actress and it was unfortunate that in Marion's effort to get the child to express her feelings, Marion's grief about the demise of her favorite actress was sometimes louder than Chassi's and often took center stage. Chassi saw Marion in her frilly office after school once a week for most of seventh and eighth grades. She thought of her as an older, pudgy kind of aunt, sort of; sad, and dopey, somebody who probably didn't have any friends.

Chassi checked her face in the rearview mirror of the BMW and changed lanes. Well, that was then, now she was all grown up, *big girl. How big is my baby?* Mommy said. *Big girl.* Her arms in the air, Sally across from her at the kitchen table; the last drop of milk, the last bite of scrambly eggs and you could throw your arms in the air and shout with your mommy, "Big girl." Did she clap in the highchair, did she remember it, or did she think she remembered it because she was clapping in the highchair in a silver frame on Saul's desk?

Chassi made the right off Hillgard onto Sunset, joined the two lanes of expensive cars taking the curves at a fast clip through L.A.'s most premium zip code.

Dr. Costello was certainly not a dopey aunt figure and certainly not pudgy. Was she sad? Chassi kept her foot steady on the gas. No. She swerved around the lady in the old diesel Mercedes and moved the mighty BMW into the left lane. Well, maybe a little. Maybe everybody was a little sad or maybe just everybody she knew. But then she really didn't know anything about Dr. Costello, did she? Eleanor. Dr. Eleanor Costello. Chassi's eyes flickered up to the rearview mirror and back to the road. Thalosinos. What did she remember about Thalosinos? Was he sad?

No. Laughing, and . . . hey, he smoked cigarettes. That's right, always had that cigarette in his hand. Talking fast, gesturing, explaining, his head bent into the cloud of smoke. Hey, she could do this remember stuff. Once he had a little blob of shaving cream still stuck to his face, she watched it move on his cheek while he talked but she didn't say anything, you weren't supposed to say anything when Mommy was working, she just watched. Black eyes. Or were they? Gray maybe. Yeah, gray. Intense eyebrows, black and pointy, and moving, like crows. Thick hair, curly, mussed. Did he ever comb it? And funny shoes.

Chassi smiled now as she maneuvered the fast car into the curtain of twilight. Wallabees? Wow. Is that what they were called? Mukluks? Okay, so she couldn't remember the name but soft and bulky and cuddly brown. She had to tell Dr. Costello. Eleanor. She would like it that she could remember, she would be pleased.

Cuddly shoes with ties.

She pulled the red-orange Crayola out of the box, the color of her mommy's toenails, and colored in the top of the rainbow. Mommy's bare toes and Mr. Thalosinos's big brown shoes, Chassi spread-eagled in between them, drawing, on her stomach under the trailer table, but her elbows had gotten itchy from the rug. She put down the crayon and rolled onto her back. She studied her mommy's bare legs upside down, the hem of the white terry bathrobe tucked under her knees, a dusting of freckles on the perfumed skin, the delicate chain of the gold anklet twinkling at the sticky-out bone. Mr. Thalosinos's socks were white, and for when you played tennis; Daddy never wore white socks with fuzzy brown shoes.

Chassi squinted at Mr. Thalosinos's shoes; they could be baby beavers that could talk but only she could hear, a boy one and a girl one. She lay there a moment and then edged over on her side, moved her hand toward the shoe, the girl one. She would pull on the laces, re-form the bow into baby beaver eyes, and he wouldn't feel it because she was invisible under there, like a ghost, no, like the invisible man, the invisible girl, or a genie that had come from a pouf of his smoke. Chassi, I am Chassi, the invisible girl genie who no one can see or feel. She tugged on the shoelace and Mommy said something, a soft laugh; Chassi smiled under the table, she loved Mommy's laugh. *Oh, Sally,* Mr. Thalosinos said in a low rumble and her mother's foot rose and came down on the baby brown beaver; Mommy's cool bare toes as they covered Mr. Thalosinos's cuddly shoe collided with Chassi's hand.

• • •

ELEANOR SAT AT HER DESK, studied the page in the notepad where she had scribbled "Thalosinos." Thalosinos under "Peroni" in spindly letters, and then an attempt at Chassi's profile, which looked more like what? A shoe? A schmoo was probably more like it. Eleanor smirked, tilted the notepad. She hesitated turning the lights on. It was more than twilight, more than time to go home, but if she turned the lights on she would stay. She rubbed her knee, leaned back in the chair, swiveled it slowly toward the windows. Her eyes followed the outlines of the buildings across the way.

She'd worked enough, she had a whole menu out there to choose from: go home, go to the movies, go to dinner, go to hell. Eleanor snickered, pushed her hands up over her face and into her hair. There was never enough time and now there was too much, giant hollow spaces filled with no sound. Evenings, she had come to hate evenings, which used to be her favorite hunk of the day. Jimmy was always home before she was, she would hear the music from the garage. Hear the music, smell the garlic, a drink in the chair. He'd cook, she'd watch him bang the pots, the baby playing on the floor; Eleanor's idea of dinner was anything on a piece of bread in her hand. Even when he wasn't home and she had to cook for Caroline she rarely put her own portion on a plate or sat down. Macaroni and cheese from the bottom of the pot as she walked around the kitchen, any leftover from the Tupperware container at the open door of the fridge, a bunch of grapes sticking out of her pocket, a bag of chips in her purse. "Your mommy's a trapeze artist with food," Jimmy said to Caroline. "Here, babe, try a napkin," he would say, pushing a paper towel into Eleanor's hand. When he cooked they sat at the table with cloth napkins and china because, as Jimmy put it, Sis had "taught him good." Eleanor sat at the table next to him; even after they had Caroline she still sat next to him, not across from him with the baby in the middle. Jimmy was the center, their middle, she and Caroline's middleman. The sweet white cream in between the two layers of cookie. Eleanor swiveled the chair around.

She was hungry, that's what it was; the hell with Thalosinos and Peroni, the only peroni she wanted now was on a pizza. Very funny. No, not pizza, Chinese. Mr. Hong would be so happy, *Herrow, Dr. Erranore, so good see you, sweet and sawa poke, shreemp in robster sauce*, grinning, *Misser Hong know* he would recite before she opened her mouth. All the dishes Jimmy used to eat. She couldn't bear to tell him how she could no longer swallow sweet and sour pork, that the mere thought of shrimp in lobster sauce made her want to vomit. Dear Mr. Hong, maybe he would like to go eat with her, she could fold him into one of the little white boxes and take him home with the fried rice.

The hell with it. What she really wanted was Mexican. Enchiladas dripping with cheese and those awful beans. Grease city to fill up the holes. This is pathetic, Eleanor, go home, but she didn't get up from the chair.

"You know I won't eat that, Mom, it's grease city," Caroline had said.

"I thought maybe just for fun. Just this once you could put something delicious in your body."

"I like what I eat," and then quiet, just breathing across the wire, "it's Daddy who likes Mexican food, not me."

"I know, but Daddy won't be home." The wrong thing, she had said the wrong thing once again. "Okay," Eleanor said, the smile fixed somewhere at the top of her cheekbones, "I'll pick up something else."

"No, it's okay."

"Then how about you make us something? Vegetables, hey, steamed vegetables with that rice you like." Come on, come on, kid, open up just a little, the phone tucked in between Eleanor's chin and shoulder, her eyes surveying the office: purse under the arm, appointment book, keys.

Caroline laughed. "*What?*"

"Hey, I like vegetables, I just don't like sprouts. And asparagus. And okra." That's it. Look, oh, God, look, we're doing it, we're laughing like mothers and daughters everywhere.

"Mom, you'll hate it. Look, just don't count on me, okay? I really want to get out."

The air rushing out of Eleanor. Not get out with you, Mom, not why don't I meet you somewhere? Quiet, Eleanor, shut up, don't say a word.

A lump of silence.

"What?" Caroline said. The *what* of *What do you want from me?* Oh, yeah, that *what*, with a definite edge.

"Nothing. I just thought maybe the two of us"—careful, careful, watch it—"you know, we could just have dinner and talk."

"What do you want to talk about, Mom?" Fast, no waiting; come on, Mom, the daughter said, step up to the plate, take your best shot.

Eleanor clutching her purse and the receiver, the flesh of her leg bruising against the corner of the desk. How 'bout the gaffe, how 'bout the whopper hole between us, how about how you can hardly stand me, I can see it in your eyes.

"Oh, I don't know, just two girls, two *women*, having dinner together," Eleanor said softly. Oh, be careful here, oh, step carefully, watch your big mouth. She listened to her child breathing, weighing her words, Eleanor thought, and Caroline said, "Mom, I don't want to talk, I get what you're doing here. We're fine, okay?"

And Eleanor said, "Oh, sure, okay." You bet, oh, sure, so much for trying, and a week later Caroline was gone. Clothes strewn around her room as if she'd left in a fever and a note on the kitchen table about going to San Francisco to be with Jono. Jono, whom Caroline had met when he played at Berkeley. Jono, who was English and the drummer for something called Demon Fever that played something called "hard core." Jono, who had dropped out long ago. Jono, who called Caroline collect. Jono, who was thirty-two years old to Caroline's twenty-one. Jono of the no last name and no forwarding address. Jono, whom Caroline refused to discuss. Jono, whom Eleanor and Jimmy had never laid eyes on.

Eleanor stood up, ripped the page where she had written "Thalosinos" and "Peroni" out of the notebook, looked at it again and slipped it into the Chassi Jennings file. Too tired. Too hungry. Too out of gas. She tucked her purse under her arm and scooped up her car keys, hit the star key and 63 to punch her phone into voice mail, and crossed the dark office to the door. Hey, maybe Chassi Jennings would like some grease-city Mexican food, or *sweet and sawa poke*, or a mother to love.

• • •

IT TURNED OUT that Jones was tight with Robby Peroni, that they'd shot two pictures together, one when Peroni was fresh out of USC film school, a short about some guy who walked in his sleep, appropriately titled *Sleepwalk*, and then *Trucks*, the one that hadn't done much at the box office when it first came out, but the one all the critics went wild over. Ionie was stunned. She'd seen *Trucks* three times but she hadn't known that Jones had shot it. It was only since she'd been in Los Angeles that she paid attention to the credits that roll before and after a film. There were lots of other things she hadn't known about Jones: that he'd been nominated for an Academy Award for *Trucks* but hadn't won—she could hardly believe it, she had no idea she'd even met anyone who'd been nominated for an Academy Award—that he had won two Emmys and an Ace Award and a whatever you got from the commercial awards people for that black-and-white thing he did for diet Pepsi that Ionie had adored when she was maybe twelve. That his brother had died of a heart attack on a basketball court when they were both in college; that Jones was a fanatic about diet and exercise, he wouldn't eat a French fry if you paid him, or a fried anything or butter or sour cream. "Not even a hot fudge sundae?" "Especially not a hot fudge sundae," he'd said, laughing, and then kissed her palm. That he practically had to have scripts read to him because of his dyslexia. That he sang in his church choir. "You don't." "Oh, yes I do." That he owned two horses he kept at The Paddock in Burbank. "Can we ride them?" "Sure." And that he never wore shorts or a bathing suit because of the scars.

"Why didn't they take you to the hospital?"

"Because they didn't know, they put me to bed, put butter all over my legs and put me to bed."

"Butter?"

Jones laughed. "It was the old days, Ionie."

She shook her head. "Why did the water heater blow up?"

"No, it was the pilot light, vapors from the gas fumes to the pilot light on the water heater, my dad had spilled some gasoline."

"How old were you?"

"Five."

"What were you doing in the basement?"

"Playing with my brother."

Ionie ran the fingers of her right hand tentatively over the scars across the tops of his legs under the sheet and blanket. "It feels like satin," she whispered, her lips skimming the stubble at the side of his cheek. "Can I see?"

He was already in the bed when she'd come out of the bathroom. He'd closed the draperies, blocking the glaring blue-white light that was reflecting off the Ramada swimming pool and the three lone little boys who were racing around it because it really wasn't warm enough to go in, their mother said, her eyes focused on the magazine in her lap, shouting, "No running, no running" as if it was her mantra or the words to a song. Jones had folded the flowered bedspread into perfect thick rectangles and had laid it across the seat cushion of the club chair, his shirt hanging from one shoulder on the back of that chair and his pants rearranged into their pressed creases on top of the spread. Socks across the loafers and a white T-shirt on top of the pants. If there were shorts Ionie didn't see them. He was leaning back on the pillows propped against the headboard when she came out of the bathroom, the sheet and blanket pulled to his waist.

The mad freedom of the night in the trailer was long gone. The longing in his eyes, the halting conversation, the tentative touch of his hand, the slow ride to the Burbank Ramada, Ionie's smoking Datsun following Jones's dark green Explorer, her eyes fastened on his license plate, her hands slick on the wheel; this was not mad freedom, there was no rush of spontaneity here. Ionie's soul-searching in the Ramada bathroom mirror had only shown her what she already knew: that what she was doing she was doing because she wanted to, in the sober white light of day. It was the *why* she didn't want to look at, not her flushed face staring back at her in the glass. He had a crush on her. She slipped out of her sandals and stepped out of her jeans. He was dear. She took a Kleenex and blotted away her lipstick, held her hands under the cold water in the sink and splashed some on her face. She liked him. She crossed her arms and pulled the T-shirt off over her head and let it fall from her hand to the floor. She did, she liked him. Oh, God. She sat on the closed toilet seat and stood up, circled the beige terry bathmat heel to toe. It wasn't a big deal, people did this all the time. She unfastened her bra. It wasn't a big deal. She slid her arms through the straps and placed the bra across the bathtub ledge, then picked it up and dropped it to the rest of her clothes in the pile on the floor. Ionie did not look at herself in the mirror again, she did not fluff at her hair, or check different views of her body, she just crossed one arm over her breasts and opened the door.

She wore white cotton bikini panties and her father's class ring, nothing more. She knew she looked beautiful, it wasn't a matter of how she felt; Jones's eyes took her in and she knew. He sat up slightly, away from the pillows, offered his hand. Ionie took the eight steps to the side of the bed, eight, she counted in her head as her toes skimmed the flat hotel rug and she walked to him through the lunchtime light. Lunchtime is what she thought, nooner, the clock at his elbow read 12:20 and Ionie thought, Oh, God, we are a nooner, just like all the jokes. She faltered and he reached for her, clasped his fingers through hers and pulled her to him, her forehead finding a place under his chin. He settled them back against the pillows. Jones was thinner than she was, taller and thinner, the hair on his chest soft and gray and brown, the rest of him all angles. Ribs hard under her breasts, his slender arm pressing into her shoulder, one hipbone in the flesh of her thigh, her left hand tucked under his neck and the jut of his chin and the stubble, her right palm and fingertips quiet now on the scars. Sea Breeze and soap and coffee and peppermint, and other than that Ionie didn't remember any of Jones from the night in the trailer; it was as if she hadn't touched his skin until now.

"Satin," she whispered, her lips in the stubble at the side of his cheek, her breath in her chest and the bass slam of one of their hearts through her skin, and one of the boys must have jumped into the pool, a shriek and a splash and the other boys whooping. "Andy, you bad boy!" the mother screamed. "You bad boy! You get out of there right now!," and Ionie moved her hand slowly and whispered, "Jones, can I see your scars?"

It turned out that Jones had shot two pictures with Robby Peroni, and as Jones said, it would be easy to call, but Ionie didn't know that until after, she hadn't asked him if he knew Peroni until after and he might not have, what were the odds? Even if you went with the theory of six degrees of separation, which in Hollywood was called six degrees of Kevin Bacon, since everybody knew everybody, Jones still might not have known Peroni. But he did, *Sure, I do,* he said, *Sure, I could call him*, but she hadn't asked him until after, she reassured herself as she drove home in the afternoon traffic, it was after, at least she could give herself that.

CHAPTER 12

There had always been postcards, a hatboxful. Lavender roses and green leaves were stenciled around the paper cardboard, fading cardboard now, a few small rips that she had painstakingly glued so the paper where it had torn and lifted fit perfectly back in place. The braided rope was purple. Chassi pulled the silk ties of the bow, lifted the lid off Nana's hatbox. The smell of Nana flooded her face. She wasn't sure if the box still smelled of Nana's hat and Nana or whether the smell of tuberoses was just locked in her head.

"Mommy's just got a little hankerin' for New York, baby, and then I'll be right back home." Sally's whisper, the hug, high heels across the parquet, the slam of the car door. Postcards of St. Patrick's Cathedral and Times Square lit up at night and the tree at Rockefeller Center and Central Park green in the spring.

> *Chassi, baby, I miss you, I saw six plays so far and bought five pairs of shoes. Love, Mommy.*
> *P.S. Don't tell Daddy about the shoes. Ha. Ha.*

Skipping with the postcard up to her room, smelling the orange lipstick kiss that her mother had smacked on the bottom, kissing the lipstick print with her own little-girl lips and placing the card with the others in Nana's big hatbox. The colors of the painted roses and leaves were vivid then, the edges of the purple silk braid had not yet frayed.

"Mommy's just gonna toodle down to Nana's, baby, I'll be back in four little days." Postcards of the map of Texas, a dot her mother had made with red ink where they hadn't put Gun Barrel City, cowboys riding across the plain, the University of Texas at Austin, cactus flowers, Texas longhorns, and shooting six-guns. At least they appeared to be shooting; Chassi had traced her finger across the silver streaks flying out of the barrels of the guns.

Dear Chassi,
I miss you. I helped Nana put up peaches and went with her to church. Ugh. Skipper is getting old but when I say Chassi loves you, he flops his head and nuzzles my neck. I gave him an extra carrot for breakfast and he took part of my apple on his own! Nana and I are making barbecue to take to the fair. I told her let's make pies from the peaches but she said oh, no. I'm not telling your daddy I'm going because he gets all mad about crowd control but it's just the neighborhood and I'm not gonna let Nana down. She likes to show me off 'cause I'm still her baby and you're mine and I can't wait to squeeze you. Love,
Mommy.

Chassi showed the postcard with the shooting guns to Andrew, told him how her nana let her ride Skipper bareback, how she weaved her fingers through his mane. Andrew and Chassi whooping and galloping around the garden smacking their own rear ends, the postcard left on one of the patio tables where the sprinklers hit it, blurring Sally's up-and-down script into shadow lines of smudge.

"Mommy's just goin' to run to Paris with Daddy, baby, and come right on home." Postcards of the Eiffel Tower, the Champs-Elysée and the Arc deTriomphe, also lit up at night but the headlights from the Parisian cars were fuzzy with rain, the Seine, the flower market, the staircase at Chanel, a Renoir of a red-haired mother cuddling a blonde baby—Chassi couldn't tell if the baby was a boy or a girl but her mother must have definitely decided it was a girl because she wrote:

Sweet baby,
look, here's you and me by Renoir. Daddy and I are staying in a fancy hotel where everybody speaks French except us. Well, Daddy a little bit. The press loooves *his movie and he's* sooo *happy. Me too. We miss*

you, miss you, miss you. I'm buying you lots of things. A stuffed black panther with her baby with fuzzy baby fur and three stuffed rabbits, all different, big and small, and a pink suitcase to put treasures and a dolly that speaks French when you pull her string! Wait till you see. Love, Mommy.

The dolly had straight brown hair that you could comb (the comb came with her and a tiny brush and a tiny mirror that was really silver paper and not a mirror at all but it worked, you just looked wobbly) and a red straw hat with a black ribbon that hung down and a string under her plaid school dress (Sally said it was a school dress, that all the little girls in Paris had to wear that kind of dress to school) and flat black-patent-leather shoes. When you pulled the string she said either: "*Bonjour, Papa,*" "*Bonne Nuit, Mama,*" or "*Merci.*" The ribbon came off the hat and one of the shiny shoes disappeared but the dolly never lost her ability to speak.

"Mommy's just got to get herself together, baby, get her poor ole body fluffed up to shoot." Postcards from the Golden Door where Sally went before a picture to get fluffed up, a fistful.

Dear Chassi,
I'm trying to keep up with the instructors but I would much rather lie around the pool and eat hamburgers than actually swim. Lost four pounds and an inch here and there. I'm especially working on firming up my derriere. (That's French for you-know-what.) When I get out of here I am never going to eat lettuce again. Hooray. I miss you. How's school? Kiss Andrew and Tia and Daddy. And kiss yourself, tip your head over and kiss your shouldie. I adore you,
Mommy.

"Shouldie" was what Chassi called her shoulder. "Mr. Bluebird's on my shouldie," she sang from the movie *Song of the South* when she was two.

"Mommy's gotta go on location, baby, and Tia will bring you on the airplane to see me real soon." Postcards from every location of every picture Sally Brash had made since Chassi was born. Postcards from Seattle and Ann Arbor, Michigan, and Eureka, California, and

Chicago, Illinois, postcards from Miami Beach with tan coconuts on green palm fronds way up high in a deep blue sky and postcards from Lone Pine, California, where they must have not had anything famous to put on the front because it only said "Lone Pine" in fat red script. Postcards from *In the City* and *A Hollywood Life* and *Life and Death on 10 West* and *The Canary Trainer* and *North of Montana* and *A Dance at the Slaughterhouse* and *No Trumpets, No Drums*. Nana's hatbox full of postcards that Chassi had memorized as if they were lines from a script. But the ribbon that she had taken from her mother's dressing table, the curl of white satin that Sally had used to tie up her hair, that ribbon was only wrapped around three:

Dear Chassi,
We are in Rome together having a wonderful time. I know you will think it's silly that I'm writing you while we're together but this way you won't forget anything, it will all be written down. See? Isn't your mommy smart? Today we stood in line at the Vatican in the hot sun and walked and walked and saw everything that we could. The Sistine Chapel didn't move me as much as the Pietà *did. You loved it. You said you especially loved the little angels, their faces and their wings. We just took showers back at the hotel and put bandages all over our feet. You want to go out by yourself to get a* gelati *and I'm going to let you because you're such a big girl.*
I love you,
Mommy

The front of the postcard was a piece of the ceiling, Michelangelo e la Cappella Sistina (*dopo la pulitura*), which meant a part, two angels behind a woman with a yellow tunic and a blue headdress, her arm chopped out of frame. There was not enough room for all the writing, Sally had wedged a lot of words close together at the end.

Dear Chassi,
I'm so happy we took this trip. You are so much fun to be with, even though you're a little pushy about us having to look at EVERYTHING. I have never been in so many churches and looked at so many paintings in my whole life. Nana would have loved it, you said. Yes, she would have, my sweet. You know, you are very much like your nana. Kind and sooo *smart and especially thoughtful and certainly not a knucklehead like me.*

You are growing into a beautiful woman, just like a butterfly, and I am so lucky to have had you since you were in my cocoon. Isn't your mommy silly? Today we went to the Galerie Borghese and stood transfixed at the Bernini statues, especially the one where Zeus is turning Daphne into a tree to save her from Apollo, which you said really wasn't such a good thing for a Daddy to do, and I laughed, and the one where Hades is pulling Persephone into hell and I cried. The tear on her face was so real.
I will always love you, Chassi, always remember that,
Mommy

Apollo e Dafne, it said on the card in black and white. Apollo catching up with Daphne as she ran from him, her feet freezing into branches, her arm extended, the fingers turning into leaves. On this one Sally had tried to write smaller and squeeze the words closer together from the beginning so they wouldn't get all messed up at the end. She hadn't succeeded.

Dear Chassi,
We are leaving Rome tomorrow. I meant to write a postcard every day but we've been so busy that I wrote only two others and just found them in my purse. I will mail them now when we go out. Today you had a long talk with a very old man who had plunked his dog right into the Trastevere fountain. You are so good at Italian, the two of you had a very animated conversation with a lot of laughing and hand gestures of pantomime, I'm not sure about what. When you get home, why don't you make a list of all the things we saw and did so you won't ever forget? (You know how I love to make lists!) You could call it the "TWO GIRLS IN ITALY" list. You are already dressed and I have to hurry and get ready, we're going to this restaurant where they make an artichoke filled with crumbs. Thank you for coming to Rome with me, my sweet girl. I'm so glad you didn't get Ireland for your report in school! I love you forever and ever. Always remember that, no matter what. Love,
Mommy

This one was another piece of the Sistine Chapel, a hand on either side of the card, the fingers extended toward each other as if they were about to hold on. Sally had run out of room again and had ended up writing tiny print around the border of the card, so you had to keep turning it as you read it, round and round in your hand.

Chassi held the three cards in the white ribbon. She didn't untie them, she didn't read them, she didn't look at the pictures on their fronts. The *gelati* had been a deep, rich blackberry, the dog in the fountain had been black and scrappy, the dress her mother wore to the restaurant was white chiffon. The *gelati* owner had praised Chassi's feeble Italian, the conversation she had with the old man was about the hot weather, and she threw up the artichoke with the crumbs in the police car.

The cards came after the funeral, after Chassi had climbed the slick green hill in the blinding sun, her fingers clutching Saul's, their palms stuck with sweat. Daddy, and Tia, who had what looked like a square of black lace net bobby-pinned to the top of her head, and Andrew somewhere with Baudelio and Andrew's mother, Mrs. Baudelio, who Chassi had never met, and Tom, who always drove Mommy, pushing Nana in the wheelchair with the lady who took care of Nana from Gun Barrel City, Mrs. Eula Mae Soames, and Daddy's brother, Uncle Walter, who came from New York with his wife who had dyed her hair red so she could look just like Mommy, Mommy said once, *fat chance*, and their two boys who were obnoxious, and lots of people whose names she couldn't remember, a blur of black suits and sunglasses marching up the hill like a silly parade following what they told her was her mother, in a long wood box. The cards came after all the people eating and drinking and telling stories about her mother, after all their stupid cars left, after Daddy didn't go to work, after Tia cried in the kitchen, after Andrew kissed her, after Nana went back to Texas with Mrs. Eula Mae Soames, clutching Chassi so desperately from her chair in the hallway that her fingers left marks, after she went back to school, and after she thought somehow she had made the whole thing up and Mommy would come home from one of her trips, open suitcases in the foyer, a hurricane of wrapping paper and ribbons across the floor. The cards came then to remind her, her mother was dead. In the irony of life and death and the postal service of Italy, the last one came second and the first one came last. Chassi hated that Daddy had to give them to her, hated the way his mouth curved down and the way he wouldn't look at her as he held them out when they arrived one by one.

Chassi sat with the open hatbox on her lap, the three cards tied with her mother's hair ribbon in the palm of her hand. The light was changing, she watched the dusk descend. The tuberoses of her grandmother, the gardenias of her mother, honeysuckle through the open window, Chassi sat in the chair. It occurred to her that she had never made the "TWO GIRLS IN ITALY" list, that she hadn't even tried.

The house was extraordinary, the girl told Eleanor, the house of the cinematographer, Jones, who would shoot *No Trumpets, No Drums*. Not big but somehow magical and extraordinary because she'd never seen anything like it except in Italy.

Eleanor watched her from the chair.

Low and flat and pale yellow stucco, Chassi went on, with thick white curlicues as if it had been made from an icing of butter cream and most certainly Italian, as if a helicopter had raised it up from one of the hills above Rome, flown it dangling over the sea, and set it down in the hills above Santa Barbara only an hour and a half from L.A.

"Jones's wife is a lawyer. Linda, an entertainment lawyer, a partner at Hergott and Bloom and Jones and whatever, very smart and very"—she thought for a minute—"very elegant, like her house. Clipped gardens, lollipop trees, and these meticulously shaped hedges, as if they were part of a maze, like in *Alice*, remember?" And then in a little girl voice Chassi said, "And the ugly, fat, angry queen of hearts, with her tiny king husband snipped their clippers in a mad chase for Alice through wonderland." She laughed. "That's what I thought about when I saw it. Wonderland for the movie rich, my dear, known by the locals as Montecito, California, very la-de-da." Chassi frowned. "Well, they're not really rich, I don't think, I have no idea what cinematographers make, but I saw these gardens and all I could hear was that mean, chubby queen yelling 'Off with her head,' do you remember?" Chassi asked, turning slightly toward Eleanor. "From *Alice in Wonderland*?"

Eleanor was quiet.

Chassi's voice softening, "God, I hated that movie. It was so scary." She took a breath, sat there staring into space and then went on. "That awful queen and that cat with the smile that wasn't on his face and those crazy rabbits with all those teapots, they were insane, and mostly—" She sat up but stopped talking.

"What?" Eleanor said.

"She couldn't find her way. I hated that so much that she couldn't find her way."

Quiet. Too quiet. "Hey," Chassi said, "by the way, what happened to Big Ben?"

"I put him in a drawer."

"I see," Chassi said, mimicking Eleanor perfectly.

"Go on," Eleanor said and they both smiled.

"Go on . . . well." She turned back, resettled herself on the couch. "The driver pulled the car up into the driveway; did I tell you Robby sent a car?"

Eleanor nodded.

"He was already up there, he's looking to buy a place up there, and I didn't want to drive, I told him—" She stopped then, as if she was going to say something and stopped herself.

"Why?" Eleanor asked.

"Why what?"

"Why didn't you want to drive?"

"Oh"—she gave the little shrug laugh—"who wants to drive all the way to Santa Barbara and I'm not much for parties anyway but he wanted me to meet Jones, since he's going to shoot the picture, he wanted us to meet . . . anyway, these twinkling lights, you know, the teeny ones, like people have for Christmas. Outlining every piece of shaped greenery, they flashed on just as we pulled up, I mean, at that very instant, as if it had been cued, like in a movie, as if it were rigged. You know, right as the light was changing from violet to navy, from day to night, as they say." Her face angled again toward Eleanor. "Hey, you know, maybe he did rig it, Jones, after all he is a DP, he could have had one of his guys do it." She paused. "Magic hour, that's what it's called."

Eleanor waited.

"You know, I thought my mother made up that expression, I didn't know that it was part of the Hollywood jargon, you know, like Tinsel Town. 'Magic hour,' she told me, 'when things can disappear.' "

She paused again.

"You know, the edges of things, when it gets dark, they blur into something else . . ." Her voice drifted off, Eleanor watched her; it was clear she was somewhere else.

"Chassi?"

"Chassi, Mommy's Chassi," Sally crooned. You couldn't see her, you could only feel her in your room, the thin yellow wedge of hall light receding as your eyes opened and closed, Mommy's low drawl in the dark, the heady smell of the white flowers, the dip of the bed and then she was next to you under the covers, pulling you close in, oh, so good, to be cozy-cozyed by Mommy, one arm wrapped around her middle, one hand on her back up under her pajamas, Mommy's fingernail painting a delicious, invisible picture on her skin.

"Is it time to get up?"

"Only me." Sally's whisper, her breath in Chassi's hair.

"Are you going to work?"

"Mm-hm."

"Is it still dark?"

"Mm-hm."

"I feel the wheels." Trying so hard to concentrate on Mommy's finger.

"What wheels?"

"Circles."

"Those are the circles in I love you."

"What circles?"

"The *o*'s."

"Oh"—pushing her backside into her mommy's tummy—"it feels like wheels."

"I gotta go to work, good mornin', my little love."

"Do I have to get up?"

"No, baby . . ."

"Is it still dark?"

"Mm-hm."

And the dip of the bed and the wedge of yellow light coming and going if you could keep your eyes open and Mommy would be gone. That's how Chassi learned that there were two times when things could disappear, two magic hours: the dusk and the dawn.

"Chassi?"

The girl blinked and stared at Eleanor. "What was I talking about?"

"The lights in the driveway, magic hour."

Frozen and then she took a breath. "Sometimes I miss my mother."

Eleanor nodded but didn't move in the chair.

"And sometimes, I'm"—another breath, this time with a fast exhale—"a little dizzy."

"Okay," Eleanor said, "we'll talk about it," and she could feel her own heart turn as she gave the child a smile.

• • •

SHE COULD NEVER REMEMBER the exact words of that morning, which was so unlike her. "Don't ever fight with Eleanor," Jimmy would carry on with anybody, "I'm telling you, she remembers everything, every word you said, she'll drag up your goddamn dialogue and hit you over the head with it later on." Miss Verbatim, he called her, she should have been a lawyer, he said, instead of a psychiatrist. But words hurled in the heat of an argument burned into Eleanor's brain like the brand on a calf and words said in a good-bye to a husband after twenty-eight years of hello and good-bye and I'll see you and later and call me and okay and what time and Jimmy, hey, Jimmy just didn't burn. She was in the bed, he'd already gone to the kitchen and made the coffee before dawn. Put it in a thermos to take on the boat like he always did because, "Are you kidding? D.R.'s coffee tastes like wet dirt." Made eight sandwiches like he always did, two for each of them, lining up the slices of bread on the edge of the sink, mayonnaise on the tomato side, mustard on the bologna side, a little salt, too much pepper, Costello's assembly line. She could see him even though she was in the bed, she knew his routine. He had the radio on. Like he always did. KCRW, National Public Radio, doodeedoodee-doo, Eleanor hummed into the pillow. Bluegrass, soft and twangy, nice, a banjo, a guitar, and he smelled of coffee and his shower when he leaned in for the kiss. "I'm goin', babe." Scratchy cheek. "Mm-hm." "See ya' later." "Mmm." His hand on her ass through the comforter. " 'Bye." " 'Bye." But had she said " 'Bye"? Or had she just rolled over, his kiss on her neck? Rolled over and back to sleep and gotten up after nine; after all, it was Sunday, the boys would be on the boat until right before dark, meet him at D.R.'s and Rose's for dinner, it was Rose's turn. Their Sunday ritual: wives on land, husbands out to sea. No kids to take care of anymore, all their kids grown and gone. No *other* suppers of macaroni and cheese, no Caroline to be read to or tucked in early, the entire day for herself. The entire *New York Times* back in the bed with the coffee and the bagel, Eleanor put the "Week in Review" on top of the front section, picked up the "Arts and Leisure" and the phone rang. Had she said "Good-bye"?

The aneurysm hit him, D.R. said, after the second sandwich. "Jesus, honey," Rose said, "what a thing to say." "What? I'm just telling her, what?" The look to his wife, the helpless anger, D.R. slumped against the wall of the hallway leading to intensive care. D.R. as pale as Jimmy. Pale but alive and Jimmy was alive but not so fast, kiddo, not exactly alive. "Jokin' around, El, you know Jimmy." Kenny's big hands at his sides, gesturing. "You know, the way he did, that's what I thought when he fell." Jimmy's hands were also at his sides but not gesturing, oh no, those fingers through the thin hospital blanket were now just dead lumps of flesh. Okay, not dead, what should we call them? *Sleeping* lumps of flesh?

"You want something, El? Coffee?" Vernon behind her, and Linda, "No, Vern, I'll go." "I'll go," from Kenny's ex-wife because what did it matter if you were an ex-wife when you were standing in a hospital hallway with your friends waiting for the death of a brain stem? "Get me a yogurt," Rose said, "a muffin, a sandwich, anything." Her touching look to Eleanor. "I'm sorry, I'm starving." As if she should be sorry that she was hungry, when really why she was sorry was because they were standing, that Eleanor could see them standing, that three husbands were still standing and Jimmy would never stand, and alive, three husbands were alive because Jimmy was . . . well, technically alive, but not exactly. After all, what good was a husband who wasn't exactly alive? After all, she was a doctor, let's use the proper terminology here, you can say it, "c-o-m-a," coma, short for comatose, anoxic brain injury in addition to the berry aneurysmal bleed; thatagirl, after all. Styrofoam boxes, crusts of whole wheat, Cheez Doodles, the rip of the bag, warm Pepsi, cold coffee, gum, toothpaste out of Rose's purse on her finger the morning of the second day.

The second day, the second sandwich, the winds were at how many knots and from what direction, as if it mattered, and his fall was at how many knots and in what direction, as if it mattered; "I thought it was a heart attack, I mean, man, do I know from a heart attack or what?" Kenny's voice low and his shoulders and the angle of his head. Kenny of the two heart attacks and the plastic valve, and D.R. doing a dance with his high cholesterol, and Vernon the diabetic, not shooting insulin yet but right on the edge, and Jimmy, "Hey, Sulka said I have the body of a forty-year-old," Jimmy carrying on after his last checkup. "Oh, yeah?" Eleanor laughing, "Show me. Where?" The forty-year-old body of a fifty-two-year-old Jimmy falling over the side of D.R.'s thirty-four-foot Hinkley. Man overboard, Kenny laughing, only it was no joke. Hey, did you hear the one about the guy who had the aneurysm and fell in? Vernon and D.R. hitting the water, Kenny screaming on the radio, Kenny, who was the oldest, who had been a radio operator in Korea but had never radioed an important message, "only shit about paint, bring white paint to Barracks B," he mumbled, pantomiming, his big hands spelling out the code. The three of them hauling him in, up and over, the boat pitched nearly vertical, pulling and pushing him in hand by hand—"Hell, you know how big Jimmy is, El, and being dead weight," "dead" being the operative word for Vernon's red face and the tender stammer. The details of D.R. doing CPR, how she was going to make a smart remark about it surely being his job because he was captain, but didn't because she knew if she opened her mouth she would scream. The arrival of the Coast Guard, the chop of the helicopter, Jimmy's body attached to the lifeline hanging over their heads in the spray, "Like some goddamned movie," D.R. said, his head falling into his hands. What each one of them did and saw and felt, every stinking detail, they only stopped telling her when Caroline joined them in the hallway, that was the only time any of the middle-aged sailors shut up.

You couldn't talk to Caroline, you couldn't touch her, you couldn't get near. Rage encircled her like a cloak across her shoulders, like a stormcloud. Rage at the men, at the boat, at the day, at the doctors, and especially at Eleanor, as if Eleanor had pushed Jimmy in. The rage covered her fear, and it covered her heartache, and it covered her grief, because the grief was already there with them, because they knew he was gone. It was machines breathing, not Jimmy, that much they knew. The grief stood beside them at his bed, hovered like a shadow over the beeping machines, and walked between them up and down the hall. As formed as if it were a person, the grief was only missing a shirt and pants and shoes.

"Matt, this is D.R." and "Oh, yeah, you guys play softball, huh?

How you doing?," rising to his feet, and Matt's "This is Moonie, my wife," and D.R.'s "Hey, this is my wife, Rose." Hushed hellos and whispered introductions from all of his friends; "How ya doin'?" from the sailors, and "What's up?" from the ballplayers, and "How is he?" from the gardeners. As if in a trance, Eleanor observed the sides of her husband's life come together in a deathwatch next to a bed and up and down a pale green hall. All of his friends and her friends caught in a jumble of not knowing what to say or do. Rose brought her clothes and Moonie kept going to the cafeteria to get her chicken soup as if she had a bad cold. Okay, everybody who has a husband take two aspirins and call me in the morning. Whoops, not so fast, Eleanor.

They stood in a half circle, the handsome one with the mustache, the schlubby chubby one in the blue scrubs, and the big tall one with the solemn eyes. They were in agreement, the three doctors, the handsome one said, "That, uh"—he shuffled his shoe, he was wearing green paper booties over Nikes, Eleanor could see the Nike logo through the green—"that the results of the CAT scan showed that between the aneurysm bleed"—he stopped—"and the secondary drowning," and the chubby internist chimed in, "That, uh" and the handsome one from emergency continued as if they were a trio, "the brain is dead." No one moved. *Hiss, squoosh* went the ventilator and no one moved. The tall one from neurology cleared his throat, looked at her, bent his head, and cleared his throat again. Eleanor held fast to Jimmy's puffy fingers—why were his fingers puffy? He'd never had puffy fingers before. She had refused to move away from him, go with them down some hallway, sit with them in some little room; she held tight to his hand. How could she hear bad news without Jimmy? It wouldn't make any sense.

Quiet. The taste of blood in her mouth. *Hiss, squoosh.* The discussion of the disconnection of the ventilator, or in plain English, the pulling of the plug. The tall one bent his head to her; hadn't he wanted to be a basketball player, he was at least six-seven, what had possessed him to be a neurologist when he could have been a New York Knick? Mumble, mumble, something organs. Did he say organ?

Liver, kidneys, heart, corneas; pieces of Jimmy, is that what he said? Caroline's eyes on her hard, Eleanor looked at her husband, tubes and lines going in and out of what was still her husband, she looked at Jimmy, she looked at the tall neurologist, she said, "Yes." Yes, you can take pieces of him, just don't make me let go of his hand.

There was no problem about remembering that part, the hospital part, words and sounds and colors, the tall one mumbling "organs," the hiss of the appalling ventilator, the green gloves on the handsome one's shoes, she remembered every bit of it, oh, yeah.

"Mom, please, not yet."

"Caroline, he's not going to change."

Panic in her child's eyes. "How do you know that? I don't care what they say, how do you know that for sure?" The white face, the rage, the horror that Eleanor could do such a thing, that Eleanor would pull the plug on her daddy, let her daddy die.

"Caroline, please, this is hard enough . . ." Caroline, please.

The aneurysm had hit him after the second sandwich, his kidneys had gone to Baltimore, oh, she remembered all of that, but had she said "Good-bye"?

Not that she didn't have a lot of time to think about it, reconstruct the dawn morning, restore the words and actions of the night before. He said this and she said that and they had leftover pot roast for supper and mashed potatoes and no salad and cold apple pie and why did he go to bed before her and why did he have to go sailing and why did she stay downstairs watching *Two for the Road* and why did he have to die?

"Come on up."

"It's too early."

"Hey, El—"

"Come on, babe, I want to see the end."

His look to her. "They end up together."

Her smirk to him. "I know that."

"Then why do you have to watch it?"

She shook her head, sighed. He shook his head and left the room.

Her feet on the coffee table, his feet going up the stairs. The crunch of the leather cushions under her, the creak of his body above her head. When she slid in next to him he was gone, deep in sleep, curled on his side, facing away. She tucked herself behind him, cool knees against warm thighs, one arm under the pillow, the other around his chest. Twenty-eight years of sleeping with a husband, how could you know which night would be the last?

Eleanor swiveled her chair toward the bank of windows and back around. There was a picture of Caroline in the bookcase, Rose had taken it on one of the Sundays. Not that Sunday, nor were there any more Sundays, sailing Sundays, the wind had definitely blown out of Eleanor's sail. She would never look at D.R.'s boat, she would never look at the ocean, she didn't even want to drive as far west as Santa Monica for fear she would see the blue.

A happy ten-year-old Caroline sailing with Daddy in the photograph, laughing in black-and-white, head back, all that hair floating about in the wind. Well, not anymore, now she had the new haircut, now she was a new girl. And how could she think that Eleanor would have possibly considered a Viking funeral or anything else that had to do with the sea? Miss Sensitive. He was an earth man who had been taken by water. Where was her head?

Eleanor got out of the chair and walked to the windows, watched the traffic below. The phone rang. Some patient needing her. She would let the service get it, she was in no mood. Green light, red light, yellow. Caroline had mittens like that, one green, one red, no yellow. Three rings and the service picked up. Eleanor sighed, let her forehead rest against the cool glass. Was there a traffic light on the Via Emelia? Did Chassi Jennings remember the exact words of the last conversation with her mother? Did Chassi Jennings get to tell her mother good-bye?

CHAPTER 13

The callback was in one of those big office buildings in Century City on the Avenue of the Stars. Ionie wasn't sure if the name of the street was a good omen or bad. "Jennings" was all it said on the lobby directory, not Jennings Films or Jennings Productions, just "Jennings, 27th floor." The office was spacious, high in the sky and sleek; pale blond wood, the glint of steel against thick black leather, bookcases of scripts bound in caramel rawhide, antique Chinese jars made into lamps, lush Persian carpets, everything stark, either pale or dark, but monotone, except for the flame of Sally Brash's hair. She was everywhere, photographs and posters in every language from every one of her movies, including the early ones that Ionie had never seen. Ionie sat directly across from *Ni Trompets, Ni Tambours*. Bold black type, the gray sky of war, the white of the nurse's uniform, the red of her hair. Full face, all Sally, the soldier was behind her and then farther in the distance, the other nurse/girlfriend/sidekick, whatever you wanted to call her, the second banana, Ionie's part. Ionie studied the poster.

Of course, this time the nurse in *No Trumpets, No Drums* would not be a redhead but a honey-blonde, the honey-blonde daughter of that gorgeous face over there. Ionie turned the page of the script, ran her finger down the dialogue. Oh, God. Unless they were going to dye Chassi's hair red, which would mean they couldn't afford another redhead in one of the leads and certainly not to play the second banana, oh, God. Ionie glanced up at the receptionist and back down to the page. Don't be ridiculous, they'd already seen her, they knew she was a redhead; if they wanted, she'd be a blond. Hell, for this part she'd be bald.

Ionie turned the page of the script. At least this time she was there on her own. Not because of Jones, not because of a phone call. Hey, please see my girlfriend, my ladyfriend, my who-knows-what he'd said for the first audition. "What did you say?"

He'd looked at her, blank.

"To Peroni."

"That you were a good actress."

"I know, but what did you *say*?"

"That you were a good actress."

"Uh-huh, okay."

She gave it up. Jones, a man of few words, wasn't one for remembering a conversation. But that was the first audition, now she was there on her own. It was what she'd done in that room that had gotten her the callback, the way she'd read the scenes.

The words on the page blurred, Ionie blinked and refocused. Oh, God, what was she doing with sweet Jones? And why was she looking at the lines anyway? She knew them, she could recite them as if they were the Lord's Prayer. Concentrate on who the character is, be the character, be the character.

"Are you sure you wouldn't like some coffee?"

The receptionist was wearing a suit that probably cost as much as the entire contents of Ionie's closet.

"Oh, no, thank you."

Coffee? Cuppa Joe had ruined her for coffee, she could hardly stand the smell. And pearls. How could a receptionist afford pearls? Well, they probably weren't real. Ionie tried to retuck her T-shirt where it had slipped out of the back of her jeans. It wasn't as if she had a nurse's uniform, not that she would have worn one if she had one, she wore the same thing for every audition: jeans, boots, and a T-shirt, callback or no callback. It was her theory that if she was comfortable and nondescript, she could become the part as if she were a chameleon, and if they needed to see her in the wardrobe of the character, then they could just give her the damn job. Ionie scanned the top of the receptionist's desk. Where were the other actresses? There were eight the last time but today there were none so far. No sign-in sheet, no nothing, why was she the only one there? Maybe they were keeping them apart from each other, hiding them in separate rooms.

She took a sip of the water the receptionist had brought. Crystal, a crystal glass of water. Holy cow. She could hear Kitty Ray: "I wonder what the poor people are doin', Ionie?" *Oh, Mama, look at me now.* Ionie eyed the receptionist, she was reading something behind a vase of lilies. Certainly not *The Enquirer* or even a lowly magazine, but something in a hardcover book, probably something in another language that she was translating in her head. She'd probably gone to Radcliffe and gotten a master's just to answer the phone. Ionie wasn't sure if it was all right to put the glass on the table but she certainly wasn't going to ask; she held it in her hand.

Okay, she was nervous. No, anxious. Not about being good, she'd be good, but about the whole setup. Why couldn't they just decide who they wanted without making everybody go through this? Torture, she thought, Hollywood torture, and the receptionist looked up at that very second from whatever she was reading and Ionie looked down. Where was everybody, anyway? What was going on? Ionie raised her eyes again and the receptionist smiled.

There were eight of them the first time. Eight hopeful second bananas, and the audition was way out on Ventura, deep in the valley, and it was hot. Terribly hot, and there would be traffic. Terrible traffic. Why did they always set up auditions so late in the afternoon? Nine-to-fivers going home from work, freeways jammed, she knew what was going to be in front of her and then, dumbfounded, she stood in the street with her mouth open—the Datsun had a flat.

"Why do you have to do everything at the last minute?" he'd said.

"It isn't the last minute."

"Sure it is."

Static on the line, crackle, crackle, something and then Al said loud and clear, "You should have checked the car."

She blotted her upper lip. "It just came out of the shop."

"You should have checked it."

Okay, she wasn't going to say anything.

"Gone out earlier and started it."

She was absolutely not going to say anything.

"Checked it."

No way.

"This is your big-deal interview, right?"

She moved to the other foot.

"You should have been more responsible."

She took a breath; she certainly didn't need him to lecture her, she opened her mouth and Al said, "Isn't this the one where you got that camera guy to call? What's his name?"

"Jones," she said. Oh, God.

He breathed into the telephone, "Ionie?"

What. "What?" she said.

He didn't answer, just the static of the cellular and the guys hammering away on the job. It occurred to her that he might say, *Hey, why don't you call him, that Jones, let him take you, that Jones, what's with you and that Jones?*, but that was ridiculous. Al didn't know, he couldn't—twice a week for about four hours she disappeared. She altered her route to the Burbank Ramada, she gave detailed descriptions of what had happened at yoga class, acting class, Cuppa Joe, the gym. How could he know? He didn't know and she couldn't think about it now. "Never mind," Ionie shouted over the din.

"What did you say?"

"I said I'll take a cab," she yelled.

"What have you got? Eight bucks in your purse? You can't get close to the valley with eight bucks, Ionie, you can't even get to Sunset, much less—"

"Al—"

Static.

"Goddamn it," he said, crackle, crackle, "I'm on my way."

She made it. He was covered in sawdust, smelled of sweat, and drove like a maniac. She kept her eyes closed, her feet in front of her, and didn't open her mouth. She made it, she read last. Eight women, she counted on the sign-in sheet, the last one leaving just as Ionie sat down. The connection as their eyes met, the uncanny camaraderie with the enemy, which was shocking and at the same time completely natural because only another actress could understand. The mutual anxiety, the mutual hunger, the *Oh, God, I need this job*, like the song in *A Chorus Line*. The deepest bond between actors being, Ionie had figured out, the pain. You were too tall, short, weak, strong, too collegiate, urban, rural, too today, too yesterday, too old, young, too motherly, immature, dumb, smart, dark, pale, it didn't matter; we need a name, we need an unknown, we need whatever we need and you're not it, we don't want you, get the picture? Okay. Only another one clutching her picture and resumé can know that pain. Eight actresses in their late twenties, early thirties. Ionie smiled. No black guys. Not this time. Just eight women all wanting to be the second banana. So where were they? She couldn't be the only one reading, they had to have narrowed it down to at least three.

She'd read last that hot day in the valley and she thought she'd read well. Peroni was on the opposite side of the table from where she sat, she knew it was him as soon as she walked into the room, she'd seen his picture plenty. No banter, no how are you, no putting you at ease. She'd walked in with the casting guy; he said Ionie St. John as if she were an announcement, as if she were a Dallas Cowboy running onto the field. She sat in the appointed chair; you could always tell which chair was the hot seat at any audition, it was the lone one, the one pulled aside with nothing next to it, as if it were under a single spot. *And where were you the night of the seventeenth, ma'am?* The casting guy took the chair next to Peroni to read with her. Peroni didn't look at her head shot, at her resumé, at the table, at his shoe, he looked right at her. Steady. She asked if she could stand. He didn't answer; the casting guy kind of waited and then said, "Sure."

The scene was loaded, a fight between her character and the lead character, Chassi Jennings's part; rage, tears, laughter, the role was a basket of goodies for an actor, a gift. Ionie had the opening line; the casting guy would wait until she began. She stood, walked to the corner of the room and turned, her back to them. A deep breath, focus. Take your moment, relish the knowledge that this is the last and first and only time during the interview when you are in control. Breathe. Let them anticipate you, not the you that is Ionie St. John from Texas, an actress reading for a part, but be the you that is Razel Palevsky from Bensonhurst, a nurse who just lost her husband in the war. Ionie breathed and remembered everything, she lifted the character of the Jewish nurse from Brooklyn as if it were a winter picture hat with a moss green veil and dull yellow roses and put it on her head. She could smell it, smell Brooklyn, taste, feel she was Razel Palevsky; Ionie stepped off the cliff and turned. Somewhere in the middle of the scene she sat in the hot seat, dragged it up to the table and sat directly across from Peroni, she had no idea when. They finished. Her hands were trembling; she didn't realize it until she saw them jumping around on her knees.

Nothing. The casting guy didn't move or change his facial expression, it was clear he was petrified of Peroni. Peroni studied her, frowned, adjusted his glasses, mumbled, "Yeah, okay," and the casting guy sprang to his feet to usher her away. She had no sense of what had happened, no take on the room. None. She cried all the way home. Al had never seen her so upset, he came over and made dinner and practically fed it to her with a spoon. Three weeks later, this callback.

Ionie finished the water in the crystal glass and put the glass on the table. What the heck.

Sally Brash didn't look like Chassi in the posters, or Chassi didn't look like Sally Brash, not at first, but then there was something. Ionie got up, she could feel the receptionist watching, she circled the room.

There were several photographs in blond wooden frames across the shelf of one of the bookcases. Sally and what-must-be Saul Jennings, Chassi in between. Sally holding Chassi when she was a baby, Sally holding Chassi when she was a little girl, Sally holding Saul Jennings's arm, Sally holding the Academy Award. Sally kissing Chassi, Sally kissing Saul Jennings, Sally kissing President Carter, President Reagan, Sophia Loren, Henry Kissinger, Jacques Cousteau, and some very handsome guy Ionie had never seen before who was also holding an Academy Award. Squinting through cigarette smoke, not looking at the camera, his hair was a mess, he wasn't wearing a tux, and he had his hand on her hip.

"Ms. St. John?"

Ionie turned.

"They're ready to see you now," the receptionist said.

No hot seat, no table, no casting guy. An office that looked more like a living room. Elegant, comfortable. A view all the way to the blue ocean from the windows, Peroni at the windows, his small frame practically a silhouette cutout against the wash of backlight. The large man who Ionie had assumed was Saul Jennings walked toward her, said "Saul Jennings" extending his hand, and then, in a welcoming gesture, his fingers barely grazing the back of her T-shirt, moved her with him to the figure on the couch. The slender young woman with the honey hair raised her eyes; Chassi Jennings looked at Ionie, Ionie looked at Chassi, Chassi smiled.

"She knew me right away," Ionie said to Kitty Ray on the telephone.

"Well, of course she did."

"Mama, it's not like I was wearing my uniform, I was totally out of context for her."

"A beautiful redhead is never out of context. Did you talk to her? What did you say?"

"Mama, I didn't talk to her, I did the scenes."

"You could have said somethin' about the two of you in the coffee place or about comin' from Texas to warm her up. Was she nice to you?"

"Kitty, let her tell it," Lyman St. John said on the extension.

Ionie pulled the telephone wire with her as she circled the coffee table, flopped on the couch. "We read the scene, two scenes actually, we did them twice. Peroni is very intense, steam coming out of him—"

"Is he married?"

"Mama, really."

"What? Is he?"

"Divorced, three times."

"They're all crazy out there," Lyman St. John said.

"Ly," Kitty Ray said, "you're talkin' too loud."

" 'Cause I'm on the extension."

"Ionie, is he attractive?"

"I don't know, I guess."

"How old?"

Ionie could hear the lighter, her mother's intake of smoke. "Mama, I can't believe that's what you're interested in."

"Neither can I," Lyman said.

"Well, goodness, I was only askin'. Did you get the part?"

"I don't know."

How could she think she knew? If she knew, wouldn't she have told her as soon as she picked up?

"Do you think you got it, baby?" her father said.

Oh, God. "Daddy, I don't know."

"Well, you must have a feelin'," Kitty Ray said and it was all Ionie could do to not hang up.

"Did you get it?" Al asked.

You could scream, you could throw things. She stared at him. "I don't know."

"You don't even have an idea?"

She bit the inside of her right cheek.

"Well, were you good?"

"I was remarkable, Al." Deadpan.

His eyes on her; he frowned, she glared. He slumped, shrugged his shoulders. "Do you want a sandwich?" he asked.

"No."

The only one who didn't ask if she got it was Jones. He reassured her that she had probably been wonderful, he reminded her of the contrast between her and Chassi and how beautifully that would work on film. He was sure they were thinking of that, he said, he was sure she'd been wonderful, he said again, kissing the bone at the top of her shoulder, he was sure. Ionie wasn't sure of anything except that the next time she saw Chassi Jennings she didn't want it to be wiping foam off a cardboard container behind the counter at Cuppa Joe.

CHAPTER 14

Eleanor stood in line for her coffee, gave her order to someone new. The other girl usually made it as soon as she saw her, the tall, gangly redhead, she knew Eleanor was a regular, knew her order, whipped up her double cappuccino as soon as Eleanor opened the door. Where was she? Maybe she'd given up, gone back to Texas, or was it Oklahoma? Eleanor couldn't remember. She was trying to make it as an actress, she did remember that. So many of them, a town full of hopefuls struggling to attain a life full of rejection, what a joke. All struggling to be Chassi Jennings, who was probably waiting in her outer office upstairs. Where the hell was her coffee? Eleanor took a step to the side, the guy behind her was practically on top of her and wearing too much aftershave. Of course, Chassi's problem was not the hateful town of rejection but it was probably this girl's. How could they all think they would make it? Especially without connections. Maybe she'd given up. Maybe Eleanor would have a sticky bun. Maybe the girl had thought better of it, decided to have a regular life and gone home. To her mother. To an old boyfriend. To no one.

Caroline had come home twice during the year she'd spent with the fugitive Jono. She would arrive unannounced with no visible belongings except a ragged duffle bag. She would refuse food, mumble through a curtain of dirty hair, and retreat to her room. She would not ask for help or conversation, only to sleep. And in between those sleeps she would emerge, pale, and wander the house as if she were still in a dream. And in between those sleeps, Eleanor and Jimmy would fight about what to do and what to say to their only child, upstairs, Jimmy shaking his head, slumped against the refrigerator, saying "You try, El, I'm not getting anywhere," and retreating to his beloved garage.

"Mom, please—"

"Is this what you're going to do with your life?"

"It's *my* life."

"I'm asking you because you're in *my* house."

"Okay, next time I come I'll stay somewhere else."

"Caroline, look what you're saying, you already know there'll be a next time. He's no good for you, he's—"

Up from the table, pinched, angry. "Don't. I won't discuss him with you. I won't."

"Caroline—"

"You couldn't know, you don't know about any man but Daddy."

A wave of memories like fast film. An astonishing gray afternoon when she was seventeen, with a boy named Ed Barber under a blanket in Sheep's Meadow. A tussle against the front door of Tommy Smith's aunt Cookie's apartment in Bayside when Tommy's mother and everybody else was in the kitchen playing mah-jongg. A resident named Louie Fishman who had the softest brown eyes and the most incredible hands imaginable. Would it make any difference if she shared her life with her kid? Described every boy who had meant something to her before and after she'd met Jimmy? Would Caroline listen better if she knew her mother's best-kept secrets with love?

The big eyes in the white face—"You wouldn't be so hard on me if I were a boy." The foot on the stair, the slam of the door.

A boy? Was that true? Would it have been easier if Caroline had been a boy? And by the time she had an answer, a whole hatful of answers about mothers and daughters and continuation and possibly how Eleanor was being more critical, no, not critical but concerned, possibly it was because she wanted so much for Caroline, and how Caroline had such potential and could do so much better, how it was hard to stomach and even deplorable that she would follow some mediocre drugged-out drummer into hell—but she would leave that last part out—Eleanor stood with the answers caught in her throat at the door to Caroline's empty room. Gone. A trace of spice, a scribbled note. All it took was a phone call from him and she ran. Mindless. Low. So hard to swallow that her child had no spine. She convinced Jimmy that their only choice was to cut her off financially—no more checks, no more credit card, no more collect calls when things got bad. Tough love, she called it. Mean love, Jimmy said, but she pushed him until he toppled. Eleanor was sure their daughter knew who had severed the cord.

At the completion of what Jimmy called "the Jono years," because it's so wonderfully freeing to laugh at the bad times when they are past tense, Caroline came home. To start over, she told them both at the kitchen table, her eyes only for her dad. She was finally finished with Jono, she told *only* Jimmy, because in the end the relationship had "emptied her out" and "sickened" her. No surprise—she looked as if she had been hit by a truck.There were no other details. She asked if she could stay there until she got on her feet. She immersed herself in swimming, exercise, and books. She went to a lot of classes, she was rarely home. She got a part-time job as a receptionist in a trendy beauty shop on Beverly Boulevard and a part-time job in the hosiery-scarf-glove-hat department at Saks. She did not want a job from Jimmy at the nursery; she was going to do what she had to do to achieve her goal, she said, by herself. And when asked what this goal was she would only answer, "Something spiritual, something that has more to do with the soul." Eleanor held tight to her eyelids so her eyes wouldn't roll. Could she just have her room for a little while? "Yes," they said together. And six months later she got her own place and moved out.

They saw her occasionally. She looked good. Healthy, strong.

Working and lots of class, she said, exercise, dancing, yoga. Lots of fasts. Studying shamanism, she said. Studying Ayurveda, she said, an ancient discipline for the body. Jimmy kicked part of Eleanor's ancient body under the table, she shut up, kept her lip clamped between her teeth. They went on like that. Polite, distant. Punishing but no more punching, no circling in the ring. Jimmy talked to her more, saw her more than Eleanor. She could always tell. Bottles of herbs appeared on the kitchen sink, mysterious green juice in the refrigerator, a StairMaster in the garage. He kept the contact. And then he died. One dazzling Sunday morning, he went out and died.

"Caroline, I would appreciate it if you would come home." Too soon. Cemetery dirt still on their shoes, too much black and too many flowers, but Eleanor couldn't help herself.

The blank stare, the tiniest hint of suspicion in the whisper, Caroline leaning forward, "What?"

Eleanor could hear Rose and Moonie in her kitchen, opening and closing cabinet doors.

"What do you mean?" Caroline's eyes wide and big like Jimmy's, the same rich brown.

She was dizzy. "Sleep here."

"When?"

"Tonight."

Incredulous. The look on the face of her only child. Rose's laugh, the particular squeak of Eleanor's dishwasher. "I have my own place," Caroline said.

"I know that."

"I don't live here."

Their eyes locked.

"Caroline—"

"I have a life."

She, on the other hand, did not have a life. "Life Without Jimmy," a title for a bad play. It had slipped out, had to have slipped out, could her own daughter consciously be so cruel?

"For how long do you want me to sleep here?"

I can't do this, I can't do this, I can't do this. "I can't do this by myself, Caroline."

"Jesus." Tears, big ones flooding the big eyes, Caroline bent her head fast, turning around, her back to her mother. "Jesus," she said again.

She should have waited, should have tried to wait it out, try it for a day, two days, a week, knew it was a mistake, knew it, but one morning you have a husband and two mornings later you don't. You leave your house married and return a widow, and why did she have to go to sleep and wake up with no one and who better to ask to be with her than her only child.

Crumpled napkins, lipstick prints across the coffee-cup rims, crumbs from a pecan stollen across the floor. What do you call the aftermath of a funeral if you aren't Irish? She'd asked D.R., leaning toward him across the sofa; she'd meant, Is it still called a wake? His puzzled look to her—"I don't know," he'd said, eyeing her house full of people. "Sad?"

It had dwindled down to Matt and Moonie and then just Moonie; Kenny, D.R., and Rose, and then just Rose. The women. She could hear them in her kitchen, the low hum of two women ripping Saran Wrap, rinsing glasses, scraping plates. The room reeked. Empty chairs pushed away from the table, a wineglass left on the piano, a plate someone had missed on the floor. Rye-crust smiles, a streak of gold mustard, a fork turned upside down. Why did people send deli? Jimmy's story about the first time he was asked home to supper by a Jewish kid in his elementary school. "And the kid says his name was Izzy"—the light in Jimmy's eyes as he tells this—"great shortstop, Izzy, and he ate at our house all the time—macaroni, Sis's pizza, shells, and I say, "Sure, whatcha havin'?" and he says, 'Deli, we're havin' deli.' *Deli*," Jimmy repeats, rolling the word off his tongue, "and I conjure up deli: It's a fish, maybe it's like calamari, it's somethin' they eat in the North? What's deli? And Sis says you go to someone's house, you be polite, you eat what the lady puts in front of you, and I say, 'Okay, Ma.' " He laughs, remembering. "By the time I got there I was a wreck."

Trays of deli. Food no one eats anymore, everyone terribly cholesterol conscious now except in the face of death. Lower the casket, raise the corned beef, down with the husband, up with the pickle, the chopped liver, the coleslaw; she was dizzy.

"I would appreciate it if you would come home, Caroline," Eleanor said, straightening her spine against the chair, appealing to the back of her daughter. "Sleep here"—her head reeling—"for a little while."

It didn't last very long, it was a terrible mistake for both of them, but Eleanor asked and Caroline did what her mother asked of her, she came home.

• • •

"TELL ME ABOUT BEING DIZZY," Eleanor said to Chassi.

"I just am sometimes."

"When did it start?"

"I don't know."

"You don't have any idea?"

"No."

Eleanor drew the tic-tac-toe crossed lines on her pad.

"During the last picture? When the studio sent you to me?"

Chassi didn't answer.

"Why do you think you're dizzy?"

"I don't know."

"Tell me about missing your mother."

"Skipping around, huh?"

Eleanor put an *x* in the upper left corner of the diagram.

"I was just thinking about her," Chassi said.

"More than usual?"

"No, I don't know."

"A particular memory?"

"No."

Eleanor drew a heart around the tic-tac-toe box. "What do you miss?"

"Her hands," Chassi said, and sat up. "Isn't that funny that I said that? What a weird thing to say."

The slender back of the girl, the sway of her hair as she moved, the down at the base of her neck, white in the light. "My mother was very affectionate," she went on, "and she had beautiful hands." Eleanor laid the pen on the pad.

"She had her hand on your arm," Eleanor said.

Chassi turned. "What?"

"In Rome, she had her hand on your arm."

"Oh, yeah."

"Why?"

"Why?" She hesitated. "What do you mean?"

"Why did she have her hand on your arm?"

"Because we were walking, she was holding my arm and we were walking."

"Why?"

"Why what?"

"Why was she holding your arm?"

"We had crossed arms, I told you, like in a film."

"Your hand or your arm?"

"My arm, she had her hand on my arm." The change in the voice, the look, the set of the shoulders.

"Why?" Eleanor asked again.

"I don't know, what's your problem?"

"Did your mother usually hold your arm?"

"No. What are you doing?"

"Where had you been?"

"Dinner, I told you."

"Do you remember the dinner?"

"Yes."

"What did you talk about?"

"I don't know."

"I thought you remembered."

The slightest falter. "No."

"What are you thinking about?"

"Nothing."

"Are you dizzy now?"

"No."

"Do you think you have a brain tumor?"

"No."

"Are you looking forward to your next picture?"

"No." The eyes up, fast. "I mean yes, I wasn't paying attention. You're going too fast."

"Are you dizzy?"

"No."

"What happened at the dinner?"

"Nothing, why are you being so pushy?"

"Was your mother ever pushy?"

"No."

"Never?"

"Not to me."

"To whom?"

"I don't know, I was just trying to tell you—"

"To your father?"

"No."

"Did they argue?"

"No."

"Did you argue?"

"No."

"You never argued with your mother?"

No answer.

"Chassi?"

"What?"

You could see it. "Chassi?" Eleanor said again.

Bewildered eyes moving to Eleanor. "She was holding my hand, not my arm, I just remembered, she was holding my hand."

Sally's hand moving the lipstick brush, painting in the red; the thick orange waves pulled back from her forehead, the white ribbon tied in a loose knot. There were two small crystal lamps with pleated ivory shades lit at the corners of her dressing table; other than that soft spill of light, the big bedroom was dark. Chassi yawned and stretched back against Mommy's pile of pillows; she had fallen asleep with her Spanish book, the corner of the pages had punched a pink mark in her wrist. She wiggled out from under the soft throw her mother had tucked around her and spread herself flat and belly down across the foot of her parents' bed to watch. She didn't say anything, Sally thought she was still asleep. The spread was silk and kind of knubby, ice blue. Her elbows poking into the nubs, her chin propped up on two fists, she kept her eyes glued to her mother's hand. "Any woman worth her salt better know how to put on makeup," was the quote Mommy had given to the interviewer, but contrary to the glossy colored pictures in the magazine, Sally Brash was not wearing a hunter-green velvet dressing gown or a black, slinky kimono as she put on her face, there were no movie star marabou slippers on the famous feet—she sat at the table of mystery jars and brushes in a faded red-plaid flannel bathrobe and thick red socks. Chassi happened to know it was the bathrobe Sally had worn all through her pregnancy, the bathrobe she had worn to the hospital the night Chassi was born. "Walked right out of the house in it and big pink socks and old tennis shoes and my hair up with a pin"—Mommy's fingers making the spider on Chassi's shoulder—"but with my lipstick on"—she laughed—"just like Nana says, 'You know my Sally, lipstick and rags.' " The tip of her mother's pale elbow poked through a fraying hole in the right sleeve. She had misplaced the matching sash, a kelly-green braided rope from a long-ago summer dress held the robe at her waist. The only thing that might have been deemed theatrical in the setting was the sweating Baccarat tumbler half-filled with amber liquid set in between the perfume bottles and the powder puffs. Sally dabbed the brush at the top of the tube of Chinese red lipstick; Chassi was mesmerized.

Saul emerged from the room-size walk-in closet and stood behind his wife. A big and looming Daddy, like a mountain in black and white: black serge tuxedo pants, a shiny stripe cascading down each leg; black-patent shiny shoes; an open white shirt. He held a fistful of shirt studs, stood behind Mommy, stared at her in the glass.

Chassi smiled, tilted her chin to one hand and tried to keep the in and out of her breath really quiet. From her vantage position in the dark, it was like watching her parents on film.

Sally put down the lipstick brush and picked up a long black pencil.

"We're going to be late," Saul said.

Her mother moved the pencil in a deliberate thin line around the lashes of her right eye. Steady, no bumps, perfect. When Chassi tried it, at her own dressing table, the line went all over the place. Once it shot down across her cheek, like a monster scar all the way to her ear.

"Do you know what you're wearing?" her father said to her mother.

Sally shifted the pencil to the other eye.

Saul rocked on one foot, lifted the Baccarat tumbler from her dressing table, and took a swig of the scotch. "I hate it when you do this."

Sally squinted, lifted her chin slightly to the right and then to the left, put down the pencil.

"What do you think it's going to get you?" he said.

She didn't acknowledge him, picked up a brush, ran it across an open case of olive powder, blew some of the powder off the brush and stroked it across both half-closed eyelids, then opened her green eyes wide, studying the effect in the glass. She reapplied the powder, slightly darker at the crease in each lid.

Saul held the tumbler of scotch, watched her. "It's not going to get you anywhere," he said.

Sally didn't lift her eyes. She picked up a crystal bottle, uncapped it, tipped the bottle to her fingers, ran the liquid on her fingertips behind her ears and down the front of her white throat into that space between her breasts. Gardenias. Chassi had already decided that she would never wear perfume, it was phony, she had decided and told her mother it wasn't the way people smelled.

Saul took another swig of the scotch, Chassi rolled quietly more on her side, Sally put the perfume bottle back in place.

He drained the glass and stood there. An ice cube clinked.

Her mother raised her hands to the ribbon and released her hair. The red waves lifted at the top of the wide, creamy forehead, split perfectly at the center part, and descended to the top of each arched eyebrow as if taking a bow. Sally ran her hands through it, shook her head slightly, tumbling the mass this way and that.

Saul opened his fist, threw the studs over his wife's head at the mirror in front of them. They hit and fell, clattering across the glass of her dressing table, one tumbling in a silent drop and a little bounce on the rug next to Sally's foot. Chassi could hear her own breath, feel it in the fingers of her hand that were now slapped flat across her lips like a bandage, a tight bandage or a bandanna that you tied across your mouth if you were a cowboy about to rob a bank. Nothing moved, there was no sound. Scotch and gardenias and no sound but Chassi's breath and the beat of her heart.

Saul turned and walked back into the closet. He hadn't taken his eyes off his wife, she hadn't taken her eyes off her mirror, neither of them had noticed their daughter listening and watching from the shadows across the room, sprawled on the foot of their bed.

It was true when she'd told Dr. Costello that her mother didn't argue, at least not so that she could be heard. No harsh words, no shouting coming from their bedroom or his office or the cabana by the pool. Sally's choice of weapon was always silence, the silence of cutting off and leaving cold. The particular argument the night of the flying shirt studs—which was how Chassi catalogued it in her head—was about the picture. Most arguments were not about the picture, but most discussions were; "the picture" not being specific, the picture being any picture of the moment, the picture she was doing, the picture he was doing, the picture that was in their lives at the given time. But the picture that night, and the three days that had led up to that night and the twelve days after that night, because Chassi had counted, marked them off in her head like red *x*'s across a calendar leading up to Christmas or the last day of school, those fifteen days were loud with her mother's silence, the silence of the argument of Sally doing *No Trumpets, No Drums*.

When she'd first said she wanted to do the picture, Saul had laughed. But she was serious, he could see then that she was serious so he made his stand, he appealed, stated the realistic flaws—that was what he called them—"realistic flaws"—and Chassi said the phrase in her head to remember. Sally gave her side, but there was really no bending, even Chassi could see that and she was just a kid. Mostly they side-stepped, pretended to listen to each other but stood firm. Chassi knew all about that, it was just like when she fought with Andrew, she half-listened to his side but she really didn't care what he was saying, all she was doing was planning what she would say as soon as he shut up. Mommy acquiesced about the low budget; yes, she said, she knew how difficult the shoot would be with no money, yes, she agreed that the young writer-director had come out of nowhere with no credentials, no background, "No track record," Saul said, and Sally said, "Okay," and Daddy muttered, "A two-bit nothing from nowhere," slamming his briefcase against the sink.

Chassi's spoon in the Cheerios, Daddy circling the table, her mother searching for where she'd set her coffee cup. "He's not a two-bit nothing, Saul."

"Okay, what is he?"

The cup was next to the toaster, Chassi could see it. Her mother was always losing her coffee cup, it was a thing with her. "It's a great script, don't tell me it isn't a great script," Sally said.

"It's a fucking world of hurt," Saul said. "You make that picture, you ruin your career."

"I'm not going to ruin my career, Saul."

She reached into the cabinet for another cup and Chassi said, "Mommy, it's by the toaster," and Saul said, "Have you lost your mind? Sally, use your head. This is America, you can't do a fucking antiwar picture about Vietnam!"

She turned, the color high in her face. "What do you mean I can't?"

"I mean you can't," Saul said.

"Tia, I have to go to the library after school," Chassi said. She was doing a report on Italy, they'd each picked a country and she'd picked Ireland but there were too many of them who'd picked Ireland so they'd had to draw out of a hat. "I take you," Tia said. Tia, holding the coffeepot over Mommy's second cup.

"I told you I want to make this picture for Joey," her mother said to her father with a tone. Chassi knew all about Joey, had seen all the pictures of her uncle who had died in the war. Mommy's baby brother, watching him get taller, page after page in Nana's albums, the boy with the lopsided grin and the orange hair.

"Don't mix sentiment with business," Saul said, and Tia said, "Chassi, eating the breakfast."

"I'm eating, I'm eating." At least Italy was better than Iceland. Judgie Vallely got Iceland and had a fit. She told the teacher she wasn't doing it and the teacher said oh, yes she was, and Sally said, "Saul, I'm making this picture," and Saul just stood there and her mother said again, "Saul, I'm making it," and her father said, "I won't let you," and her mother said, "Saul," and then everything stopped. Across the kitchen, over the Cheerios and the orange juice and the scrambly eggs, in a soft but firm voice her father said, "No."

Chassi looked up from the bowl, Tia stopped whatever she was doing at the counter. Sally gave him a look, one long look and walked out of the room. Saul poised at the French doors, Chassi's arm half-raised with a spoon of Cheerios, Tia's hand adrift, holding a pink sponge. Her mother's second cup of coffee remained where it was, getting cold on the kitchen desk next to the telephone when the silence began.

Chassi stood now in the doorway of her parents' room in the hush of evening. The lamps were no longer lit on the dressing table, Tia never turned them on. Mommy had won, of course, Mommy could hold out; Saul crumbled after fifteen days. "Women are tougher than men, baby, never forget that, a woman always has the upper hand." Chassi had no idea what "the upper hand" meant, all she knew then was that Mommy was learning the lines to the drum picture and going to wardrobe and getting fluffed up to shoot. There were no two ways about it, Mommy had won.

Chassi backed out of the doorway, the script from *No Trumpets, No Drums* in her hand. Her eyes lingered on the foot of the big bed. No trace of sweet gardenia, no tiny golden shirt stud twinkling at her from the rug. Her mother had not only won the toss but had also won the Oscar, and the mystery then to eleven-year-old Chassi was that she'd credited Saul. Watching from two steps away, her hand tucked into Daddy's big one, Mommy beaming in the garnet silk gown, her arms wrapped around the golden man, had said to the reporters, "I never would have had the courage to make *No Trumpets, No Drums* if it hadn't have been for Saul." It was only later Chassi realized that the line her mother had given to the reporters could have garnered her another Academy Award.

CHAPTER 15

Ionie sat in her car behind the Ramada. She was parked next to Jones's Explorer. She should have gone in, it was 1:10, he was waiting, she should have gone in. The note was in plain sight through his window on the driver's seat; a scrap of paper, his shaky script: $25.00, which meant he was in room 250. It was absurd. Did he really think they were being followed? She sat in her car, holding the cell phone, sweating on the cell phone, waiting for Nicki to pick up. Maybe she should buy Jones a trench coat, maybe she should get a hat with a veil. She poked her finger into a small hole in the seat of the vinyl upholstery under her thigh, pulled at the edge; the car was disintegrating, she could imagine a cartoon version of herself on the 101, her hair whipping across her face as she took the Cahuenga off ramp at 70 mph, music blasting, her and the steering wheel and the dashboard and just a piece of the frame remaining, the tires falling off to the left and right of her, one by one.

"Hello? Ionie?"

Her heart gave a little lurch up against her ribs. "Nicki? Yes?"

"She's still talking," Nicki's assistant, whose tone was more in keeping with the tone of the chairman of the board of the agency or the president or the—"We'll get back to you," the assistant said.

"I, uh—" *What's happened to all the secretaries?* Kitty Ray had said. *Where did all these assistants come from? Isn't a plain old secretary good enough anymore?* Kitty Ray had been a secretary, a crackerjack, she would tell you, able to take shorthand faster than the speed of light. *Why, in my day I could type like a bat out of—*

"Ionie? We'll get back to you."

"It's fine, I'll hold."

"She's late for a lunch," said the tone.

Didn't they work for her? Didn't she pay them 10 percent of every penny she made? Not that it was that much, but, "I'll hold," Ionie said again, clutching the steering wheel with her other hand. *Ding, ding, ding* went the adding machine of the cell waves, it was costing her a fortune to sit in the car in the middle of goddamn Burbank while she waited for a woman who worked for her to get off the phone.

"She's supposed to be at LeDome," said the tone.

"Okay."

"Ionie, I don't know if she'll have time to pick up, she's supposed to be at LeDome."

LeDome, LeDome. "I really need to talk to her." Soft voice, sweet, oh come on, who are you, anyway? Please don't do this to me, please.

An audible sigh. "We'll get back to you right after lunch."

Oh, sure, call me in room 250 here at the Ramada, I'll tell Jones that it's for me if it rings and hopefully we will have finished, hopefully when you call I'll be able to talk, I won't have his cock in my mouth.

"Ionie?"

Oh, God, Nicki's voice. "Yes, hi, it's me," Ionie said.

"What's up?"

Ionie ran her fingers around the wheel, tried to keep breathing. What's up? What did she think was up? "Have you heard anything?"

"About what?"

"*No Trumpets, No Drums.*"

"No."

"But it's the end of May, it's nearly June, don't they go in August? Don't they have to cast the part?"

Static, then Nicki, "I said I'd call you, didn't I?" Static. Ionie swung the door wide, got out of the car with the phone, slipped on the gravel, righted herself, clutching the door. "Did they hire somebody else?"

"Not that I know of."

"But would you know?"

"Ionie, they'll call with an offer if they want you, that's what I know."

You could lose all your breath, you could pass out, you could have a coronary in a parking lot behind a Ramada in downtown Burbank and no one would know.

"They just cast the other part," Nicki said.

"What other part?"

"The soldier, opposite Jennings, the second lead. They got who they wanted, Tim Burke."

Tim Burke was a major player, Tim Burke was a name. "Oh," Ionie said. Her hand was shaking. "Okay," she said brightly into the phone, "okay, I was just, uh, checking."

"You're up for a pilot."

"Uh-huh, okay." A pilot? Did that mean Nicki had given up on the movie? Oh, please don't give up on the movie . . .

"Look, I have a lunch. The MOW airs in two weeks, the network's high on it, let me handle this, sweetie, okay?"

"Okay."

"I gotta go."

"Okay. But will you—"

The line went dead, Nicki had clicked off or Ionie was losing her battery. She slumped against Jones's Explorer, studied the note through his car window, and closed the phone. "Tim Burke," she mumbled with an exhale. Tim Burke was dark and lean and mysterious, Tim Burke had a dreamboat face but eyes that stripped you; he was like a hand grenade about to be de-pinned. She took her bag out of the Datsun, along with the crumpled yellow paper from the Taco Bell burrito supremo and the rest of her diet Coke. Tim Burke and Chassi Jennings were both stars. The ice had melted and the soda was flat. She slammed the door and a strip of chrome along the frame of the car sprang loose. Ionie looked at it, stood where she was clutching her bag and the drink and the greasy paper, her eyes on the chrome. There was a guy in her acting class, an old guy, not that he acted old, he was really funny, Earl was his name, definitely in his sixties, and he told stories all the time about the "golden olden" days, that's what he called them—cowboy movies at Republic, gangster movies at RKO, stuff they'd shot in fourteen days or whatever, and he told a story about a guy who had done really well, a pal of his, made movies with John Wayne and Steve McQueen and whoever, a guy Ionie had never heard of but who Earl'd said had a real career. *Nearly,* he had nearly made it, one of those guys where you know his face but not his name, he was the sidekick in everything, the second banana right next to the star and once he was even the star but it didn't go anywhere, and over the years it slid to nothing, downhill, the parts got smaller and smaller until there weren't any parts at all. Not that this was a new story, Earl said, but right before the end the two of them were doing some submarine picture where the company didn't have money for a real submarine, much less to go to San Pedro to shoot, or even Santa Monica, and Earl and this guy were under the floor of a crummy soundstage at Monogram, the lowest of the low of studios, in their frogman gear and flippers, "in the pitch black," he said, "you couldn't see dick," he said, waiting for their cue to break through the floorboards. And Earl says that this guy, who'd been *nearly* something, he turns to Earl and mumbles, "Under the floor at Monogram, the end of the line."

Under the floor at Monogram. Oh, God.

The MOW would be on and it wouldn't change anything, she wouldn't get the movie, they would go for a name or someone older or someone younger or a petite brunette, or this time for sure a black guy. The MOW would be on in two Sundays and they probably wouldn't even see it. What did movie people care about TV? *Don't whine, Ionie,* Kitty Ray would have said, *Don't be a Sarah Heartburn, you look at the rest of the people and thank your stars,* but she wasn't the rest of the people, she was an actress and she suddenly hated it, hated the whole thing. She should have gone to school, studied to be something else; she was smart, she could have been anything, even an assistant with a tone. Ionie kicked up gravel as she crossed the parking lot and thought about her agent eating lunch at LeDome.

• • •

"WHAT ABOUT THE DIRECTOR?" Andrew said. He didn't look at Chassi, his eyes were only for the delicate roots of the cyclamen as he loosened them from the packing dirt.

"Let me do one," she said, her hand out.

"Chass—"

"What?"

"You hate to plant."

She punched his shoulder. "I do not."

They were side by side on their knees in the bricked circle at the turnaround end of the long driveway, surrounded by flats of pink and white plants.

"What about the director? Do you like him? What's his name? Burrito?" Andrew said.

She toppled him, pushed him hard in the same shoulder and he went over into the newly turned mud. "*Perino*," Chassi said. "Why are you only planting white?"

Andrew, grinning, rolled over onto his back on the grass, stared up at her and the sky. "White first. White cyclamen, pink vincas, that's the plan. Not Spanish, huh? Señor *Perino*?"

"There are no Spanish directors," Chassi said.

"Your ass, Chass. What about Buñuel?"

"Okay, Buñuel, and . . . ?"

"Almdomovar."

She laughed. "That's not his name."

"You know who I mean. The one with the woman and the fire in her bed."

"Almodóvar. And?"

He lifted the tender white cyclamen from his chest and handed it to her. "Jorge Semprun."

"Who?"

"Jorge Semprun, *chica*, and Carlos Saura, the guy who made all those stomping-their-feet things. And Cassavetes. Be careful with that."

Chassi smirked. "John Cassavetes was not Spanish, Mr. Moviefone."

"You sure? Just jiggle the dirt off and put it in, it's not brain surgery, Chass."

"Yes, sir, *jefe*." She leaned forward, placed the plant in the hole and pushed the dirt around the roots. "He was Greek."

"Very good, you planted a cyclamen." Andrew said, "Who was Greek?"

"Cassavetes." She looked at Andrew. "And Thalosinos. Do you remember him?"

"Nope. Yeah, maybe. Rehearsed with your mama in the garden? Dark? Smoked?"

"Yeah." Chassi poked at the dirt with the spade.

"Yeah, Pop didn't like him."

She looked up. "Baudelio didn't?"

"No, put his butts out in the garden, never used the ashtray. So you like this Burrito guy?"

"Yes."

The deep brown eyes of Andrew. Chassi shrugged. "No, not like that. Well . . . I don't know."

Andrew nodded. "At least we're clear here."

"He's . . . I don't know . . ." Chassi collapsed backward like a rag doll, the back of her head on Andrew's chest, her legs stretched out in front of her at an angle to him, both of them on their backs across the dirt looking up.

"What do you see?" Andrew said.

Her eyes searching the marching clouds. "Three elephants."

"They're dogs, *niña*."

"Elephants."

"You going to go out with him, Perino?"

"*Burrito,* Andres."

"Yeah." He put his hand on her head, "Are you?"

"I don't know. You smell like soap."

"I read about him. Very bad boy."

Chassi kept her eyes on the clouds.

"Not too good-looking," Andrew said.

"No."

They were quiet.

"Smart, right?" Andrew muttered.

"Yeah. The elephants are getting mushy."

He pulled a piece of her hair through his fingers. "You'll go out with him. All the leading ladies fall in love with their directors."

Her head rode the up and down of his chest and she could hear his heart beat, feel the twist of her hair around his long fingers, the heat of the sun, the smell of the mud and the grass and the flowers. "I thought that was patients with their psychiatrists," Chassi said and Andrew laughed.

She hadn't considered Perino. Chassi moved the taupe pencil around the lashes of her right eye. Her hand was steady now, like her mother's, no more skid marks. She usually didn't consider any man until it happened, until she tripped over him. She smudged the pencil with her fingertip into a soft blur and moved to the other eye. Someone on location, someone accidental, not planned. So far the acquiring of men didn't matter, so far she had been satisfied with the playing with them and the moving on. No holds, no ropes, no commitments. She could get laid or not get laid, she had Andrew to talk to, and she had her work. Perino would be on purpose, quite another thing. She dabbed her fingers at the top of a pale lavender lipstick and rubbed the soft color into the apples of her cheeks. She had never thought of herself as being a . . . what? Femme fatale? A woman who sets her mark on a man and does whatever it takes to catch him? Chassi pursed her lips, half-closed her eyes into slits, and in the glass stretched like a cat. Then she picked up the lip pencil.

Perino had a bad track record. Andrew was right, he was a very bad boy. Three divorces, three ex-wives, three babies—bad, bad, bad. But there was something appealing about him, he was terrifically smart with no arrogance, and he had that funny edge . . . and . . . wasn't that funny for Andrew to have said what he said? Actresses and their directors, Chassi had never gone out with a director, good boy or bad. She leaned forward, raised the mauve pencil; the memory caught her before she'd finished her lips.

It was in the commissary, but in the tablecloth part, not in the where-you-pushed-your-tray part, not in the where-you-go-to-pick-the-things-as-you-went part that Chassi most loved. Wiggling squares of red Jell-O in a pretty glass dish, or a smile of orange cantaloupe, or chocolate pudding, or vanilla, or even butterscotch, all lined up next to each other on the ice, and you could scoop them right off of there and put them on your tray. That was the part Chassi liked, but Mommy didn't usually go in there. Too many people stopped her, too many folks, she said, who wanted to talk to her about some picture they'd worked on with her and by the time each one came up and stopped her she had no time left to eat. In the tablecloth part nobody bothered Mommy except maybe another movie star or some dopey stuffed man in a suit, the unwritten law of the studio commissary being: Leave them alone. Of course, you could still get the chocolate pudding, but the waitress had to bring it, which was not half the fun of seeing everything in front of you and getting to stick your finger in the ice.

Today it was her and Mommy and Mr. Thalosinos and he was smoking while he ate. Chassi kept her eyes on him until Mommy told her to stop. A bite of sandwich, a puff and a blow out, a slurp of the coffee, two more big puffs, and Mommy said, "Chassi." Chassi lowered her eyes, smoothed the pudding over the dent where she had just lifted out a spoonful. If you moved the pudding in a particular way with the back of your spoon, it could look like you hadn't eaten any. Of course, it got lower but there were no telltale holes. Lower and lower until you clinked. "Drink your milk, Chassi."

He drank a lot of coffee, Mr. Thalosinos, and he had stickeeoutee hair. Chassi slapped her heels, one foot and then the other, against the puffed aqua booth. "Baby, you're kicking," Sally said. And little hairs on his face like his razor didn't work. Chassi loved to watch Daddy shave. Sometimes he'd let her pat the white cream all over, if he wasn't in a hurry he would. "Baby, stop staring," Sally said. Mr. Thalosinos smelled of smoke.

"Do you want another pudding, sweetie?" Bonnie, the waitress with the smiling teeth, Chassi's favorite, who kind of pushed out of her uniform in places like she was really made out of balloons, little diamond shapes in between the buttons where it was pulling, and you could see her slip. Pink.

Chassi slapped her heels back against the leather. "Can I, Mom?"

"Hmm?" Sally said. "Chassi, you're kicking."

"Can she have another pudding, Ms. Brash?"

"All right, Bonnie, I guess so," Mommy said.

Yippee, yippee. Hooray for Mr. Thalosinos, because she'd really left the horrible hamburger, disguised it, changed its shape by pulling it apart and hiding various pieces of it under things: under a slice of tomato, under a glob of ketchup, under a lettuce leaf, under the table. She'd buried a large portion of it under the mound of stinky potato salad and put some of it, the chewed-up part, in her napkin, which was rolled up in her lap, because she hated it, hated all meat, even hamburgers and hot dogs, even chicken nuggets, all those awful things they were always trying to make her eat. Steak, that you had to chew and chew and if you looked down you could see that it was bleeding all over your plate into your potatoes, like a cut on your leg. And lamb chops, Tia said lamb chops, which smelled, no matter what Tia said, and how could anybody eat baby lambs? She would throw up if she had to eat a baby anything, she would.

Mommy usually found her out, pushed at the crusts, searched

under the potato chips, rearranged everything with the orange fingernails until she found where Chassi had hidden the meat. "Three bites, just eat three bites," she would croon at Chassi with big green eyes all pleading. "Baby, please." Chassi wiggled in the booth now, excited, thrilled with the knowledge that she would always ask Mommy to bring Mr. Thalosinos along to lunch with them, Mr. Good Old Smoking Thalosinos, because if he came to lunch, Mommy's eyes were on Mr. Thalosinos and not searching around Chassi's plate.

She sat there now, stunned at her reflection, at the mauve pencil line skidding from her lip to her chin.

• • •

SHE WAS SLEEPING WITH TWO MEN, she had to face that. Well, maybe not. Oh, yes, she did. Ionie stepped to the right, a woman with a baby in a stroller and a sulking, teary toddler reeking of apple juice pushed past her and through Cuppa Joe's back door. White sun in the parking lot; she walked in between the parked cars, held her hand up against the glare. There had always been men. She was pretty. If you were pretty, there were always men. "So many men, so little time," she said out loud in a thick drawl. A man two cars over looked up; Ionie stared right at him, smiled. She opened the door of the Datsun, pulled the Cuppa Joe uniform top over her head, threw it in onto the seat next to her, tugged at her T-shirt, and slid in. She left her legs out and the door open. She'd never had two men going on at the same time. Not like this. She popped the tab on the diet Coke.

She could talk to Jones. Oh, about everything—her work, her dreams, her fears, her worries, everything. She perched her elbows on her knees, took a long drink of the cold soda. He listened, he knew things. He cared. Did she want a sandwich? She had a half-hour break before she had to face another frozen mocha and the reek of coffee beans, she could get a tuna at Art's. She took another swallow of Coke. She could talk to Jones about everything; she could talk to Al about the now: what to eat now and which movie to see at seven and let's go to the beach tomorrow, no, let's go to the mountains, and can you pick up my shirts on Tuesday? Oh, right, she'd said she'd pick up his shirts.

They argued. Probably too much but they were both pigheaded, as her mother had pointed out the last time they'd had an argument and she had been blue enough to blab to Kitty Ray about it on the phone. She wiped her lips with the back of her hand. She didn't want a whole tuna, she wanted a half. Why didn't they do that? Restaurants. Most people only wanted a half.

Not that Al didn't care. He cared plenty. He was probably even in love with her but didn't want to get into it, which was typical. "Feelings" was definitely not Al's favorite song. Jones, on the other hand, was all feelings. In his eyes, the way he touched her, held her, everything he did and said. Ionie moved her Nikes on the asphalt, swung them up and into the car. He said things, he could actually turn her on with his words. Well, not turn her on exactly, but make her melt. Ionie lifted the cold can, put it to her cheek. Oh, to not have to go back to work, to turn on the motor and drive into that white sun, burn the hideous uniform right there in the parking lot, a smoldering heap of purple polyester, sprinkle the ashes among the Colombia Supremo beans—*For Rudy, with love from Ionie, drink this.*

Jones knew about Al, knew he was her boyfriend but never asked for details. Knew that she didn't live with him, but didn't know that Al was campaigning for that, wanted her to move into his place. Some things were better left unsaid. Sometimes Jones called when Al was there. Well, that couldn't be helped, he had to be the one who called, she couldn't call him, it's not like he had an office, it's not like she could call him at home. "Hello, Mrs. Jones?" "Oh, call me Linda," says the blonde wife. "Oh, thank you," says Ionie, the red-haired mistress. "May I please speak to Jones?" "Who was that?" says Al, leaning against the refrigerator. "Oh, my yoga instructor," Ionie says with a straight face. Talk about being a good actress. Being a good liar. Ah, there you go.

Ionie moved the can to her other cheek, rolled the icy aluminum across her skin. Al could make her melt too. But mostly, it wasn't her heart melting, it was another part. And he didn't do that with words.

Ionie sat forward, checked her face in the rearview. She needed a haircut, a trim. Not that Jones wasn't a good lover, he was fine. In her vast experience. Ionie grimaced, sat back, drained the rest of the can. Fifteen men. She had no idea if that was a lot or a little for a woman of twenty-eight, okay, nearly twenty-nine, okay, okay, who'd lost her virginity when she was thirteen. A man a year, not that it happened that way, but if you counted, a man a year. Not that they all counted, that was for damn sure, some of them certainly didn't measure up. Wait, what was that thing her mother said about hindsight? She couldn't remember. Well, you couldn't go back and change things, that much she knew. Fifteen men, fifteen minutes until coffeeland. Cripes. She wouldn't have tuna, she'd run.

She grabbed the top of her uniform and got out of the car, threw the uniform top on the hood. All that mattered, Jones said, was to give to her, oh, to make her happy, he said, his eyes on hers—with his mouth, his hands, his everything, that's what he said, his fingers warm against her skin. Ionie blew out, frowned, stretched the other leg. Al would never say anything like that, not even close. More likely he would say, "Baby, I'm gonna make you crazy."

Ionie slammed the door of the Datsun, and took off around the parking lot at a clip. It was too much. Jones and Al and the job or not the job; she hadn't heard a word from Nicki, she hadn't seen a thing in the trades about anybody getting the part and it was getting closer to the shoot. She tried not to think about it but that was next to impossible.

"Well, what did that agent say?" Kitty Ray asked again.

"I told you, she said she'd let me know."

"I never heard of such a thing."

It could make your teeth hurt. The waiting and the hoping and the praying. Gramma had said, "Honey, don't ever pray for money," but was praying to get a job the same as praying for money? Ionie wasn't sure and there was no way to call Gramma and ask her now. Al's blue eyes and Jones's soft brown ones, and if it wasn't bad enough, she was his first affair. Oh, yeah, he'd said it and she believed him, there wasn't a trace of anything false about Jones, and the truth was she didn't feel guilty. She didn't. Was she supposed to worry about his wife and his kids too? She couldn't worry about everything. God. She hadn't planned on being a mistress. She hadn't planned on ever sleeping with two men. Boy, that would be one for her mother. "Mama, I'm having a little problem here besides the job." "Oh, honey, tell me." She could hear Kitty Ray trying to secretly light her Marlboro as she cuddled the phone. Too much. She'd figure it out for herself, there were some things you couldn't discuss with your mother. Ionie tossed her head, pulled her fingers into fists and punched at the air as she ran.

• • •

SAUL DIDN'T WANT HER. The girl from the coffee place was perfect, her timing was perfect, her look, but Saul said no. "A long, tall drink of water," Saul said.

Chassi sat on the edge of the desk, tried to concentrate. "Dad, she was perfect."

"Okay, the way she read the role, okay, perfect, I'll give you that, but what for?"

Chassi looked to Robby. He was pacing the room, head down.

"We get nothing from her," Saul went on.

Robby looked up. "You mean box office?"

Saul nodded.

"I don't give a shit about that," Robby said.

"You should give a shit about that," Saul growled.

Her mother's face was everywhere—posters, photographs. "You don't need her for box office, Daddy, you've got the press about the picture, about Mommy, you've got—"

"You've got your daughter for box office, Saul," Robby interrupted, "and Tim Burke, and me." He laughed. "You got enough box office to choke a horse. The girl's got something, let's give her a shot."

Chassi studied Perino's face; he caught her looking at him, smiled.

His two front teeth weren't even, one stuck out a little, the one on the left. It was kind of sweet, actually. He wasn't even good-looking, it was the way he used his brain.

"She was very good in the clip from the movie of the week," the casting guy piped in from a chair in the corner; none of them acknowledged him or turned around.

"Television," Saul said, as if he had a bad taste in his mouth.

He was back, her father, prepping a picture, at the top of his game, funny, vital, as if he'd awakened from a coma; he was back.

Saul looked at Peroni. "She's a long drink of water."

"She knocked the others out of the box," Robby said, standing in front of Saul's desk.

Chassi studied him. Skinny, short, really. What was he? Five-nine?

"I don't know," Saul said.

"What don't you know?"

Perino stood there. Scrappy, smart, talented, standing up to her father as if they were peers. But with respect, he had respect for Saul, that was clear. With that tooth and that silly hair. Chassi smiled and Saul saw her.

"What?" he said to his daughter but didn't wait for the answer, shook his head. "No one's ever heard of her. You got five, ten names here would die for this part. A little older, a little more established, I got every agent in town calling, and you—"

"I want an unknown," Robby interrupted.

"I know that," Saul muttered. "What the hell for?"

"An unknown in the middle of two movie stars. You of all people," Robby said with a savvy look. "Saul, are you forgetting? You hire her, she'll be great in the picture, she'll be forever indebted, and you'll have done it again. Think of the press. Jennings hasn't lost his touch, Jennings picks a nobody from a java joint, Jennings discovers another dazzling unknown."

The man knew everything. Her mother was the first—Saul had discovered Sally, picked her out of a roomful, the little broad from Texas with the big tits and the red hair and put her in a big picture with two male movie stars. How many times had she heard "The joint was packed with girls and your daddy walked through, took one look at me"—Sally's arm lifting, the beautiful fingers playfully punching her father's shoulder—"tell her, honey, tell her how you gave me my first job." Leave it to Robby to know that and judiciously use it to get what he wanted from Saul.

A smile curving the corners of her father's mouth, Saul Jennings leaned back in his chair. "All right, you two, stop ganging up on me. What's her name again?"

"Ionie St. John," the casting guy squeaked from the corner.

"Ionie St. John," Saul repeated. "Sounds like something we cooked up in the fifties." He laughed his big laugh. "Catchy and goyishe, give 'em a name that's catchy and goyishe, Freeman used to say, and he knew, named some of the best of them . . . head of publicity, Freeman, always wore a hat, summer, winter, damnedest thing, behind that desk in a hat . . ." They were both staring at him. He frowned at his daughter. "You want this St. John dame, huh?"

"Yes."

"Why?"

Chassi smiled. "Because she's a good actress, Dad."

His look to Peroni. "You think she can cut it?"

"Yeah."

"I don't want her towering over Chassi."

"I wouldn't let that happen, Saul."

Peroni looked at Chassi. Something in his eyes. He was attractive, not good-looking but attractive. Not that it mattered, but he was.

She looked to her father.

Saul shrugged, sat there, pursed his lips, shrugged again. "All right, you two"—he laughed and then growled like Rod Steiger in *On the Waterfront*—"you want her, you got her." He looked at both of them. "All right, already. We'll give the drink of water the job."

CHAPTER 16

Stardom, breathless stardom, the speed of breathless stardom. Reviews, exposure, a woman recognizing you over the potatoes in the produce section getting all giggly and red, a man asking for your autograph at the cleaners, his voice shaky as he rips the cleaning ticket from the plastic so that you can write your name. The phone ringing, appointments, the phone ringing, interviews, the phone ringing some more. "Can you make it? Are you available? Could you *possibly* come in?" The new tone of respect, awe, possibly even reverence. The loss of reality, the high of prominence, the flutter of fame. The false power of who you are, that *isn't* who you are, but *is*, and most of all, how you lose your place.

• • •

"THAT'S BEAUTIFUL, DEAR, lovely, lovely, beautiful," said Zuck the photographer, backing up a few steps, still looking through the camera, still babbling, the shutter still clicking as he moved. "Beautiful, beautiful, lift your chin, lovely, to the left, lovely, *left* dear, lovely, beautiful." The smile emerged from behind the lens; a big smile, on a big, gangly, dowdy man with big teeth, a man you could not possibly imagine using the word "lovely." Dirty chinos, a brilliant white shirt that he must have stolen from a sailboat mast, far too wide and half tucked, thick glasses and flyaway hair; like an overgrown Woody

Allen. Ionie thought, like a Russian wolfhound with shoes. Big shoes, terrible shoes, the worst shoes.

"Beautiful," he said. "Now pop into the black. Lovely, dear."

He dropped the camera into the arms of a hovering assistant and walked toward the bagels and cream cheese. Bagels and cream cheese and smoked salmon and rye toasts cut into perfect triangles, and a platter of zucchini-and-rice *frittata*, they called it, which Ionie's mother would have said "tastes like your Daddy's left-over eggs," trays of sweet rolls and croissants and jams, cottage cheese, sour cream (Ionie had no idea where you were supposed to put the sour cream), plates of sliced tomatoes and sliced onions, seven cheeses (she had counted), pots of coffee and tea, a case of bottled water, sodas, and a full bar. For a photo shoot at eleven o'clock in the morning, a full bar.

Ionie slid off the gray cube and went into the dressing room. Pulled the curtain. Slipped off the dark red silk Helmut Lang tee they had given her and the Ralph Lauren gray flannel pleated slacks. Took off the Gucci loafers and slid into the tube of sleek Jil Sander black cashmere and the Manolo Blahnik black suede heels. She noted every label, studied it, ran her finger over every buttonhole and seam, cradled the handful of silk that was fine enough to fit into a letter-sized envelope, inhaled the cashmere that caressed her breasts. Ionie, who just last month had shopped the aisles of Target adding the prices as she pushed the cart, who had replaced three items that she knew would topple her checkbook, was now wearing clothes that equaled more than what Al made in a month, clothes from one of Chassi Jennings's $17.00 magazines. She turned, eyed herself in the mirror. One red wave fell seductively across her forehead, one dark red wave newly highlighted and styled by Armando fell over one newly plucked eyebrow by Marie across one forehead powdered by Robin.

"Do you need help, Miss St. John?" A chewed, chipped, purple-painted fingernail poked through the curtain; one of Mr. Zuckerman, *Zuck's* assistants, the toe of a black boot. Not a Gucci boot, Ionie figured. No assistant could afford Gucci boots, they cost more than new tires.

"No, thank you," Ionie said toward the curtain. Not that she was getting new tires because she was thinking of burning the Datsun, possibly shooting it, driving it into the ocean, pushing it into the ocean, shooting it, then torching it, watching it sink. She was getting a new car. A Ford Explorer. Black. Inside and out. Or red maybe.

"Champagne?" said the purple fingernail.

"Oh, no, thank you," Ionie said. No, not red, a black Ford Explorer to match her new black Gucci boots.

Breathless stardom, the speed of breathless stardom. Okay, not stardom, not stardom, okay, but *something*; she just didn't have the word. The offer for *Trumpets*, which was what *they* called it—they didn't say the drum part—the *they*, the *them*. The offer for *Trumpets*, just *Trumpets*, after she was sure they must have found somebody else, after she was actually beginning to consider walking into traffic or moving back to Tyler, which was practically the same thing, it was then that the offer came. The deal, the minute details and fine points that were still being negotiated, as per Nicki. "Don't worry, kid, it's as good as closed." Closed. She was going to be in a movie with Chassi Jennings and Tim Burke. Ionie St. John from Tyler, Texas, was going to be the third lead of a major motion picture being produced by Saul Jennings and directed by Robby Peroni. Ionie St. John was going to make $225,000, plus per diem, plus first-class travel on Philippine Air, first-class accommodations in Manila, and be on a separate card right after the title, Nicki explained, as a "with." *With Ionie St. John* was all she could see in front of her, *With Ionie St. John*, awake and asleep. And before she could even begin to comprehend that reality, the movie of the week aired. Didn't just air, aired on prime-time network television, nine o'clock on a Sunday night, "from coast to coast," Kitty Ray cried, and they singled Ionie out in the reviews. Really. In the *New York Times*, the *Los Angeles Times*, the *Hollywood Reporter*, even in her daddy's faithful *Dallas Morning News*: "Miss St. John radiates," "Ionie St. John will break your heart," "Wait till you get a load of newcomer Ionie St. John."

"What do you mean, you don't have a fax machine?" Nicki carrying on. "Messenger her this stuff," she was yelling at the tone. Even the tone was carrying on—"Oh, you were magnificent," she said to Ionie, "magnificent," with hardly any tone at all.

Al, making like she was suddenly one of the cast of *Friends*, her mother hysterical, her father stuttering, stammering, it could make you breathless, all this whatever it was, and then quitting Cuppa Joe. Oh, that was better than being singled out, that was the whipped cream and the cherry, telling Rudy what he could do with his coffee beans.

Ionie sucked in her cheeks.

She looked like a million bucks in all this cashmere. Strapless cashmere, her mother would absolutely collapse. Her mother would buy a hundred copies of *Marie Claire* magazine, her mother would paper the bathroom with the covers, her mother was coming in three weeks—

"Ms. St. John?" The chipped nail was back.

"Coming," Ionie said.

"Zuck will be ready in ten," the nail said and left.

Ionie sat on the stool in front of the three-way mirror. Her mother was coming. She lifted her chin.

"I'll help you move," Kitty Ray had drawled.

She was moving out of the rathole and into a fabulous guest house behind a sprawling Tudor in Brentwood. "There's nothing to move, Mama, I don't have anything worth putting on a truck."

"I'll fold your undies then."

Ionie held tightly to the phone.

"I'll line your drawers with new paper," Kitty Ray said. "I know, nothin' pink."

She could picture her mother hunched over an open dresser drawer studying her underwear, lifting a red silk thong with one finger as if it were a jellyfish. "Lord have mercy, Ionie St. John, what is this?"

"Why don't you just come when I'm settled?"

"I wouldn't hear of my baby movin' all by herself, my movie-star baby."

"Mama, I won't be able to be with you, I have wardrobe fittings and camera tests and lots of things—"

"Well, I'll just drop you off at all your things and pick you up when you're through."

The image of her mother honking the horn on the other side of the studio gates practically made her knees buckle. Ionie stood there speechless, holding her breath.

"What?" Kitty Ray said over the distinct sound of the flip of a Zippo lighter. "Is there some reason why you don't want me there?"

Yes, yes, yes, I could make you a list. Ionie exhaled and said, "No, Mama, don't be silly, of course I want you here."

Ionie tilted her face to the left in the mirror. He was right, Zuck, it was her better side; the laugh line from her nose to her chin was definitely softer on the right. She smiled at herself in the glass and then released the smile. Definitely softer. She would have to remember that, she *would* remember that, and she would deal with her mother coming, and with Al wanting to move into the new place with her—no way—and the fact that Jones was going to shoot *Trumpets* and would see her every day and was definitely in love with her, couldn't take his eyes off her, looked at her like she was a box of candy, like Gramma used to look at her cherry creams, and she would figure out a way to get in close with Chassi Jennings, be her friend—

"Ms. St. John?" said the fingernail.

She probably needed a friend, Chassi Jennings, she looked like a loner for sure. *Ionie St. John and Chassi Jennings were seen leaving the Viper Room and heading for the Sky Bar. . . .*

"Coming," said Ionie and slid off the stool. She adjusted the cashmere at the top of her breasts and where it cupped her ass, and before she opened the curtain she remembered to angle her face just slightly to the left and lift her chin.

• • •

"IT'S THE FIRST TIME it's happened to me," Chassi said to Eleanor. The jingle of the bracelets. She'd gotten used to being on that couch, hearing Dr. Costello behind her, the swish of fabric when she crossed her knees, the silver bangles making their slide.

"Tell me about it," Eleanor said.

"I just can't get in. It makes no sense, the part's more like me than any part I've ever played before, but I can't get in. You know the story, don't you? It's the same as when my mother did it, they're going with the original script."

Quiet. The sun was warm, white light. There were those little specks in the beams that were playing across her and the couch. She raised her hand and they went all berserk around her fingers as if they had life.

"Actually, I have her script. My father gave it to me. Her script, her notes, everything. You'd think that would be . . . incentive . . . I don't know." She'd read the notes, her mother's scribble about the character in blue ink, the same blue ink as the postcards. The jingle and a swish behind her, the swish of nylon. Panty hose probably, not stockings. She didn't know anybody who wore stockings except her mother, or dancers, chorus girls in *Chicago* or *Cabaret*, or somebody trying to get laid, going out of their way to be sexy, stockings with a purpose, not stockings as a matter of routine. Sally wore stockings as a matter of routine; stockings or she went bare-legged, she said panty hose had no allure. Chassi had looked up "allure" in the dictionary and it said something about "enticing." Did that mean her mother was always going out of her way to entice? Entice: to—

"Chassi? What are you thinking about?" La Shrink said.

"I don't know, something stupid." Black lace, white satin, red silk, Sally's enticing garter belts lined up in little plumped piles like flowers without the leaves, the slide of the drawer, the cool brass of the handle, the smell of the sachet as it hit you in the nose, everything just as she'd left it and then it was all gone. Empty hangers, blank drawers, the smell of nothing. Chassi racing to the kitchen, screaming, "Tia, where are Mommy's things?" Tia crying and Daddy saying he'd had no idea how upsetting and how could she explain that she had found comfort standing in that closet, letting her hand touch every shred she had left of her mother in the silk and the scent.

"Stupid," she said again. There was no movement from Eleanor. "I was thinking about stockings," Chassi said.

Two weeks at Nana's and when she got home, everything gone.

She bent her legs now at the knees through the rays of white light, reached down and pulled at the tops of her socks. Well, how could he know, Daddy. It's not like she told anybody that she'd sneak in there when they all thought she was in her own room down the hall. Chassi let her eyes wander La Shrink's office. She had come to love this room: the books, the furniture, the way the sun streamed in or the expanse of gray clouds building on the other side of the glass; she had even begun to love the terrible little black clay sculptures across the top of that shelf. "I told you it was stupid."

No jingle.

"Who's the little girl in the picture? Over there."

A crunch in the leather.

"Huh?" Chassi said. "Is that your daughter? Did she make the statues when she was little?"

Nothing.

"Is it your daughter?"

"Yes."

"It is? Hey." Chassi slid off the couch, went to the bookcase, held the small silver frame in her hand. "Hey, she's pretty, what's her name?"

"Why were you thinking about stockings?" The tilt of Eleanor's eyebrows.

"Huh? Oh, I don't know."

"Does the nurse wear stockings in the movie?"

"I don't know." The little girl was probably nine or ten, she looked a little like Dr. Costello, but not much, probably more like her dad. Chassi, on the other hand, didn't look like her mom or her dad, she had the features of her mother's kid brother, Joey, they told her, the one who had died in the war, with her daddy's mother's coloring, they said, the grandmother who had died before she was born. Great, she looked like two dead people, how great. "Honey hair," Saul had said, "you have honey hair just like Mama, *afasholem*," the last word being some kind of blessing you said if you were Jewish and you mentioned the name of someone who was dead. She knew that much about being Jewish from her father but not much more, and nothing from her mother about being Presbyterian except that you were supposed to go to church, which Sally gave up when she left Gun Barrel, when she left Nana's house, "Adios, amen, and good-bye," her mother drawled with a ha-ha. "No more church." The little girl in the photograph had Dr. Costello's mouth.

"She has your mouth."

"Are you having trouble with the part?"

"Sort of." Sort of. Talk about a joke. She was so lost she'd actually smelled the script. If anybody had seen her they would have thought she was insane, standing in her father's bedroom, the pages pressed against her face. "What's her name, your daughter?"

"Chassi?"

"What?"

"We're not here to talk about my family."

"Is it a big deal?" What was the big deal? What wasn't she supposed to know?

"I'd appreciate it if you'd sit down,"

"Lay down, you mean. No, *lie* down. Right? How old is she now?"

Why was it so difficult? Why was everything so difficult? Why didn't the spirit of her mother just come back and help her learn the lines? Big hair, big eyes, the daughter of Dr. Costello.

"She doesn't look like you, I mean, not too much except that she's dark. She looks more like your husband, right? You know, I don't even know if you're married."

"Chassi, we don't have much time."

"Are you married?"

Nothing. It was ludicrous. "I don't know anything about you." Dr. Costello held her gaze, didn't say anything but held her gaze. "Is it such a big deal to tell me?"

The swish of the nylon. Suede boots, chocolate brown. She hadn't seen them before. Chassi studied the face of the girl. "She's laughing," Chassi said, "in the picture. Why is she laughing? Do you remember?"

The shrink was expressionless.

There was no reason to cry. She could feel it coming. Ridiculous, what for? She didn't cry, hadn't cried, why would she want to cry? "You could tell me one thing." Tears, so stupid. It didn't change anything. "Does she live here? Is she married?"

Dr. Costello stood up. They were the same height, she hadn't realized that, their eyes were even, head to head, across the room.

"Does she have a regular life?" She couldn't stop, it was insanity. "What's the big deal to tell me one thing?"

"Chassi—"

"What? What's it like to be a mother and daughter when you're grown up? Is it, I don't know . . . wonderful?"

She walked toward the doctor.

"Do you talk all the time? Are you best friends?" So stupid, wiping her nose with her T-shirt sleeve and clutching the stupid picture and Dr. Costello was in front of her and she couldn't help it, she held on to her and the stupid picture while she cried.

• • •

A MOTHER AND A DAUGHTER in Italy, a mother and a daughter who were friends. Eleanor stood at the windows of her office. Smog and fog and whatever else that made the sky colorless, timeless, more opaque than gray. Remembering, hearing his words.

"You're cool with her," Jimmy had said, sitting next to her on the couch in the den.

"I am not."

"Okay."

Eleanor went back to the article, realized she had finished it, crumpled the newspaper as she turned the page.

Jimmy looked up, off into the distance, and then refocused on the magazine in his hand.

"What?" she said.

"Nothing."

"I'm anything but cool with her."

"Mmm-hmm," he said.

Eleanor slammed her feet up onto the coffee table, Jimmy didn't move. She refolded the newspaper, the bracelets on her arm jingling as they slid. He looked up, not at her but lifted his eyes from the page.

"How can you sit there and read an article about mulch?" she said.

"It's not about mulch, El, it's about composting."

"Same difference."

"No"—he leaned forward to explain, that look she knew, that set of his mouth—"organic composts—"

"Don't tell me," Eleanor interrupted, "just don't tell me."

"Mad, huh?"

"I'm not mad and I'm not cool with her."

Jimmy closed the magazine, pitched it onto the table near Eleanor's feet. "Okay, wrong word. Not cool, annoyed."

"She says she'll be home, she doesn't come home, she doesn't call. Right, I'm annoyed."

"Most of the time."

"What most of the time?"

"You're annoyed with Caroline."

She stood at the office windows replaying the conversation, her eyes on the milk-glass sky, his words in her head.

"I am not."

"Okay." He picked up the clicker, on came the TV.

"It's too loud," she said. "I'm only annoyed when her behavior is annoying."

"Okay"—he flipped through the stations, lowered the volume—"I just don't have the word. What channel is the cop thing?"

"What cop thing?"

He gave her a look. "The cop thing, El, with the cops, with that guy with the mustache and the girl with the voice."

She stared at him.

"Friendly," he said.

"What?"

"You're not friendly, that's the word, it's like you've always got an edge with her, like you're not friends."

"I'm not her friend, I'm her mother," Eleanor said.

Jimmy gestured with the clicker. "I rest my case."

"What? I'm supposed to be her friend now?"

"She's going to hear you," he said.

"She can't hear anything in that room but the music, the music that's melting the paint off the walls."

"It's always something."

Eleanor didn't answer.

"You're always in her face."

"I'm in her face because she messes up. If she didn't mess up, I wouldn't be in her face."

"She's sixteen."

"And?"

"Okay, El." He picked up the paper, searched through the sections. "Where's the TV thing?"

"You want me to condone her behavior?"

"You sound like a doctor. And that's not what I said."

"I can't be her friend and her mother."

"Why can't you?"

"Because I can't."

Not intelligent, not even clever, and certainly not worthy of the education she had under her belt. She knew it, and she knew it wasn't because Caroline was sixteen and rebellious, or eleven and stubborn, or seven and moody, or three and spoiled. It had nothing to do with age; she couldn't be Caroline's friend because she'd never been her friend, she'd always been the bad guy.

Eleanor stood at the bank of windows and saw nothing but Caroline's face.

Stomp, stomp went the little red tennis shoes. "Mommy, I'm not your friend." Frowning, her lower lip stuck out, and with perfect two-year-old petulance, Caroline looked up at her mother. "Mommy, go 'way my room."

Before the first sleep-over, before begging to go on the Matterhorn at Disneyland or the flying thing at Magic Mountain or having another soda or staying up late or seeing scary movies or anything that Eleanor thought wasn't safe or was foolish or would hurt in the long run. It was the only time they really fought—Jimmy was always ready with the okay, Eleanor was always waiting with the no.

And by the time Caroline became a teenager the gap had become a chasm, or more likely a pit, with steep sides and no place to get a leg up, sliding gravel pummeling you as you fell back down. Constantly aware of what could happen if she took her eye away, Eleanor didn't, and maybe that very eye is what pushed Caroline over the edge. Boys, grass, alcohol, lying, especially lying, that was her specialty. "I'll be at Susan's." "I'll be home at eleven." "I didn't have any." "I didn't do that." "I didn't. No, Mom." With a straight face, with the big brown eyes wide open she would deny. Would it all have been different if Eleanor had been less of a mother and more of a friend? Could she have been both? They had walked on eggshells from the very beginning, maybe the very eggshell that had broken for Caroline's birth.

She hadn't wanted her. She hadn't wanted a child. Standing here now at the windows, the mere thought of it still torture, the still shameful, guilt-making truth. She hadn't. She hadn't wanted anyone to be with her and Jimmy, near her and Jimmy, between her and Jimmy, no way. She had Caroline *for* Jimmy, and as much as she thought she had conquered that, smudged it, fixed it, covered it, coated it, hidden it, swallowed it, choked on it, buried it, maybe the child had always known. Maybe all the love that had bloomed in Eleanor for Caroline had never erased Eleanor's initial rage. She had not embraced motherhood immediately, she had run screaming in silence the other way, allowed herself to be pushed to the side, and could never recoup the lost ground. They had never been friends, Caroline and Eleanor, not from the time the child could say his name. "No, Mommy, let Daddy." "I'll wait for Daddy." "I want Daddy." But maybe "I want Daddy" really meant "Mommy doesn't want me." Was it possible that's what she had led Caroline to believe?

CHAPTER 17

Al threw the cell phone into the ivy. It wasn't the way Ionie had envisioned it ending, but it ended it just the same. The cell phone thrown into the ivy, his dry cleaning flung at him across the two steps up into her apartment, bad words hurled between them into the night air.

Ionie had known the evening would be rocky from the very beginning; she hadn't wanted to take him with her but he was standing right next to her when they'd called. A dinner at Ago, could she make a dinner at Ago being given by Saul Jennings, asked the tone. You bet. You and a guest, gushed the tone, and Ionie had scribbled it on the pad, along with the name of the restaurant, the time and the address, she was so excited, *you and a guest*, she'd scrawled. She didn't even realize she'd written it, but there he was reading it and how could she take it back?

"Great," he said, "dinner with the phonies."

"You don't have to go with me."

"Why? You got somebody else?"

The steady gaze of his baby blues; there was no way.

Twinkly lights, Spanish valet parkers who smiled at each other over the hood of Al's pickup. Ionie's Explorer wasn't in yet, the dealer'd had to send it someplace special to blacken all the chrome. Black paint, black chrome, black leather interior, Darth Vader, look out. They went in Al's truck; he had washed it, waxed it, even Armoralled the tires and he was wearing a jacket and tie. They were early. "Not *early*," Al carried on, "*on time*. They said eight o'clock. Why do people say eight o'clock if they don't mean eight o'clock? Why don't they just say eight-fifteen?" Crumpling his forehead—"It's too late to eat anyhow, it's no good to eat this late"—staring at the people at the bar, his hands shoved into his pockets, frowning at the room. She was not going to say anything, she was not going to remind him that he didn't have to come with her, she was not going to remind him that she could have gone alone. This was a big night for her and she wasn't going to get into it, she wasn't going to open her mouth. Besides, he was nervous, she knew that, with all of his bravado, this was certainly not Al's turf.

They were whisked to a table, "This way, signorina," a table for seven on the second tier, which Ionie assumed was an "A" table considering who was who. A round table for seven. Saul and Chassi, and Robby Peroni, she figured, maybe with a date, and her and Al, and who? It couldn't be Tim Burke, she knew he was shooting something in Utah and wouldn't be back until rehearsals in July. Never in a million years would Ionie have thought her dream dinner would include Mr. *and Mrs.* David Jones.

"Linda Jones," said the pale blond, extending her hand, the pale blond with the pale eyes and no mascara, no makeup as far as Ionie could tell, pale stubby eyelashes, tiny diamonds, an ivory sweater, all angles and bones like Jones. Not as tall as Ionie, much taller than Chassi, she must have been wearing very high heels. Hello, hello, push back the chairs, the men standing, the shaking of hands, the so good to meet you, Ionie's heart in her throat, Linda's warm hand in hers, and somehow in all the introducing, Ionie wound up sitting next to Jones. Jones, who didn't look at her, Jones on her right and Al on her left and Chassi next to Al, and then Peroni, who came alone, and Saul and then Linda, Jones in between her and Linda. Ionie ordered a vodka martini straight up. Al gave her a look. Jones touched her lap, his palm, just for a second, his fingers clutched the tops of her legs. Not sexual, not even intimate, more like a shipwrecked sailor grasping for a piece of debris, and when the waiter was in between them, under the scrape of his chair Jones leaned in and said, "Ionie, I didn't know." Ionie smiled as if he'd said something lovely and nodded her head.

She'd tried to swallow the unthinkable rush and the terror and the hysteria along with the first sip of her drink. She hadn't talked to Jones in four days, she never talked to him over the weekends, he was in Santa Barbara every weekend with Linda and the boys, and Friday he'd left messages and Monday they'd missed each other again. Later she found out that Peroni had arranged it at the last minute, asked Saul to invite Jones. Later she remembered the evening mostly in a speeded-up blur.

Did she want the risotto and Chassi wanted to split the scallopini and the little space between Peroni's front teeth and his crew cut, she'd wanted to skim her hand across that crew cut, what was it about him that was such a turn-on? Al's studying the menu and the look on his face when Saul asked if he'd ever done set construction and Jones's aftershave mixed with the smell of marinara, and Linda's eyes like pale blue water, eyes on Jones. Jones telling a story and Chassi laughing and Saul telling a joke and everybody laughing and Peroni talking about how he saw the picture, visualized it on film, and Jones intent on Peroni's words, bowed forward, chair legs hovering, stick drawings on the linen, the two of them speaking a private language of light and dark. The glint of Saul's cuff links and his big glasses and his big fingers caressing the sheen of Chassi's hair, her face when she talked about Texas, about her mother, Al's knee hard against Ionie's under the table, Jones's shoulder, the nub of his jacket scraping Ionie's arm, the tang of the veal, the bitter coffee, the hysteria of kissing the air at the top of Linda's cheek on the lean-in, like football players in a huddle, good-bye, good-bye, all one big blur.

The ride in the truck, the rain, rain in June, which was ridiculous, she'd said, where was summer, the groan of the heater, and it started . . . how had it started? She went back over it again in her head.

Funny, that was it, she'd asked him, hadn't she been funny, on the way home. Funny, lively, interesting. Didn't he think she'd been funny? Hadn't it gone well?

"Funny?" Al said. "You were loaded, Ionie, for crissakes."

She patted the purse in her lap, adjusted her skirt on the seat. She wasn't going to take the bait, no way. A couple of blocks in silence.

"That Peroni can talk your ear off," Al said.

"I think he's fascinating, all those stories."

"Yeah," Al said, "I could tell you were fascinated, you practically drooled on his arm."

She would keep her eyes focused on the window, the cars on Melrose sliding by like skaters, the lights glazed over with rain.

"You stumbled when you got up to go to the bathroom with what's-her-name . . . Linda. Slurring your words. You know that? What was going on with you and the martinis? You never drank a goddamned martini in your life."

Ionie recrossed her legs, turned the heater to high. She thought she had handled the perilous trip with Linda Jones to the bathroom with grace and style. Drunk? Okay, drunk, but only on the reality of who she was with; following the black high heels, the slender legs, the straight back in the ivory sweater and the perfume across the room, the perfume that she had occasionally smelled on Jones, no wonder she stumbled. The reality of that face in Jones's wallet standing next to her in the flesh. That face that was smart, the pale yellow eyelashes of a lawyer, who happened to also be the wife of Jones, who slept with him and made his supper and folded his socks and mothered his sons, who handed Ionie a paper towel, smiled back at her over her shoulder, and thoughtfully held the door. No wonder she slurred. Al would have slurred, you betcha, if she'd told him what was really going on. Ionie turned down the visor mirror and checked her hair.

"Saul was okay," Al said.

An opening. "I hope he realizes how grateful I am," said Ionie.

Al laughed. " 'Beholdin',' that was the word you used," and Al did an imitation of Ionie thick with drawl and a fluttering of lashes. "'I'm so beholdin' to you, Saul.'"

"Well, I am beholden. It's a real word, you know."

"Well, there was no reason to get all sloppy."

Flip, flip went the wipers, Ionie ran her hand across her face, pushed at some curls.

"You shouldn't have brought up Sally Brash, it upset Chassi and nobody gives a rat's ass that you're from Texas anyway. Turn that thing down, will ya? It's burning my pants."

They did too give a rat's ass that she was from Texas. She was from Texas just like Sally Brash, had red hair just like Sally Brash, and her very own daddy even knew Sally Brash, which was incredible, simply incredible that of all the places in the world such a connection could exist—in Tyler, Texas. Tyler, Texas, of all places, incredible, anybody could see that and there was no reason to not bring that up. Ionie lifted her chin, reapplied her lipstick. She certainly had not upset Chassi. Absolutely not. Chassi leaning forward, that beautiful hair falling across one cheekbone, listening to the story about her very own mother when she was in high school. She was not upset. What did Al know about what upset people? He didn't know anything. Flip, flip went the wipers, and a rush of adrenaline walloped her, caught her and fueled her with mean words.

Ionie said that Al couldn't possibly have a take on the evening because he probably had no idea what anybody was talking about, and he said oh, yeah?, which was so typical and precisely her point, he wasn't on a level with those people, she said, and Al said that was fine, he wouldn't stoop so low, and she said he was a reverse snob and these people were her new life, she'd waited her whole life for this new life and she couldn't wait, and he said she should walk away from it while she had the chance, the bunch of phonies, especially that Jones, who sure had his hand on her back a lot (which was true), and she said something about how Al had fallen all over Chassi (which wasn't true), and he said something about Ionie's head being up her ass, and what the hell was he supposed to do when she never said a word to him at the table, didn't even look at him, and she said what was the matter, was he too stupid to try and make conversation on his own, was she supposed to take care of him, and next time she'd go alone. And he said if suddenly she thought he was *stupid* then there wouldn't be a next time and that was just fine with him. And they were home and rain and car door slamming and she grabbed for the keys to stop him, to tell him she hadn't meant stupid, she'd meant unsophisticated, but she missed and somehow caught him with her nails across his cheek and he pushed her out of his way hard as he threw the cell phone and she stumbled across the concrete and fell into the ivy with the phone and he went for her and she ran away from him and into the apartment and came back screaming and hit him in the face with the flying shirts. And, oh, it had been coming, this fight, for such a long time, it was like somebody had opened the valves.

And that was the end, it had to be the end of it, because no matter what they said or did after that, there was just too much to take back.

• • •

"HER FATHER KNEW MY MOTHER," Chassi said.

Eleanor looked up from her pad.

"She told me at dinner, Daddy had a dinner at Ago. Isn't that kind of amazing? That I kind of know her, well, not know her but I've seen her, you know, and then that her father knew my mother. Kind of amazing, don't you think?"

Ago, Eleanor had never been to Ago. What was the point in going to a fabulous restaurant alone?

"Of all the gin joints, huh?" Chassi said.

"How did they know each other?"

"High school in Tyler, Texas," Chassi said. "They won a dance contest. They were the champions of Texas swing"—Chassi sighed—"their junior year."

"Go on."

"My mother . . ." She stopped.

"What?" Eleanor asked.

". . . I was just thinking how she did everything. Danced, sang, was on the debate team, was head cheerleader, was the queen of the Flutter Ball, was an Apache Belle. All those pictures in Nana's house lining the walls."

Eleanor didn't say anything, Chassi moved on the couch. "Do you know what that is? An Apache Belle?"

"No."

"It's Texas. It's what you want to be, *have* to be, if you're from Texas; they start to teach you practically at birth, baby girls in cribs in tiny baby boots with baby tassels . . ." She stopped, shrugged. "It's the drill team. There's one in every town in Texas. You know, marching, in those white boots with the little tassels and those flirty, short skirts. Kicking their legs high against the night sky, trombones and drums and crickets, sitting in the bleachers and scratching chigger bites, the air thick with wood smoke. I went plenty of times with Mommy and Nana"—Chassi's sigh—"Apache Belles kick the highest, my mother said."

Eleanor nodded. She couldn't imagine herself in white boots with tassels. Had there ever been such a thing in New York?

Quiet.

Probably the only white boot that had ever been worn in New York had been on a Rockette. Eleanor frowned. She tried to fashion a tassel on the boot she'd drawn on her pad. A shaky boot and the heel was too high or maybe it was just the perspective, which was definitely off; no matter what, it was awful. She scribbled over the deformed boot, obliterated it with black ink in a poufy cloud shape and then wrote Tyler, Texas, above the cloud three times.

"Roses," Chassi said. "Tyler is full of roses and trees and more roses, and it's hotter than hell there, *hotter than hell itself,* Nana said. Nana and Charlie lived there until Mama finished high school. Then they moved to Gun Barrel to live on the lake and Mama came to California. I went with her lots of times back to Tyler. Anyway, her father and my mother were an item, Ionie said, in high school. As she put it, they were dancing fools."

"Did they ever see each other again?"

"Nope. Not as far as we know."

She was edgy, there was something going on with her. Eleanor lowered her pen. "She's going to play the other part, this girl, the actress-waitress you told me about, she's going to play the other nurse in the picture?"

"Ionie," Chassi said, "Ionie St. John."

Chassi recrossed her legs at the ankles, the big, white marshmallow sneakers replaced today with some kind of low, black spaceship-looking shoes, a far cry from white boots. Ionie, Eleanor had never heard the name Ionie. "Do you like her?" Eleanor asked.

"She's very . . . friendly."

Quiet. Eleanor drew a star, the six-pointed kind that you make by overlapping two opposite triangles, a sheriff's badge star, which is actually the same as a Star of David, a Jewish star, which is kind of strange.

Chassi went on, "Kind of flirty, funny, tall." She stopped and then started, "She has this really red hair, like my mother's."

Quiet.

"Do you not like it that she's flirty?"

"What do you mean?"

"You said 'flirty' as if you didn't like it."

"Oh."

"Did she flirt at the dinner?"

"Yes."

"Did she flirt with someone specific?"

Chassi gave the shrug laugh. "All of us, I guess."

"Was she an Apache Belle when she was in high school?" quipped Eleanor.

Chassi laughed again. "I don't know."

Eleanor remembered, couldn't remember the *name* of the actress who had played the part the first time but vaguely remembered her face. This time the part would be played by a girl Chassi used to see in some coffee shop; Chassi'd had no idea the girl was an actress, she'd said, it was a complete surprise. Probably like the waitress who used to work downstairs, another starstruck, innocent hopeful from a little town named Podunk who'd come with big eyes to the phony Hollywood to make good. A little town where they walked around in cowboy boots and drove trucks. Where they scratched chigger bites. Eleanor made a tic-tac-toe outline on her pad. And now this girl would become a movie star and never go home again. And never wear cowboy boots. And never drive a truck. Eleanor tried to draw a truck but gave it up, it looked more like an animal with a hood ornament for a nose. Chassi shifted on the couch, recrossed her legs again.

"Maybe you'll be friends," Eleanor said, "you and Ionie."

Chassi didn't answer.

"You could be," Eleanor said.

"You know, I used to march around Nana's yard in those boots, my mother's Apache Belle boots, when I was little. They were in the closet in what used to be her room."

Quiet.

"My feet were too little, they made a *squoosh* sound inside, you know? Against the leather, and I could feel my toes."

Eleanor put an *x* in the center of the crossed lines. Caroline used to walk around in her shoes too, she'd forgotten. One high heel clopping and one bare baby foot making a *squoosh* sound across the kitchen floor.

"She used to watch me, Mommy, I could feel her eyes from the window . . ."

Eleanor studied the back of the girl's head, the slope of the perfect gold haircut moving like a whisk broom.

". . . or from the steps. Sometimes she'd sit on Nana's back steps and watch me parade around the edge of the fence in her boots. Mommy barefoot . . . in short shorts . . . clapping . . ."

Quiet. The girl holding her breath, remembering, seeing her mother and the steps. Maybe the steps were peeling, blue paint peeling. Eleanor tried to imagine, steadied her pen on the paper, imagined the blue of the paint and the big sky. The mother and the daughter framed against the big sky. Texas, what did she know from Texas?

Eleanor lowered the pad and pen into her lap, released them, felt the soft weight of them hit the skirt fabric across her thighs. "Your mother and you had fun together," she said to the back of the girl's head.

"Yes."

"You were close to her."

"Yes," Chassi said.

"You loved her."

"Yes."

Eleanor ran her fingers across her lips. "Did you ever not love your mother?"

Quiet, a thin second of quiet and then, "No."

"You said you were never angry with her."

They both sat motionless, Eleanor's eyes on the child's hair.

"Were you ever angry with her?"

"I don't know." Chassi moved on the couch, moved herself up on the leather. "Don't all kids get angry with their mothers?"

"You said you remembered your mother was holding your hand, in Rome, not your arm but your hand. You said you remembered."

A slight tilt of the head.

"You were having a good time in Rome."

A slight lift of the right shoulder.

"Do you remember the street?"

Quiet.

"Where you were standing?" Eleanor said. "Before the car?"

Nothing from Chassi.

"Do you remember going to the restaurant?"

"Yes."

"What happened that day?"

"Nothing."

Eleanor waited.

"I mean, I guess we went to a museum or something . . . oh"—she stopped and then started—"Trastevere," the smile back in her voice, "we were at the fountain with the old man and his dog."

Eleanor listening, then Chassi's soft laugh. "He put the dog in the fountain. It's on the postcard, I just forgot."

Eleanor leaned forward. Postcard? What postcard?

"It was hot and he just plunked him right in. A squatty, black dog"—she hesitated—"what was his name? I can't remember, the man's name was Pasquale, and he didn't know who Mommy was; didn't know that she was famous, I mean. People always knew, they would get all funny, try not to stare at her while they were staring, try not to react with their mouths wide open, but he didn't, Pasquale. '*La bellissima donna*' he called her. '*Una bellissima figlia.*' " She turned and looked at Eleanor, her face luminous. "That's what he called me."

"The postcard?" Eleanor said.

Chassi just looked at her.

"What postcards?"

"The ones my mother sent."

Eleanor waited. "To your father?"

"No, to me." Incredulous, as if Eleanor knew about the postcards, as if Eleanor shouldn't be interrupting, Chassi turned away. "The beautiful lady and her beautiful daughter, that's what he called us. He had white hair and stubble on his face"—a quick breath—"and he wore a cap. Oh, and he peeled an orange for us, he had an orange in his shirt pocket." She laughed. "I thought it was a ball for the dog."

"Why did she send you postcards?"

The shrug. "I don't know, so that I would remember, I guess, so I could make the 'Two Girls in Italy' list, which, of course, I never did."

"The what?"

"The Two Girls in Italy list, a list of everything we did."

"When did you get the postcards?"

"After she was dead."

Eleanor rubbed her knee. She could go with the postcards, she could go with the two girls in Italy list, she could go with the memory. A buffet of choice always in the back and forth of a doctor and her patient, but the memory was Eleanor's priority. The memory, she felt, was the key to Chassi, and at the top of her list.

"What happened at the fountain?"

"We played with the dog, I don't know, ate the orange, washed our fingers in the water, tried to talk to Pasquale, then we went back to the hotel."

Thinking, remembering.

"She let me go out by myself to get a *gelati*, by myself on the street." She lifted her legs, recrossed her feet at the ankles. "We walked to the restaurant. She couldn't walk in L.A., people would jump all over her, but she could walk in Rome."

"Do people jump all over you when you walk?"

"Sometimes."

Thinking about that, she was thinking about that, Eleanor knew now by just the tilt of her head.

"Tell me about the restaurant."

Quiet.

"Chassi?"

"What?"

"Do you remember the restaurant?"

"I don't know, I guess."

"Tell me about the restaurant."

She moved, she breathed deeply, a big rush of air in and out. "It was happy," Chassi said, her voice full.

"What did it look like?"

"I don't know."

"Yes, you do."

Quiet.

"What did you see when you opened the door?"

No answer.

"Chassi, open the door, you can remember, you and your mother, what do you see?"

She turned. "What is this? Some new memory game?"

Eleanor waited.

"A walk down memory lane to the moment of your mother's death." A flash of the eyes. "Boy, do I want to play that, I've been looking forward to that all week. Don't you have to swing something in front of my eyes to get me into a trance?"

"Are you afraid to remember the restaurant?"

"I told you I've done this, I've been shrunk by the best of 'em. This is no big deal."

"Why are you here if you don't want to remember?"

"Why are you pushing me?"

"I don't have to push you, you can leave. Are you afraid to remember the restaurant?"

"Why do you want to rehash this?"

"Are you afraid to remember the restaurant?" *That's it, babe,* Jimmy would have said, *you're the doctor, stick to your guns.*

"Why should I be afraid to remember the goddamn restaurant?"

Okay, okay.

Chassi tossed her head, the yellow silk tumbling around her face. Irate eyes and the toss of the head. "Black-and-white tiles on the floor like hopscotch."

I'll show you said the eyes that never left Eleanor's.

"It smelled good . . . a long table with antipasti . . . flowers . . ."

You got her, babe. Eleanor didn't move in the chair.

". . . they were short, the waiters, like uncles, not handsome . . . smiling, all smiling, all speaking Italian, there was a rush of them when you went in"—she took a breath—"they must have been waiting for her, my mother. The maître d', the waiters, the owner, I don't know, his wife, I think, his mother, they were all there." The anger dissipating. "She actually twirled, Mommy, she was so happy, the white dress . . . the skirt was full and when she twirled it went out"—an intake of air, a gulp—"like a cloud."

A cloud about to get hit, Eleanor thought and took a breath.

"Mommy was trying to speak Italian"—Chassi's soft laugh—"hopeless, and this one waiter who was trying to speak English, he had his hair combed, you know"—her hand lifting in one swoop across the top of her head—"like black strings from ear to ear."

Smiling now, remembering.

"And I had my artichoke . . ."

Remembering.

". . . and my own glass of wine, she let me . . ." And then she stopped, stopped speaking but kept thinking, you could see it across her face. Like a slide, an unstoppable slide into somewhere else. Like Pete Rose, Jimmy would have said, like a headfirst skid, dirt flying and the crowd roaring while he skidded into home plate.

Chassi sat forward, her back lifting off the leather, head bending, the whiskbroom hair parting at the back of her head like water and falling forward across both cheeks.

What? What was she remembering? Come on, come on . . . but the room was still.

"She let me do grown-up things," Chassi finally said, her voice drifting.

"What?" Eleanor said in a whisper.

The lift of the head. "She let me."

"Do grown-up things?"

Breathing, thinking, the almond eyes searching Eleanor's. "Why did she do that?" Chassi said.

"Let you drink the wine?"

No answer.

"What kind of grown-up things?"

No answer, the almond eyes didn't waver but there was no answer from the child.

"She shouldn't have let you drink the wine?"

No answer.

"She shouldn't have let you go alone to get an ice cream?"

No answer.

"Did something happen when you went alone to get the ice cream?"

The bottom lip caught between the teeth.

"Chassi, what grown-up things shouldn't your mother have let you do?"

Chassi got off the couch, slid off, walked the length of it and back. *Easy, babe . . . easy.*

The silence of the shoes, flat black shoes, back and forth on Eleanor's carpet.

Shoes . . . that's right, Chassi's mother had let her buy her first heels, she'd said that the first session, the heels that she'd wound up wearing to the funeral, the grass stuck on the heels that she'd said were still in the box. Okay, okay, so Sally Brash had let her kid buy her first heels maybe when she was a little too young, and have a glass of wine on special occasions, and walk around the corner alone for an ice cream, but what else had Sally Brash done?

"I was only twelve."

Eleanor leaning forward.

"I was only twelve," she said again.

Twelve, twelve . . .

"I couldn't be her girlfriend," the child said.

The light went on, the yellow light on Eleanor's wall flashed on like neon over Chassi's head. Another patient had arrived, was sitting out there in the waiting room, waiting to come in. Eleanor had forgotten to look at the clock, wanted to swivel her head now to the clock, Chassi's eyes on her and no sound of the clock. No ticking from the new one, no nothing from the new one, stupid, stupid to have replaced it and because of that she hadn't paced herself, because of that The Shoelace had arrived to interrupt the memory, and what might have been.

CHAPTER 18

Girlfriends. "Girlfriends are paramount, and I don't mean the studio," Sally had said. Chassi'd had girlfriends from day one: Danielle in nursery school, Danielle with the big brown eyes and the mommy and the daddy who were not in the movies, which was how Chassi determined who was who—mommies and daddies were either in the movies or not in the movies. Later the perception became more defined—those who were above the line and those who were below, which was Hollywood talk for whose name went above or below the title of the picture, and the whole thing only had to do with where you played and how you got there; someone's mommy picking you up instead of a driver, someone's mommy making the snack instead of Tia, someone's mommy driving you home, from a mansion, from a regular house, from an apartment in a neighborhood where they didn't have swimming pools. Sally was never a snob about who could be your friend, she opened her arms to—in or out of the movies—above or below.

Danielle's mommy taught at the nursery school and her daddy worked in a bank but then they got a divorce and Danielle and her mommy had to move away to live with her grandma in someplace called the Bronx. A clinging good-bye in Chassi's driveway with an exchange of stuffed animals and a lot of sobbing into Sally's front. In first grade there was Allison. Allison of the blue eyes and yellow hair in two braids that were pulled too tight, it seemed to Chassi, and made her eyes thin. Allison, who only wore pants and hated girl things, who didn't give a goodgoddamn (an expression Allison had learned from her mother) about learning to read because she was going to be a baseball player, and whose daddy worked on a set. In the movies but below the line, which meant if you went to visit the set and didn't want to play in Sally's trailer you could play in Allison's daddy's truck. That friendship only lasted the length of the picture. What Chassi didn't know then was that most friendships made in the movie business only lasted that long. Mara was Chassi's best friend in second grade. Mara, whose mommy was a movie star just like Sally and whose daddy was a producer just like daddy and who lived in a big house just like Chassi's that was only three blocks away. Yellow afternoons of riding your bike like the wind to Mara's, but then you had to wait up for Tia puffing behind you because you couldn't go anywhere by yourself for fear of being kidnapped. Sally never said the word "kidnap," but Chassi knew. Unfortunately, Daddy had a fight with Mara's daddy over a deal and that was the end of that. Janie, in third grade, was a little too dull, Sally thought, and Suze, in fourth, was a little too wild. Joy's daddy was a bum, Saul said. Joy and Chassi were what Sally called "a summer romance" since they had met and pledged undying devotion at camp. It was over before Tia had unpacked the sand out of Chassi's shorts. Maggie was Chassi's best friend in fifth grade. Maggie had freckles everywhere, even on her toes, and her grandpa, who lived with them and used to be in something called vaudeville, taught the girls all the words to "How Ya Gonna Keep 'Em Down on the Farm?" and how to play the big casino and gin rummy. "Breast your cards, girls," he would mutter and they would go nearly unconscious with giggles. In sixth grade Maggie became Chassi's second-best friend because Sissy Danziger became Chassi's first. Sissy Danziger had the biggest bed and the biggest bedroom for sleep-overs and her parents were never home. Her nanny was planted like a dead geranium in front of a droning television set and she either didn't hear or didn't care to hear what was going on upstairs. Sissy also got points for having a cook who would make you pizza or chocolate chip pancakes, or whatever you wanted, in the middle of the night. Chassi moved from nursery school through sixth grade loaded with friends. Then she went to Rome.

Chassi slid lower in the window seat, the backs of her knees against the pillows, her legs raised, socks flat on the glass. It was a navy night, clear and balmy, you could even count stars. She punched at the bolster behind her head, fanned her hair out at both ears.

Junior high was a new school and should have been thick with new friends, but if Sally's death over the summer had added to Chassi's cachet, given her already established colorful aura an air of mystique rare for twelve-year-olds, it had also pinned her to a new role. Unapproachable. The downcast daughter of the dead movie star. No one was about to sidle up to the elusive, sorrowful Chassi Jennings who had seen her mother fly up into the air and come down again dead. No telephone conversations and putting your hair up in rollers, giggling over boys and gossiping, sleep-overs and pillow fights, painting your fingernails, shopping, swapping secrets over endless Cokes—shades of *Grease* in Chassi's head, images from *Bye Bye Birdie*, even yellowing pages from *The Group*. The loathsome shrink, Marion, tried to push her: "Say hello, have a party and invite everyone, join a group." A group? Chassi took stock of herself and came up with a handful of zero. She wasn't athletic, she wasn't honor roll, she wasn't popular, she wasn't a geek, she wasn't in Spanish club, she wasn't in drama, she wasn't even—she smiled to herself now, watching the night sky from the window seat—she wasn't even an Apache Belle. There was no place for her to make friends. And that was fine. She didn't need friends. She went to school, she went to sessions with the loathsome Marion, she went to dinner with Daddy, she stayed in her room.

Chassi wiggled her toes in the socks, lifted the small book off her chest and fanned the pages. There were no lines on the paper, thick ivory paper with rough edges and a thin red ribbon fastened at the top to mark your place. The covering was slick, a red-and-gold paisley pattern on an ivory ground.

"It's a journal," Ionie had said. "Oh, I always do that, tell people before they get the wrapping off, but it's a journal," she said again with a fetching grin.

"Thank you." She was beautiful, Chassi thought. All that hair and skin and red and white. Beautiful.

"I always buy them and then never write in them, it's insane."

"I've never had a journal," Chassi said.

"You haven't? Oh, I just thought . . . well, I don't know you and I didn't know what you like and I just thought—"

Chassi interrupted, "I mean, I'm happy to have it, I just never bought one for myself."

"Did you have a diary when you were little?"

"No."

"It's the same, isn't it, they just don't call them that anymore. I had one with the sweetest little key. I always think I'm going to write in them," Ionie said, "but I guess I'm too self-conscious; as I'm about to, I think what if I don't like what I write, what if it's just stupid and then it's written right there in ink. It's not like you can rip out the pages. Well, I guess you could." Ionie grinned again. "Maybe I'm just not brave enough, more of a scribble-on-a-piece-of-paper-towel kind of person, you know? Cocktail napkins, scraps of paper shoved in my pockets, notes to myself"—she laughed, pulling bits of white stuff from her sweater pockets—"on crumpled Kleenex, see?"

Tentative, unfolding, showing, getting to know you, Chassi heard in her head, Deborah Kerr singing to the children in *The King and I,* Deborah Kerr of the beautiful hands and the ivory-white skin and the red hair . . . like Ionie . . . like Chassi's mother. Sally's smile, a faint whoop of dizzy, Chassi took a long drink of her Coke. They sat across from each other in a cracked orange booth for four at Swingers, the diner on Beverly, it had been Robby's idea.

"You two should hang," he said.

Saul's open mouth, his stare, Robby laughing. "Hang, Saul, as in spend time together."

"Such an expression," Saul said.

Chassi had suggested coffee.

"Oh, God, anything but coffee," moaned Ionie. "I'll never drink coffee again." The quick grin, then, "How did you get that name? Considering it's the frame of a car, a chassis. I know all about cars from my dad."

Chassi shook her head, grimaced. "Oh, God. My nana's husband, Charlie, used to work on the line, you know, a hundred years ago at Ford, and it seems he said to my mother one day, 'Without a chassis you ain't got nothin', Sal.' " Chassi shrugged, made a face. "My father says he fought her, but I guess she won."

"Mothers. 'Ionie St. John' sounds like a stripper. I said to Mama, 'You should have given me fans and pasties, how could you possibly name me that?' "

She was animated, she was funny, passionate. She was easy, loose with her body, her talk. She didn't hold back, didn't hold back anything as far as Chassi could tell. Everything that Chassi wasn't, it seemed, Ionie was.

"Are you dating him?"

"Who?"

"Robby Peroni," Ionie said, mid-burger, eyes bright.

"Oh," Chassi said, "no."

"Don't you find him remarkable? So terribly unattractive and yet so terribly attractive all at the same time. I've never met a man like that. Are you attracted to him? Please, eat my fries. If I eat them all, I'll kill myself."

"I, uh—"

Ionie's bottom lip caught by her teeth—"Oh, God, I'm sorry, I didn't mean to offend you, asking you about men and all, it's certainly none of my business."

Watching her step, finding the boundaries. "No, it's fine," Chassi said.

"I bet that's what Onassis was like, don't you think?" Popping a french fry into her mouth, "Carlo Ponti, you know, men like that, attractive because of their enormous talent, their big brains—"

"Their money," Chassi said and Ionie laughed.

"Right, their money, pots of money—God, do you think Peroni has money? He must pay tons of alimony. Oh, and child support. He has three kids. Three wives, three kids, my mother would call him a scoundrel. Do you want ketchup?"

"Okay."

"Am I drawling?" She glared and then laughed. "I mean, can you hear my Texas?"

Chassi smiled. "A little."

"Oh, man, it always happens when I feel comfortable, you know, safe. You're going to have to help me, I mean, my character in *Trumpets* is from New York!"

Heady, like having too much champagne. Chummy and familiar and close and intimate, as if they had known each other for a long time, as if this wasn't their first secret swapping, their first lunch, their first Coke. Friends, Chassi thought, as if they were friends. She hadn't had a girlfriend since sixth grade.

She studied the journal in her hands, turned it over, pulled the thin satin ribbon out from between the pages and then smiled. "Made in Italy," said the small inscribed sticker on the inside back cover. Chassi smiled at the sky from the window seat. Maybe it was an omen, she thought, reading the words in script on the tiny sticker, maybe it meant something, maybe her mother had sent her a friend.

• • •

"CHASSI'S QUIET," Ionie said in the mirror to Jones. Side by side, facing the mirror above the Ramada sink, Jones combing his hair, Ionie dabbing her lipstick brush into a tube of dark red.

"She's wounded," he said.

"Jesus," Ionie sighed, but it came out 'Cheesus,' the brush on her mouth. "I like her," she said.

Jones frowned at his shirt, pulled at the collar.

Ionie watched him. "What?" she said.

"This shirt gives me the willies." He moved his neck, straightened and wiggled his shoulders. "I don't know," he said, jamming his hand over his shoulder and down the back of his neck.

"Let me see," she said. He turned and bent, she was behind him, ran her fingers under the collar. "It's a label."

"Great."

"You got a scissors?"

"Not that I know of." Jones laughed. He straightened, turned back toward the glass. Her breasts against his back, she wrapped her arms around him, clasped her hands at his chest. She peered from around his right forearm, red curls to Jones's elbow covering half of Ionie's right eye. "Hi, there," she said to him in the mirror. He smiled, a faint blush edging across his face. The dark red lipstick of Ionie's grin. "You're blushing," she said.

Jones put his hands over hers. "I have a meeting at Technicolor in twenty-five minutes." She didn't say anything, just held her ground. "Ionie?"

"What?"

He rocked, swayed softly to the outside edge of his right foot and then his left. They studied each other. "I've decided to buy stock in Ramada," Jones said. Ionie laughed.

"I have a meeting at Nicki's," she said. "Meeting everyone in the movie department, very la-de-da."

"Good, about time they made over you."

She took a deep breath, her nipples hard up against the gray cashmere of her sweater. She could feel the muscles in Jones's back. "You now have a meeting at Technicolor in twenty-*three* minutes," she said.

He didn't reply, his gaze steady and adoring in the glass.

"It's different," she said, with a breath, "you know, now that I've seen her."

He nodded.

"I mean Mrs. Jones—"

"I know." His eyes never left hers, his hands on her hands.

"—not Chassi."

"I know."

"When you don't see someone, it's like"—the tiny frown between the brows, the hesitation—"like they're not real. They don't exist, they're a . . ."

He nodded.

"She's real," Ionie said.

He squeezed her hands, she rubbed her cheek against his forearm.

"You shouldn't fall in love with me," Ionie said. "Jones?"

"Yep?"

"You shouldn't fall in love with me."

"I knew from the beginning, the first time I saw you."

"But we have to consider—"

His fingers hard on hers, interrupting. "I love you," Jones said.

Their eyes locked, they swayed in the mirror. What was there to say unless they said everything, and to say everything was something neither of them wanted to do. Eventually Ionie smiled and Jones released her hands, she took her arms from around his chest, came out from behind him.

She pushed at her hair, he slipped his comb into his back pocket, she took a Kleenex from the dispenser and blotted her lips, he turned and walked to the chest of drawers. Something in the ease of being with him, something that warmed her every time, pushed away the bad thoughts, the reality. She picked up her purse, he grabbed his car keys and sunglasses. He bent and flipped up the spread where it had fallen, she pushed at the pillows. Their eyes met over the bed. They had been here many times, in this room and in this place, and sometimes Ionie felt that their intimacy was as deep as if they were married and then she stopped herself from those thoughts. She slipped her hand in his, they walked the length of the room together.

Jones held her at the door. "I don't ever want to see your boys," Ionie whispered into his neck, "I couldn't take it."

He bent to kiss her. "Sweetie, you'll have red lipstick at Technicolor," Ionie said, but maybe he didn't hear.

She missed Al but not too much, she didn't let herself. It was all about *Trumpets*, getting ready. It was all about her mother coming, moving into the new place. It was all about seeing Jones, getting to know Chassi. It was all about running, going to the gym, going to yoga, learning lines. If she missed Al—no, when she missed Al—she missed his feet planted firmly, his ability to bring everything down to black and white, good and bad. No grays, no wavering. Part of that made life easier, part of that made you want to scream. Al would never have had an affair with a married woman, it was a *no*, a no-matter-what no. And when she thought about Jones, Ionie tried to block out all illusions of Linda, tried to blend her pale demeanor into an ivory blur, tried to think of her as Mrs. Jones, a name that wasn't accessible. Not Linda, not the blonde Linda of the stubby yellow eyelashes and the good calves, not the Linda that Jones had married, that he looked at first in the morning and last at night. Images of Linda only brought up images of that night, brought up images of Al, images of the phone in the ivy, images of the hurt on his face. It was hard enough that she kept finding traces of him as she sorted through things to be tossed or packed. She tossed: one white T-shirt with a grease spot in the shape of a hand, instructions for installing a CD player in his truck, four copies of *Men's Health* magazine, his toothbrush, his shampoo for silver or gray hair that took the yellow out, his Mennen original aftershave, his Speed Stick deodorant, his comb. She kept the three pipe wrenches he'd left, the hammer, the WD-40, the tiny portable radio that he kept by the side of her bed to listen to ball scores, and the scrap of sandpaper he'd used to work on her closet door. When she found the sheriff's badge she had given him, she told herself they would never have made it anyway, that they were about to be in two different worlds.

Ionie held on to the tin badge for three days. When she walked out the door to follow the movers to the new apartment, she dropped it in the trash.

• • •

"I LIKE YOUR PANTS," La Shrink said.

"What? Oh. Thanks." They were new, for exercise, for yoga, for whatever she decided to do to fluff up for the picture, as her mother would have said. Flared, navy, made out of sweatshirt stuff but flared at the ankle, Chassi felt like a sailor about to swab the deck.

Eleanor mumbled, "I've never understood why people wear pants that go in at the bottom, makes them look like a pear." She swiveled slightly as she sat in her chair.

Chassi was familiar with the creak, the creak of the swivel. Most times now she knew what Eleanor was doing back there without turning around. She moved to the couch, stretched out on it, the leather cool under her head. She lifted her legs in the new pants, her eyes on the flare as she balanced the heel of her left shoe on top of the toe of her right. She also didn't like pants that went in at the bottom, she preferred a bootleg or—wait a minute, La Shrink had never connected personally before, had she? Brought up her own point of view? No. What was going on? Wow, a slip, a shrink slip, and what an image, she couldn't imagine the doctor wearing anything but her drippy skirts and boots and . . . amazing—flared pants. . . . "Did you wear bell-bottoms in the sixties?"

"Yes. We were talking about you and your mother."

"You wore bell-bottoms? I love it." She turned, she wanted to see her. "Tie-dye? Love beads? Flowers in your hair?"

Such an open look on Dr. Costello's face. "I had a medal on a chain that read 'War is unhealthy for children and other living things.' "

"You did?"

"Yes." She put her hand on her knee, absently rubbed the kneecap. She did that often. "And a copper bracelet," the shrink said.

Chassi sat up, halfway, propped herself with her elbow. "What do you mean, a copper bracelet?"

"For a soldier. Chassi, we were talking about you and your mother."

It was amazing, you could think you know somebody but you know only the tiniest part of them, and that's only the tiniest part of them that's right now. "God. Do you remember his name?"

"Major Leonard Rubin, United States Army, missing in action September 2, 1968." Softly, she said it softly, like the lines of a poem, like a child who had been asked to recite. Amazing.

"Did they find him?"

"No." She took a breath. "Chassi, we have to—"

"You were a protester? Like I've seen in the clips?"

La Shrink didn't answer right away. Shook her head, slightly, yes.

"How long did you wear the bracelet?"

"For a time."

"Do you still have it?"

"We were talking about you and your mother."

"I know, but do you still have the bracelet?"

Dr. Costello sighed, sat forward. "Why is it so important to you?"

"I don't know, I was thinking, maybe you would let me wear it for the movie. You know, it's a movie about Vietnam, maybe it would give me . . . I'm having such a hard time getting the lines, getting the . . . I don't know."

Eleanor was watching her, she could feel her eyes. Her eyes then must have been circled in black, wasn't that what they wore? Black eyeliner? Pale lipstick. Maybe no lipstick. La Shrink Hippie, long hair down her back or in braids, dodging tear gas in bell-bottoms, *Hey, Hey, LBJ, how many boys did you kill today?* She'd been watching it, all the news footage, Robby had sent over boxes of tapes. Running, screaming, La Shrink raising her fist against the war, a glint of light flashing off the bracelet, the bracelet she wore for Major Leonard Rubin, missing in action since— "Hey, why did you stop wearing it if they didn't find him?"

"Chassi—"

"No, really."

"Chassi, I never should have—"

"Please, Dr. Costello."

The shrink looked up, waited.

"Please," Chassi said again.

"I took it off when I met my husband because he had been in Vietnam."

"He had?" God, it was unbelievable what you didn't know about people. Her husband had been in Vietnam . . . but, wait a minute . . . "But they still hadn't found the guy."

"Chassi—"

"But I don't get it—you mean your husband didn't want you to wear the bracelet?"

"Chassi, please—"

Pissy. Okay, now she was pissy. Well, if she wasn't going to tell her, she wasn't going to tell her, but it certainly was ludicrous, you start a conversation about something and then—

"We were talking about Rome."

"I wasn't." Just like that, she thinks you can flip back.

"Last time. We were talking about the restaurant. Please concentrate."

She can just talk about it herself. Chassi settled back on the couch, away from the doctor, her eyes.

"What did you mean when you said you couldn't be your mother's girlfriend?"

A wave of dizzy. But here and gone.

Creak went the swivel.

I don't care, turn circles in your chair. You too can be dizzy—

"Chassi?"

"What?" Let her wait.

Bracelets.

She had lines to learn, she had camera tests, she had more important things to do than sit here and do the dance of the goddamn restaurant. Again. But she was dizzy, she couldn't shoot a picture if she was spinning.

"Chassi?"

"What?" No way.

"In the restaurant, what did you and your mother talk about?"

"What?"

"Please concentrate, we were talking about Rome."

"We were talking about Vietnam."

"That was my mistake."

"Why does it have to be a mistake? It's relevant."

"It's not relevant."

She sat up, turned to her. "Goddamn it, it's what I'm about to do. Don't you see that?" Oh, Jesus, no, spinning again, she was going to fall off the couch. She shut her eyes, covered her face with her hands. "It's my work, it's about the movie—don't you see?—and I have to be ready and I'm having a hard time, and you could help me, why don't you want to help me?" If she concentrated, kept her eyes shut, her feet flat.

Swish of the legs, a jingle.

She steadied some, a little . . . okay . . .

Quiet.

"How can I help you?" Eleanor said. "You're having a hard time with this movie. Do you know why?"

Okay . . . open your eyes . . . you can do it . . . not so bad. "Can I talk to your husband about the war?"

The soft face of Eleanor, pieces of her through the shadows of Chassi's fingers, melting, it seemed, melting and softer, this woman who was probably the same age as her mother, if her mother— It occurred then to Chassi, then, at that exact moment; she spread her fingers to the sides of her eyes. "How old are you?" she said to Dr. Costello.

"Are you all right?"

"Are you the same age as my mother?"

"I don't know," Eleanor said. "Are you dizzy?"

"I was."

"Tell me how you feel about this movie."

Staying put, Chassi's chin propped in her palms, elbows on her knees, sitting forward on the couch; they didn't speak for a few moments.

"My mind is racing," Chassi said.

"Tell me."

"My mother's face if she were here today, if she were your age now instead of the age she was . . . what it would be like, what I would say to her. God, what a mess. Please, Dr. Costello, may I talk to your husband about Vietnam?"

A moment, half a moment, and then Eleanor said, face-to-face, "Chassi, my husband is dead."

"Just go out with him," Eleanor's best friend, Iva, had said, "you don't have to marry him. Anyway, he's not your type." Eleanor studied him sitting at the tiny table of the noisy Greek diner as she returned from the ladies' room. James George Costello, all six-four of him, stuffed into the cracked red booth. His knees didn't fit, he didn't seem to be sitting as much as he seemed to be wedged. Stick-straight brown hair, warm brown eyes with astounding lashes that any girl would have killed for, and big. Big all over. Big arms with big muscles that she'd felt as she'd brushed against him when he'd held open the door. Big shoulders, big hands on the menu, big fingers opening the tiny packets of sugar and moving the spoon, big feet sticking out into the aisle in gigantic black shoes.

A waiter balancing three Reubens dodged Eleanor where she lingered, half hidden by the cold case. James George Costello through the streaked glass, on the other side of the cantaloupe halves and the squares of red Jell-O and mounds of rice pudding and pitchers of iced tea. She had picked at her salad, he'd relished every bite of the hot roast beef open-face with extra gravy and mashed. He'd had two glasses of milk, a cup of coffee, and a wedge of deep-dish blueberry à la mode, she'd barely finished her Coke. He wasn't anything Eleanor had ever known. He wasn't driven, he wasn't an intellectual, he wasn't Jewish, he wasn't Upper East Side or the Village, he wasn't city at all. He was shy, conservative, old-fashioned. He was Italian. He was Brooklyn. He was street. He loved his mother, he said, even though she was a little pushy, he added, carefully choosing the word "pushy," and he grinned. His dad was dead. He was the one and only, he said, no brothers or sisters. He was living with his mom in his old room where his feet hung off the bed, he said, for now. His smile was like Christmas. He was working for his uncle Vinny and his uncle Frank, his dad's brothers, at the place. The place turned out to be a discount house for small electrical appliances: blenders, irons, toasters, he said, Mixmasters, stuff like that. He was managing the warehouse but it wouldn't be for long. His words were thick with Brooklyn, and when he talked he used his hands. Great, sweeping gestures, his head bent in concentration, his brown eyes intent. He wasn't sure what he was going to do, he'd said when she'd asked him, it's not like he had a particular plan. He liked it outside. He wasn't quite sure what to do with that; he laughed—not a lot of forest ranger jobs in New York, but he wanted a job outside where he could taste the sun. Or the rain, the snow, whatever was out there. If he had a horse he could drive a hansom cab, he said, and Eleanor melted a little in the booth, toppled by a picture in her head of him in a top hat, pulling the reins on a brown horse that matched those eyes. She felt silly all of a sudden, rearranged herself on the sticky leather, put a paper napkin under her glass. He weighed his words, he was careful. He cared about things. He was sensitive and kind, which wasn't a word Eleanor had ever thought of before for someone in their age group. He had been to war, twenty-six and already back from a war, which was shocking to Eleanor and not something, he said when she asked him, he thought about much. Except in dreams, he added softly, and then he shrugged. The sweetest lift of those big shoulders, the angle of his chin, his warm eyes, and Eleanor was filled with what he must have seen and didn't know what to say, and she touched his arm with her fingers and he covered her hand with his big one and she didn't even know him, but in that tiny second of nothing, that insignificant second that passed between them in a crowded coffee shop on Sixty-fourth and Madison, in the middle of screaming Greek waiters and people glaring at them for the little booth, Eleanor decided James George Costello was very much her type, that her friend Iva was wrong.

She never got over thinking that, she never tired of him, she never lost interest, no matter the years, no matter the ups and downs of their marriage. They walked out of the Viand coffee shop together and stayed that way until the morning he left to go sailing, leaning in, the smell of coffee and soap from his shower, his hand warm on her backside through the comforter, his lips on her neck. Eleanor had never expected Jimmy to die before her, the truth was she'd never expected Jimmy to die at all. She walked across her office, threw the yogurt top into the wastebasket and sat in her chair. The therapist doesn't tell the patient sacred information about the therapist, the therapist doesn't tell that her husband is dead. Do not collect $200, go immediately to shrink jail. Eleanor dunked the banana into the yogurt, tried to catch some of the peaches on the bottom, but it broke off partway up. What was so hard about remembering to buy plastic spoons? She could even grab some with her cappuccino from the coffee place. She poked her finger into the yogurt, pushed at the tip of the banana and it sank. Great. In order to get the banana she would have to stick her hand in.

What had possessed her? It had started with the pants, schmoozing with Chassi as if they were friends, talking about pants, telling her things she'd done when she was young, things she'd never even told Caroline. She knew better, she didn't do that, didn't talk to her patients about personal things. Jimmy and the war and bell-bottoms, she hadn't just fallen off the shrink truck. So, what had happened? What was she—lonely, talking to Chassi as if she were a friend?

As if she were a daughter. Eleanor's breath caught. Is that what it was?

It had seemed so cold to not tell her the truth, to not answer the girl when she'd asked to talk to Jimmy about the war, so cold to say no without the why of it. Her maternal instincts told her to speak.

Is that what it was, is that what had gotten the best of her, slipped through? Eleanor sat with her fingers dipped in the cold yogurt. Maternal instincts. She had maternal instincts even if she'd failed as a mother. "Mom, I don't want to talk to you, I don't want to see you." What more did she need for proof?

Okay. The truth was, she had to watch herself, she had to be careful not to make a transference, a substitution, a switch. She'd lost her place and she wouldn't do it again, she wouldn't let herself. Talking to Chassi as if she were a daughter; she wouldn't do it again.

She took her boots off her desk, swiveled toward the windows. She wasn't Chassi's mother, couldn't be Chassi's mother, didn't want to be Chassi's mother. Eleanor caught the piece of banana in her fingers and raised it to her lips.

The truth was, she wanted to be Caroline's mother. The truth was, she didn't know how.

CHAPTER 19

First there was: "Well, I could just sit there and rot," Kitty Ray said, "sit there and look at that phone, it doesn't ring, it doesn't do nothin'," she went on, rummaging through a pale pink train case that she had gotten as a gift for her high school graduation, removing things and placing them all around her on Ionie's new oatmeal-silk couch.

"Mama." She had only been in Ionie's new place maybe forty minutes, tops.

"And talkin' to your daddy is like battin' your head against a wall, he's about as understandin' as the dog; he says, 'Kitty Ray, you better get outta that house, stop lookin' at the g.d. phone,' and then last week after I left you three messages about my airplane and you didn't have the courtesy, common courtesy, to call me back, which is not the way I raised you, missy, and here I have to call you again and you say, 'Mama, I can't talk to you now,' well, your daddy says to me, 'Kitty Ray, she ain't got time to talk to you, you shouldn't even go.' "

Remorse, shame, contrition, guilt—the words cut painfully across Ionie's brain like nail heads, along with her bottom lip between her teeth. "Mama, I had a photo shoot."

"Well, it's always somethin', isn't it?" Tubes and jars and pieces of Scotch-taped folded paper towels flooded her lap and the pillows.

Which was worse—hurting your mother's feelings or watching your mother stain your new couch? "What *are* you looking for?" Ionie said.

Kitty Ray looked up, her lips pressed into thin strips, deep up-and-down lines between her eyebrows; she frowned at her daughter. "Well, I don't know. I'm so riled up here that I don't know."

Ionie laughed out loud. There was no way to stop it, it just flew right out. She said, "You're looking for your cigarettes, aren't you?" and Kitty Ray said, "I don't smoke," and Ionie fell off the new oatmeal-and-taupe-striped club chair. You couldn't help but laugh, you couldn't help but fall into the comfort of it, the satisfying good-and-bad of it, this ancient mother-daughter dance, wanting to throttle the one who comes before you and at the same time embrace her.

Kitty Ray threw one of the folded taped paper towels at her daughter, laughing on the floor. "You stop that right now."

"What is this?" Ionie said, recovering, fingering the soft, neat package that had dropped on her chest.

"Oh, never mind."

"What is it? Mama, come on."

"Oh, herbs," Kitty Ray said and tucked a loose pale-strawberry-blonde wisp back up into her French roll.

"I can't believe it," Ionie said, sitting up, lifting the tape from the paper. "You're into herbs?"

"Oh, your aunt Dorothy went to some meeting for this women's group about the 'this and the that' of the menopause, they're supposed to help you with your nerves."

Ionie laughed. "They're not working."

"Ionie, give me those."

Herbs, her mother was into Chinese herbs, a nineties woman with nineties herbs tucked into a pale pink train case from 1954. "There's no stopping you," she said to her mother.

"Well, I should hope not," Kitty Ray said. "Give me those."

Then: She thought the guest house was too white. After a slow inspection, "Honey, did it cost more for colors?" was her review. She was in every drawer and every cabinet, moved her hand along every bit of molding and ran every window up and down. She disapproved of, and not necessarily in that order: the electric stove—"We'll just have it changed to gas"; the difficult faucets in the bathroom—"Well, I don't know, maybe I just have arthritis"; and the blond hardwood floors—"Don't you think wall-to-wall is more *prestigious*?" She approved of: the large closets—"bigger than your aunt Dorothy's house in Dallas and you know how much they paid"; the kitchen—"Plants will just thrive along this window ledge here"; and the trash compactor—"Granny would have loved one of these." She was a little confused about the fact that it was really not an apartment but a guest house: "Do you have to be friends with them?" "What about your comings and goings?" "Are they nice people?" "What do they do?" She was reassured when Ionie told her that Dr. and Mrs. Fox were older and retired, that they were friends of a friend who knew a friend. Ionie did not give details: that she had lucked out on finding the place with the help of Jones.

Her mother had come and was ready to take on Hollywood, with her pale pink train case and her pale blue pants suit, with her T-shirt emblazoned with a sequined golden retriever (didn't it look just like her Sparky?), and her white Reeboks with the black stirrup pants that she wore for her walk. She was ready to see them make a movie—"It couldn't be much different than when I saw Channel 2 cover that fire in Lubbock"; and go to that Spago place that she'd read about in the *Enquirer*; and meet Chassi Jennings and her daddy and see their house—"I hear they have a picture of her, Sally Brash, may she rest in peace, in their living room that's the size of the Taj Mahal." Ionie couldn't decide if it was better to pretend she didn't know her mother or to leave town.

After three days of sight-seeing, after a trip to Universal Studios where she had dropped her mother off and picked her up six hours later—"I don't need you to go with me, I'm just fine by myself"; and a trip to the front of Mann's Chinese Theatre where Kitty Ray put her shoes into each and every cement footprint, including John Wayne's—"Those were boots, I'm sure, not shoes"; and a trip to the beach where she'd actually watched her mother slip off the stirrups, delicately roll her pants to the ankles and walk partway into the water, standing strong as the waves splashed around her calves. On the fourth day,

Ionie braved it out for a few hours, leaving her mother at home—"You just go on about your business, I don't need you to baby-sit me."

"Drinks at Saul Jennings's," said Kitty Ray, beaming at Ionie from the couch when she returned. Ionie shut the front door, dropped her tote, put down her water bottle, and wiped her face with the sweatshirt sleeve. How had her mother moved the couch all by herself? When she'd left, it was facing the windows. And where did she get the camellias in that vase? "Mama, I asked you to let the machine answer."

"Well, I was standin' right here, it just goes against everything to not pick up a ringing phone." She fluttered the scrap of paper in her hand at Ionie. "And I certainly know how to take a message, I took messages for more than fifteen years at Milvain, Hall, and Thompson, I'll have you know."

"I do know."

Kitty Ray lifted her chin. "Well, I'm thrilled to be invited."

Oh, Jesus. "How do you know you're invited?"

"Well, that's what she said, that she would clear it, but she was sure it would be fine. After all, I am stayin' here, it doesn't look nice to just rush off and leave your mama, it's not like it's a business meeting, it's drinks."

"Who 'she'?"

"The *she* who called, Ionie, the lovely young woman who works for your agent. Cheryl is her name."

"Ah, the tone," Ionie mumbled.

"What? She was lovely and very efficient, it seemed to me, especially with all those problems, and that reminds me, you need notepads by your telephones, I had to look all over to find somethin' to write on. I'll pick some up for you at Neiman's when I get my hair done. It's a shame about her and that boy, isn't it?"

Oh, Jesus. The tone had a beau. Ionie picked up the water bottle and took a long swig. "What boy?"

"The boy who wants to come back, the one who's on drugs even though she says he's been clean for three weeks. I told her all about Daddy's cousin Earl and the drinking, how you just can't trust them no matter what they say." She smirked. "It's amazin' to me how you young people think compulsive-obsessive behavior belongs to the nineties, as if those of us from back then don't know our you-know-whats from a hole in the ground."

Maybe she wasn't still damp from yoga, maybe she was damp because she was about to pass out. "When are you getting your hair done?"

"Well, before the drinks. And you don't have to worry about taking me, I refuse to be a bother, there's a bus I can take that goes right down Sunset, I get off at"—she studied another scrap of paper—"Bedford Drive, walk down to Wilshire, and it's right there." She beamed again. "The operator at Neiman's was very helpful; of course, they always go out of their way."

It was too much. The couch, the conversation with the tone, the invitation to Saul Jennings . . .

"Mrs. Fox and I cut these camellias after we had lunch in her garden. Aren't they beautiful? Such a nice woman, what a shame she couldn't have children. Ionie, did you know her husband was head of pediatrics at that big Jewish hospital they have here, for over thirty years?"

There was absolutely no leaving her alone anymore. For all Ionie knew, Kitty Ray had promised Mr. and Mrs. Fox her firstborn. She studied the tall, wiry woman with the spray-fixed strawberry blonde hairdo smiling at her, had another swig of the water, and sat down.

Then, there were the drinks at Saul Jennings's: Kitty Ray didn't understand why anyone would serve those dreadful little pickles—"Well, I don't care if they are French, since when do pickles go with drinks?"—or the fresh mozzarella dribbled with olive oil—with pursed lips she hissed to Ionie, "It doesn't even taste like cheese." She had them scurrying in the kitchen to find a recipe for a whiskey sour, they'd probably had to send a runner for maraschino cherries, and after all that, she'd tilted her head at the waiter in Saul Jennings's living room and said, "Oh, no, dear, I wanted it with ice." She patted Chassi's arm when she met her, gushed, "Oh, my, you look so like your mother, rest in peace," a sheen of tears in her eyes. She picked up every framed photograph on the piano and put it down again in a slightly different place, Ionie was certain, and then she sat on the bench next to the man playing the piano and asked him if he knew the song "Many a New Day" from *Oklahoma!*, which she confessed to him she had sung in the school play. Jones gave Ionie a reassuring smile from across the room, she made a face as if she were about to fall down. And then Kitty Ray shyly suggested to Mr. Jennings that she would love to see the *whole* house, "a tour," was how she put it, practically flapping her eyelashes, "the grand tour." Ionie staggered as if she'd been slapped. "Mama, I don't think that Mr. Jennings—" And before she could get another word out Saul Jennings rose to his feet as if he were 007, extended his arm to Kitty Ray, and said, "Absolutely, madam, the grand tour, including the pool and cabana, and call me Saul."

"It's fine," Jones said to Ionie.

"I'm going to walk into traffic," she said with her teeth clenched.

"You'll have a very hard time, there's not a lot of it in Holmby Hills."

She exhaled.

"It's fine," he said again and touched her arm with his fingertips. It was so hard to know when a touch was normal. A touch between friends was just a touch between friends and as far as everyone knew she and Jones had done the television movie together but if you'd done a television movie together would you touch the other person's arm?

From behind them a voice said, "Hey, what's goin' on?" Ionie spun around to Robby Peroni's crooked smile.

"Hi," he said.

"Oh, hi."

"What's up, Jones?"

The two men shook hands.

"Your mother's the bomb," Peroni said to Ionie.

"I was just telling her," said Jones.

And Ionie laughed; she had no way of knowing what the night would bring.

"You were flirting with him, I was waiting for you across the room, you never looked up."

"Jones, please."

Hiding, the din of the party noise two rooms away, in their ears. "I wanted to hit you. Me. Hit. You." A space in between each word, a sharp space. He was white and clipped. "I wanted to hit him."

"Someone is going to hear us," she said.

Side by side in the hall by the bathroom, as if they were—waiting to go in? Go out? Had accidentally met there? Were talking? About what?

"Please," she said.

"I can't stand it."

"Jones—"

His hand on her—"I didn't bring her, I didn't want her here." His eyes—"And I don't want to go home." Hard fingers making marks on her arm. "Jesus," he hissed.

A woman with a tray nodded as she went by; Ionie gave her a big smile.

"Are you going out with Peroni?"

"No." Would she? Would she if he asked her? Did she want to? Yes. No. Yes.

"I love you," he said.

She didn't look at him.

"I love you," Jones said again.

"That man is married," Kitty Ray said.

Ionie kicked off the other shoe and looked up. "What man?"

"You know what man, and you certainly know what I'm talkin' about and I certainly did not raise you to go after another's woman's husband, let me make that clear."

Oh, God, oh, Jesus. "Mama—"

"You had better stop what you're doin' before I'm ashamed to be your mama." She glared at Ionie, the flush of the party now drained from her face. She turned her back to her daughter, walked into the kitchen. Ionie stood where she was. The refrigerator door opening, jars and things being put on the countertop, the slide of a drawer. Ionie's hand on the wall, cold stucco. Don't move, just stay here, don't move.

Kitty Ray in the doorway, waving a package of bologna."What do you think? I don't have eyes?" and then she left and then she returned, like a jump cut, like Jones had taught her, *when you have two masters and you cut from one to one*; what a thing to think of, her mother back in the doorway cradling the bread. "Who did you think you were kidding?" Such despair, such pain, such anger, Ionie took a breath, tried to swallow. Kitty Ray turned on her heel.

Cold sweat, the chill of cold sweat, a bead of it running down her side surely staining the olive silk of the dress, the sweat of being six years old and getting caught in the lie and the bile of peanut butter and chocolate milk backing up in her throat and the smack of Kitty Ray's hand and, oh, if only it would be that easy, because this time Ionie knew there would only be the smack of her words.

She steadied herself; there was nowhere to go, there was nothing to do but do it. She crossed the room, stood in the doorway of the kitchen. The rip of cellophane, the clink of the knife hitting the inside of the mayonnaise jar, Ionie stood there; Kitty Ray didn't lift her head.

She moved around her mother, folded into a kitchen chair.

"It doesn't matter to me if you love him," the mother said to the daughter, "not one bit."

Don't say anything.

"Does he have children?"

"Two boys."

Disgust across her mother's face, as vivid as the stink of bologna. Kitty Ray placed the second piece of bread across the lunch meat, ran the knife through the sandwich on a diagonal, and pushed one half across the cutting board toward her daughter. "Here."

"I'm not hungry."

"Yes, you are. You only ate some of those pickles they had and two shrimps. Probably couldn't eat from all the play-acting."

Ionie picked up the triangle. She was suddenly starving, she took a big bite.

"It's a dangerous game, what you're playin'."

"I didn't plan it."

"Oh, explain it to me then—was it an accident? He accidentally found you . . . where? In his arms?"

"He loves me."

"Oh, for goodness sakes, you sound like a country song, and I don't care." Kitty Ray went to the refrigerator, took out a diet Pepsi and popped the tab. She set it on the table in front of her daughter. "He's a married man, that's all there is to it, he's a married man." She stood there, picked up the other half of the sandwich and put it down. "You have a whole world of men out there, how could you?"

There was no way to explain it. How it had come this far, how tangled, how he looked at her, what he said. Ionie took a long drink of the soda. "There's no way you could understand."

"Try me."

"You live in another world."

"What? In the sticks? I'm not sophisticated enough to understand adultery?"

"That's not what I'm saying. You're different from me, your life is different from mine—"

"It certainly is."

"It just happened, we were together, and—"

"Do you ever think about her?"

Sick in the pit of her stomach.

"How she feels?" Her mother's eyes—"You don't, do you?"

Clammy. "I do sometimes."

"Then how could you?"

"I don't know."

"Yes, you do. Tell me how."

Hot. Red. She could feel it. What right did she have to ask? She wasn't a child anymore, what right did her mother have to mess around in her life? "What do you want to know? Details?"

"That's right, tell me. I'm only familiar with the other side." Blotched pink circles of color high on her mother's white face.

"For crissakes, I'm not telling you any details."

"You watch your mouth, watch how you take the Lord's name."

"Don't start with me, Mama," and then it hit her, no, not a hit, a sinking, sick feeling that she wanted to go away, her look to her mother. "What did you say? What did you say about being familiar with the other side?"

"Oh, Ionie, I'm so disappointed in you."

Her mother's eyes, the slam in Ionie's gut and Kitty Ray's eyes.

"When you were seven your daddy started an affair with his bookkeeper that lasted four years." Ionie's mother lifted her chin, her look to her daughter. "That's right. It's always different, isn't it? When it happens to you."

Her father in bed with someone other than her mother. Oh, Jesus. Ionie turned over. She couldn't picture it, she didn't want to, didn't want to picture her father in bed with her mother, much less with somebody else. And Kitty Ray crying that it was a mistake, that she shouldn't have told her, that she just got riled up, carried away. That she never should have told her what her daddy had done, she shouldn't have talked to her as if she were a girlfriend, she just got carried away.

Ionie punched the pillow. How could he? When she was seven, what did she remember from when she was seven? Nothing. Just being a little girl. She punched the pillow, smoothed the cotton under her cheek. Daddy kissing Mommy in the kitchen, the bowl between them in her arms. "Ionie, you want to lick these beaters, you better get in here now." The slam of the screen door and she made a beeline for the kitchen in her new sandals with the skinny straps. How could he? Jesus. Her very own daddy. Her very own mommy. The distress in her mother's eyes as she looked to her very own daughter and said, "How could you?" about Jones.

Fooling around with a married man. Fooling, fooling. Having an affair. Other people's words. Other people's, not hers. She pushed at the pillow, changed her legs on the sheet. This wasn't fooling. Fooling meant not being real, not from the heart, this wasn't fooling. She loved Jones. She did. Dawn seeping through the curtains, that gray over there around the edges of the window, that was dawn. She had to close her eyes, she had to stop thinking about this, she had to get some sleep. Ionie sighed, turned over, away from the window of morning, toward the wall.

How had it happened? What could she say to that? She wasn't even sure she knew. Okay, she slept with him. She wanted him to help her and she slept with him, but she also cared. Did that make her a bad person? He was sweet and kind, she was charmed by him from the very beginning, she just never thought about the end. After all, women have needs too. Wants and needs. After all. Ionie pushed at the pillow. The problem was, Jones fell for her. Hard. And the whole thing had run away with itself, snowballed across some invisible line into some kind of commitment that she didn't want and hadn't asked for and now . . .

Sadness changing his face, the slump of his shoulders. "I don't want to go home," he'd said at Saul's, and what could she say? Come live with me? That wasn't what she wanted, not deep down. She loved Jones, but . . . She slid her hand under the pillowcase and unclenched her fist. Granny had said, "Let's call a spade a you-know-what," and Ionie knew what was a spade, she knew deep down: She didn't love Jones for forever. "Look to yourself, baby girl," Granny had said. Ionie rolled to the other side. There was no forever with

Jones in her dreams. No prayers that he would ever leave Linda. No prayers, no wishes, none of that. Just fear.

She flipped the pillow, turned it to the cool. Just fear. Jones at the door with suitcases, hopeful eyes, arms wide, and what would she say to him then? If that happened—what would she say? I'm sorry, I made a mistake . . . oops, I wasn't thinking . . . you better go on back home. She couldn't do that to him. How could she do that to him? *Look to yourself, Ionie*. She had no pretty pictures of Jones living with her in the tiny guest house, Jones's boys joining them every weekend and a month in the summer, taking them to McDonald's and dropping them at soccer practice and cutting their crusts off or whatever you did. She wasn't ready to raise two boys, she didn't even want to; Jones showing up would ruin everything, she had a life to live.

Ionie rolled onto her back. Morning was definitely lighting the room. She pulled the comforter up over her face, felt her breath come back at her. Jones in the bed next to her, Jones over the coffee cup rim, Jones cutting the Sunday night chicken, in the shower, in the car, in the kitchen. Jones on Saturday and next Tuesday and then September and then December and then next year. That wasn't what she wanted. By next year she could be a rising star, by next year she could be a somebody, the movie would be out and her life could change. It would change. And what would she do with him then?

She pushed the comforter off her face, tucked the softness under her chin.

She hadn't made him any promises. She hadn't said please marry me, please live with me, please anything. So what did he want from her?

Ionie concentrated. It was clear to her, suddenly and horribly clear to her, incongruous really, because in some cockeyed way she had to face all of this because of her mother. Absurd even, but suddenly clear, as she closed her eyes and tried to breathe evenly, that she had to stop it, she had to break it off with Jones.

CHAPTER 20

"Take a moment," Ionie said to Chassi, "and center . . . and relax."

Cross-legged on thin rubber mats the same purple as Chassi's leotard, Ionie sat across from her and breathed. They did the sun salute, hands together and up, "up, up," she persuaded, leaning forward and then bending, their heads down to their knees. Ionie's head, that is, Chassi's head didn't quite reach. "How long have you been doing this?" "Forever," Ionie said, grinning through the tumble of red hair. They did the cobra, the cat, the downward dog. "Even Stanislavsky wasn't this many animals," Ionie drawled. They did something that Chassi couldn't remember the name of where they stretched forward and moved their hands "like stringing pearls." They did a triangle pose, the two of them making triangles of their bodies across the wide stripes of sun streaming through Saul Jennings's den. "That's good, that's good," Ionie coaxed, pushing Chassi's leg into position with a firm hand. When they did the one where they held their ankles in a fan and then hooked the right leg behind the left, or maybe it was supposed to be the left leg behind the right, or maybe she hadn't been listening, Chassi crashed to the floor. When they did the relaxation at the end lying on their backs with their arms and legs spread and stretched and open, Ionie fell asleep with a soft snore. Chassi loved it.

. . .

"Yoga, schmoga," Saul had said.

"Dad—"

The clink of ice cubes against crystal, he'd taken a sip of his scotch, eyed her from his wing chair. "So, what does it do for you?"

"It helps you find your center."

"I could have told you that, it's in your middle."

"Dad—"

"Okay, okay."

"She can do this, huh? The *drink of water*?"

Chassi had made a playful punch at his shoulder. "Dad, you have to stop calling her that."

"Ionie, Ionie, I know."

"She says it gives you greater focus, calms you down."

"Since when do you need calming?"

"You know, for stress?"

"Chassi, sweetheart, your life is a cakewalk. What do you know from stress?"

What did she know from stress? Why did he think she was still going to Dr. Costello? Chassi turned away from the jets of water pummeling her face and shut off the shower. Of course, he was probably only thinking about the picture, he'd been to Manila twice with Peroni to lock down some locations, it was already the second week in July. She pushed open the glass door and reached for the towel.

She had been dizzy again, that day talking with Ionie in the garden, and every now and then, and it wouldn't add up. No matter how she tried to pinpoint what set it off, it was too soft to nail; it was something about the picture and then it wasn't, and something about her mother and then it wasn't; none of it made sense—getting dizzy in the middle of camera tests, camera tests for hair, for makeup, typical, normal—why would she get dizzy then? Chassi lifted the hair dryer from the drawer. She couldn't worry about it, she felt fine now.

• • •

That was the third time Ionie had come to the house to do yoga. They'd gone twice to a class on Robertson but there were too many eyes. *Oh, let's look at the movie star and pretend like we're not.* Chassi had asked Ionie if she'd come to the house and teach her, could she just make a fool of herself at home?

Chassi leveled her eyes at herself in the wall of bathroom mirrors, took stock. Beige. Beige hair, beige skin, beige person. Okay, nice eyes. Normal body, maybe too thin, but just normal. A normal beige movie star. But she certainly didn't look anything like her mother. She ruffled her hair with the hot blast from the dryer, rolled a thick hunk around the brush. Not anything like her mother, not her face, her body, her hair—that's how the discussion had begun. Ionie was talking about her mother—who had just gone back to Texas—how strong she was, and Chassi had commented that Kitty Ray looked kind of wiry but she certainly didn't look strong.

Ionie laughed. "That's the steel they talk about, that wire, that's what they mean when they say 'steel magnolia,' honey. It wasn't just the title of a book. Southern women are tough cookies, no matter how they look."

Chassi said Ionie looked like her mother, a longer, leaner version of her mother.

"I do?" Ionie's eyes big, a strawberry between her teeth. "I look like Kitty Ray?"

"Uh-huh."

"Well, at least I don't dress like her, she won't give up those stirrup pants for anything." Ionie grinned. "You know, in Texas the boys used to say, 'Just check out the mother and you'll know what the daughter will look like in twenty years.' "

"I don't look anything like my mother," Chassi said.

"Sure you do."

"I don't."

"Well, it's a resemblance, not an actual lookalike," Ionie said, reaching for the bowl. "You're gonna have to get me away from this whipped cream."

"I've never seen it," Chassi said, "when I look at myself, I mean."

"You have her light. Of course, I only saw her in the movies. She was a looker," Ionie said, raising her eyes from the berries. "I mean, is that all right to say?"

The sun was good and the sky was clear blue and a hummingbird was doing a dance in front of them in and out of the orange blossoms. The two of them stretched across two thickly padded dark green lounges in the shade of Saul's garden, peaceful after yoga, picking at a huge bowl of strawberries, Ionie dredging them with brown sugar and cream, Chassi dunking them in cold tea.

"I liked your mother," Chassi said.

"She talked her head off about you, spent about eighty-three dollars on the phone with my daddy in Tyler, tellin' him all about the cocktail party and how you even took her up to see your room."

They were quiet. Ionie licked some whipped cream off her finger. "I thought she'd never leave."

Chassi looked up from her tea. "Are you serious?"

"Only a little."

"I can't imagine what it's like to have your mother around when you're a grown-up," Chassi said.

"It's hell." Ionie laughed, looked at Chassi. "Do you remember your mother?" She clapped her fingers at the edge of her lips. "Is it out of line for me to ask you that?"

"No. I remember her very well, I was twelve when she died."

"God, when I was twelve, Kitty Ray and I nearly strangled each other." Chassi laughed. "I'm not kidding," Ionie said. "I had discovered boys. And everything good that went along with boys: cigarettes and boys, convertibles and boys, beer and boys . . ."

"But you get along now."

"Pretty much. Like I said, she's tough, a steel magnolia."

Chassi looked at her. "But so are you."

Ionie smiled. "Am I?" She took a long drink of her tea. "Well, you have to be tough to be an actress."

"Did your mother ever want to be an actress?"

"No way. Strictly a businesswoman, Kitty Ray."

Chassi let a strawberry drop into her tea, rubbed a piece of mint around the rim of her glass, took a drink. "Did you always want to be an actress?"

"Since I could stand," Ionie said. "I didn't even know what acting meant, I just knew I wanted to be in front of the curtain, in front of the people. I never wanted to do anything else."

Chassi took another drink.

"I guess I'd do anything to be an actress," Ionie said.

"You would?"

"Well, within reason. I wouldn't shoot anybody." She ate another berry, stretched her arms up over her head, tousled the waves of red hair. "Well, maybe—" A flash of the eyes to Chassi, then "I'm kidding." Ionie stretched long on the chaise and gave a big sigh. "You sure are lucky," she said.

Chassi looked up.

"The way you fell into it, never had to go through the torture or the rejection."

"No."

"The auditions, the waiting, the praying, the hoping—you don't even know what that's like. Did your mother?"

"No, I don't think so."

Chassi blew the last hunk of hair dry now, studied her face in the bathroom mirrors to see if she could see any of her mother; her thighs cold up against the tile, she pulled the hair back hard with the brush.

• • •

TWO DEER WERE EATING the roses off Eleanor's fence, standing poised against the green and brown of the mountain, just munching away. She didn't do anything, didn't make a noise to stop them, just watched. Sunday, another horrible Sunday. Eleanor leaned her chin in her hand. Jimmy had died on a Sunday, everything bad happened on a Sunday. The letters of the crossword blurred. She downed the aspirins, put down the pen.

"Caroline, what are you doing?" That was a Sunday, indeed, another dreaded Sunday.

"I'm making an altar for Daddy," her daughter had said.

Dumbfounded, Eleanor had moved farther into the room, put down her keys, her purse. "You're what?"

A month after the funeral. Caroline in the house with her, sleeping most of the time in the house with her, but against her will, that much was clear. Back and forth to her apartment, shuffling clothes, and Eleanor knew she should let her go, release her, but the thought of being alone in the house, the thought of being forever alone in the house, because that's how she felt, that no one would ever come home again. One steak in the pan, one baked potato, one plate dripping in the drainer, one towel, one toothbrush—the thought of it so terrifying. What had Caroline said?

"An altar?"

"To help him go."

Sweet Jesus.

"You have to release him, Mom."

Eleanor's face hot. "What are you saying to me? I'll never release your father."

"Hey, I didn't mean forget him or anything, just cut him from our energetic field. He has to make the transition to move on, you have to help him go."

The same Sunday, horrible Sunday of her fit in the store.

Pushing herself to get out, she had driven to the mall. Caroline, nowhere to be found when she got up, Eleanor had shuffled around with her coffee cup. Get out. You're smart, you know better than this, don't sit here listening for his footstep, his "Hey, El." She'd thrown on some clothes, driven to the mall.

Store after store, drifting, not even looking, not even knowing where she was and then standing there at that register in the men's department, the two shirts in her arms pushed up against her chest. Two polo shirts, just like he liked, on sale. Soft knit and short sleeves, a navy and a green. Proud of her find, holding out her credit card. "Oh, he'll love those," the saleswoman had said. All gushy and friendly. *He'll love those*. She didn't even know him, didn't know Jimmy, some nerve to be all warm and friendly and say such a thing. How could she say that to Eleanor? How could he love them? He was dead.

Smacked over the head with the knowledge of it, staggering with the knowledge of it, the way he must have staggered when he'd fallen in. She could see it so clearly in her mind's eye, Jimmy dropping over the side of the boat. Dropping the shirts as he had dropped into the water. Ashen, she guessed from the reaction of the saleswoman. Ashen, weak, her bad knee buckling and toppling her to the floor. And what was she doing in the men's department, what was she doing buying shirts when her husband was dead? A fool, slumped on the floor of Macy's having a crying fit. And now this.

Caroline's smile. "See?"

A piece of fabric—what was that? Oh, yes, she remembered, a piece of something from Bali or somewhere that Sis had brought back from one of her trips. A scrap of fabric she'd brought them and Eleanor had thought, Well, what the hell am I supposed to do with that, and Caroline had said, "I'll take it, Mom, I want it for my room." Her scavenger daughter. Eleanor's eyes focused on the square of purple-and-lavender silk with a dull gold-green thread across the rickety table Caroline had brought down from her room. And sitting on the fabric, three roses floating in a bowl. Three lavender roses she must have cut from the fence, in the Peter Rabbit bowl that Jimmy had bought for her first cereal, her first mashed banana, her first tomato sauce. The tiny spoon in his huge hand, the baby across from him in the high chair laughing at his antics, her eyes big. Incense burning next to the bowl and next to that a candle, one of those big church candles like they sold in the grocery stores in the Spanish section with an angel painted on the glass, an angel with a blue-flamed sword, as if that could help him now. An altar to help her dead husband; she wanted to hit her child. A photograph of Jimmy holding Caroline when she was a baby. Look how big he was, look how he smiled, look how he held her like a football in the crook of his arm. How could he be dead? The sweet incense sickening her, Eleanor sat in the chair.

"See," Caroline said, "to help release him, so his spirit can go."

She didn't want his spirit to go, she wanted him back, she wanted him to hold her, she wanted to knock everything off the table. She was shaking. It went against everything she was holding on to, this altar to let him go.

"Take it down."

"What?"

"Take it down, take it out of my living room."

Caroline's eyes hard. "Then I'll put it in my room."

She couldn't speak, no air, no words.

Her daughter cradling the objects the way Jimmy had cradled her. "It always has to be your way, you don't even want to hear."

"No, I don't."

"You're holding him back."

"You bet I am."

Tears, the clatter of the bowl dropping, the roses falling to the floor. Caroline at her feet in front of her. "You're hurting him."

"Don't tell me about hurting him. You hurt him, you're the one who hurt your daddy."

"Is that what you want to do? Bring it all up? Everywhere I went wrong? Quitting school and running away with Jono and what else have you got, Mom? A list of everything I did?"

Trying to find air.

"I've changed, Mom."

Standing, shaking. "A bunch of New Age bullshit."

Her daughter's flushed face. "No matter what I do, it isn't good enough for you."

No breath in her chest.

"Why do you want me here?" Caroline on her knees in front of her. "If everything I do and say means nothing to you, why do you want me here?"

"I'm going upstairs." Pushing herself up from the chair, stepping gingerly around her, knowing if she stayed she'd slap her, Eleanor left the room.

• • •

"DID YOU STOP IT?" Kitty Ray said, her voice distinct and clear across the wire.

Pushing, it was the third time she'd asked this week. "I told him," Ionie said.

"You told him to go back to his wife?"

"I told him, Mama," she said back distinctly. She sat with the phone on the balcony of the guest house, her bare feet up on the rail. Mrs. Fox waved to her from the midst of the camellias. "Your friend is in her garden."

"What? What did you say?"

"I said Mrs. Fox is in her garden, she's wearing a big sun hat and green rubber hip boots, she looks like an ad."

"Don't try to change the subject."

Ionie laughed.

"You have static," Kitty Ray said.

"I sure do," Ionie said, "and I'm supposed to be somewhere, really, Mama, I gotta go."

"Ionie, wait a minute, did you go out with Mr. Peroni? Did he ask you?"

"I—"

"I think you should, he could do lots of things for you. It doesn't matter that he's not handsome, he's such an interestin' man. You have to always think about what you want, Ionie, what's best for your career."

"I'll call you later, I gotta go," Ionie said and clicked off the phone.

Ionie rocked on the chair legs, watched Mrs. Fox shuffle around her garden, then she picked up the pale blush nail polish and started on the other hand. She'd told Jones, she'd said they had to stop, said it couldn't continue, said she loved him but . . . but the telling didn't mean the ending because he didn't want it to end. Persistent phone calls of him saying how much he loved her, endless pleading—how he was in this way over his head, how he wouldn't be able to look at her when they started shooting, he wouldn't be able to look at her knowing that she didn't want to be with him anymore.

"Jones—"

"No, please, Ionie, not now."

Looming in the open doorway of her little guest house, the stooped silhouette of his bony frame caught against the dawn, she'd told him. Sleep in her eyes, hair across her face, clutching a sweatshirt to the front of her, Jones at the door pacing before the sun broke and of course she'd let him in and of course he'd caught her unawares, or maybe she was aware, because she *did* care, it wasn't as if she didn't care, and how could she hurt him, and it wasn't as if she had someone, the sweetness of him tentatively wrapping her up in his arms along with the coffeepot. The safety of Jones, the pure comfort. But she'd told him.

"You're my fantasy."

"But, Jones—"

"But nothing. We shoot in less than a month, we'll be in Manila. Together. Let's just see what happens, Ionie, please."

"You're supposed to be at the studio," she said.

"I love you." Sea Breeze and coffee.

"Jones—"

His lips, his hands, his fingers. "What time is your call?" His low sound.

"After lunch—me first, then Chassi."

"Big day for me," he said.

She blinked up at him. "You've done camera tests a billion times."

"I'm photographing you."

"You photographed me on the television thing."

His lips on her shoulder. "I didn't love you on the television thing."

"You didn't?"

She had told him, she had told him it was over but there he was. His hand tucking the comforter over his kiss and under her chin. Safe, warm, his fingers firmly grazing the length of her as he left the bed. "I'll see you this afternoon, my love," Jones said.

A soundstage, a floor, two chairs, a black backdrop. Two makeup artists, two hairdressers, two stand-ins, the costume designer, Ms. Marley, her assistant Bud, the set wardrobe mistress who would dress Ionie and Chassi, a full camera and lighting crew under the direction of Jones, and then Peroni, off to the side. Frowning, mumbling, technical talk of filters and diffusions and whether to tech the nurses' uniforms cool or warm. "It's too bright, Ruth," said Jones, and a 24 lens versus a 100, and Chassi's skin had more olive and Ionie's skin had more red, and the makeup man working with different tones of base, she could smell the sponges before they touched her skin. Stock and contrast and exposure, Chassi on the left and Ionie on the right, the stretch of Jones behind the camera, the way he curled into the lens, the way he bent his knees, the way he pulled up his chin.

Ionie making faces at Chassi while they blew her curls into straight sticks, kidding with Bud, trying to grab the light meter from the gaffer, tugging at the uniform—"I look pasty in white"—smiling into the lens, playing with her New York accent, crossing her eyes, licking tiny bits of chocolate glaze from the top of a doughnut, guzzling diet Coke, and then kissing Peroni behind the backdrop where he'd pulled her to him, the shock of his hands on her back out of nowhere, in the dark, in the hush, hot close up against her, tough and short up against her, young up against her. The shock, the heat, the breath, she could feel him hard up against her, she hadn't stopped him, why hadn't she stopped him, melting against him, and there was Jones.

Her face pulled back from Peroni's, lips wet, her pulse at the top of her chest, heart slamming, and Peroni tilted his head to the side, his eyes over her right shoulder looking at someone else, someone behind her, and he said, his arms still holding Ionie as if it were the most natural thing in the world, "Yeah? What's up? You need me, Jones?"

She had told him. Told him that it should be over, that it wasn't right, that it had to end. And she reminded herself that she had told him, oh, so many times when she saw the look on his face.

• • •

"WOULD YOU CHEAT on Blanca?"

"Whoa," Andrew said to Chassi, "what?"

"Would you cheat?"

She put her hand on his arm through the open window of the truck; he killed the motor, he was behind the wheel of Baudelio's red pickup. "Big-deal discussion, Chass, to have in a driveway."

She shrugged. He put his hand over her hand. "Are you saying me, now in time, or me as a man in general?"

"I didn't think it was so complicated."

"*Ay, Dios,* it's always complicated."

She made a face.

"I would with you"—he took a breath—"but you know that."

You could fall right into his eyes they were so deep.

"I thought you knew that," Andrew said.

She stood there, didn't say anything.

"Chass?"

"Ionie's having a thing with the cinematographer, he's married, older. Just a regular guy with two kids, nice, I've met his wife."

"Ionie told you?"

"No."

He ran his thumb across her knuckles.

"I can tell," she said.

She turned her hand over into his, palm to palm, encircling their fingers, the calluses, the mud from her mother's garden under his nails. It occurred to her that she'd known these hands forever.

"And?" he said.

Chassi inhaled. "I don't know." She frowned. "He's in love with her. You know, he looks at her all desperate."

"Yeah? Is she in love with him?"

"No, I don't think so," Chassi said.

"Poor jerk," Andew said. He squeezed her fingers. They stared at each other, he finally smiled. "What, Chass?"

"I don't know."

"It's not like it's the first time you've seen it."

"Yeah, I know."

"Hollywood, Hollywood. Don't you know the old joke?"

She shrugged.

"A single female movie star is having an affair with a married male movie star, goes to a party only to run into the guy's wife. Major confrontation. The wife says, 'How can you do this?,' and the movie star says, 'Hey, lady, if your husband hasn't got any respect for your marriage, why should I?' "

No laughter from Chassi. "Not funny, huh?" Andrew said.

Chassi looked at him. "I don't know. It makes me sad."

CHAPTER 21

Commotion. In her chest, in her tummy, a jumble of commotion, a roar in her ears, Mommy's face across the table, red-orange lips moving, no words, no sound but that sound, she was up, the chair tipping, running, the black-and-white tiles speeded up, the "Don't do this," the black-and-white waiters with their aprons and slick hair parting, "Chassi, please, baby," as if she were a big girl, she wasn't a big girl, and the door and the steps—"Don't leave me"—and the street and the heat—"Don't leave me"—and the Vespas and the little cars racing, the little horns bleating like baby sheep. Mommy's hand on her arm, running, Mommy's fingernails grabbing, red orange. Pulling her arm, yanking—"Chassi, wait"—Mommy's fingers clutching, nails in her skin, noise in her head, gardenias and artichoke crumbs; she jerked her fingers, dragging her mother with her, jerked her fingers away, ran, slid in between the high-pitched squeals, blurry, screaming; behind her, Mommy flew in the air.

The words tumbling out of her as the color drained from her face, Eleanor leaning forward in her chair. "You were running?"

It was time for the words, she had pushed her and pulled her to say the words, now it was time.

Breathless, white, back and forth in front of the bank of windows, Chassi turned to her. "Yes."

The memory, the unraveling of the memory like loose yarn filling the room. "You were running," she said again, her eyes on Chassi, "no crossed arms like two girls in a film."

As if she'd slapped her, in barely a whisper, "No."

"It's all right, Chassi." The realization as it unraveled between them, stitch by stitch.

Astonished, "We weren't holding arms."

"I know."

"We weren't."

"No."

"I pulled away from her hand."

Eleanor waited. She was seeing it, she was getting it.

"She was holding me hard, tight, with her fingers, but I got away."

"And you ran."

"Yes." Stricken, ashen, smaller.

"Into the street."

"Into the street," the child repeated and began to sob, "I didn't know it was the street."

"I know you didn't."

Choking, "I didn't know."

"You didn't know, I know you didn't know. And she followed."

Barely standing, the child shook her head up and down. "I didn't know."

"And the car hit her."

"The car hit her," she repeated as if it were a line from a play.

Jesus. Eleanor could feel her own breath in her chest, it actually hurt. "Tell me why you ran."

Pacing again, head down, charging back and forth in front of the windows like a tin duck at a shooting gallery.

"I'm here," Eleanor said, her throat full. "Put it out in the room, Chassi, I know it's scary but you can say it. Tell me why you ran."

"I can't."

"I'll help you."

The child stopped, turned in the flood of light from the windows, stared.

"I'll help you," Eleanor said again.

Exposed, defenseless. "I don't know."

"Just say it."

Laid open.

"You can say it. Talk to me, sweetheart, just talk to me," Eleanor said. It slipped out, the "sweetheart," slipped out in the need and the grief and the face of the child battling this appalling memory. Eleanor said "sweetheart" to the daughter who wasn't her own.

I need to talk to you, sweetheart, her mother had said. Okay, okay, to be Mommy's girlfriend, to hear the secrets Mommy had to tell. She was twelve, after all, twelve was practically a teenager, and here they were together, just the two of them, in a foreign land. She pushed another artichoke leaf into her mouth, sucked the olive oil off the tips of her fingers, watched her mother's beautiful face. She was old enough, she could be her mother's girlfriend, after all.

Sally took another sip of the wine, kept the glass in her hand. "Sometimes, when you're big, sweetheart, when you're a grown-up, when you're a woman"—a secret smile—"sometimes things happen that you can't predict."

"Like if you spilled that on your dress," Chassi said.

Sally just looked at her.

"It would make a terrible stain."

"Yes, that's right."

"And probably not come out and it would be an accident but you'd be mad."

"Yes, but I meant things that you can't predict that have to do with people"—her lips to the glass—"people who are friends, people who love each other, people who are married."

"Like you and Daddy," Chassi said.

"Like me and Daddy," Sally said.

Chassi smiled, her mother's lips looked very red tonight, red like the red of the sauce on top of her spaghetti that was sitting where she had left it and hadn't even picked up her fork. "I think it's sweet that he calls you a humdinger."

"So, sometimes, people are married and they love each other."

She could talk about love, people who loved each other, her mother could tell her about her father and she would tell her mother about Andrew, about how she really felt, really loved him, wanted to end up marrying him, Sally would understand. "Can I taste the wine, Mom?"

Her mother poured a little wine from her glass into Chassi's. Chassi lifted it, clinked it against her mother's glass and took a sip. She didn't really like it but she'd never say that, she'd just act like it was the best wine she'd ever had. It was really the second wine she'd ever had, the first wine was at—

"Chassi, I need you to listen."

"I'm listening, you didn't say anything. Why aren't you eating your spaghetti?"

"I—" Sally stopped.

"I'm listening," Chassi said again, her eyes big.

"I have to leave you and Daddy."

See? They were talking about grown-up things. "Go on location? When? After I start school? What's the picture? What's it about?"

"Not on location."

"Oh. Can I taste your spaghetti?"

"Chassi, listen to me."

What was it? She was listening. "I'm listening, I'm listening."

"I have to leave you and Daddy."

"Mom, you said that." She dipped her fork into her mother's plate, wound the noodles around and around and up.

"I've fallen in love." Her mother's face as white as her dress. "Oh, God," Sally drawled.

Chassi stared at her mother, a mouthful of noodles. "Cool. You mean with Daddy again like a second honeymoon? Sissy Danziger's parents did that, they went to Negril. I can't remember, where exactly is Negril?" One noodle slipped off, slid down her chin. "Oops, sorry." She dabbed at her face with the napkin, grown women didn't let spaghetti do that, she would have to be careful or Mommy wouldn't tell her grown-up things. She sat tall in the chair like her mother, took another sip of the wine.

"Chassi."

She lowered the glass to the cloth. "Mom, what's the matter?" She'd never seen her look like that, she didn't even look like that when her dog died. "Mom?"

"Chassi."

"All you keep saying is Chassi."

It was bad, very bad, whatever the thing was she wanted to tell, the secret. Chassi leaned forward, and quietly, lowering her eyes from anyone who might be watching, said, "You can tell me, honest, Mom, I won't say anything, go ahead."

"Oh, sweetheart." Sally leaning forward too, the red waves splitting, making scallops over her mother's eyebrows. "It's not your daddy, I've fallen in love with somebody else."

Running, screaming, but that wasn't first, first she was leaving, leaving her and Daddy, running, Chassi running from the words, Sally running from the two of them, don't leave, how can you leave me, Mommy, please. She had her hand on her wrist, like the picture postcards, she could see the two of them scuffling as they ran.

Stop telling me, don't tell me, let go of my arm.

Why can't you stay, don't do this, Mommy, please.

Don't go with him, I hate him.

Don't do this, don't leave me.

Don't tell me, I hate you.

Don't go. Out of the grasp of the orange fingernails, Sally screaming, Chassi ran.

• • •

"I ran," Chassi said.

Quietly, in the still of the room and the light, Eleanor up from the chair. "I understand,"

"I ran and she ran after me."

"It's okay."

"She wanted to tell me, she was trying to tell me . . ."

Eleanor nodded.

". . . I didn't want to hear . . ."

"I know you didn't."

It was there, right there, all she had to do was say it. "Tell me, Chassi," Eleanor said, her eyes on the girl breathing, reliving every step, every word, "you can tell me, tell me what she said . . ."

"She wanted to go."

That's right, that's right. Lord in Heaven. "Where did she want to go?" Eleanor said softly.

She didn't look up, sitting there on the floor of Eleanor's office, the girl didn't look at Eleanor.

"It's okay, you can say it now, Chassi."

Slowly, the whiskbroom hair swinging from side to side, covering her face.

"It's okay," Eleanor said again.

"I never—"

"I know you didn't."

"—I didn't . . ."

"You can now."

Breathing, both of them caught in the light of the room and the breathing. "You can say it now, Chassi," Eleanor said.

Breaking, the child was breaking and Eleanor was breaking right along with her. "Say it, Chassi."

". . . to live with him," the words falling out of her mouth in front of her as if she had been sick on the rug.

Nodding, Eleanor walked to where she was sitting, bent to where she was sitting. "It's okay," she murmured to the child's bent head.

"Thalosinos . . ."

"Thalosinos," Eleanor repeated, extended her hand to Chassi.

"She wanted to live with Thalosinos . . ."

"Go on," Eleanor whispered.

". . . instead of with Daddy and me. . . ."

Eleanor's hand on the child's shoulder, "It's okay."

". . . I never told . . ."

"It's okay now."

". . . never. . . ."

Her arms around the child, cradling her. "I know you didn't."

Fragile, finished, as if the air had gone out of her, the almond eyes lifted to Eleanor. "I never told Daddy what she said."

The street and the waiters and the owner of the restaurant, and his mother and his wife and the police and the ambulance, and the cars and the people and the flashbulbs, and the shock and the blood and the horror of what the child had seen. *She was holding my arm. Not exactly holding it, but we had crossed arms for a second, not like a mother and daughter, but more like two girls . . . in a film.* Before, it had to have been before the restaurant, Eleanor had always thought that had to have been before the restaurant, that picture in Chassi's head. Before the words, the shock of whatever words the mother had spoken, the hideous words.

How long did it take for them to reach the father, how many hours did it take for him to get to Rome, and where did they hold her, the one who now had no mother, where did they hold her until the father got there? And did any of them, any one of them hold her until the father got there? Police and wives of restaurant owners, did anyone hold the little girl? Eleanor sat motionless in her chair.

I never told Daddy what she said.

The hideous words that the child never told the father, words that the child probably never told herself. Words that were buried with the woman who said them, the words and the woman who said them flying into the air.

Eleanor got up from her chair and walked to the windows.

A person says something, opens their mouth and says something and from that second onward, everyone's life is changed. One unremarkable instant and nothing remains the same. Eleanor watched the people crossing the street below the window. She couldn't have planned it, not an act so selfish, this Sally Brash who surely loved her daughter, it must have been a mistake. Words that slid out of her mouth and into the air between them, like the splatter of red sauce across the white cloth.

Words that you can't take back.

Words that cross the line between being a mother and being a confidante, between being a mother and being a friend. The fine line of knowing what is right to say. There ought to be a rule book, Eleanor thought, instructions. A faint smile pulled at her lips—with her luck, if there had been an instruction book for Caroline it probably would have been written in Japanese.

She bent her head at the bank of windows.

Words that you can't take back.

She'd made a mistake, the stunning movie star who was just another mother loving her daughter. Just another mother loving her daughter, just like Eleanor, she hadn't gotten any instructions, she'd said the wrong thing, she'd made a mistake.

It had ended with Caroline walking out, it had ended with, "Mom, I don't want to see you. Don't call me, okay?," but it had started with something so silly, it had started with the furniture, of all things, in the living room. The couch specifically, but as Caroline had pointed out, "Really, the whole room."

"You want to rearrange the living room?"

A hopeful smile on her daughter's face. "How about just the couch to start with?"

"Why?"

"I just explained it. To promote the best flow of energy."

"What's the matter with the energy?"

"You're not allowing the good to come in."

She wasn't kidding. How could she not be kidding? "I'm not?"

"You're sitting with your back to the door, Mom."

"What is this crap? The living room has been like this since you were two years old, since we bought this house."

"That doesn't mean it's right."

She was tired, she didn't have the heart for this, she was so tired. She spent most of her nights waking up for him, the soft sound of his snore, his back against hers, his knees, his hand, his head on the pillow, thinking he would be there only to discover and relive the whole thing. "Caroline, where would you put the couch?"

"To the side. Open it up."

Eleanor's hand tight on the chair behind her, holding on. "But then you're not facing the fireplace."

"Not exactly, but you won't have your back to the door."

"We like facing the fireplace."

The "we" stuck out like a cuss word. "We." There was no "we" anymore. How could she not be a "we"? She'd been a "we" for all these years, how could Jimmy have left her and made her an "I"? "Your daddy liked it this way," Eleanor said.

Caroline stood her ground, her hands on the couch arm. "Why don't we just try it?"

She didn't want to try it, she didn't want it to look different, she didn't want to change anything. This was her house with Jimmy, she had to remember each and every moment, it had to stay the same.

"Just help me with the other arm. I've been studying this, it's the art of placement, ancient Chinese, Mom, it's amazing really, let's just see." Lifting one side of the sofa, waiting for Eleanor to grab the other end.

"Please don't do that."

"Mom, we can put it back. Don't make such a big deal."

She could see him on that couch smiling at her. Laughing with her. Angry at her. Just sitting with her. His head in her lap. Her feet in his lap. Both of them asleep. Both of them awake. Making love. Making decisions. Playing dominoes. Playing strip poker when Caroline was a baby, asleep. Reading the papers. Reading the tax forms. Watching the afternoon. Watching the flames as the logs went up. Having a drink. Having friends for dinner. Having a sandwich. Having a life. "Leave it where it is."

"Why are you making such a big deal?"

"I want it where he left it."

His brown eyes looking at her out of her daughter's face. "You're never going to move anything?"

"No."

"You're going to leave everything the way it was when Daddy left the house?"

"Yes."

"You're kidding."

Eleanor moved to the stairs.

"Mom, that's sick."

"Thank you, I'll see if I can go to someone."

"I think you should."

"You don't know anything about it."

"His shirt on the chair, his razor in the shower with the muck on it, his reading glasses in every room? His clippers in the garage? The way he parked the Jeep crooked, you can't get out of the other door? You're going to leave it like that?"

"Stop it."

"You're not going to touch anything?"

"No."

"You're losing it."

"You don't know what it's like to lose a husband, you can't possibly understand."

"My God."

"I know you lost your father, it's not the same."

"You're going to compare grief?"

"Caroline—"

"Whose grief is bigger? Is that it? It's a contest? Where are you going?"

"Upstairs."

"Don't walk away, please don't walk away. You've been walking away ever since I got here. Why did you ask me to come?"

"Everything you do hurts me."

Quiet.

"Then I shouldn't be here," Caroline said.

Eleanor's hand on the bannister, thinking, Why can't she take care of me? Why do I have to take care of her?

"If that's the way you feel then I shouldn't be here," Caroline said again.

Oh, there were so many somethings Eleanor could have said then. She could have said I didn't mean that, she could have said don't pay any attention to me, I'm just tired. She could have said I'm sorry. Why didn't she say I'm sorry?

Quietly, Caroline said, "If everything I do hurts you, then I should go."

"Then you should go."

That's what she'd said. *Then you should go*. Not I'm sorry. Not I didn't mean that, my Caroline. *Then you should go.* That's what she had said to her daughter. As she climbed the stairs, with her back to her only child, Eleanor had said those hideous words.

As if her grief was separate from Caroline's, she had felt inconsolable and alone. She had asked her daughter to come home and had then ignored her, as if all she needed was the sound, the presence of someone else in the house to assure her that she wasn't alone. Eleanor's forehead against the glass, crying for Sally Brash and Chassi, and crying for what she had done to Caroline, standing at the glass looking out, but seeing only her child.

CHAPTER 22

She was flooded now with the memory, like the soap popping up and dancing across the bathwater, there was no way now to hold it back down. Chassi let in more hot from the tap, slid down the tile, her head underwater, her hair floating out from her face. Like seaweed. Dr. Costello said not to fight the memories, to let them come. She lifted her face out of the water, rested the back of her head against the tile of the tub. She covered her breasts with the steaming washcloth, raised her legs and put her feet on the hot and cold. She wasn't dizzy anymore, she hadn't been dizzy since the day in Dr. Costello's office when everything had come out. A physical something from an emotional something . . . what? . . . what had she said? It didn't matter, she didn't have to remember, the only thing that was important now was to let it be. That's what she'd said, Dr. Costello, *Chassi, let yourself be.*

She scooped the washcloth off her chest and put it over her face, breathed the wet air and the scent of lavender through the terry. It was as if she hadn't been across the table from her mother until now. As if no one had ever asked her what went on before the street. Had they? She didn't remember. It was awful and horrible and ugly and then Daddy came. She didn't remember the in between.

Chassi dipped the washcloth into the hot and put it back over her chest. Her mother's face across the table. The red of her mouth, the black and white of the waiters' coats and their hair and the tiles. She breathed it in, let the memory wash over her, replayed it, reheard it, rethought it; she hated her, she slid under the water again. Daddy's face, loose and sunken and ugly, as if Daddy were dead too, she'd told Dr. Costello, that was the main thing, when she'd seen his face, when he got there, the bow of his shoulders, his eyes, his mouth, his big hands limp and hanging, Chassi was terrified that he would die too.

Her father suddenly old and broken, and she knew she couldn't let that happen, she would make sure that didn't happen, that was all she would do. She remembered that clearly, telling herself not to think about her mother, she wouldn't think about her mother, she would only think about him. Make sure that he wasn't too sad, make him happy, be with him, take care of him, protect him and make sure. She wouldn't let anything happen to her daddy. She never had, not in all these years.

I love you forever and ever, always remember that, no matter what. No matter what, it had said on the postcard in loops of blue ink. Chassi sat up in the bath. Thalosinos. That's what it meant. *No matter what,* that her mother loved him, that she was going to leave and run away with him. Chassi shook her head hard, wet hair flying. Look at what she did. Look at what she did to me and look at what I did to her. Chassi reached again for the hot, turned it on full blast until she had to pull her feet away.

• • •

LET'S CALL A SPADE a you-know-what. The point was, Chassi Jennings could have her fired, that was the real point. She had the power, she had the father, she had the everything, let's call a spade a spade. Ionie took a long swig from the water bottle. She wiped her face with her hand, took a deep breath and exhaled. You just be smart, Ionie, you just sit here and don't do anything else, you just calm yourself and think things through.

Really, the girl had come at her out of nowhere, sitting there quietly in all that sunset, peaceful after the swim, the yoga, the crystal goblets of French wine, watching the evening sky. What a life she had up there in all that splendor, it's not like she had to make her own living or take care of herself. *Tia, could you bring us some wine and cheese in the garden? Tia, could you make us a sandwich? Tia, could you wipe our ass?* Everybody was a goddamn servant. *Ionie, could you come up and do yoga? Ionie, could you come up and do lines?* What was she gonna say to her—no? Walking around in that Taj Mahal, beckoning people to do for her, her life was one big bowl of strawberries and cream. She didn't even have to cut the strawberries herself, she'd probably never cut strawberries, she'd probably never even been to a market, much less . . . okay, okay.

Ionie exhaled, slammed her feet around on the railing, chugged the last two inches of water. Chassi Jennings's life was a slam dunk. Oh, to have a father with the power and big bucks of Saul. Her heart was still racing, she didn't even remember the drive home. She put her hand on her chest. Just breathe. Just stay focused and think this through. Go back to the beginning. "What are you doing with Jones?" That was how it had started, out of nowhere, in between whatever they'd been talking about, the look to Ionie, the tone in Chassi's voice that Ionie had never heard before and then the "You're sleeping with Jones. He's in love with you. What are you doing with Jones?" What was she supposed to answer? Hey, no I'm not, you must be mistaken, we're just friends, me and Jones. Weren't they girlfriends, her and Chassi? Weren't they supposed to talk about stuff like that? Men?

Who knew she'd come on to her like a g.d. priest. All that guilt trip about his wife and how could she look at herself, and then all that shit about his kids. She'd never even seen his boys, she wasn't doing anything to them, it was just . . . well, how could you explain it, and why did she have to? And it wasn't like she would even still be seeing Jones, she'd tried to end it, but he'd practically shot himself after seeing the kiss between her and Peroni. Showing up that night at her place like that—thank God she hadn't brought Peroni home with her—literally crying, Jones falling apart totally—talk about a scene.

She had to promise him that she would keep seeing him, at least for the length of the picture. It was two weeks away from rehearsal, just two weeks. What else could she do?

She got up from the chair, walked around the balcony in a little circle and sat back down. And what right did Chassi Jennings have to lay shit on her about how she lived her life? It wasn't her business. Carrying on about how it was beneath her, Miss High and Mighty, as if living up there in paradise she knew about problems that happened to regular folks. Who did she think she was?

Ionie got up from the chair. She was the one who could have her fired, that's who Chassi Jennings was. She could really have her fired and this was her big chance. Oh, God, it could be her only chance. It could be her everything. Ionie paced the balcony. Fired right before the damn rehearsals, she'd never get another job, Nicki would drop her, it would be over before it began.

On the one hand, she couldn't let Jones hate her, couldn't let him shoot her badly, literally light her so she looked bad on film. And he could do that, oh, yeah, cross a cinematographer and they can do that, light an actor so they look like shit. No way. She had to hold on to him in some way, give him something to go on. But on the other hand, she couldn't let Chassi Jennings be her enemy. She had to be careful how she behaved in front of Chassi with Jones. Make it look like it was over. They had to shoot together, her and Chassi, reams and reams of pages and pages of scenes together, she had to be cool. Stop pacing, Ionie, breathe.

She put her hands on her hips, focused on Mrs. Fox's garden, the way the yellow light splashed across the lemon leaves.

Wait a minute. There was always the outside possibility that when Chassi Jennings got all pissed off and carried on like that and said she was having "second thoughts," that maybe she didn't mean about Ionie playing the part. Maybe she'd meant . . . what? Ionie put her hands on the railing of the balcony. What else could she have meant? Could she have meant she was having second thoughts about Jones shooting it?

Wow, wouldn't that be a relief? Maybe Ionie could make Chassi think she was Jones's obsession and that she had tried to stop him and the affair, but he wouldn't let go. Which was partially true. And then Chassi could have *him* fired. Tah-dah, no more worries. Oh, God.

She bent at the waist, let her head hang to her knees, her hair fall across her face. She blew at it. Shampoo and orange blossoms. Could she have meant she didn't want Peroni to direct it? No, no way. Peroni was one of the hottest directors in town. That was crazy, that made absolutely no sense. She stood up straight.

Could Chassi have meant that she was having second thoughts about doing the picture herself? Ionie rolled her eyes at the night sky. Oh, that was a good one. That was ludicrous—why would Chassi Jennings not want to be in *Trumpets*? Her brain must be failing, Ionie thought as she slammed into the guest house; she would not come up with a plan until she was thinking clearly, and hopefully she would be smarter after she got some sleep.

• • •

"HELLO? CAROLINE? Uh, it's your, uh—" *Beep* went Caroline's machine and Eleanor said, "mother," and hung up. Well, how could you leave a message if the thing went *beep*? She staggered as she got out of the chair, actually staggered and then laughed at the thought of staggering around her own kitchen in her suit skirt and bra and pearls, sliding on the tile in her panty hose, her black suede heels collapsed on top of each other where she'd stepped out of them at the refrigerator door. She tilted the wine bottle over the glass and then thought better of it, lifted the bottle to her lips and took a swig. What a thought: Caroline seeing her mother drink wine directly from the bottle. Not something a prude would do. No, not a prude, a prune. No, not a prune. Giggling, Eleanor steadied herself on the corner of the table, swiped at the pile of her silk blouse but it slipped to the floor. Stiff, that's what Caroline thought about her mother, that she was stiff. Not *a* stiff, just stiff. Fixed in her ways, not open. Closed. Oops, watch the doorway there.

She rumbaed her way through the dining room into the living room, her left hand on the shoulder of the imaginary Jimmy, her right hand high in his hand, *with* the bottle of Cabernet. No more blind dates, that was it, *fini*, kaput. Better to stay home. He'd seemed like a nice man, presentable, good-looking, short but good-looking, losing his hair but good-looking, he'd seemed nice. "He's nice," Moonie had said, "go out with him." Nice restaurant, nice conversation, nice kiss at her car. Okay, nice.

Eleanor looked up into the eyes of the imaginary Jimmy. One kiss, a kiss, honey. Jimmy's hand pulled her in closer, his broad fingers on the small of her back. Eleanor took another swig. She could smell him. Jimmy. She shook her head, danced by the CD player and hit the volume up another notch. Tito Puente and a trumpet and a conga drum.

He'd said it was early, the nice man, Jeff, Jeff the ophthalmologist had said it was early, "Only ten after ten," he'd said, with a nice smile and a nice voice and a nice suit and tie, he'd sit with her a moment in her car.

Eleanor crashed into the corner of the coffee table, backed up and surveyed the damage. One ripped black opaque leg. No big ting, mon. That's what they said in Jamaica, she'd been to Jamaica, wasn't a stiff in Jamaica, that's for damn sure. Jimmy and her in Ocho Rios making love *outside*. Wouldn't that throw the kid?

She continued the rumba or was it a samba or maybe more like a meringue up the stairs, did a little striptease at the edge of the bed until she lost her footing pulling off the panty hose and kind of slipped to the floor. She sat there, her back against the bed and carefully set the wine bottle down on the carpet to the left of her hip. A sit in the car, a little conversation, my ex-wife does this to me, he says, and that to me, he says, and she's manipulative and punitive and lots of other things with "tive"—did he think it was a session?—she hardly lets me see my kids, he says with big eyes. Oh, I'm so sorry, says Eleanor, the good shrink, and out of nowhere, pounce and grab? What the hell was that? Was she supposed to feel sorry for him? Enough to let him stick his hand in her blouse? And then he's the one who's astounded when she says, "Get out of my car." Looking at her with that expression, his hand caught where she had trapped it with her hand, slamming his fingers, she was so shocked, someone else's fingers on her skin, his other hand suddenly pushing her back against the seat hard, his knee between hers, and how had he wedged it in with the steering wheel there? And all the while feeling like she was being taped for a segment on *20/20*. "Is fifty-three too old for date rape?" says Barbara Walters to Hugh Downs.

Eleanor unhooked her bra, slid one strap from one shoulder but couldn't manage the other one, let both shoulders slide across the bedspread until she was all the way down, lying on her side.

She stared at the bottom of the wine bottle and the turf of the rug. She'd left the music on downstairs. Oh, and the lights. She hadn't had this much to drink since she was a kid. She closed her eyes and then opened them. Oh, no, she'd called the kid. Hadn't she? Yep. Left a message. Yep. Chicken to call in the middle of the night. Hey, I was thinking I hurt you. Oh, okay, Mom, cool, I'll be right there, I'll come over and hold your head. Yeah, sure.

Eleanor lay there, moved her cheek against the thick wool. She'd never known how to talk to Caroline, never. They were always at odds, always at opposite ends of whatever was in question. "You're the same, El," Jimmy had said. Incredulous—the man was batty—she shook her head. "How can you say that? We're as different as, I don't know what . . ." "Nah, you butt heads," Jimmy said, " 'cause you're just the same." She closed her eyes again and opened them.

But she'd held Caroline's head. Hadn't she? Sure. When she had the flu, when she went on that flying thing at Magic Mountain, and on those horrible tea cups at the dreaded Disneyland, and when she ate all that macaroni with too much cheese at Sis's house. God. Eleanor pulled at a tuft of the carpet.

And dusted her with cornstarch when she got poison oak, whisked her into the garden, stripped her clothes off and sprinkled her like a piece of chicken about to go into the pan. And put calamine on the chicken pox and told her not to scratch. No, Jimmy did that. He wound her little fingers in a soft piece of his old T-shirt so she couldn't scratch. Oh, Jimmy, so sweet with his baby.

She had to get up, her cheek was tingling from the wool. And . . . what else? Well, all the things you do when you're a mother. Right? She'd been a mother, she knew. Laundry and carpool and picking up after her and making those sandwiches *without mayonnnaise, Mom,* with that look, all those things you do too numeral to mention, numerous, right, numerous to mention, but the list, the other list of what you do, what one does—a tear slid out of Eleanor's left eye and across the bridge of her nose, she didn't move her hand to swipe it, she wasn't going to pay it any attention—folding the little shirts and tying the laces and zipping the zippers, slipping the wiry curls up into the ponytail—*You're pulling, Mom;* and wiping the dirty face—*Don't do that;* and the tushie— *I'm ready*, yelled the little voice from the potty. The thump of the tiny red tennis shoes as they hit the sand, watching her from the bench, holding your breath, biting the inside of your mouth so you didn't scream while she did terrifying flips off the jungle gym, and helping her with take-away, otherwise known as subtraction, and going through the entire laundry of the Drake Hotel in New York with the concierge hovering at her elbow—*But, madam, really, I don't think* . . . —when the maid had accidentally picked up Caroline's precious stuffed Rabbity along with the sheets. Caroline sobbing in the room upstairs in Jimmy's arms while she rummaged through people's dirty socks and jock straps and . . . and . . . Eleanor pushed herself up, pushed herself with her palm against the thick plush of the wool.

She hadn't held her. Eleanor blinked, shook her head. Oh, God. Not like that. It was true. She hadn't held her.

Eleanor slumped back against the bed. Not since she was little.

Wash the scrape, clean out the gravel, tell those mean old boys, but not since she was little. A little girl with a dirty face and a splinter, a spider bite and a runny nose, hiccups and measles and a tooth hanging by a bloody thread. But not big. Not grown-up. No.

Not like she'd held Chassi.

Chassi, someone else's child. Someone else's daughter crying into her. But not her own.

Eleanor looked at her feet, the slither of black panty hose across the floor, followed it across the bedroom carpet and up into the mirror on the closet door. A bedraggled woman with her bra half off and half on; a bedraggled, lonely woman who hadn't held her only child, didn't have the heart for it. A standoffish, stiff, cold, ungiving mother who hadn't had the heart to hold her only child. Who was this woman who hadn't held Caroline the way she'd held Chassi? Hadn't let Caroline cry into her when Jimmy died? On top of everything else she'd done to her, how could she have let the gap grow wider when Jimmy died? It wasn't Caroline who had kept them apart, it was Eleanor. The reality of it sobered her like a slap in the face.

• • •

"I WAS THINKING I should change my life."

"You'll never make it as a gardener," Andrew said.

"Thanks."

"In case you were considering it, Chass, you do not have a green thumb." He looked at her. "You don't have a green anything if the truth be known . . . well, maybe your eyes, but they're more chartreuse." He smiled, she didn't smile back. "Change your life, huh? Don't you have to shoot in a month?"

"Less than a month. Rehearsals start next week, but I don't know."

"Don't know what?"

Chassi patted the seat of the big chaise lounge. "Could you please sit down? Stop standing there like a tree?"

Andrew sat. "Are you pissed at me about something?"

"No. I don't think I want to do the picture."

"I don't think I want to be on the premises when you tell Saul."

She leaned her head on his shoulder. "I'm trying to figure out how I got into this."

"This particular movie, this conversation, being an actress—should I go on?"

"All of it," Chassi said.

"Ahhh, well, as I recall"—he stopped, tipped his head to look at her—"you're serious."

"Yeah."

"Once upon a time . . ."

"I'm serious, Andres," she said.

He shrugged, moved his chin against her forehead. "I don't know, I guess I always thought we were the followers in their footsteps. You know, me into Baudelio's gloves and boots and manure and rose clippers, you into your mother's scripts and limousines and high heels. The only thing you don't do like her is barbecue."

"That's what I mean."

"I missed something."

"You have a life, Andrew, you have Blanca, and a house together, you're making a baby. If you take over the business, you'll make it your own. Maybe you're following Baudelio, but you're your own person. You made a choice. You have a life."

"Okay, I have a life."

"Well, maybe I've spent my whole life not having a life."

"Chass—"

"I don't know. I never set out to be an actress, I kind of fell into it and look at what I'm about to do now—step into my mother's actual wardrobe, play her actual role. Why am I doing that?"

"I thought you wanted to."

Chassi was quiet.

Andrew said, "For your dad?"

She didn't answer. They sat there quietly, she tilted her face up to the sun. "Maybe I can't take care of him anymore, Andres."

It was his turn to not say anything. He placed his hand on her knee.

"*Ay, Dios,*" Chassi said, turning his hand over, slipping her fingers into his, "huh?"

To not say anything, to keep the secret. Her mother told the secret and look what had happened. It was all she thought about. Not the learning of her lines, not the ins and outs of the character, not how she would breathe life into the character, none of that, no. She didn't want to do the picture and the picture was connected to all of it. If she didn't do the picture, she would have to tell. Do you tell the bad thing, look what happens if you tell the bad thing, over and over in her head, because to tell Saul she wasn't going to do the picture would be to tell him everything.

"There's no other way," Chassi said to Eleanor. "He won't buy it that I've just changed my mind. It wouldn't make sense to him, he'd know better, he'd know there was more."

"Go on," Eleanor said.

"If I tell him I hurt him."

La Shrink didn't say anything.

"I give him pain. Why would I do that after all these years?"

Not even a jingle from the bracelets.

Chassi sighed. "I even made the list. I didn't want to, I don't want to do anything she told me to do, but then I thought, well, that's silly . . . I mean, I can't spend my whole life not doing anything that's remotely connected to my mother . . ."

"Good," La Shrink said.

"Did you say good?"

"Yes."

Chassi waited but Eleanor didn't say anything else. "Well, I made it. Everything that was on the pro side was still there: work, a terrific picture, a hot director, a great part; except my heart isn't in it, it doesn't mean anything to me, it's like the pro side became the con." She sighed again, it slid out of her loud in the room. "I'm full of sighs, it's all connected to my mother, isn't it? The picture, my mother, my mother, the picture, it's like Faye Dunaway in *Chinatown*."

No answer.

"I know, it's not funny. I wasn't trying to be funny, I'm just trying to . . . I guess I kind of know what it is . . . sort of"—she shrugged—"real definitive, huh?"

"Go on," Eleanor said.

"It's like I took over her life, my mother's, like I became her. Not totally, but, you know"—she moved her hands through the dust specks in the sunbeam—"I was thinking about it, and"—she sat up—"can I turn around?"

"Yes."

No hesitation, she let her; Chassi turned. "What I think is, I don't want to do it anymore. Any of it."

"Go on," Eleanor said again.

"I don't want to be in the picture, I don't even know if I want to be an actress and in order to not do that, I have to tell him. Everything. Because it's all connected. I have to tell him even if I hurt him, don't I? Come clean."

La Shrink nodded.

"If I want to have a real relationship with my father, I have to tell him, I have to be honest. I'm gonna sigh again."

"Go on."

"In a way, I've always been pretending to be my mother. I've never really talked to him. Been myself. As me."

They were both quiet.

Chassi studied Eleanor's face. "You understand, don't you?"

Eleanor leaned forward. "What was on the other side of the list, Chassi?"

"You mean if I tell him? If I don't do the picture?"

La Shrink nodded.

"Oh, it sounds very dramatic. You know, saying it out loud, not just writing it on a piece of paper alone in your room."

She was waiting.

"Very high drama," Chassi said.

"Try me."

"Well, if I tell him," Chassi said, and then her eyes were full and she gave the little shrug laugh because she was embarrassed, "it sounds corny."

A reassuring look on La Shrink's face. "I can take it, tell me," she said.

Chassi's eyes on hers. "If I tell him, I'll be free."

• • •

ELEANOR SAT IN HER CAR, parked across from the apartment. It was an old courtyard apartment between Wilshire and Olympic in lower Beverly Hills. Easy to find. She'd never been there, Jimmy had been there but not her.

Jacaranda trees quietly dropping sticky purple blossoms, birds of paradise fronting the clipped hedges like stiff orange soldiers, the hum of a gardener's blower, a small white-haired woman walking a small white-haired dog. Hardly a car, hardly a stirring, as if the neighborhood were taking its nap. The air was soft, heady with mock orange and jasmine. She looked at her watch again: 2:10. Stalling. Get out of the car. It's enough with the sitting and stalling, you've gone over it and over it, get out of the car. She shut the windows and got out of the car.

338A was upstairs, up a narrow flight of white cement steps after a curved pathway through a small garden. One hand on the painted railing, one palm grazing the grainy stucco as she moved up the steps. She should have taken two aspirins, her knee hurt. Her head hurt. Her heart hurt. Poised in front of the door, she considered falling back down the staircase, landing on her head. She pushed the bell. Chimes. Footsteps. A blurry face in the peephole, brown eyes.

"What?" Caroline said, opening the door.

"I need to talk to you."

"Why?"

"Because I need to. Please, Caroline."

"Why are you doing this when I asked you not to?" the girl said to her mother, but she let the door swing wide. Eleanor took it as a sign, this door opening, maybe it hadn't all gone bad. Sunlight through the crystals hanging in the windows, rainbows dancing along the thick cream walls. A quilt across a sofa, a rag rug, light wood floors. Beautiful. Serene. Silent. Eleanor wanted to collapse across the pale blue sofa and pull the quilt up over her head.

"What do you want, Mom?"

Begin at the beginning, just begin at the beginning and say what you have to say. "I made a lot of mistakes."

Caroline in ballet second position in front of her but she would take it as another sign: feet open, not closed.

"I hurt you," she said and took a gulp of breath. "I hurt you terribly." She hadn't realized she had practically stopped breathing. "May I have some water?" Her daughter turned, Eleanor followed her into a tiny kitchen, wanting so desperately to reach out and touch Caroline's hair. "I was never good with you," she said, "I don't know why, I'm trying to figure it out."

The child said nothing, took a glass out of the drainboard, filled it, handed it to her.

"It won't matter how many times I say I'm sorry, the wounds will still be there," Eleanor said, her finger accidentally grazing Caroline's when she took the glass, "but I'm so sorry, I'm sorry for so many things."

"Mom, what good is this going to do?"

"I'm sorry, Caroline."

"You think if you say you're sorry, it will change anything?"

"I don't know. If you could just listen, I've been trying to think it all through—"

"I've always listened to you, I've spent my life listening to you, it's no good for me."

"Because I didn't listen back."

Her child's sweet face. "No. You never listened back. Not about anything."

"I'm sorry, Caroline."

"Not about school, not about what I wanted, who I am. Mostly who I am. I was never what you wanted. You wanted to remake me like a before and after in a magazine."

"That isn't true, I always loved you."

"No, you didn't. You had no time for me, it was always about Daddy."

"Caroline—"

"No. I don't need your approval anymore. I've learned to get along without it."

Eleanor held tightly to the glass. "Caroline, I love you."

"I don't need you to love me. Not anymore."

All the preparation, all the writing it out, thinking it through, planning what to say and how she wouldn't cry. Listing the things, all the bad things she'd done and said, telling her how it would be different, she would be different. How she had taken stock of herself, how sick she was about all of it, how she wanted to make it okay. How she would say it, not lose her way, not get lost in tears, but there she was against the sink breaking down, choking with tears. "You can't mean that. Caroline, please."

"Mom, why are you here?"

"To tell you I'm sorry."

"Okay, you did that."

"To ask you to let me try."

"Try what?"

"We can't go back but we could start over."

"Mom—"

"Please, I would be different."

"No, you wouldn't."

"I promise I would."

"You're kidding yourself."

"It wouldn't be the way it was. It was me, it was my fault."

"You just miss Daddy."

"I do miss Daddy but I miss you too. Please, I need you, Caroline, and you need me."

"It's a waste of energy."

"It could be positive."

A breath, a second, Eleanor kept going. "You don't know. It could be positive. I wasn't a very good mother, maybe I could be . . . something else . . ."

"What?"

"A friend?"

"Are you kidding?"

"You could let me try."

"It's ridiculous."

"Just say you'll think about it."

"Mom, we can't be friends."

"Please, Caroline, just think about it. Please let me try."

Neither of them moving, neither of them speaking. "Please," Eleanor said again.

"God, you're pushy. Even when you're apologizing you're pushy."

But it was an opening, Eleanor was sure it was an opening, a hint of something on her daughter's face, a lightness, and she would take it as a sign. She stood where she was. The quiet of the room, the soft, white light, Eleanor's knees were trembling, she could feel them moving lightly against her skirt.

"I think you should go."

"Please, think about it."

Caroline took the glass out of her hands. Eleanor tentatively touched her daughter's arm with her fingers. Just for a second.

"Mom," Caroline said and Eleanor tried to breathe. "Okay, I'll think about it," Caroline said.

CHAPTER 23

The ice cubes shifted against the crystal. "So, my little sweetheart, we got ourselves a problem," Saul Jennings said to his daughter. He ran his big fingers along the nail heads studding the arm of the caramel leather wing chair and raised his glass. He downed the inch of amber liquid, got up, and walked across the room to the bar.

"Dad," Chassi said.

Saul lifted his hand. She stopped, she waited.

"Between a rock and a hard place, huh?" he said. He lifted the bottle of Dewar's and tilted some into the glass. "A lot to take in all at once, even for an old fart like me who thought he'd heard everything."

"Nothing will happen to the picture."

"I'm not worried about the picture."

"You're not?"

He shrugged. "Okay, you got me. A little, I'm a little worried."

"The whole world will want to replace me."

"I didn't want the whole world."

"Dad—"

He held his hand up again. "I know, I know, I'm just mulling on it." He took a swig of the scotch. "Kind of a dream I had, you know, seeing you play your mother's part, kind of a dream."

"Dad—"

"I know, I know." He crossed the room. "You explained it.

Plenty." He did not sit in the wing chair, he crossed in front of it and sat next to Chassi on the couch. She'd never seen him sit on the couch, not that it should be a big deal to see your father sit on a couch but her whole life she had never seen him sit anywhere in that room except in that chair. He put his hand on her knee, gave it a little pat. "Let's not talk about the picture. Everybody's pay or play. You want me to replace you, I'll replace you. The picture is not our problem." Chin down, he took a breath, raised his eyes to her.

Chassi had never seen him like this, she had never seen him so exposed, so open, so—

"So, when are you moving?" Saul said, the slightest gleam in his eye. "Tuesday?"

Chassi smiled. "No, I'm not moving Tuesday."

"Uh-huh. Well, that's good." A moment, Saul took a moment, his eyes on his daughter. "Big adjustment for me, your not being here"—he stopped—"maybe we'll meet for dinner."

"Daddy, I'm not walking out of your life."

"I used to go to my mama every Friday night when I still lived in New York, have supper." He jiggled the ice cubes in the glass. "Another story." He nodded his head, shrugged again. He patted her knee again. "So, I've got something to say."

"Okay."

"In light of what you said, what you told me—" He took a breath. "I sound like I'm negotiating a deal."

"It's okay."

"I understand what you told me."

She didn't remember being this close to her father, maybe ever.

He frowned. "Why you don't want to do the picture . . . all of it, the way it's all tied together . . . well, maybe 'understand' is too big a word. But I . . . understand."

"Okay."

"You gotta figure out what you want to do now, by yourself, I see that. I say to myself, maybe I pushed you, I don't know . . ."

"Daddy—"

"No, it's okay. Who knows how to be a father? You do what you do."

Chassi put her hand on Saul's hand. "Look how little," he said.

She was overwhelmed, stunned by his openness, by the all of it. He nodded. "I don't know, I'm not too good at this stuff."

"Me neither."

"Maybe I'll have to go to your Dr. Costello."

"Do you want to?"

"Nah." He took a swig of the scotch, smiled at Chassi. "I don't know, does she really look like Bancroft?"

Chassi grinned.

"I'm trying to change the subject. You gotta watch me, I'm a very smart old man."

"Dad—"

"No, let me do this. I have something to say and maybe I shouldn't, because what's the point now, in light of what you told me and what happened, and I don't want to make it worse, but . . . then . . . I figure, with all that went on with you, better we shouldn't have any more secrets, better to just get it out in the open"—his eyes so full of love for her, so tender—"so we can go on. That's the point, right? For us to go on?"

Chassi couldn't get the words out, she just nodded.

"Okay." He took another breath, polished off the scotch. "You tell me about your mother and Thalosinos"—he stopped, shook his head—"this is very hard for me."

"It's okay, Dad."

"I don't know if it's okay, it is what it is." He took her hand in his. "Chassi, your mother never would have left us." She started to speak, but the timbre in his voice stopped her. "I don't know what went on that day, what was in her head, what she was thinking . . . who knows with your mother? It could have been the way the light came in the room—" his face softened—"hell, with Sally, it could have been the spaghetti." He took a breath. "Your mother was a romantic, sweetheart, to beat the band. A peach, a song, she didn't even need a sunset, and she fell in love. Your mother could fall in love with a pancake, a spray of gardenias, somebody else's dog." He bent his head to hers. "Do you understand what I'm saying?"

Saul took a moment, an intake of breath. "Thalosinos, the guy before him, the guy before that . . . you think I didn't know? Chassi, your mother fell in and out of love with every director she ever worked with"—a shrug of Saul's shoulders—"hell, a director, sometimes even an actor"—his hand in the air—"a this, a that, a sound man with a smile, a driver who had a mustache, a God-knows-what . . . I knew 'em all . . . some little thing and it got to her and off she went. That's the way it was with her." His eyes on Chassi's, he continued, "That's all it was. I made my peace with it. Your mother was an actress, she fell in love." He clutched her fingers in his big hand. "She would never have left us. I don't know what went on that day, what she was thinking, God knows what she was thinking, but I'm telling you, you take it from your daddy, sweetheart, my Sally would never have left us, that much I know."

• • •

· THE HOLLYWOOD REPORTER ·

NO TRUMPETS, NO DRUMS, NO CHASSI

by C. R. Smith

LOS ANGELES—Under tight security and amid intense speculation, leading actress Chassi Jennings, daughter of former studio head Saul Jennings and his Academy Award–winning wife, Sally Brash, walked away from her starring role in the much-awaited remake of her parents' greatest triumph, *No Trumpets, No Drums*. Principal photography is scheduled to start in the Philippines in three weeks. No decision on a replacement for Chassi Jennings has been announced but a Jennings Films spokesperson confirmed that several other well-known actresses are available and anxious to play the part. Sources close to Saul Jennings feel that he planned this film as a tribute to his beloved late wife with his actress daughter in her mother's role, and that he will shut down the production at great expense rather than cast it with another actress.

Ionie sighed, let the glossy trade paper slip out of her hand and fall to the floor. It had practically been enough to give her a heart attack—to think that it could all fall apart after being so close, that she might have to go back to auditioning for simpy television roles when she had the movie right in her hand. But it was okay now, it was okay, Saul Jennings was definitely not going to shut down. She'd gotten it directly from Jones who had gotten it from Peroni who had gotten it from Saul. Chassi was out and nobody knew why; Ionie certainly didn't care why, she just wanted the part.

She was the redhead, after all, why shouldn't she have Sally Brash's part? No. Really. It was perfect. She was a real actress, working at it all these years, not getting it handed to her on a spoon or a silver platter or whatever, and if Chassi Jennings was stupid enough to walk away from one of the most incredible parts in the world, who knows why, and Ionie certainly didn't care enough to find out, it's not like they were really friends, but if Chassi Jennings wasn't going to play it, why shouldn't Ionie St. John?

She had to be smart. She had to look at this clearly and think it through. It was the most incredible part. It could be the pinnacle. Talk about articles in the trades, talk about something falling into her lap, talk about stepping into the role at the last minute, two weeks from principal photography, saving Saul Jennings's ass and his picture . . . if she played her cards right she could even win an Academy Award. Jones groaned in his sleep, Ionie pulled the comforter up and tucked it around his shoulder, he moved his butt back against her thigh. He always fell asleep right after. She had to wake him, he had to get up and go home to the wife and kiddies, and she had important things to do. She'd wake him at—she lifted her head to see the clock over Jones's shoulder—she'd wake him at six.

Ionie breathed deeply, relaxed, her eyes looking up. She was okay now, now that Jones had told her the articles about shutting down the picture weren't true. A plan was everything. She had to be fast and she had to be convincing and she could do both. She would do both. The timing was perfect and her positioning was perfect—she was accessible, she was available—she could be his first choice, she was already right there. And he'd given her the eye, he'd certainly given her the eye—there was no question that he'd given her the eye. She had his private phone number and she would get the part. That was the plan.

Ionie turned into Jones's backside, tucked her knees behind his, put her arm around his shoulder, her breasts pushed into his warmth. She held him and smoothed his hair, breathed in his skin, ran her lips softly against the poke of his shoulder bone. She would get this part. It wouldn't be hard, it would just be tricky. And it wasn't like she couldn't be tricky, she was an actress, after all, she could be tricky, and besides, now that she thought about it, Saul Jennings wasn't just powerful, he was also a very attractive man.

• • •

"THE SKINNY IN TOWN is that I need a rest," Chassi said and laughed. "A rest as in a butterfly net, I bet."

"How do you feel about that?" Eleanor said.

Chassi could feel her smile lift her face. “Fine.” It was true, she did feel fine. “They’re probably saying I had another *episode.*” She took a breath, “Hell of an episode.”

Eleanor laughed. It was barely audible but Chassi knew it was a laugh. “Are you laughing back there?” she said from the couch.

“Yes.”

“Okay.” La Shrink was waiting, Chassi knew now when she was waiting. “I’m trying to make peace with what my father told me. Not peace, but . . . I don’t know . . . not let it, you know, hurt me, because I could . . . get trapped in that it wasn’t necessary, that I lived my whole life in a particular way because of what happened on a particular afternoon in a particular restaurant and that it wasn’t necessary.”

The creak of La Shrink’s chair.

“But maybe that’s how everybody lives their life. Boy. And then I think . . .” Chassi stopped.

“Go on.”

“I think maybe he doesn’t really know, that maybe that one time was different, that maybe that one time she really would have gone—not that it makes any difference—and then I think maybe he’s just protecting himself, and then I think all the thoughts again about if only she wouldn’t have told me, if only I wouldn’t have run, if only, *if only*. . . . It’s another T-shirt for us to make.” She recrossed her feet, the squeak of the big tennis shoes against the leather of the couch. “I bet you’re smiling back there.”

Eleanor jingled.

“I know I can’t change it. If only I could change it—that’s the biggest *if only*—but I can’t.” Chassi exhaled. “I know that. I can only change *now*”—she took a breath—“that’s all I’m supposed to know now, is that I can only change *now* . . .” She laughed. “Right?” She turned to Eleanor and smiled.

• • •

ELEANOR PUSHED THE PLASTIC SPOON through the raspberry yogurt, took another bite. She swiveled around in her chair, lifted her legs and set the heels of her boots on her desk. Chassi, Chassi, Chassi. She licked the pink off the back of the plastic. Parents and the things they do. Things we do. That's more like it, "we." Parents messing up their kids, we parents messing up our kids. Did anybody ever do it right? Eleanor scooped up the last spoonful of yogurt. Probably not.

She'll be okay, that Chassi, she'll probably end up staying in the business. Hard to think of someone already so immersed being able to regroup anywhere else, and especially the way it seemed to hook people, the movie business; the intoxication of living a life of rejection never ceases to amaze. Eleanor smiled. But you never know what a person will do, which way they'll go. When you least expect it, they can turn around and knock you off your feet. *It's a crap shoot, babe,* Jimmy would have said. Eleanor scraped the spoon around the empty carton. You bet.

The phone rang; she didn't make a move for it, she'd let the service pick it up. She had forty-five minutes before The Shoelace arrived, she was going to take a walk, maybe mosey through Bloomingdale's. Not think about Caroline, not think about anything, maybe buy herself a new skirt. She licked the raspberry off the carton top, pitched it in the trash. A new beginning for Chassi, a turning point. Now that was a movie she loved, *The Turning Point*, that fight with Anne Bancroft and Shirley MacLaine, smacking each other on their behinds with their pocketbooks, turning in that circle. Maybe she'd rent that on the way home.

She slid her boots off the desk, stood up, threw the empty carton and the spoon in the wastebasket, frowned at the ringing phone. Probably The Sad Lady falling apart again over the crafty doings of the evil husband; maybe The Shoelace saying he would be late. Hey, she'd never named Chassi. Just as well, she might have had to rename her. Damn it, why didn't they pick up?

Eleanor groaned, licked a smudge of yogurt off the top of her finger. Damn. Maybe it was somebody in trouble trying to ring through.

She brushed her finger across her skirt and picked up the receiver. "Dr. Costello."

"Hi."

Eleanor's fingers flew to her lips, pressed hard.

"Mom, it's me."

No breath to speak, Eleanor nodded.

"Mom? It's Caroline. Do you have a new answering machine? Where's your service?" She hesitated. "Well, okay, so I thought I'd get you in between . . . there goes my big plan . . ." She hesitated, exhaled. "Okay, so I've been thinking about what you said . . ."

Eleanor could see her, the tilt of Caroline's head, the way she did when she was thinking, that little frown that was just beginning over her right eyebrow.

". . . the friend thing . . ."

That stance that was so Caroline, that straight back, the set of those wide shoulders.

". . . I don't know . . . it seems so ridiculous . . ."

Space, air on the line, her daughter taking another breath, probably turning one foot into the other the way she did, that endearing way she'd done since she was two. Just like Jimmy. Eleanor's face wet, her fingers pressing hard against her mouth, seeing her child.

". . . but I guess, you know, for Daddy, because, I was thinking, this would really piss him off, you and me not speaking, you know how he hated that, he would have been stomping around . . ."

Her smile, Caroline's gorgeous, open smile.

". . . you know, the way he did . . . so, I guess I have to say yes. And for me, I guess I should be more open. So, don't get all excited, I'm just saying we'll see. We'll probably come to blows the first time." She laughed. "Anyway, so, you can call me. I mean, it's okay. Okay?"

A click and the line went dead.

Her eyes brimming over, Eleanor smiled at nobody in her office, just hung up the phone and stood there smiling and crying and saying "Okay."

• The Hollywood Reporter •

by C. R. Smith

The show must go on. . . . In keeping with a time-honored show-biz tradition, producer Saul Jennings and director Robby Peroni have awarded the coveted lead actress role in the remake of *No Trumpets, No Drums*, which garnered seven Academy Awards, including a best actress for the magnificent Sally Brash, to virtually unknown Ionie St. John. St. John was originally cast to play the smaller role of Razel Palevsky, in same pic. Cameras start rolling in the Philippines on August 20. Jennings and Peroni still refuse to comment on why young Chassi walked *Trumpets*. . . . Hooray for Hollywood—stay tuned!